#TagMe for Murder

#TagMe for Murder

A Trending Topic Mystery

Sarah E. Burr

LEVEL BEST BOOKS

Author Photo Credit: Doug Walters Photography

First edition

ISBN: 978-1-68512-317-8

Cover art by Level Best Designs

This book was professionally typeset on Reedsy.
Find out more at reedsy.com

To my squad

Praise for #FollowMe for Murder and the Trending Topic Mysteries

"This book is the perfect mix of Nancy Drew and Instagram and a fun and enjoyable read."—*What Angela Reads* podcast

"I love Coco Cline...She is like a breath of fresh air in the cozy world."—Dollycas Great Escapes

"*#FollowMe for Murder*'s sleuth Coco Cline is confident, chic, and cool."—Lane Stone, author of the Buckingham Pet Palace Mysteries

"I absolutely loved the characters. Everyone was strong, and I can't wait to hang out with Coco and her friends again."—Carstairs Considers, book blogger

"Ms. Burr has her finger right on the pulse."—J.C. Kenney, bestselling author of the Allie Cobb Mysteries and the Darcy Gaughan Mysteries

"Sarah Burr's *#FollowMe for Murder* is an accomplished, witty, and perfectly delightful mystery. The narrative unfolds with clear, precise details, and the heroine, Coco Cline, is indeed, someone we'd all want to follow."—Lori Robbins, award-winning author of the On Pointe Mysteries

Chapter One

"How did I get stuck driving?" Jasper Hastings muttered as he navigated his sporty Porsche out of our quiet, beachside development.

I shifted around in the backseat so Jasper could see my pointed gaze in his tiny rearview mirror. "Because *you* were late."

Beside me on the cramped buttery leather seat, Charlotte Whittaker giggled as she wagged a disapproving finger in Jasper's direction.

Despite our teasing, my stomach flipped with anxiety. "We were supposed to be there at six thirty."

"And you know how punctual Coco likes to be." My boyfriend, Hudson Caruthers, offered sage advice from his coveted spot in the passenger seat.

Jasper, who'd been my best friend since second grade, sighed. "Don't make me regret moving here more than I already do."

His grumpy attitude made the rest of us laugh, the cheery sound filling the small car. Jasper had officially been moved into his new condo for all of five minutes before he'd started moaning with remorse, although most of it had been feigned. I knew deep down he was glad to be back in our hometown of Central Shores, Delaware.

"You just need some time to adjust." I snaked my arm around his seat and patted his broad shoulder. "It took me a while to settle in."

Jasper snorted. "Oh, please. I remember exactly how it went down. You got your check from Zuckerberg, moved back home, and went so stir-crazy that you launched a new business a week later. Quarter-life crisis, if I've ever heard of one."

1

"Hey, Coco started a new business because of *me*." Charlotte swatted the back of Jasper's seat in retaliation. "Not because she was having a crisis."

I smiled at the memory. Center of Attention Consulting had indeed taken flight with Charlotte as my first client. It all started a little over three years ago, just after I moved back to Central Shores, when I literally fell into Charlotte's life. Well, more like tripped. After a round of apologies (me for making a scene in her coffee shop and her for her sticky doormat), we struck up a conversation that eventually led to ideas of increasing foot traffic through social media campaigns. I offered her my social media marketing expertise, and voila, Center of Attention—or CoA, as I lovingly abbreviated it—was born.

I turned my attention to Jasper's reflection in the rearview mirror, arching my eyebrows. "And *Zuckerberg* didn't cut me a check." His lawyers were the ones to do that honor back when the artist formally known as Facebook purchased the LiveIt lifestyle app I had developed with five of my girlfriends after graduating college.

Jasper waved a hand, batting the thought aside. "Tomato, tah-mah-to."

Hudson shifted in his seat so he could meet my gaze. With his short, dark hair, warm brown eyes, and bronze skin, the mere sight of him gave me shivers of delight. "Speaking of CoA, are you on the clock tonight?"

I grinned in triumph. "Nope! I officially sunset my engagement with Andre yesterday. My little sommelier must now spread his metaphorical wings across the web and fly."

Charlotte pulled her smartphone out of her black leather clutch, and her fingers danced across the screen. "Well, he's already posted some gorgeous promo shots. You taught him well."

I tugged her wrist toward me to scope out Vine's professional Instagram profile. Beautifully cropped and filtered pictures of Central Shores' new wine bar lit up the screen. I glowed with pride at what my consulting services had helped Andre Nunez achieve. When I'd met him a few weeks ago, Andre had been on the verge of giving up on his business before Vine's doors had even opened. Now, my friends and I were on our way to a glitzy private event to celebrate the bar's first week post-launch.

Hudson grinned, shooting me a wink. "Then it's all play and no work tonight."

My suntanned skin sizzled under his dark, sexy gaze. It had been a while since Hudson and I had had a fun night out on the town. "It can't be *too* much play. I do have to be down at the police station tomorrow morning."

Charlotte leaned closer to me so she could see Hudson's profile. "Hey, Mr. WMTG, how did *you* manage to swing a Friday night off?"

Hudson zipped his lips, forcing Charlotte to look to me for answers with her big, ethereal gray eyes.

"Hudson and his producer are working on a top-secret project, and apparently, he made her so happy this morning that she gave him the night off as a reward." I shared the Hudson-approved blurb with my friends. Of course, I knew what the project was, but I'd been sworn to secrecy by Hudson and Millicent Stabler, his boss and executive producer at the local TV news station in Milton. They were piloting a new true crime show that featured both solved and unsolved murder investigations throughout the Delaware region. Hudson described it as a "*48-Hours*-Featuring-Your-Neighbors" type program, and if the higher-ups at WMTG green-lit the pilot, Hudson would be the show's full-time host. Until that happened, though, he'd continue to juggle research and filming with his current nighttime anchor duties.

"Giving someone the night off as a reward for good work," Jasper mused while stroking his clean-shaven chin in exaggeration. "An interesting concept. I usually reward my employees with *more* work."

"I'm sure that's effective management," I said dryly, although I knew how successful Jasper's society and fashion magazine, *Divulge,* was.

Hudson tossed Charlotte and me a sly look. "You know what they say. It's better to be feared than loved."

"Who says that?" Jasper quipped. "Angelina Jolie?"

Our playful banter continued for the rest of the twelve-minute drive down to Central Shores' beachfront strip. Located across from the pristine Atlantic, the strip was considered the social hub of our little town. Restaurants, shops, and galleries lined one side of the road, giving tourists and locals easy access to our renowned beach. Though Central Shores had a population of under three thousand, tonight, the main road that ran down the strip was packed with cars and foot traffic. Red, white, and blue streamers hung from the lampposts lining the sidewalk, a clear sign the Fourth of July holiday was rapidly approaching. And with that came Central Shores' annual Salute to Summer festival.

"Did you get your residential parking sticker yet?" I asked Jasper, trying to turn myself around in the tight quarters to check his back window. Despite all the tourists milling about, if Jasper had his parking sticker, we shouldn't have any problem nabbing a spot in the residential zone.

Jasper's broad, muscular body shook in a visible cringe as he sighed. "Yes. I was forced to mar my precious baby with it." He patted the steering wheel of his Porsche with fondness.

Since I affectionately called my British racing green MINI Cooper "Jolly," I could relate to Jasper's relationship with his car, his first major high-end purchase as an adult.

Five minutes later, Charlotte and I struggled to climb out of the cramped backseat and through Hudson's passenger side door.

"Maybe next time, we should just call a Lyft." Once she was free from the car's clutches, Charlotte tugged down her slinky, black mini that had ridden up, revealing her enviable long, lean legs in all their glory.

Trying not to feel self-conscious standing next to such a natural beauty, I brushed the wrinkles out of my A-line cocktail dress and nodded my agreement. By punishing Jasper for his tardiness, we had effectively punished ourselves.

"Don't say I didn't warn you." Jasper grinned wickedly as if he could read my thoughts. "Ready to party?"

With a whooping cheer, Charlotte laced her arm through Jasper's, and I took Hudson's hand as we made our way through the packed parking lot tucked behind the row of buildings that made up the strip.

Hudson let out a low whistle. "Man, it's busy, even for a Friday night."

Charlotte tossed her silky amber locks over her shoulder. "You should see it during the daytime. The beach is crawling with people. It's been great for business. I hit my profit goal for June two weeks ago."

Jasper snorted. "You'd think tourism would have taken a hit given what happened this spring."

Goosebumps peppered my skin, and Jasper hadn't even mentioned *what* had happened in our cozy little town earlier this year. Stumbling into the break room of a former client's consignment shop and finding an employee lying in a pool of her own blood was something I would never, ever forget. Not to mention everything that happened afterward. In an effort to prove my two clients innocent of the young woman's murder, I'd taken it upon myself to investigate her death. After digging into her messy private life, I'd come face-to-face with her killer and had been dangerously close to losing my own life in the process. However, thanks to an unintended Facebook LIVE broadcast, my online followers witnessed the confrontation through social media, including the local police, who came to my rescue. With the killer apprehended, I barely had time to recover from the attack before learning my virtual takedown of the criminal had ended up on CNN, MSNBC, *The Colbert Report, The View*...you name it. At one point, "Celebrity Blogger Coco Cline" was trending on Twitter and Google News, so it took a few months for things to go back to normal. Or as normal as life can be when you're a twenty-eight-year-old influencer who writes a popular lifestyle blog with over three million subscribers.

"I still can't believe you had the courage to go inside Vine in the first place, Cokes." Charlotte gave an exaggerated shudder.

I'd found Stacy Lockner's body in the back of the very same building Vine now occupied. "Believe me, I was super nervous when I went to meet Andre for a consultation. But the new owners did a great job with their renovations. You can hardly tell it's the same place." I swallowed the white lie. When Andre first gave me a tour of the newly constructed wine bar, I'd felt sick to my stomach, dreading I would find a dead body in the wine fridge or something.

Hudson hugged me close. "I'm so proud of you, you know that? Tons of folks at the station are already buzzing about how Vine will be *the* summer hotspot. And Andre has *you* to thank for that."

Warm fuzzies pulsed through me at Hudson's praise. He'd been my rock in the aftermath of unmasking Stacy's killer. There'd been one too many nights when I'd woken up screaming, feeling like someone was choking me. Yet, without fail, Hudson was there to comfort me, to reassure me that he'd never let anything happen to me. No matter how much work he had or how busy he was, Hudson always made it home to share our bed and make me feel safe.

The four of us continued along the footpath between Jewel's Ice Cream and Harper's Pub, the aroma of fried fish and potato skins lacing the air.

My stomach rumbled. I'd advised my friends to skip dinner, as Andre promised a catered spread at the party, but Harper's deliciously crispy breading had me rethinking my strategy.

"Ooh! The line for the party goes down the strip. Poor plebs." The glee in Jasper's tone was evident. He reveled in having VIP access to an event.

"I thought you said this was a private party?" Charlotte unlinked her arm from Jasper's and slowed her pace to walk beside Hudson and me.

I wrinkled my nose. "It is. Andre did mention the possibility of opening Vine up to the public once things were well underway, but after realizing what a nightmare that would be for catering, he decided against it."

Charlotte giggled. "It looks like he may have gone overboard with the guest list, then."

Jasper stopped and turned to face us, his pale, stony façade darkening. "I am *not* standing in line."

I waved away his concerns. "Well, sometimes it does pay to be friends with me. Come on. I've got an in."

We wove our way through the gathered crowd lining the sidewalk. While I was more focused on the ivy-covered archway of Vine's entrance, I managed to take stock of the people around us. Most were young, dressed in cocktail attire, with glam hairdos and vampy makeup. I didn't recognize any of their faces either. Since I'd helped Andre curate the guest list, it appeared that Vine had attracted a horde of party crashers. Word had undoubtedly gotten out about the new boutique wine bar, and the long line of eager partygoers boded well for the new business's continued success.

We eased past grumbling complaints that we were cutting the line and arrived at the front door, only to be greeted by a hulking white guy dressed all in black. He sported a buzzed head of blond hair and sunglasses, even though the sun straddled the western skyline. He blocked our way, tapping impatiently on the iPad in his beefy hands.

While I couldn't be sure, due to his covered eyes, he didn't even glance at us before asking, "Name?"

"Coco Cline. Along with Hudson Caruthers, Jasper Hastings, and Charlotte Whittaker."

The bouncer paused and lowered his shades. Big brown eyes widened as recognition filled his face. "Ms. Cline! Nice to see you. Mr. Nunez has been waiting for your arrival."

I had never met or seen this guy in my life, so I assumed he recognized me from the media attention I received earlier this April. He didn't strike me as the type to be a *Trending Topic* subscriber or even one of my social media followers. But who knew? You couldn't judge a book by its cover.

I smiled and thanked him as he held the door open. I had to admit, there was something intoxicating about notoriety, and I felt a little bit giddy as I waltzed inside the elegant bar with my friends in tow. Despite all its privacy pitfalls, fame, even a little of it, had its perks.

Polished mahogany paneling and gilded-framed mirrors lined the walls of the sizable room. I'd never realized, back when this space had been filled with shelving and boxes packed with consignment goods, how big the main floor really was. Vacant spots on the strip were rarely empty long, as it was prime real estate for business owners. Andre had certainly struck gold when he'd secured a lease on the newly renovated building...even if it had once been a crime scene.

Vine was already packed with enthusiastic guests. Smooth Latin music pulsed from the speakers mounted along the walls. Uniformed waiters circulated among the attendees, trays of wine samples bobbing up and down amid the sea of faces. Given that most of the guest list were affluent members of Central Shores and nearby communities, designer emblems shimmered on the suits and dresses surrounding us. It looked like a scene out of *Succession* rather than our sleepy little coastal community.

Jasper's jaw fell slack for a beat before he recovered.

"Hard to believe this is the Central Shores of our youth, right?" I nudged him in the side.

He rubbed his hands together, his icy blue eyes gleaming. "Maybe I can get used to living here after all."

"Coco, darling! So glad you could make it." A tall, lanky figure bounded through the crowd with a broad smile. The debonair man kissed both my cheeks in greeting. "I know you have an early start tomorrow with another one of your engagements."

I hugged him tightly. "Please, a chance to celebrate one of my favorite clients? I wouldn't miss it for the world."

"So, what do you think of the fruits of our labor?" Andre Nunez motioned to the extravagant scene in front of us. Local politicians, entrepreneurs, and town movers and shakers mingled, clearly enjoying the occasion. "Can you believe it?"

"This is all you, Andre." I gave him a congratulatory pat on the back. "All I did was create a few hashtags and add a little flair to your branding."

He clicked his tongue. "So modest." Turning to my friends, Andre's smile widened, his radiant teeth almost blinding. "Hudson Caruthers, I'd recognize your handsome face anywhere."

My boyfriend's skin darkened as he blushed. A true investigative journalist at heart, Hudson wasn't wholly comfortable with the fame that ensued from his career at WMTG. Truth be told, I was still getting used to it, too. When we first started dating, I was the one recognized everywhere we went. But once LiveIt was in my rearview, my life and career took a different direction. I retreated from the public eye, focusing on matters closer to home, while Hudson continued to climb his way to the top at WMTG. Many times in recent months, Hudson's local celebrity had outshone my own, and it'd been an adjustment. But regardless of my ego's inner struggles, I was beyond proud of Hudson and what he had accomplished.

"Pleased to meet you, Andre." Hudson shook our host's hand. "Coco's really enjoyed working with you."

"She's an angel." Andre clasped his hands together and looked toward the heavens. "I would be a little lost lamb without her."

His hyperbolic adoration elicited an awkward chuckle from both Hudson and me before I turned to introduce Andre to Jasper and Charlotte.

Andre waved away the need for introductions. "Please, I'm in Brewed to Perfection nearly every day," he said, referring to Charlotte's popular coffee shop in the strip, "and *Divulge* is practically my Bible." He shook Jasper's hand and hugged Charlotte. "Even if Coco hadn't added you to the guest list, I would have invited you both myself."

Charlotte beamed. She had worked hard to solidify herself as one of Central Shores' respected business owners, and it visibly pleased her to hear a fellow entrepreneur's praise. "The place looks wonderful, Andre."

"Would you be open to renting the space out?" Jasper asked. "I'd love to do a *Divulge* event here sometime."

Andre looked like he might faint at the opportunity as he nodded and continued to pepper my friends with more questions about their lives in Central Shores. Andre had moved to the area only two months ago and had been so busy with Vine that he hadn't gotten to know many folks in the community. "Am I right in saying that you *all* live up in the Sunny Shores development on the south side of town?"

"We're starting our own little commune," Jasper said with a straight face.

Andre twisted one of the ends of his mustache in deep thought. "Someone else mentioned Sunny Shores to me tonight. Who was it? Who was it?" His eyes narrowed as he surveyed his domain before pointing a finger to one of the high-top tables tucked away in the back of the room. "Ah-ha! That couple told me they moved into a Sunny Shores condo recently. Have you met them?"

My stomach convulsed with sudden dread as I followed the trail made by Andre's finger. I feared I knew what—sorry, who—lay at the end: Larry and Rosalynn Dunmer.

Hudson, Charlotte, and I visibly recoiled as our gazes settled on the newest members of our little neighborhood. Jasper groaned aloud at what we were all thinking. "Who in the name of Lizzo invited *them*?"

Chapter Two

Okay, Hudson probably didn't think those *exact* words, but I digress.

Andre frowned at our unified reaction. "What's wrong? Isn't the husband the guy the state department sent in to do the town audit?"

I raised an eyebrow. "Is *that* how the Dunmers scored an invite? They weren't on the guest list you sent me last week." *If they had, I might not have come.*

Andre shrugged nonchalantly. "I added them on a whim a few days ago. I figured it couldn't hurt to have someone looking out for the interests of new businesses while reviewing the government's budget." He glanced nervously at each of our pinched expressions. "You four look like you smell a dead skunk or something. Sure, they're a little off-brand," he paused to eye the dress code-violating Hawaiian shirt Larry wore, "but they can't be that bad, can they?"

I didn't like to speak ill about people I didn't know very well. Still, the arrival of Larry and Rosalynn Dunmer had me seriously considering selling my beloved beachfront condo and fleeing Sunny Shores. My new next-door neighbors had been moved in all but two hours before an irate Larry was rapping at my front door, demanding I remove my lawn furniture because it sullied his wife's view of the ocean. Since their one-story home was situated on a slight incline and at an angle, my two-story condo blocked most of their waterfront view, not *just* my wicker lounge chair set. Given that Larry hadn't even issued a greeting or introduced himself before laying into me, I'd been sorely tempted to reply in an equally rude manner, but for the sake of neighborhood peace, I offered to move my patio furniture off the grass when I wasn't using it.

My compromise turned out to be a huge mistake. The well-intentioned peace offering opened the floodgates for Larry to complain about anything and everything in our small, secluded neighborhood. Ranging from Charlotte's lawn being too dry, to Jasper having too many cars parked in his driveway, to the color of the flowers on the bushes that lined my property (what is so offensive about purple lilacs?), Larry's smorgasbord of complaints had become a daily part of my routine. He once even yelled at Hudson for leaving our garage door open while Hudson mowed the lawn as if seeing my boyfriend's BMW was somehow an egregious affront.

Even more unsettling, Rosalynn Dunmer saw her husband's frequent visits to my doorstep as a threat to their blissfully wedded union. Whenever Rosalynn cornered me alone, she never failed to remind me that she and Larry had been happily married for twenty-two years and that she didn't appreciate me *throwing* myself at him every chance I got. That's right. She'd convinced herself that I was flirting with her oaf of a husband every time he assaulted me with his list of grievances. I tried to take pity on her and be nice...but she made it really, *really* hard with her endless, snide comments about my "trampy" wardrobe and "loose-moraled" friends.

Due to their odious personalities, I did my best to avoid the Dunmers and not ruffle any feathers, which was much easier said than done. Not a day went by when I didn't ask myself, *Why couldn't Jasper have bought their condo instead of the one up the road?* My only saving grace was that Larry and Rosalynn were just renting for the summer while Larry was stationed in Central Shores on business. He was a state auditor who'd been assigned to evaluate Central Shore's finances and help make budget adjustments for the upcoming year. After scrambling to deal with the abrupt resignation of Mayor Beaufort this past April, the town council was less than thrilled to have a state audit dumped onto their laps, especially one done by such a lovable character as Larry. Why couldn't the state department have sent the Delaware version of Ben Wyatt or Chris Traeger from *Parks & Recreation*?

"Let's just say," Jasper sneered in answer to Andre's question, "that Larry accuses me daily of running a brothel, all because I invite my creative team over to the house to workshop *Divulge* layout ideas every now and then."

Andre wrinkled his nose. "Well, that's quite rude."

Jasper's scowl deepened. "Come to find out, Lechy Larry catcalls my female employees any chance he can get. The guy is a total creep."

Charlotte tucked a stray strand of hair behind her ear. "I'd tell your catering staff to watch out for the two of them, Andre. Larry is handsy, and Rosalynn loves to make a scene about it." She winced as a disgusted look enveloped her pretty face. "Only Rosalynn deludes herself into believing it was the *other* person's fault that her husband groped them." As the nicest person I'd ever met, the fact that even Charlotte didn't have a kind thing to say about the Dunmers should have been telling.

Andre raised an eyebrow with intrigue. "Sounds like you know from personal experience?"

Charlotte self-consciously tugged at the hem of her black dress. "He may have made a few lewd comments about my work attire at the café, which prompted Rosalynn to accuse me of being, and this is a direct quote, 'a total skank' in front of my customers."

I wrapped an arm around Charlotte's shoulders, knowing how much the recent incident had humiliated and angered her. There was nothing skanky about Charlotte's Brewed to Perfection uniform. Rosalynn was just jealous that Charlotte looked like a million bucks in Bermuda shorts and a polo.

"I'm thankful Gavin walked in for a latte before things escalated any further." Charlotte leaned into my comforting embrace. "A uniformed officer seems to be the only thing that shuts those two up."

Jasper and I glared at the couple, who were seemingly oblivious to our conversation. In fact, Larry was busy eyeing the breasts of a passing waitress.

"Deacon told me I'm within my rights to ban them from the café," Charlotte continued. "I think I might have to. I don't want Larry harassing Bethany or Maria when I'm not around to defend them." Bethany had been working for Charlotte for quite some time, but since she was heading off to college in the fall, Charlotte had also hired Maria Ortiz, a recent Delaware State graduate.

Andre's coppery brown skin had lost its luster by now. "Goodness. Their reputation failed to precede them. Should I ask them to leave?"

I bit my lower lip. "That would cause more of a scene at this point. Just warn the waitstaff, and you should be fine."

"I don't know." Jasper growled. "I wouldn't trust Larry to behave in public."

"Oh, dear. This is karma for adding someone to the guest list without your approval, Coco." Andre wrung his hands, a line of sweat developing on his brow. "Most of the servers here are from Cyprus. I'll track down their event coordinator and tell her to be on the lookout." The posh beach club in Cherry Springs touted one of the best catering teams in the area.

With Cyprus's world-class executive chef in mind, I redirected the conversation, as we'd clearly put our host on edge. "Andre, you promised me premium hors d'oeuvres. Where might we get a bite to eat before we begin wine tasting?"

Andre's tense demeanor turned on a dime. "We have a selection laid out along the back with recommended pairings," he chirped brightly. "And don't forget to swing by that station over there." He pointed to a half-moon tabletop with a few people milling around it. "I had personalized corkscrews made, engraved with the names of each guest. Make sure to pick yours up."

"What a clever party favor!" Charlotte gushed.

Andre sighed. "I'm afraid I can't take all the credit." He winked at me. I floated the idea during our first CoA consultation session, and Andre had run with it.

"We'll leave you to deal with the horde of party-crashers at the door." I motioned to the faces outside pressed against the window, eager to catch a glimpse of the goings-on. "Congrats on the perfect end to a fabulous opening week." I kissed him goodbye on the cheek before ushering my friends toward the shiny souvenirs.

We fawned over the elegant design of the corkscrews before skimming the engravings for our names. The silver and copper handles had been braided into grapevines, an ode to the wine bar's moniker. The favors were laid out in alphabetical order, so it didn't take us long to locate our own.

I slipped mine and Hudson's into my flashy, gold clutch. "Want me to hold yours?" I asked Jasper, as he likely wouldn't want to put something so sharp into the pocket of his blue Calvin Klein trousers.

Jasper shook his head. "I'll just grab mine on the way out."

Charlotte reached for another corkscrew. "Aw, Andre had one made up for Deacon, just in case." She picked up the souvenir and tucked it into her black clutch alongside her own.

"Speaking of Deacon," Hudson said as we redirected ourselves toward the buffet at the back of the bustling room, "where is he? Still out of town?"

"He's flying in later tonight. He's been at a seminar in Chicago all week." The off-the-cuff way Charlotte answered made it sound like her boyfriend of three months was a boring old businessman. In reality, Deacon Lait was a forensic technician with the Sussex County Crime Lab who'd been reassigned to the Central Shores Police Department for the foreseeable future. After the murder of Stacy Lockner, Chief Lloyd McInnis insisted his department be allowed a few crime techs should a situation like Stacy's death ever happen again. The seminar Deacon had been attending was about new techniques for analyzing blood spatter patterns.

"Is that the one you mentioned going to?" Hudson turned his curious gaze on me.

I nodded. "Deacon asked if I wanted to tag along to document the department participating in the seminar. He thinks it would be a great feature for the new police bulletin I've added to their website." The online bulletin board was one of the ways I'd incorporated technology and social media at the Central Shores PD. "I would've loved to have been a fly on the wall, but I promised Andre I'd be here to support him, and I had too many webinars to do this week for my remote CoA clients. So, Deacon's homework is to write about the conference for the website."

Judging by the impressive spread of cured meats, pasta, cheeses, salads, and fruit on display as we arrived at the buffet, I was glad I'd passed on the invitation to attend the forensics seminar. As much as I loved TV crime shows, I doubted I had the constitution to sit and look at gory crime scene photos in a stuffy lecture hall for a week. Experiencing one in real life had been more than enough for me.

With our sights set on the expansive buffet, my friends and I split up, heading for the sections boasting our preferred cuisine. Charlotte and Hudson made a beeline for the seafood tower while Jasper and I hit up carb city.

"How is your consulting gig with the po-po going these days? You've barely mentioned it in the last few weeks." Beside me, Jasper loaded a plate with gnocchi, pumpkin ravioli, and rice pilaf. "Is bringing the Central Shores PD into the twenty-first century not as glamorous as you'd hoped?"

I laughed as I scooped some black truffle mac and cheese onto my plate. "I'm honestly surprised by how well it's going. At first, I worked mostly with Gavin and Maude, but Adrian now joins our little pow-wow sessions. We have a good time."

Chief McInnis initially contracted Center of Attention to redesign the PD's website and create social media profiles across Facebook, Instagram, and Twitter. Once those had been implemented, the chief asked me to stay on to update and post on the department's behalf. Since I had other CoA engagements to manage, I proposed I teach Maude and Gavin how to maintain the website and keep the public informed via social media campaigns. Gavin McInnis was the chief's nephew and the lone lieutenant among the ranks of the station's officers. He also was my good friend from high school. Maude Longford was the station's daytime receptionist. While Maude had been slower on the social media uptake, Gavin had developed a natural flair for poignant, engaging posts. I was so impressed with what we had achieved that I planned to wind down the engagement within the next couple of weeks, although I'd still serve as the department's spokesperson if the need ever arose.

"Who's Adrian?" Jasper scrunched his nose in confusion.

"He transferred down here from Dover earlier this year and is incredibly tech-savvy. He's been helping me with the PD's website configuration since Maude struggles a bit."

"She must be ancient. I remember her being old when we were kids," Jasper replied with a smirk.

"It's scary, but she's hardly aged a day. I wonder if we seem old to kids now?" I asked thoughtfully, knowing that when I was ten years old, anyone over the age of thirty was practically geriatric. But, considering my twenty-ninth birthday loomed on the horizon, those assumptions felt utterly absurd now.

"Hardly. I still have my youthful glow." Jasper put down his overloaded plate next to a vat of white bean chili and used Vanna White hands to showcase his baby-faced skin.

"Thanks to your over-priced facial regimen," I clapped back.

Jasper merely shrugged at my exaggerated remark. "Hey, when you can afford the best…." As the Editor-in-Chief of *Divulge*, Jasper had access to top-of-the-line beauty products that he very much put to good use.

Leaving Hudson and Charlotte to finish gathering their food down at the smelly end of the buffet, Jasper and I grabbed an empty high-top table. A waiter materialized next to us, offering us a glass of white wine to kick things off.

Jasper and I each took a tentative sip, then nodded our appreciation to the waiter, who promptly disappeared into the crowd.

"Then why settle here of all places?" I asked, my bestie's last comment still bouncing around in my head. "I still can't believe you made the move back."

At my question, Jasper looked embarrassed. Quite a shocking reaction from someone who rarely had any shame. "As much as I hate to admit this, especially to your face, I missed our days as a little family."

During my LiveIt years, Jasper had been my roommate in Dover, so our adventures together had been nonstop. Once Hudson entered the picture, Jasper affectionately labeled us "Mom and Dad," and he never failed to joke that he was our grown-up child whenever the three of us went out on the town. After Hudson and I had moved out to Central Shores, our outings together had grown fewer and far between. Until now.

Jasper sighed. "Home is where the heart is, you know? I'm hoping to recapture some of our glory days. With Charlotte in tow, of course." Since I had introduced them to one another three years ago, Charlotte and Jasper had grown thick as thieves.

I raised my glass and clinked it against his. "Here's to those days never-ending."

Charlotte shimmied next to me, balancing her plate and a glass of red wine she must have picked up from a roaming server. "Excellent vintage," she deemed in a mockingly haughty tone.

As Jasper chuckled, I glanced over my shoulder toward the buffet. "Where's Hudson?"

"He spotted someone from work and went to go say hello. Something about the station president...maybe?" Charlotte answered before inserting a forkful of seared salmon into her mouth.

Andre and I had added Gordon Lane to the guest list on a hopeful whim, so it surprised me that he'd accepted the invite. Mr. Lane usually didn't make an appearance for anything less than a lavish fundraiser. Maybe Vine would be *the* summer hotspot after all.

I decided to join Charlotte in sampling the delectable spread and stabbed my fork through a piece of juicy braised short rib before bringing it to my lips.

As we gushed over the savory bites, we waved to familiar faces and chatted with folks as they passed us on their way to the buffet or the bar. Not a single person had a negative thing to say about the party. I made a note to share the good news with Andre. He'd been banking on this event, cementing Vine's status as a distinguished Central Shores business.

Twenty minutes had already flown by when my phone vibrated with a text alert. It was from Hudson.

Stuck @ shrimp cocktail w/ Lane and the new studio VP. U didn't mention he was coming.

My heart tightened with guilt as I tried to catch of glimpse of Hudson in the crowd but had no luck. He had been looking forward to a night off from station politics. **Sorry. Didn't think he would come. Need me 2 bail u out?**

Hudson's reply came a few seconds later. **No. Enjoy urself. U earned it. Lane keeps saying how gr8 the party is.**

Slipping my phone back into the handy pocket of my burgundy dress, I greeted a pretty, young Black woman dressed in a Cyprus catering uniform as she arrived at our table. With a bright smile, she offered us a glass of smoky Malbec. Unfortunately, I had an early morning meeting, so I opted out. Charlotte and Jasper, though, murmured their appreciation and grabbed glasses, with Jasper promising it was his last one of the evening since he was our ride home.

The server, who had the name "Bonnie" embroidered onto her blouse, turned to leave when a gurgling, wheezing voice startled her from behind. "I'd sure like you to service me, little lady."

The vulgar comment made my shoulder muscles spasm as my gaze darted to an oversized Hawaiian shirt flapping through the parting crowd.

Larry Dunmer licked his lips as his beady eyes roamed up and down the young woman's figure.

Bonnie tugged nervously at her braided hair with a free hand, her cheeks darkening with unease. "Can I offer you a drink, sir?" she asked, holding out the tray she carried.

"I was kinda hoping you'd offer me something a bit more *full-bodied*." Larry's salt-and-pepper eyebrows wriggled against his sunburned forehead.

"That's enough, Larry," I snapped. "Leave her alone."

With my neighbor's attention now on me, Charlotte motioned for Bonnie to escape the scene. The mortified young woman needed no additional coaxing before booking it out of there.

Larry's saggy features tightened as he stared me down. "I'm surprised they let you in here, Coco, given your history with the place."

Slinking up beside Larry's burly form, bottle-blond Rosalynn cackled at her husband's lousy attempt at a joke.

Jasper answered indignantly on my behalf. "Andre begged for Coco's assistance launching this place, Dunmer. Without her, you two would be stuck at home drowning kittens, or whatever it is you do for fun."

Larry bristled at the barbed comment, puffing his chest out. "Nice to see you outside your little den of iniquity, Hastings."

"Please," Charlotte whispered to the both of us, placing a hand on Jasper's forearm. "Bonnie got away. Just ignore them. Don't take the bait."

Jasper simply reached for his wine glass and took a deep swig.

"I think I'm going to make a complaint to the condo association about you, after all, Hastings. Parading scantily clad women *and* men in and out of your house at all hours of the day?" Larry wiped a little line of slobber from his chin. "It's disgraceful, the way you conduct your 'business.'"

I eyed the empty wine glass in Larry's hand. Based on his slurred yet brazen speech, it couldn't have been his first drink.

"What's disgraceful is how you conduct yourself around women." Jasper set his glass down, his icy blue gaze making even me go a little bit cold. "You better watch it, Larry, or you're going to land yourself in some serious trouble."

His chilly retort left the ornery couple momentarily speechless. Rosalynn recovered first, her petite figure vibrating with outrage. "How dare you say such things about my husband? He's been nothing but an upstanding citizen since we moved to Central Shores."

Jasper scoffed, his tone incredulous. "Did you not just hear him proposition our poor server?"

"How dare you, indeed!" Larry bellowed, sending a spray of spittle into the air. His red face morphed to an unhealthy shade of violet. "I would never act in such a crass manner."

"You've been acting nothing *but* crass since you moved here." Jasper folded his arms. With his six-foot-three muscular frame, he cut an imposing figure in his navy suit. "Why can't you just leave us all alone, do your little audit, and get out of our lives?"

I shot Jasper a silencing glare. I was all for putting Larry in his place, but Jasper was dangerously close to crossing a line. It was one thing for us to complain about the Dunmers behind their backs but another to say it directly to their faces. *I* had to live next door to them, after all.

Andre materialized out of nowhere, his expression riddled with concern. "Everything all right here?" he asked tentatively through smiling, yet gritted, teeth.

Before Larry could respond, Jasper's lips stretched into a tight smirk. "Just some neighborly chitchat."

Andre did not look convinced. "Mr. and Mrs. Dunmer, was it? Why don't we go have a drink over at the bar?"

"Why? So this sleazeball and his skanky friends can continue to debase me?" Larry jabbed an accusing finger between Jasper, Charlotte, and me.

"Come now, Mr. Dunmer." Andre reached for the man's elbow, only to have Larry slap his hand away.

"Get your hands off me," Larry roared. "Why don't you just go back to whatever country you came from."

Jovial chatter evaporated from the room as a stunned silence settled all around, save for the rhythm of the soft, twinkling music.

Andre, French and Latino in ethnicity and one hundred percent American by birth, turned red as he looked at his feet. "Mr. Dunmer, I must ask you and your wife to leave my establishment." Then, with renewed courage, he lifted his fiery gaze and straightened his shoulders as he glared at the couple. "You will not be welcomed back."

Rosalynn had the audacity to be offended. "Well, I never. Who would want to come back after hearing how you treat prominent state officials?"

Jasper snorted. "The only place you'd be listed as prominent officials is in the state of denial."

Andre shot Jasper a pleading glance, silently begging him to be quiet.

I stepped in to help, taking a firm stance at Andre's side. "Larry, Rosalynn. Mr. Nunez asked you to leave. Unless you'd like us to get the police involved?"

Larry grabbed his wife's hand. "You'll regret this." He glowered at Jasper and me. "Both of you. We're done being neighborly."

"Wow. *This* was you being neighborly?" Jasper scoffed. "You're a Weinsteining, jerkwad, Dunmer. You know that?"

Larry's humiliated anger practically radiated off him. "I have friends in your industry, Hastings. I can ruin your stupid, vapid, piece-of-trash magazine with a few phone calls."

Jasper growled. "I'd like to see you try."

I elbowed my friend's side a little more forcefully than I intended. "Can you just *shut up* so they'll get out of here?" I hissed under my breath.

"Go grab our corkscrews, Ros. We might as well get something out of this wretched evening." Larry continued to scowl at us as his wife swiftly disappeared to collect their party favors. "I'll be surprised if you even have a job this time tomorrow, Hastings." He flashed a deadly sneer that had my insides wriggling. "I'd also keep an eye out in the comments section of your little blog, Coco. Something interesting might pop up."

Chapter Three

Hudson pushed through the crowd and arrived at my side just as Vine's front door slammed shut behind Larry and Rosalynn. "What the heck just happened?" His left arm encircled me like protective armor as he looked from Jasper to Charlotte and then back to me. "I leave you guys alone to talk shop for a few minutes, and you start World War III?"

I ignored Hudson's concerned questions for the time being and turned to comfort our shaken host. "Andre, I'm so sorry about that horrid scene." Larry's lecherous comments toward Bonnie and his racist remark about Andre's ethnicity still rang in my ears.

Andre smoothed invisible wrinkles from his peach jacket. "You have nothing to be sorry for, Coco." He buried his lingering frustrations and slipped a tired smile into place. "Bonnie came to warn me about Larry and told me how you all stepped in to help her ward off his unsavory advances. You and your friends aren't to blame. Larry is responsible for the filth that comes out of his own mouth." Andre pressed his hands together while he surveyed the stunned and curious expressions of the party's attendees. With his head held high, he broke away from our little group and addressed the crowd, ever the gracious host. "I apologize for that appalling scene, everyone. Seems like some folks just don't know how to hold their liquor or how to check their racism at the door."

A few awkward chuckles dotted the room.

"I think it's time for a little something to sweeten things up." Andre's entire body swelled with bravado. "Nothing pairs better with wine than chocolate!"

On cue, the Cyprus catering staff entered from the back, carrying trays of diced fruit, accompanied by two women in chef hats rolling forward a majestic, four-tiered chocolate fountain. At the tantalizing sight, the party burst back into life.

With a steeling glance my way, Andre set off to do a sweep of the room, likely to conduct some necessary damage control. Thankfully for Andre, the arrival of dessert had diverted most of his guests' attention away from Larry's offensive outburst.

As much as I wanted to dive into that chocolate fountain, I could not afford to be so easily distracted.

"What in the name of Beyoncé were you thinking, going after the Dunmers like that in public?" I seethed, smacking Jasper on the arm, this time with intended force.

Jasper rubbed his biceps as he grimaced. "I was just giving them a taste of their own medicine."

Charlotte chewed nervously on her lower lip. "Larry sounded serious when he left, Jasper. Who knows what he could do to *Divulge?*"

"Hey, aren't we supposed to stand up to bullies? Besides, that little weasel can't do anything to me." Jasper shrugged off her concern.

Hudson's brow furrowed. "I don't know, man. He's with the state treasury department. What's to say he doesn't call the IRS or something?"

Again, Jasper shrugged but didn't look as confident this time. "What kind of operation do you think I run, Dad?" He sounded flustered. "I have a finance department of my own. Everything is above board."

Hudson's handsome features darkened. "I don't doubt you, Jasper, but I've read enough investigative reports about shady government employees. I wouldn't put it past Larry to bribe someone to make your life miserable."

Jasper's shoulders deflated as he hunched forward. "I didn't think about that."

"Yeah, it's pretty clear you didn't think. At. All." I huffed, still miffed that Jasper had let the Dunmers crawl under his porcelain skin.

Charlotte placed a hand on my forearm. "And that threat he made about your blog? Gosh, what a wretched little man."

Jasper finally had the decency to look guilty. "I didn't mean to drag you into our spat, Cokes. I just got carried away. What with Larry hitting on that poor waitress and everything. Someone had to put him and Rosalynn in their place."

I couldn't find it in my heart to stay mad at him. With a sigh, I gave Jasper a comforting pat on the back. "I know. And to be honest, they totally deserved it and more. Especially after what Larry said to Andre."

Hudson glanced around the room. The party was back in full swing, the unpleasant scene seemingly forgotten. "At least there were plenty of witnesses to hear Larry threaten you both if he does try something underhanded."

"Come on, let's grab a few glasses of the Austrian pinot floating around." Charlotte tugged on Jasper's arm, clearly intent on changing the sour mood that hung over our group. "We can't let the Dunmers ruin the swankiest event I've been to in, like, forever."

"Designated driver remem—" Jasper's reply hung interrupted in the air as he pulled his cell phone from his suit pocket. His blue eyes narrowed and widened within seconds. "Holy sh—sorry, guys. I need to bail."

My brow wrinkled in concern. "Is something wrong?" I couldn't judge from Jasper's reaction if the message on his phone had been a good or bad thing. Had Larry already made good on his threat somehow?

"Nope." Jasper grinned wickedly with a teasing twinkle in his eye. "I need to scoot out for an impromptu meeting."

"A meeting?" Hudson and Charlotte echoed. "Who sends out a meeting invite at eight on a Friday night?" Hudson glanced at his smartwatch.

Jasper pocketed his phone and scanned the room, his gaze resting on the front door. "Sorry, can't stay and chat. I'll catch you guys up tomorrow."

"Hey, wait, you drove us here!" I called out to Jasper's retreating figure, but it was too late. He'd already hightailed toward the exit and disappeared into the night.

"That was odd." Charlotte frowned.

Hudson cocked an eyebrow. "A hot date?"

I snorted at the notion my best friend might be seeing someone without my knowledge. Jasper was the definition of a perennial bachelor—in all the time Charlotte and Hudson had known him, he'd never dated anyone seriously. He often quipped that he could only handle a person's company "for one night, and one night only." Gosh, Jasper's last significant relationship had been in high school when he'd dated a receiver on the football team. He broke it off three weeks later due to "artistic differences" over the guy refusing to use deodorant.

"I guess we'll be calling a Lyft, after all," I said, thankful that the ride-sharing service had cars idling up and down the Delaware coastline this time of year.

Emerging from the buzzing crowd, Andre flitted toward our group with a crestfallen expression. "Please don't tell me Jasper left. I swear, that whole scene with the Dunmers is already water under the bridge."

I admired Andre's grit, but it seemed so unfair that Andre felt he had to brush Larry's crude comments off like they didn't matter. I suspected, though, why Andre was worried about my friend's abrupt departure. If Jasper, a local influencer in his own right, was seen leaving a party while the night was still young, it might spell trouble for Vine's fledgling hotspot status.

I placed a reassuring hand on Andre's shoulder. "Jasper wouldn't let a little thing like a public spat get in his way of a good time. He was called away for an impromptu meeting. *Divulge* business or something."

Andre nodded his understanding. "Of course, of course. Business before pleasure. Oh, there's the mayor over there with his posse. Must mingle!" Andre wiggled his fingertips in farewell and dashed away.

Charlotte giggled. "He's quite the character."

Our collective gaze followed Andre over to an assembled group of local politicians who had congregated around the souvenir table. Mayor Sullivan was joined by several council members, a state senator, and even Central Shores' former mayor, Melvin Beaufort.

Hudson nudged me in the side. "Hey, did Jasper ever pick up his corkscrew? No, right?"

I nodded, realizing my bestie hadn't swung by the table on his way out. "I'll grab it when we leave."

With Jasper gone to attend some mysterious "meeting," it fell solely on my extroverted shoulders to keep the party going for my friends. Eager to regain the festive spirit we'd been enjoying before the throwdown with Larry, I linked arms with Hudson and Charlotte and tugged them toward the bar to sample the Austrian pinot noir Charlotte had been salivating over. Even though I had an early client engagement in the morning, after surviving an encounter with the Dunmers, I required some liquid courage to forget their hostile faces.

My five-thirty alarm chirped way too early for a Saturday. Charlotte, Hudson, and I had left Vine around ten with the party still in full swing, but I'd consumed more than my fair share of vintage vino, trying to put the whole Larry Dunmer debacle behind me. I hadn't been all that successful. Now, even with my head buried in my pillow, the effects of Andre's floral pinot still lingered, pounding against my skull, as well as memories of Larry's nefarious threat to post something "interesting" on my blog.

Groaning, I quickly silenced the alarm so as not to disturb Hudson's gentle snores. I managed to drag myself out of bed, not even prying my eyes open fully until I reached the en suite bathroom sink. With my iPhone in one hand and a toothbrush in the other, I scanned every inch of *Trending Topic,* even older, archived posts, for new activity. Much to my relief, I couldn't find anything scandalous unless you counted the dating horror stories my subscribers had been sending in over the past week. I'd recently sent out an online S.O.S., asking for anecdotes to use in a new monthly featurette I planned to launch in July. The column would be about dating in the twenty-first century and how social media influenced our dating lives and habits. I'd been out of the dating game since falling for Hudson, so I relied on my fabulous followers to provide me with situations to analyze, critique, and advise.

"Looks like Larry hasn't made good on his threat." I sighed at my tired reflection. "Yet."

A sense of unease still weighed on me, and I frequently checked *Trending Topic* for new activity while I readied myself for a brief consultation visit down at the Central Shores Police Department. By the time I hopped into my MINI Cooper, I felt hopeful that Larry had forgotten about his drunken promises. Tossing my phone aside, I started Jolly and pulled out of my garage to greet the balmy late June day, pledging to put *Trending Topic* on the back burner and focus on my priority CoA client.

With Salute to Summer officially kicking off on July first, Chief McInnis had instructed his PR team—namely me—to spruce up the public safety recommendations posted on the PD's website. I'd gone the extra mile and converted the rules into a short, engaging video assembled from stock footage I'd found online. I planned to tweet and post the clip from the Central Shores Police Department's social media accounts. This morning, I was meeting up with Gavin, Maude, and Adrian to get their final approval on the video before blasting it out to the masses. We wanted the public safety notice to have plenty of time to circulate before Salute to Summer commenced this coming Friday.

At six-fifteen on the dot, I breezed into the sterile police station lobby and waved to Maude, sitting atop her ergonomic throne. Steaming beverages from Brewed to Perfection lined her desk. Wordlessly, she handed me a caramel macchiato. Something about her knowing my regular order buoyed my spirits. I really loved working with a team again. So much of the consulting work I did with Center of Attention was done remotely, interfacing with one designated person, that I hadn't realized how much I missed being surrounded by colleagues, even ones as surly as Maude. That feeling of comradery was one of the reasons CoA was currently looking to make its first hire. With the number of remote and in-person engagements I had on my plate, I decided several weeks ago to post a job listing for an assistant. The search had proved fruitless so far, but I had a few candidates to interview on Monday who sounded promising.

"Thanks, Maude." I swallowed a deliciously sweet sip of coffee. "Ahh, divine." Charlotte was such a pro. After a night out at Vine, she'd gotten less sleep than I had. Even on the weekends, she opened her coffee shop at five to catch the early-morning foot traffic, but Charlotte never let lack of sleep get in the way of quality work.

Maude pushed her thick-rimmed glasses up her nose. The station's air conditioning was underperforming, and sweat glistened from her wrinkled pores. "We'll get started once Adrian and Gavin are done with their briefing from the night patrol. I appreciate you coming in so early. My grandsons are in town, and I want to get this techie nonsense over with as soon as possible."

I giggled at Maude's unabashed loathing toward her new responsibilities. As the daytime receptionist for a small-town police department, it made sense that she'd be the one person who'd have the most time to maintain the station's Twitter, Facebook, and Instagram accounts. At least, it had made sense to everyone but Maude.

I noted a stack of fliers resting on the countertop. "These came out great!" I picked up a glossy poster that outlined the various Salute to Summer festivities. Pie baking contests, beach volleyball, sandcastle building competitions, fireworks, vendor demonstrations...the list went on.

"Your mother dropped them off yesterday," Maude commented without glancing up from her work. "The town council wants the station plastered with them."

The poster headline also touted the Swing Well, Save Lives charity tournament taking place this Wednesday at the Crestview Country Club. While it technically wasn't a part of Central Shores' Salute to Summer official lineup, our town council was co-sponsoring the golf tournament with WMTG studios in the hopes it would boost awareness for the festival. A PR move *I* had suggested to my mother, who lorded over the town council with an iron fist.

"I still can't believe WMTG convinced Jessica Barnes to host the golf tournament." I placed the flier back on the pile.

Jessica Barnes was a Hollywood ingénue who'd starred in her first blockbuster film last summer. As a Delaware native, WMTG had been thrilled to book her as the celebrity host to increase public interest in the tournament.

Maude scoffed. "I'm pretty sure Ms. Barnes is the reason why the chief weaseled himself an invitation to compete. Lord knows he's not my definition of a 'local celebrity.'"

I chuckled. All the golfers participating in the event also had some claim to local fame. Hudson, one of the most popular news anchors in the state, had received an invite as soon as the tournament was scheduled. I'd even been asked to play, but golf was most definitely not my sport. I just couldn't make my club connect with that impossibly tiny ball. Intent on not making a fool of myself but wanting to help a good cause, I ended up donating to one of the charities Swing Well, Save Lives supported.

Maude leaned in closer, keeping her voice low. "You didn't hear it from me, but Lloyd saw *Last Chance Love Match* four times in the theater."

I doubled over in abrupt laughter, picturing our burly, gruff police chief sitting in rapt attention at a rom-com movie.

"Hi there, Coco. You're in good spirits this morning." Adrian Riley's handsome, friendly face popped into view as he emerged from the singular metal door that led to the station's inner workings. "I think you'll be pleased with the captions I came up with last night."

Rubbing my hands together, I eagerly awaited Adrian's report as he was well on his way to becoming my social media protégé. We had also become good friends in the time I'd been consulting with the PD. Hudson and I joined Adrian and his wife Lana for the occasional double date on nights Lana's mother babysat their ten-month-old twins.

Digging into one of the pockets of his tailored uniform, Adrian withdrew a piece of paper covered in scribbles. As he cleared his throat, a crackling came over the radio enshrined on Maude's desk.

"Dispatch, we've got a ten, fifty-four down at the southern tip of Pelican Beach."

Maude nearly spilled her coffee, reaching for the receiver. "Did I hear you right, Frank? Ten, fifty-four?"

A brusque voice crackled a reply. "Yes, ma'am. Can you get the team in gear?"

Before Maude or Adrian could respond, Lieutenant Gavin McInnis dashed into the room, his hazel eyes pooling with concern. "What are the chances Frank mixed up his codes again?"

Adrian ran a hand over his shaved head, his dark gaze looking to Gavin for orders. "What's the plan, boss?"

Even though I'd worked alongside Gavin since the spring, I still had to remind myself that my goofy high school prom date had grown up to be one of the youngest lieutenants in the state.

"We need to get down to the beach ASAP." Gavin grabbed the keys to one of the two cruisers the station owned. "Coco, if you don't mind, I'd like you to come with us in case we need to keep the public at bay. That falls under your PR contract, right?" A crooked yet stressed smile curled on his lips.

Keep the public at bay? What is going on? "Sure, of course," I said with as much gusto as I could muster. After all, my public relations skills excelled more on online platforms than face-to-face interactions. This would be my first real test as the official Central Shores Police Department spokeswoman since I'd been hired.

Gavin motioned for Adrian and me to hustle out of the station, leaving a worried Maude behind in our wake.

"Hey, Adrian," I whispered as we hurried outside to the oversized garage the police shared with the fire department, "I guess I didn't read the manual thoroughly. What are we up against here? What's a ten, fifty-four?"

He sent a sidelong glance over his shoulder. "Ten, fifty-four...possible dead body."

Chapter Four

The remnants of my caramel macchiato corroded my stomach lining and not because I was riding in the backseat of a police car. *A possible dead body?* This was not how I envisioned my Saturday morning going.

With Gavin and Adrian stone-faced and silent up front, the short ride down to Pelican Beach gave me precious little time to prepare for what I was about to experience. Yes, I had seen a dead body before, but it wasn't like it was something I enjoyed. The unauthorized investigation my friends and I had subsequently launched *did* have its moments of fun, but ultimately, it had culminated in a rather scary confrontation leaving me lucky to be alive. Not that I had any reason to be involved with the actual crime-solving of this "ten, fifty-four" call we raced toward. Gavin had simply asked me along to keep any members of the public from prying, and that's what I intended to do.

Gavin pulled off the road and parked behind a squad car I assumed belonged to Frank Thompson, one of the other officers on the very small Central Shores police force. I had already spun up the opening line Chief McInnis could use when he made a public statement. *Early this morning, our officers responded to reports of a body...*Pulitzer-winning stuff, right?

Adrian opened the back door once he was clear of the car, allowing my release. "Hang back a bit while we see what's going on, okay?" He'd been one of the first officers on the scene when I discovered Stacy Lockner's body and knew how traumatic the experience had been for me.

I gave Adrian a half-hearted salute and leaned against the squad car as he and Gavin rushed down a sandy path that snaked toward the water. Wondering what had brought Frank Thompson this far out of town, I surveyed the rolling dunes of Pelican Beach. Due to its remote location, Pelican Beach served as an overflow when the beach across from the strip got too crowded. We were well south of the main strip, even past the Sunny Shores development, so I wasn't too surprised that we appeared to be alone for the moment. Perhaps my PR services wouldn't be required after all.

Taking off my sandals, I buried my feet in the warm sand and ambled along the road, catching a glimpse of my house in the distance up the shore. Seeing it perched over the water, looking down on Sunny Shores' private residential beach, blanketed my bubbling nerves with an elusive sense of peace. Maybe Frank Thompson *had* called in the wrong code. Perhaps he'd found a poor dead animal that had washed up. As sad as a dying sea creature made me, it was a little less worrisome than a human corpse.

A few minutes passed with only the salty air as my companion before Adrian's dark form resurfaced against the dunes. He dove into the squad car in a fluid motion, and even through the tinted windows, I could see him in the front seat doling out commands over the radio.

I walked over to the car after he'd reemerged. "Everything all right?" I cringed as soon as the words were out of my mouth. Of course, things weren't okay.

Adrian shielded his eyes against the sizzling sun, his ebony skin glistening with perspiration. "I just canceled the ambulance and called in the medical examiner. The vic's been dead a while."

His casual delivery of awful news unsettled me. "Victim...of a drowning?" Given that we were parked a mere hundred feet from the clutches of the Atlantic, it seemed the most obvious cause of death.

Adrian's lips curved downward. "We won't know for sure until the ME does an autopsy, but my guess is that a strong undercurrent isn't to blame for this one."

His cryptic words stoked the fires of my curiosity. I know I told myself there was no reason to get involved...but I *had* been hired to help the police deal with the media, and a dead body was sure to garner public interest. I needed to know what kind of PR crisis we were up against. "Do we need to warn Central Shores about sharks or something? That won't bode well for Salute to Summer." As callous as it sounded, I couldn't help but be concerned about how an ocean-related death would affect our town's bottom line. So many municipal departments depended on the funds raised by Salute to Summer, not to mention the small businesses that needed the increased tourism to make it through our quiet winters.

With his hands on his hips, Adrian glanced over at my inquisitive expression and sighed. "Why don't you come on down and see what we're dealing with? Gavin mentioned you might be able to make an affirmative I.D. for us."

My knees wobbled a bit. Make an I.D.? If Gavin needed my help, that meant whoever Frank had discovered was someone Gavin thought I *knew*. Oh, God. Who? I repeated a silent prayer that Gavin had made a mistake as I slipped my sandals back on and followed Adrian's tracks.

The seagrass thinned out as we marched down the slight embankment. Once the sand had leveled, I noticed the sickening outline of a sheet-covered body just mere yards from the clutches of the ebbing tide. Gavin and Frank stood several feet away, conferring with one another. Each shared matching grim expressions.

As we approached, Gavin folded his arms. "I'm sorry to ask this of you, Coco, but I'm hoping you can do the preliminary I.D. for me before we seek out next-of-kin. I'd hate to show up at the doorstep of the wrong person. Water damage is pretty bad, so I'd like a second opinion. Unfortunately, neither Adrian nor Frank has ever had a run-in with the victim, so they aren't much help."

I assumed he didn't state a name to ensure my unbiased assessment. "It's fine." It was *not* fine. "It's not like this is the first dead body I've come across." I chuckled weakly, trying to avoid throwing up my coffee. "At least this one is just an unfortunate accident."

Gavin shifted on his feet. "Eh, I highly doubt that."

Confused, I traipsed over to the covered victim, the sand forcing an awkward gait. Taking a deep breath, I gave Gavin the okay to pull back the white sheet.

Omigod! My hand went to my mouth, bile swirling at the back of my throat. Despite the massive bloating and eerie blue tinge to his skin, I'd recognize that face anywhere and turn around if I saw it. Larry Dunmer's lifeless eyes stared at the infinite sky above, his face a pained, frozen mask. As I continued to scan his visible upper body, I soon discovered why Gavin doubted this was a terrible swimming accident. A corkscrew had been jabbed deep into Larry's flabby neck, and even the ocean water hadn't wiped away all the traces of blood.

I finally tore my focus away from the gruesome sight and met Gavin's searching gaze. "I know him. That's Larry Dunmer."

With a curt nod, he lowered the sheet back over the dead man. "Your lovely new neighbor." Gavin sighed. "I thought it was him, but after only seeing the guy once at Charlotte's coffee shop, I wasn't a hundred percent sure. I'm sorry I had to ask you to do this, Coco." He stared at the covered body. "At least we know for certain who we are dealing with."

My head grew light, and I wished I had more than sweetened coffee in my stomach. "He's fully clothed." My spinning thoughts suddenly came into focus. "He's still wearing the outfit he wore to the party at Vine last night."

Gavin cocked his head with interest and pulled out a small notepad and pen from his breast pocket. "Ah, yes. The big party down on the strip. *My* invite must have gotten lost in the mail."

My jaw dropped. How could Gavin joke at a time like this?

He sobered at my unimpressed reaction. "You saw Dunmer there?"

Sharp words tumbled carelessly across my lips before I could stop them. "Yes, much to my dismay." *Oof. Sarcasm must be a popular crime scene coping mechanism.*

Gavin's eyes narrowed, silently requesting more information.

I sighed and continued, "Andre Nunez, Vine's owner and sommelier, enlisted CoA to help with the wine bar's official launch. That included helping to organize last night's party, but Andre invited Larry and his wife Rosalynn to the private event without my knowledge. They weren't on the guest list I vetted, or I would have advised Andre against inviting them."

The unpleasant memory of Larry's vile outburst danced to the forefront of my mind. Staring at his covered form, I shivered with guilty relief. At least Larry wouldn't be able to make good on any of those awful threats—*Oh, geez, Coco. Could you be any more insensitive?* I chided myself.

"Why would you have recommended something like that?" Gavin's question batted away my selfish thoughts.

"Like the Dunmers always do," I said, tearing my focus from the dead man, "Larry and Rosalynn ended up ruining the mood. Andre had to ask them to leave the party."

Gavin scribbled furiously, urging me to continue. "Why? What happened?"

"Larry began harassing a server, so Jasper, Charlotte, and I stepped in to help her. Larry didn't appreciate it."

"Jasper? Was Jasper at Vine with you? The whole time?"

I shook my head. "He left early for some meeting that popped up on his calendar."

"Before or after the Dunmers left?"

"Shortly after. Around eight."

"Did Jasper get along with Larry?"

Gavin's rapid-fire questions had me a bit flustered, and it reflected in my response. "Well, no one in town got along with Larry." I paused as the harshness of my comment set in. "I'm sorry. That was disrespectful." I glanced shamefully at the white sheet fluttering in the wind, revealing Larry's blue, swollen feet. Another morbid tremor ran down my back. Had he lost his shoes before or after being stabbed? What about his cell phone? Had it sunk to the bottom of the Atlantic?

"Did Jasper know the deceased well?"

The hardness in Gavin's usually kind hazel eyes chilled me to the bone, despite the morning heat. "Why are you asking so many questions about Jasper?" I snapped rather unprofessionally.

With pressed lips, Gavin knelt beside the body and lifted the corner of the sheet once more. "Take a closer look at the corkscrew, Coco, and then *you* can tell *me*."

35

Bending down, I forced myself to focus on the metal object, not the fleshy neck and body from which it protruded. The repurposed weapon was relatively shiny, so it had to be pretty new. The silver-and-copper braiding even caught prismatic glints of the sun. Silver and copper? *No way. Impossible!*

Two corkscrews, nearly identical to the one in front of me now, were lying on my kitchen counter back home, one bearing Hudson's name and the other carved with mine. A lovely, personalized party favor from Vine's invite-only event glared up at me from its fleshy home in Larry's neck, this one engraved with the name that catapulted my heart into my throat: *Jasper Hastings.*

My attention retreated from Larry's body, meeting Gavin's brooding gaze with raised eyebrows. "You can't possibly think Jasper had anything to do with this."

Gavin sighed at my astonished tone. "I've known Jasper for nearly as long as you have, Coco, but he's also changed a lot since we were kids. Of course, I don't *want* to think he had anything to do with this, but we can't rule him out when his name is literally staring back at us. And it sounds like he and Larry didn't necessarily get along."

My stunned retort was interrupted by the medical examiner's arrival. Due to the grisly circumstances, greetings were clipped, and the ME and his team got to work, forcing Gavin and me to join Adrian and Frank farther away from the scene.

Adrian's arms were folded across his chest. "I called Deacon to let him know what's going on. He's on his way down with the techs." As a former Dover police officer, Adrian was sadly used to dealing with gruesome crimes more than his other Central Shores colleagues.

"Not sure how much they'll be able to determine." Gavin scanned the surf. "The sand will make it hard to pull any possible trace evidence. No sign of a phone, keys, or wallet. Besides, I don't think Dunmer was killed anywhere around here, guys. No blood."

"I'd bet my right arm he washed ashore," Frank Thompson, junior in rank but not in age, added.

I stood alongside the three officers, watching the ME take pictures of the body and its positioning. "Have you informed the chief?"

Gavin rubbed his eyes. "I had to leave a message for him at the Crestview Country Club. He's out on the links practicing for Wednesday's tournament and has his phone off. He won't be pleased to have his golf game interrupted, especially by this."

I flinched, mentally wishing Gavin good luck delivering the unfortunate news to his formidable uncle.

"Adrian, will you take Coco back to the station?" Gavin looked past me like I wasn't even there.

I opened my mouth to protest, but the lieutenant held his hand up. "I know you are an official employee of the police department, but that doesn't mean you're a part of this investigation. We hired you to help with managing the public. I only brought you along this morning because I thought there might be beachgoers, but it looks like we've caught a break for once, given the secluded location. I'll reach out to you when it's time to make an official statement. We can figure things out then."

"But—"

"No buts, Coco." Gavin sounded as tired as he looked. "Go home and enjoy your weekend."

"What about uploading the safety PSA?" I was still a bit dazed by the sudden change in Gavin's demeanor.

Gavin sent a pointed look toward the medical examiner and his team. "Put a pin in it for now. We have other *safety* issues to deal with at the moment."

With a gentle but firm hand, Adrian led me away from the beachfront and up the embankment toward the squad car.

Gavin called over his shoulder. "And keep a tight lid on this, will you? We owe it to Larry's wife to inform her about his death before releasing her husband's name to the public."

I grunted. *Good luck keeping a secret this big in Central Shores.*

A tense silence lingered until Adrian and I were buckled in our seats. "Sorry about dragging you into this." He offered a supportive smile as he started the car and pulled away from the crime scene.

I didn't trust myself to respond. I *was* glad Gavin and Adrian had asked me to accompany them to the beach. I certainly didn't relish seeing another dead body, but the evidence poking out from Larry's neck had me even more concerned. Not to mention Gavin's condemning questions and suspicious attitude toward the situation. Even though we hadn't encountered a single soul on the dunes, I had obtained information vital to fulfilling my role. Not as a PR consultant but as a best friend.

There is no way I will let the police accuse Jasper of cold-blooded murder.

Chapter Five

When Adrian dropped me off at the police station, I was eager to follow Gavin's advice and head straight home. Although given the shocking evidence found protruding from Larry's neck, I didn't plan to "enjoy the weekend" as the solemn lieutenant had suggested.

"I'm fine, I promise," I assured a worried Adrian and relieved him of his chauffeur duties, allowing him to return to the crime scene. I waved until the police cruiser disappeared. Once I was no longer in Adrian's rearview mirror, I wiped the cheery smile off my face. I had to find Jasper before the police did and ask him how a corkscrew engraved with *his* name could have ended up in a dead body.

With determined steps, I hustled toward my parked MINI, setting a mental destination for home.

"That took longer than expected. Everything okay?" Hudson greeted me with a hesitant expression as I barged into our condo. From his seat at our kitchen island, he pushed a steaming cup of coffee toward me, eyes crinkled with concern.

It was only eight-thirty, but due to the crime scene detour, my time at the police station lasted longer than I promised Hudson it would. Saturdays and Sundays were the only time we had to enjoy each other's company these days. Late weeknights at WMTG often left Hudson completely exhausted, and I always did my consulting work in the morning, leaving us schedule-crossed lovers.

I accepted the medium roast brew gratefully and collapsed onto the cushy barstool next to him. I'd been hoping to have this conversation with Hudson *after* locating Jasper, but keeping him in the dark wasn't fair. "I'm sorry, babe. Ran into a bit of an issue."

Hudson rubbed my back. "What's wrong? Did the video file upload poorly or something?"

I gathered my long, loose, strawberry-champagne-colored hair into a bun and tied a sloppy knot on top of my head. "Oh, that I could handle." I went to work massaging my temples. "Before we could even fire up Maude's computer, Officer Thompson radioed in from the south shore."

Ever the inquisitive journalist, Hudson's back straightened. "What about? He didn't find a beached whale or something, did he?"

"You could say that…." I cringed at the rude comment that erupted from my mouth. *Wow, way to respect the dead, Coco.*

My boyfriend's brown eyes narrowed. "You've got a haunted look about you. What's going on?"

I took a reaffirming sip of coffee, reveling in the bitter aftertaste. It mirrored my mood. "You can't tell anyone about this, Hudson. This is *so* far off the record—"

He held a hand over his heart. "I solemnly swear."

"Larry Dunmer's body washed ashore down at Pelican Beach."

I should have waited until after Hudson had swallowed his coffee, as the shock of my admission made him choke back his drink. Patting him on the back to ease him through a coughing fit, I sighed. "Sorry. Not a smart move on my part."

"Ha, well, I should have been better prepared. You do have a flair for drama." Hudson wiped his mouth as he cocked a teasing eyebrow. Yet, as he continued to study my body language, the concern returned to his gaze. "Your anxiety levels suggest our charming neighbor didn't drown during his morning swim."

I had precious little time to locate Jasper before the police did, so I gave Hudson a quick rundown of the wild events that had occurred since I'd departed for the police station. "So now," I hastily concluded, "I need to find Jasper."

"Why?"

Could Hudson not connect all the dots? "Um, because Gavin wants to question him about Larry's *murder.*"

Hudson rose from his barstool and sauntered over to the Keurig to punch in another cup. "Do you think that's necessary, Cokes? I mean, Gavin can't possibly believe that Jasper had anything to do with it." As his coffee finished its final drip, he turned to face me.

Sticking my chin out in defiance, I countered, "You didn't hear the questions he asked me about Larry and Jasper. I'm sure it won't be long before the police hear how Larry threatened Jasper's livelihood before the Dunmers were tossed out of Vine." My irritated gaze meandered over to the party favors we'd left on the kitchen countertop when we'd come home the previous night. "That could be construed as motive, and Jasper's name is literally sticking out of Larry's body."

"Jasper didn't even take his corkscrew with him, remember?" Hudson paused. "You were going to grab it on our way out."

Great. If he starts saying that around town, the police will be after me next.

"But I didn't." I scooted out of my seat and grabbed my personalized party trinket to closely examine the craftsmanship. "I got sidetracked by the effects of the Austrian pinot and totally forgot."

"Okay. Still, we saw Jasper leave the party without it. He'll be fine." Hudson wandered into the living room and plopped onto the sectional couch facing our big-screen TV. He was clearly ready to move to other topics.

I wasn't. "Who's to say the police will believe us that Jasper didn't take his corkscrew?"

Hudson's raised brow had a condescending arch to it. "I'm sure they'll take our word for it. You do work for Chief McInnis, after all."

I hated how his calm, logical approach made total and complete sense. I wanted to believe him. I wanted to believe I was overreacting and that everything would turn out fine. Still, my panic over Jasper becoming embroiled in a police investigation got the better of my reasoning. "Well, I'm going over to have a little chat with him. See you later." I regretted the cool delivery of my announcement as soon as it was out of my mouth, but I didn't have it in me to apologize. This wasn't the first time Hudson's rational attitude clashed with my hotheaded emotions, and it wouldn't be the last. Luckily for us, it kept our relationship spicy.

"All right, then. But please, Coco, be careful."

Hudson's quiet plea stopped me in my tracks as I reached the front door. I should have known better by now. Hudson wasn't trying to belittle my instincts. He was just trying to keep me safe.

On impulse, I whirled around and raced to the couch, planting a deep kiss on his surprised lips. "I'm sorry. I just need to make sure Jasper's okay."

Hudson returned my apology with an even more sensual kiss that curled my toes. "I know. I've seen that sparkle in your eyes before, though. Don't put yourself in the middle of this, babes, if you can help it."

Since I wasn't even sure what was going on that I could put myself in the middle of, I backed away without another word. Hudson knew my silence indicated I wasn't ready to make a promise to him I might break, and he respected me to make my own decisions.

Once outside, I hurried along the walkway that wove around the entire Sunny Shores development. My condo was one of two properties with direct access to the water, so my place was a little farther away from Charlotte's and Jasper's homes up the road. Passing the Dunmers' rental, I kept my head forward, but my gaze darted to the side to examine the scene. Drawn curtains eclipsed every window, giving no sign of life. In an unexpected surge of compassion, I wondered if Rosalynn had been told about her husband's death yet. Telling someone their husband had been murdered seemed like it required an in-person visit. Since I hadn't spotted a police cruiser in the neighborhood, I assumed Rosalynn was still blissfully unaware of this morning's awful developments.

I reached Jasper's in record time, anxiety fueling the harsh pounding I gave to the front door. What if the police had skipped Rosalynn's home and gone straight to dragging Jasper down to the station?

"Good grief." My best friend moaned, wiping sleep from his eyes as he answered my summons. "What could you possibly need this early?"

"It's almost nine." I walked past him into the living area of his condo and claimed a seat on the couch for myself.

Jasper followed my lead, retying the knot of his rugby fleece bathrobe. Even though it was the middle of summer, his house chilled at arctic temperatures with the help of central air.

"Make yourself at home," he grumbled, rubbing his red eyes once more.

As I settled against the firm cushions and assessed his appearance, shock radiated through me. Jasper was always immaculately coifed, never a hair out of place. A habit of his since we were teenagers. Even at sleepovers, he always woke up with a dewy glow. This morning, though, crimson circles lined his baby blues, almost as if he'd been crying. His unkempt hair and frumpy slouch put me immediately on edge. "Is everything okay? You look awful...no offense." I tried to recover my gaffe with humor.

Jasper's scowl deepened. "I had a late night."

When he didn't elaborate, I pressed him for more details, as he'd never fully explained what had lured him away from the Vine party so unexpectedly. "Doing what?"

"I had a meeting." His attempt at a nonchalant shrug was stiff.

My fists clenched with frustration. "Come on, Jasper, if it's a hot date you're covering up, I promise I won't tease you. It's great you're finally taking a break from work. It's been ages since you've dated someone. Who is it? Someone I know? A guy, a girl, or—"

"It wasn't a date," he snapped.

Yikes, I'd definitely woken Jasper up on the wrong side of the bed.

"Why are you here, Coco?"

In our twenty-plus years of friendship, not once had I ever felt uncomfortable around my bestie. Until now. Something about his haggard manner put me on edge. "Look, I'm sorry to be the bearer of bad news, but something tragic happened this morning, and you need to be prepared to deal with the fallout." With a fortifying breath, I launched into the sordid tale of Larry's body being found on the beach, with Jasper's monogrammed corkscrew sticking out of his neck.

To his credit, Jasper kept calm during my spiel, reserving his comments for the end.

"Well, I hope you don't think *I* had anything to do with it."

His unmistakable sarcasm pulled a tight smile across my lips. "No, you big dummy. I don't." I paused, gnawing at the inside of my cheek. "I'm just worried about how this will play out in the court of public opinion. With the corkscrew being a key piece of evidence, the police will be forced to drag you into their investigation. Believe me, being connected to a murder is no walk in the PR park."

"I guess you have a point. This isn't good." Jasper rubbed the light stubble scattered over his chin. "Everyone at Vine did see me have words with Larry."

I snorted. "Well, who hasn't had words with that man?"

"Touché," Jasper conceded, "but I can't deny that last night's debacle doesn't paint a pretty picture for me. The douchenozzle threatened to ruin my career."

My tongue felt like sandpaper. I'd hoped talking everything out with Jasper would help me realize that I was completely overreacting. But he was right. Jasper certainly had the motive to want Larry dead. "Hey, Larry threatened to sabotage *Trending Topic,* too."

"Yeah, but your corkscrew wasn't found shoved into his neck, now, was it?"

I winced at the blunt imagery. "I'm sure once Hudson, Charlotte, and I tell the police you didn't even take your party favor with you, that will be the end of it." Oh, the irony. I'd used my boyfriend's unwelcomed logical explanation to smooth over the situation. "But when the deets about Larry's death get leaked, you might want to prepare for a boatload of press that could affect *Divulge.*"

Jasper waved a hand aside. "Please. What's the golden rule?"

We said it together. "No publicity is bad publicity."

Our in-sync delivery elicited only a half-hearted laugh from Jasper. His blasé attitude about the whole situation had suddenly evaporated.

I leaned forward in my seat. "What's wrong?"

"Well, if clearing my name relies solely on you guys saying I left without my corkscrew, we might have a problem." Jasper scratched his head. "You see, I hit up Vine on my way home from Dover to see if you all were still there."

My heart somersaulted. "Um, why didn't you just text?"

"I stupidly decided to install that new, huge software update on my cell during the car ride back. It was on an infuriating load screen for hours." He shuddered. Jasper was never without his iPhone. He clutched it in his palm as we spoke. Being without it for even a few minutes drove him up a wall. "Since I couldn't message you, I opted to stop by Vine."

I didn't like where this was going. "We left around ten. Charlotte and I had to be up early for work."

Jasper nodded. "I ran into Andre, and he told me you guys left to get your beauty sleep. He then reminded me to pick up my corkscrew because I mentioned that I hadn't had a chance to grab it. Since there was no point in hanging around the party without you, I swung by the souvenir table on my way out." An annoyed frown grew on Jasper's face. "I couldn't find one with my name on it. I checked every corkscrew left. Mine wasn't there." He sighed. "But I didn't bother telling Andre. He was too busy schmoozing some folks who reeked of Crestview privilege. So, I just pretended to take a corkscrew and split."

The implications of Jasper's polite actions rained down on me. "Oh no." His statement made anything Hudson, Charlotte, and I could tell the police irrelevant. Any investigator with half a brain could poke holes in Jasper's story. Of course, he wouldn't admit to picking up the party favor if he'd used it to kill his onerous neighbor, especially after said neighbor had threatened his media empire.

It was my turn to rub my eyes, not with weariness but with building tension. "Maybe someone else can confirm that you actually didn't grab a souvenir."

Jasper sighed as he rose from his chair and shuffled into the open-concept kitchen. "I doubt it. By the time I returned to the party, everyone was thoroughly sloshed on grapes."

I joined him at the counter as he toasted two slices of bread. I waited until he was done slathering apricot jam on his breakfast before continuing with my questions. "So, you bailed on us to drive up to Dover last night?"

"I told you. I had a meeting," Jasper mumbled through a crunchy mouthful.

I stared at him for a beat. "You've mentioned *that* much. Who was it with?"

He wrinkled his nose. "Why does it matter?"

I drummed my fingers anxiously on the countertop. "Well, for one, they might be your alibi."

Jasper shook his head. "I'm sure once I talk to the police, everything will be fine. You're getting way ahead of yourself, Coco." He eyed me curiously. "It's like you *want* me to be a suspect or something."

"*What*? Are you insane?"

He rolled his eyes. "No. But that squeaky denial voice makes me think *you* actually might be." His sly expression morphed into a grin. "You want a reason to stick your nose into Larry's death, don't you? Like you did with Stacy's murder?" He *tsked* as he wiggled a finger in front of my nose. "You're a murder mystery addict looking for a fix."

I puffed my chest out defensively. "I only got caught up in Stacy's murder because the chief tried to pin the crime on my clients."

Jasper's groomed eyebrows shot up, but he wisely held his tongue.

"This is totally different," I pressed onward. "I was there at the beach. I saw Gavin's reaction to the corkscrew." My sea-foam gaze pinned Jasper in his place. "The police are going to follow the evidence. What if all the evidence conveniently points to you?"

My best friend's confidence deflated right before me as confusion settled across his features. "You think someone is trying to *frame* me?"

Chapter Six

As ridiculous as the notion sounded, especially in our close-knit community, I couldn't ignore the nagging feeling in my gut. "Look at it this way. Someone either took an engraved party favor with your name on it by accident and ended up killing a man with it, or someone took it on purpose."

"I know I can rub people the wrong way," Jasper muttered with a sheepish shrug, "but dang, I don't think I've pissed anyone off enough to want to pin a *murder* on me."

I offered another explanation. "Maybe it was a spur-of-the-moment thing. Everyone at Vine witnessed you and Larry square off. Perhaps the killer saw it as an opportunity to cover their own tracks and acted on it."

Jasper sighed. "I can't believe I'm encouraging your *Only Murders in the Building* behavior, but we haven't even asked the most obvious question. Who in Central Shores wanted Larry Dunmer dead?"

I kept a sarcastic *Who didn't?* to myself because it really wasn't true. Larry might have been a bigot and an awful sleaze, but even those unfortunate personality traits didn't warrant murder.

"While you stew on that, I'm going to shower." Jasper disappeared down the hallway toward his primary suite.

The sound of the water running soothed my racing thoughts. I hopped down from the barstool and searched around the kitchen drawers until I found one stocked with pens and scraps of paper. While Jasper made himself presentable, I would come up with a list of potential suspects to whom Gavin could redirect his questions.

47

Who despised Larry Dunmer enough to want him dead? He and Rosalynn had been living in Central Shores for less than two months, but in that time, Larry had made a name for himself around town...and not in a good way. Besides Charlotte's café, he'd also gotten himself tossed out from Squeezed, the local juice bar owned and operated by my friend, Lacie Burbank. The thought that she could kill Larry was laughable. Lacie had been my babysitter, for Adele's sake.

Larry and his wife had also caused a scene at Beaufort's, the most upscale restaurant on the strip. Owned by Fred and Natalia Beaufort, Larry and Rosalynn had been dangerously close to losing their dining privileges after Larry "accidentally" dumped hot soup on a waiter simply because the poor kid brought a different-shaped spoon than Larry had requested. Hudson and I had been having a rare date night at Beaufort's when the dramatic scene occurred. I still couldn't believe Fred hadn't barred the Dunmers from returning. He was more forgiving than me, for sure.

The more I mulled over the situation, the more I was certain every business owner in Central Shores had a story about the Dunmers. But did hissy fits and tantrums really merit murder?

Perhaps it had something to do with the state department audit. Larry definitely wasn't above making threats. I'd learned that the hard way last night. Maybe he had threatened to cut a portion of the town budget that someone else was willing to fight for. I tapped the pen rhythmically against the marble countertop as I wrestled with the theory. Perhaps Mom could spill the tea on how the audit was progressing. As a Central Shores town councilor, she must be in the know.

Then there was Rosalynn Dunmer. I couldn't overlook the motive of love and marriage. Love caused people to do both amazing and terrible things. Rosalynn was clearly devoted to her husband and extremely territorial over him. She painted Larry as a saint, even as he ogled other women right in front of her. How could Ros look past such hurtful transgressions? Had she finally been humiliated by his antics one too many times?

I scribbled Rosalynn's name across the top of the Post-it. Ros had access to Vine last night, however briefly. She could have pocketed Jasper's party favor before she and Larry left, especially since she'd also been on the receiving end of Jasper's anger. Two birds with one stone, so to speak: kill her obnoxious husband, all while framing her adversarial neighbor.

"Wow. What an exhaustive list," Jasper commented dryly as he sauntered back into the kitchen. His dark hair was still wet, but he looked much more put together than he had just a few minutes ago.

I whistled. "That was fast."

Jasper smoothed the nonexistent wrinkles in his plaid shorts. "I'll probably get sunspots as punishment. I thought I'd better be quick, so I didn't have time to tone, exfoliate, *and* apply retinol serum." He patted his pale cheek tenderly. "I hope my canvas forgives me for only moisturizing today."

I laughed at his elaborate skincare routine. "I'm sure you'll be fine."

A sudden, fervent knock echoed from the front door.

Wordlessly questioning each other who it could be, both Jasper and I hurried to the entrance. My bestie took a breath deep enough to fill the sails of a three-masted ship before grabbing the handle and pulling open the door.

Detective Harriet Forester's sharp features greeted us. As surprised as we were to see her standing on Jasper's doorstep, she didn't appear shocked to see me standing beside my best friend.

Her pale, thin lips pressed together. "Lieutenant McInnis warned me you might be here, Ms. Cline." Then, in a fluid motion, she removed her aviator sunglasses, looking like a proper lady boss in her crisp maroon suit. Not a strand of brown hair was out of place, and her creamy skin dared the sun to make her sweat. "Jasper Hastings? I'm Detective Harriet Forester. Mind if I come in?"

The sight of the Sussex County investigator had clearly rocked Jasper to his core. He didn't move a muscle as he stared at her, open-mouthed.

I saw this as my cue to assume control of the situation. With gritted teeth, I maneuvered Jasper's stiff, bulky frame out of the doorway before welcoming Detective Forester inside. "Can I get you anything to drink?" I asked her, wringing my fidgeting hands as we moved into the living area.

"No. I'm afraid this isn't a social visit." She relaxed her face enough to send a tight smile my way. "Lieutenant McInnis thought it best for me to ask Mr. Hastings some questions about his movements last night while the forensics guys finish things up at the beach."

I bobbed my chin, doing my best to bury a surge of anxiety. Harriet's reappearance was something I had not expected. With Deacon and his team working at the police department as forensic techs, I thought the days of needing help from the county crime lab were long gone. I guessed not.

Detective Forester studied me for a moment before turning to an ashen-faced Jasper. It was evident the reality of the situation was becoming all too much for him. "Mr. Hastings, I'm sure Ms. Cline—despite being told *not* to—has informed you that Larry Dunmer was found dead this morning, yes?"

For a second, I worried Jasper wouldn't respond, but he gave a subtle nod.

The detective claimed an elegant, winged-back chair in Jasper's mid-century modern living room. Clasping her hands together, Harriet said calmly, "We're treating Mr. Dunmer's death as an active homicide investigation." She paused, allowing a moment for her words to sink in. "The police and the county crime lab will be working together to ensure justice is served for Mr. Dunmer. We plan to conduct an unbiased, thorough investigation so that the killer, once apprehended, won't be released by a jury on some technicality."

While her explanation was simple enough, the underlying message was clear. Gavin didn't think he could lead an impartial investigation where the most obvious suspect was a person he'd been friends with since elementary school. Well, either Gavin didn't think he could, or his uncle wouldn't let him. After Chief McInnis's bitter war with our former mayor over relevancy, the police department's reputation in the community was sterling, something the chief was proud of and wanted to maintain.

"What questions do you have for me, Detective?" Jasper's throat wobbled a bit.

Harriet pulled out a notepad and pen from the depths of her suit jacket, all while trying to break the tension with another smile. It lifted my spirits a smidge. She couldn't seriously believe Jasper had anything to do with

Larry's death, could she?

"Mr. Hastings, will you please recall your movements last night for me, starting at seven o'clock?"

"Sure." Jasper gulped. "I arrived at Vine for a private party, along with Ms. Cline, here, and our two friends, Hudson Caruthers and Charlotte Whittaker." He glanced at me, searching for reassurance.

I gave him an encouraging nod. Everything was going to be fine. My bestie was innocent, and the police would be able to see that in no time.

"Once we were admitted by a bouncer," Jasper continued, "the four of us spoke briefly with Andre Nunez, the proprietor, before getting drinks and food."

Detective Forester's gaze was inscrutable. "Did you speak to anyone else while you were at the event?"

"I made small talk with other guests. I also had very public words with Larry Dunmer and his wife." Jasper's hesitance turned to annoyance over the unpleasant memory.

The detective's brows drew together. "About?"

"Oh, several things. Coco and I stopped Larry from harassing our poor server. Once we rescued her, Larry turned his attention to insulting me and my magazine. He made some disparaging remarks at the expense of my female employees." Jasper's gaze grew more perturbed. "He referred to them as prostitutes."

Detective Forester scribbled a few notes before she spoke. "And this was the first time you two had ever had a disagreement?"

I jumped into the fray, hoping to paint Harriet a picture of how sleazy and mean Larry had been in life. "Jasper, didn't you tell us that Larry accused you daily of running a brothel, all because you had your creative team over to brainstorm the July layout?" I willed my friend to tell the story, but his lips remained shut. "You see, Detective," I said, turning my focus to Harriet, "Jasper's creative team consists of photographers, editors, journalists, and models. Come to find out, Larry was just making trouble due to his wounded ego. He tried flirting with the female members of Jasper's team, only to have his unwanted advances rebuffed."

51

"I see." Harriet pursed her lips. "So, Mr. Dunmer made a habit of antagonizing you, Mr. Hastings?"

I panicked at her probing tone. *Crap! What was I thinking, telling that story?* Now I'd only added fuel to the fire that Larry and Jasper had an ongoing battle of egos or something.

Jasper sent me a chastising glare but answered the question in a calm demeanor. "I wouldn't say I suffered his delusions on a regular basis, as I avoided the man as much as possible. It was tricky, though, since I lived right up the street from him."

With a dip of her chin, Detective Forester seemed to concede her point. "Please, continue telling me about your evening then."

"As I was saying before Coco's little anecdote—" Jasper sent another pointed glance my way "—I had some words with Larry and Rosalynn, which ended with Andre Nunez asking the Dunmers to leave. Shortly after the Dunmers left the party, I received a last-minute meeting invite and had to depart Vine as well. I drove to Dover, had my meeting, and was on the road by ten thirty." Jasper proceeded to explain what he'd already told me. He'd stopped by Vine once more to see if my friends and I were still there and was reminded by Andre to take a party favor. "None of the remaining gifts had my name engraved on them, so I did not take one."

"Did you point this out to Mr. Nunez? Or to anyone else at the party?" Detective Forester asked. She'd been listening to Jasper with rapt attention.

My bestie shook his head. "No. Believe me, I wish now more than anything I had. I simply chalked it up to someone taking mine by mistake and went home."

"What time did you arrive back here, Mr. Hastings?"

"A little after eleven thirty. I can't recall the exact time."

Detective Forester paused for a moment, her pen hovering over her notebook. "Can anyone confirm your arrival?"

"No, ma'am. They cannot."

I nearly snickered at the reverence in Jasper's contrite tone. The detective couldn't be older than thirty-six, but he was treating her like the Queen. Seeing my friend act so completely out of character both amused and alarmed me.

With a furrowed brow, Detective Forester continued her line of questioning. Clearly, she wasn't thrilled to be called 'ma'am,' either. "So, you arrived home sometime before midnight. What happened then?"

"I got ready for bed and was under the covers by one o'clock. I remember the time because I silenced the ringer on my phone right before I turned off the lights."

A slight smirk twitched on the detective's lips. "It took you over an hour to get ready for bed?"

Jasper brought a hand to his face. "I have a pretty intense skincare regime."

In a rare display of character, Harriet snorted. "Goodness. And I thought taking off my makeup was a pain."

I studied Jasper for a moment, a funny feeling developing in my stomach. Was he lying about the amount of time he'd spent getting ready for bed? It seemed to me like he had skipped out on his nightly ritual based on how awful he'd looked when he opened the door this morning. If Jasper hadn't been going through his nightly routine, why had he gone to bed so late? I made a mental note to question him later. I certainly wasn't going to call him out in front of the detective. He must have had his reasons...maybe a Tinder *or* Grindr date dropped by?

Still chuckling to herself, Harriet wrote a few more notes down. "Well, thank you for speaking with me, Mr. Hastings. Since we are still in the very early stages of our investigation, we may need to reach out to you again. Unfortunately, we haven't been able to notify the next-of-kin yet, so I must ask that you keep these details to yourself for now. Chief McInnis is adamant about keeping Larry Dunmer's identity confidential until his wife has been told."

"Of course." Jasper bowed his head.

I straightened in my seat now that her interview with Jasper had concluded. "Do you need anything from me, Detective Forester?"

She skillfully raised one eyebrow. "Do you have something to share that's relevant to the case, Ms. Cline?"

"Uh...." I fumbled with my words. I had nothing for the detective other than the steadfast belief that Jasper didn't have anything to do with this crime. "Not to speak ill of the dead, but Larry ticked off quite a few people since arriving in Central Shores. You have your work cut out for you."

"Yes, *my* work is correct." She pinned me with a stern glare. "I'm warning you, Ms. Cline, leave this case to the professionals. I'm willing to overlook your transgression of sharing confidential information with Mr. Hastings *if* you can promise me that. Your interference in Stacy Lockner's case may have proven fruitful, but civilians often do more harm than good when meddling with police matters."

I bristled at the term "meddling" but kept my mouth shut. I'd rightfully earned the rebuke. Gavin had ordered me to keep Larry's death under wraps, and I'd already told two people.

Jasper escorted the detective to the door and bid her goodbye, only to slink back into the living room and collapse on the couch. "That was worse than Anna Wintour forgetting my name immediately after I introduced myself to her at New York Fashion Week."

"Come on." I nudged him on the knee. "I think Harriet's on your side. Gavin certainly is, or he wouldn't have sent someone else to conduct an 'unbiased' interview."

Jasper wrung his hands, worry flooding his eyes. "You didn't hear her just now by the door. She told me not to leave town, Cokes. What more could they need from me?"

I replayed Detective Forester's visit, trying to figure out the detective's reasoning. "Of course! The timeline she asked you about was way too broad." I jumped up and paced behind the couch. "It's been like three hours since Larry's body was found. There's no way the medical examiner has done an autopsy or anything."

"I thought you said the cause of death was pretty obvious," Jasper said with dry humor.

Cringing as the image of the bloodied corkscrew once again overtook my brain, I shook my head. "Cause of death, yes, but *time* of death, no. The water damage to Larry's body will severely limit the medical examiner's ability to make an accurate assessment. I bet Harriet was covering all her bases to start, so she asked you to recount your evening beginning at seven." I folded my arms. "Once they've narrowed the timeframe to when Larry was killed...."

"She'll be back."

Jasper's spot-on *Terminator* impression did nothing to lift our punctured spirits.

Chapter Seven

My phone buzzed on Jasper's kitchen countertop. I snatched it up and felt my stomach flip-flop as I read the notification. It was a text from Gavin.

Done @ beach. Can u come down to the PD? Need ur help w/ statement.

A giant wave of relief washed over me. Detective Forester's willingness to overlook my blabbing to Jasper and, now, Gavin's summons gave me hope that the police didn't consider Jasper a real suspect in Larry's death. If they did, they wouldn't want his best friend and confidante prowling around the station with insider access. Since Gavin was reaching out for help, it meant I was still trusted to remain on board. They had hired me, after all, to help manage any press releases that needed issuing. I bet they hadn't expected my BFF to be at the center of their next big case, though.

I tapped a quick answer into my phone. **Be down in 15.**

"Will you be okay?" I asked Jasper after explaining why I had to leave so suddenly.

He waved a hand, shooing me out the door. "I'll be fine. The best place for you to be is where there's information."

"Go visit Charlotte or something. I don't like the idea of you being cooped up here all by yourself."

"Why? Because you don't want people gossiping that I've become a murderous recluse?"

Glad to see Jasper's sarcastic spirits were back, I waved my middle finger in fond farewell and jogged out the door. I'd been a little overzealous with my fifteen-minute response to Gavin, so I hurried back home, told Hudson in between breaths where I was going, and hopped back into Jolly. Thirteen minutes later, I pulled into the same parking spot I'd vacated earlier in the morning, ready for work. Again. It felt a bit like *Groundhog Day*.

The town square was ghostly quiet as I zipped across the Commons. A typical weekend sight, really, considering most of the action in Central Shores happened down at the beachside strip. The library had a few visitors milling about in its windows while the town hall was locked up tight. The fire station and police station also ringed the small park where I'd spent many afternoons as a teenager, hanging out with my friends.

Maude was already buzzing me back into the station's inner sanctum by the time I stepped over the building's threshold.

"How's everyone holding up?" I stopped by her desk to check in on the harried receptionist.

Rubbing the bridge of her nose, Maude released a low grumble. "So much for enjoying my grandsons' company. The chief asked everyone to come in today to strategize."

Strategize? "That doesn't sound like the chief," I commented dryly, pleased to pull a smile across Maude's face.

"No kidding. More like he'll tell us what to think and what to do." She issued a snort of disapproval over the chief's somewhat dictatorial leadership tactics.

I closed my mouth before I got us both in trouble and hustled down the hall into the station's lone conference room, currently filled to the brim with bodies. At first glance, I spied Adrian and Frank standing in the corner behind a seated Gavin and Rita Yoon. I didn't interact much with Rita at the station, as she was the ranking officer on the night shift. However, I'd gotten to know her through our volunteer work at a local soup kitchen, and thus, I'd become quite friendly with Rita and her partner, Heather.

Detective Forester's tightly wound bun caught my eye next. She was furiously typing away on her laptop at the conference table. Next to her, Deacon Lait lounged in a chair, his strong, dark hands drumming nervously on the tabletop. Standing behind Deacon were the vaguely familiar faces of several crime techs who'd been involved with the last murder I'd been witness to.

Lording over them at the front of the room stood Chief Lloyd McInnis, his stormy blue eyes squinting in my direction as I entered. "Nice of you to finally join us, Ms. Cline." His tone suggested his displeasure that I was the last to arrive. Or maybe, based on his visor, polo, and khakis, he was still irritated to have been summoned away from the green.

Gavin cleared his throat. "I told her she could go home, Chief. She came back as soon as I asked her to."

I gave Gavin an appreciative smile for standing up to his formidable uncle and slunk behind the conference table chairs, claiming a spot against the wall near Adrian.

Chief McInnis ignored his nephew and turned his hulking frame back to the whiteboard. Then, with a dry-erase marker, he wrote in childish scrawl: *Salute to Summer.*

Disappointment vaulted through me. Why were we talking about the Salute to Summer festival when a killer was on the loose?

Chief McInnis glowered at his confused team, agitation written all over his face. "I just got off the phone with Roger. He's concerned about how this will affect the celebrations kicking off on Friday."

Detective Forester's raptor gaze whipped up from her computer screen. "More concerned than the fact a man is dead?"

New to his position, Mayor Roger Sullivan had been doing a fine job as far as the citizens of Central Shores were concerned, so his insensitive response surprised me as well.

Chief McInnis sighed, stroking his sandy beard, speckled with strands of gray. "No. The mayor was very upset to hear about Dunmer's death, especially given that they'd become close friends over the course of the town audit." He tapped the dry-erase marker against his open palm. "Roger's demanding Larry's killer be brought to justice, but..." the chief paused, and his steely gaze landed on me, "the mayor is extremely worried about how this will affect Salute to Summer turnout. The town is counting on the festival's income. Luckily for us, we have our very own PR consultant to help navigate these murky waters."

All eyes turned to me. Heat pounded in my cheeks as I struggled to summon a response. I had not been expecting Chief McInnis to lean on me *this* extensively, considering how much he liked to be the one in charge. Now, he was all but asking me to present a media strategy off the top of my head. "It's all about the details, Chief." My voice was somewhat shaky, but I kept my head held high. I prayed he didn't expect much more at the moment.

He nodded. "Agreed. We'll have to issue a statement, but we can be blissfully brief. We also haven't been able to track down and notify Rosalynn Dunmer yet, so until we inform next-of-kin, we cannot and will not release Larry's name to the media." His stern tone left no room for argument.

No Rosalynn? Where the heck is she? Aloud, I shared, "Without a name, it will be harder for news crews and media outlets to drum up public interest in the story." As I started assembling a plan, my confidence began to rise. "A nameless person won't pull on the heartstrings of their audiences as much."

"It also makes our job tougher," Chief McInnis added with a growl. "As soon as we start asking questions about Dunmer, people will begin to speculate. So, I want locating the wife to be a priority." McInnis shot a commanding glare toward Gavin.

Detective Forester rose from her chair and joined the chief at the front of the room. "We also don't know for certain how the victim died." Her remark elicited a few snorts of barbed laughter. "I know it seems obvious, but the medical examiner's report may tell us he died due to drowning."

Mixing all the facts I'd gathered thus far, I presented my entrée in my most news-anchory-kind of voice. "*At this time, local authorities can confirm an unidentified body washed ashore at Pelican Beach this morning.*"

Chief McInnis snapped his fingers. "That'll work. Pelican Beach runs the length of a few towns, so that will keep Central Shores directly out of the spotlight for now." He folded his arms across his chest and scanned his eager team. "Which gives us precious little time to get to the bottom of this. We need to find the wife. From what we know about the Dunmers, she doesn't let her husband stray far, so it's odd we haven't been able to touch base with her."

"What's more, her cell is turned off, and she isn't answering the Dunmers' landline," Gavin added.

Deacon cleared his throat. "There might be another body out there, then."

I stilled at his remark. It hadn't crossed my mind that Rosalynn could be dead, too. Oh, God.

"Coast guard is conducting a water search as we speak," Chief McInnis replied. "We're trying to get ahold of her cell phone location data, but that will take time. Harriet, when is the ME's report due back?"

The detective glanced at her phone before answering. "He'll have it to us no later than three. Mayor Sullivan made sure we got bumped to the top at the county lab."

"Great." Chief McInnis rubbed his hands together. "Coco, you work on disseminating the statement. Loop in the neighboring police departments, too. But no names, no specifics, no nothing. Got it?"

I gave him a mock salute in response.

"Now that we've got our PR strategy worked out for the time being, you're dismissed."

The words were out of my mouth before I could stop them. "Don't you want my help figuring out who had it in for Larry? He was my neighbor, after all."

A flurry of expressions battled for dominance on the chief's features. Smug arrogance won. "Coco, we are plenty capable of solving a case without your assistance. Last time I checked, we hired you for tweeting, not interfering."

Once again, everyone's eyes fell on me as I flinched at the chief's snide glare. Yes, it had been silly to hope I would somehow be involved, but I couldn't help it. I'd blown things wide open for McInnis and his team during their last murder investigation. Didn't that mean I was kinda good at cracking a case? And how else was I going to keep apprised of how well Jasper faired in all this if I wasn't allowed access?

Chief McInnis raised a self-satisfied eyebrow as if he could hear my inner monologue.

I begrudgingly backed out of the room in defeat. With heavy footsteps,

I made my way toward the front of the station, where I found Maude FaceTiming with her little grandsons on her phone.

"I'm sorry Gam-Gam isn't there, my loves, but we'll go out for ice cream when I get back." She made kissy faces at the camera before signing off upon my arrival. "Everyone playing nice back there?"

"So far." I grinned. "At least, from what I was allowed to see."

Maude rolled her eyes. "Chief McInnis is under a lot of pressure to wrap this up quickly with Salute to Summer right around the corner. How he's supposed to do that, I don't know. Things like obtaining warrants and forensic testing take time. I swear the chief is convinced Larry did this to himself to sabotage the police station's reputation."

"Really?" I plopped down in front of Maude's abandoned computer and began pulling up the department's email, Facebook, and Twitter accounts. I'd start by emailing a brief statement to the neighboring precincts in the surrounding towns. "What makes him think that?"

"Oh, that Dunmer fellow was always in here demanding to speak with him, wanting to file a report about something or another. The first few complaints the chief took relatively seriously, but then it became clear Larry just enjoyed wasting his time." Maude lowered her voice despite the fact we were alone. "The chief didn't want me telling you this, but one morning Larry came with—well, was practically dragged in—by his wife. She berated him into asking me how to file a restraining order."

"What? Who did Larry need a restraining order from?" Whoever it was, they might have been the person who killed Larry. Maybe the police *should* have taken him seriously…

"You."

And then again, maybe not.

"*Me?* What in the name of Taylor's Version are you talking about?"

Maude chuckled. "That's exactly how Chief McInnis reacted when he came out to see what the commotion was, minus the Taylor Swift reference. Rosalynn was under the impression you were stalking her husband because he scorned unwelcome advances from you."

My jaw nearly hit the keyboard. "You're joking, aren't you? Please tell me you're joking."

Maude raised her hand to her heart. "I swear on my grandbabies."

Anger and rage mingled with confusion as I tried to wade through the incredible information Maude had just shared.

"Of course, Chief McInnis thought it was a load of crock. We've heard your horror stories about Larry's awful attitude enough times. It quickly became clear that Rosalynn felt threatened by her husband's fascination with you and was making up baseless accusations." Maude patted me on the arm. "Larry himself was more than ready to let it all go. But Rosalynn kept hounding him, and they got into a bit of a tiff. Eventually, Chief McInnis yelled at them both for wasting our time and sent them packing. Since then, our town hall friends say Larry has been looking for ways to slash our budget with his audit."

Hmm. So, even Chief McInnis had a bone to pick with Larry. Yet another reason for Detective Harriet Forester's objective presence, I presumed.

Glancing at the clock on the wall, I wrapped up my small talk with Maude and started to tackle the rest of my task list. Chief McInnis had already spoken with the mayor, so my next move was to call the *Central Shores Gazette* and relay the vague yet informative statement. After several rounds of "No comment. No comment. No comment," I moved on to the other local news outlets in the area, reading my statement word-for-word. Then I took to Twitter and Facebook, posting a brief press release for the community to read and interpret on their own. Comments began to spring up on the Facebook post almost immediately after I uploaded it. My spirits were momentarily buoyed to see people lamenting about a drowned swimmer. I didn't believe we could keep Larry's gruesome death a secret for long, but at least I'd bought the police some time.

The conference room door was still closed when I left. Chief McInnis made it clear I wasn't to be any more involved than he deemed fit, so with my PR duties completed, I decided it was time to enjoy the weekend.

I'd just clicked my seatbelt into place, ready to drive Jolly back home, when my phone rang through the car's Bluetooth system. Hitting the Receive button, I answered, concerned about why Jasper was calling me.

"What's up?"

"I just got off the phone with Detective Forester. She's requested I come down to the station to make a formal statement and answer a few additional questions."

In all the years I'd known him, I'd never heard Jasper sound so worried, and I'd talked him through *Divulge* almost going bankrupt two months after he started working at the magazine. "Why?"

He sighed, the sound crackling against my car speakers. "I guess the preliminary autopsy report came in, and they have questions about my alibi...or lack thereof."

My stomach seized as I looked at the digital clock on the dashboard. Harriet had said the report wasn't due until three. It was only eleven thirty. Had the ME done a rush job, or was Harriet fudging the truth? "I'll come get you and drive you back to the station. I'm just leaving there now."

Ending the call with a hurried "Sit tight, I'll be there in a few," I gripped the steering wheel as I tore out of the Common's parking lot. My best friend was being summoned for police questioning. So much for enjoying the weekend.

Chapter Eight

Jasper hardly spoke as I drove toward the town square. His pale skin was abnormally translucent, as if all blood had stopped flowing. His knuckles gripped the passenger door handle so hard that I thought he might rip it off.

"Everything is going to be fine," I reassured him as we pulled into the same parking spot I'd left not twenty minutes ago. I should put up a plaque and claim it as my own.

"I called my lawyer. She's meeting me here."

"That's smart." I wasn't lying. So many people thought calling their lawyer made them look guilty when, in fact, it usually saved them from serious jail time.

"This can't be happening." Jasper's hands covered his face as he moaned.

"Hey." I grabbed his arm and commanded his watery gaze. "Harriet just needs to take an official statement. They did the same for me when I found Stacy. Tell them the truth, and this will all blow over."

He nodded mutely before getting out of the car. "I'll go in alone. I don't want you getting into any hot water with the chief over this." His voice was hoarse.

"Text me as soon as you're done," I called after him through the open window. As he dragged himself toward the station, my anxiety doubled with every step. If Harriet had already gotten ahold of the preliminary autopsy report, something about it must have indicated Jasper could be responsible. Knowing with every fiber of my being that Jasper was not to blame for Larry's demise, I pondered the report's contents as I drove home for what felt like the umpteenth time that day.

"It has to be the timing," I announced to no one as I climbed out of Jolly after parking in the garage. Jasper had given Harriet a rundown of his evening, so the police already knew Jasper was alone after eleven thirty. Larry must have died sometime *after* that to have Jasper still be a person of interest.

Hudson was waiting for me in the kitchen. "Nice tweets. You've got the whole town speculating there's been a drowning somewhere down the coast." He held out his phone, showing me the viral reaction my vague statement had caused. "What's going on? I saw you drive Jasper off somewhere. Not to the airport or the border, I hope." His stiff chuckle did little to relieve the tension in his eyes.

I rubbed my temples, a brewing migraine issuing an "I'm coming for you" warning. "Detective Forester requested Jasper's presence at the station for a formal interview."

Hudson sagged against the counter as if the wind had been knocked out of him. "What? The police really think he had something to do with this?"

"How could they not? He had a huge blowout with Larry, who winds up dead hours later. It's that dang corkscrew." I slammed my bag down on the kitchen island. "Just because his name is on it, they think it's a smoking gun." I hung my head with the dejection of a sad puppy.

Hudson held his arms out.

I leaned into his strong and protective frame. "I'm the worst friend. I spaced. I completely forgot to grab Jasper's souvenir before we left last night."

He kissed the top of my head as he went to work, massaging my tense shoulders. "This is in no way your fault. I'm sure everything will be all right."

I'd told my best friend the same thing when I'd left him at the police station, but now I wasn't feeling so confident. "Chief McInnis has such a one-track mind. He did this with Stacy's death. He focused on only one suspect and didn't consider anyone else."

"But I thought Detective Forester was on the case," Hudson asked.

"Well, yes, but McInnis is still lording over everyone. Mayor Sullivan wants this wrapped up since Salute to Summer is just around the corner. I'm worried the chief might take some shortcuts to make it happen."

Hudson released my shoulders and turned me around to face him. "I take it you have a plan to make sure that *doesn't* happen?" He did not look entirely pleased.

I sighed. "I know how much it bothered you when I went looking into Stacy's death, but you can't honestly expect me to sit on the sidelines when my BFF is involved. Can you?"

Hudson eyed me for a long moment, his lips pressed in a grim line. "No, that wouldn't be fair to you." He kissed me on the nose. "Or to Jasper. Can you imagine how offended he'd be if you intervened in a relative stranger's case and not one involving him?"

Hudson's unexpected reply sent me into a fit of giggles. "There'd be no living with him." I then wrapped my arms around my boyfriend, eternally grateful he wasn't going to put up a fight over me doing a little snooping.

Hudson held me in a tight embrace before pulling back. "Okay. Where do we start?"

I rubbed my hands with glee. The last time I had dabbled in police matters, Hudson had been much more reluctant to assist. I guessed the thought of Jasper being framed for murder fueled Hudson's interest in the case, too. "While I was over at Jasper's, I started putting together a list of people who may have had it in for Larry." I scooted over to dig through my bag, as I'd tucked the Post-it inside for safekeeping.

Smoothing out the creases, I laid the list in front of Hudson.

He examined Rosalynn's name. "Wow. How are we ever going to wade through all these suspects?"

I swatted at his right biceps. "I didn't get that far before Detective Forester interrupted." Grabbing a stray pen left on our kitchen counter, I began to tap rhythmically on the marble countertop, trying to jumpstart my brainwaves.

"For the show Millie has me working on," Hudson began, "I've had to review a lot of old cases. The two motives that pop up time and time again are love," he paused, pointing at Rosalynn's name, "and money."

I nodded. "I need to ask my mom about the town audit, then. Maude told me Larry was trying to slash the police department's budget. Maybe he was planning to cut funds elsewhere, and someone decided to take matters into their own hands."

Stroking the dark stubble on his chin, Hudson pursed his lips. "Would someone really kill him over that? Wouldn't the state just send in a new auditor, who might do the same?"

"Hmm. You do have a point." I wrinkled my nose. "I'm still going to talk to Mom about Larry and see how he acted in a professional setting. Goodness knows, I never saw that side of him."

Hudson reached for an abandoned glass of water and took a sip. "What about her?" His gaze darted downward to Rosalynn's name on the paper.

"No one's been able to get ahold of her. And get this. Deacon floated the idea that Ros might be dead, too."

Hudson shuddered. "Makes sense why a bunch of uniforms were at the Dunmers' house earlier."

"Really? When?"

He glanced at his watch. "Not long after Gavin summoned you to the station."

I considered this news. Had Gavin purposely sent a team to check out my neighbors' rental when he knew I wouldn't be around? "Did you see anything?"

Hudson shook his head. "Nope. It just looked like a wellness check. They left empty-handed, too."

"So, Ros is still MIA." My brow wrinkled in concentration. "A coincidence, or something more sinister?"

"Let's say she's on the run for killing her husband," Hudson began. "Why? We know Larry was awful, but she seemed utterly besotted with him."

"Maybe her rose-colored glasses slipped. Or finally cracked." I then shared the wild news with Hudson that Rosalynn had wanted Larry to file a restraining order against me.

"Wow." Once his full-bodied laughter had subsided, Hudson grew pensive. "Okay, so Ros had serious trust issues pertaining to the sanctity of their marriage."

"Married to a guy like Larry, who wouldn't?" I scoffed. "You should have heard what he said *in front of his wife*, mind you, to our poor server at Vine."

"Oh, I saw enough of him last night to have a good idea." A scowl grew on Hudson's face. "The man drooled after anyone and anything with breasts, even the chicken croquettes."

I winced at the mental image. "I heard a rumor down at the strip a few days ago that the management team at the Crestview Country Club asked the Dunmers not to return over an incident with shrimp and koi." My gaze flicked to Rosalynn's scribbled name. "Word on the street is that Ros went off on some poor waitress Larry flirted with while they were having lunch at the clubhouse." I steepled my fingers together and propped my elbows on the countertop. "His wandering eye seems like a motive to kill."

Investigative intrigue sparkled in Hudson's dark gaze. "We need more intel on their blissfully wedded union."

Chapter Nine

As we were about to formulate our plan of attack, Hudson's cell vibrated loudly from his pocket. He dug out his phone and glanced at the Caller ID, his good mood evaporating in an instant as he answered. "What?" There was an uncharacteristic harshness to his voice as his features contorted with irritation.

I stilled in my seat. *Oh no.* There was only one person who made Hudson's expression darken so intensely.

"Can't this wait until Monday? Millie already signed off—what? Why does this have to be in person?" He paused as a voice trilled on the other end of the line. "Whatever. Fine. I'll be there in…" He paused as he glanced down at his watch, "forty minutes. I can't stay all day." Hudson punched the screen to end the call. "You've got to be kidding me."

As much as I wanted to pepper him with questions, I knew from past experiences that it was best to let Hudson do the talking. He needed to release his pent-up steam at his own pace.

Hudson ran a hand over his buzzed hair, the veins in his arms bulging with suppressed anger. "That was Tori. I guess she dug up a few more cold cases," he explained through gritted teeth. "Millie wants them vetted to see if they fit the profile for our show."

I frowned, already not liking where this was going. "Can't Tori just email the case files to you for review?"

He gave me a sad smile. "If only she would make life easy, right?"

Tori Beals had been a high-profile local TV personality from some Baltimore morning show whom WMTG had enticed aboard their news team. She was Hudson's co-anchor on the weekday evening news, and, to everyone watching, they made a great on-air team. But behind the scenes, Tori had become a serious problem for Hudson. Since getting wind of his true crime show, she'd been looking for ways to get in on the action, trying to position herself as Hudson's co-host. But that wasn't the worst of it.

When I'd first met Tori at a WMTG fundraising event this spring, she had blatantly flirted with Hudson right in front of me, so of course, our relationship—if you could call it that—had not started on the best footing. At the time, I believed it to be my own insecurities that made my hackles rise around her. Since I trusted Hudson more than anyone, I did my best to ignore her antics, even after Hudson told me Tori was trying to weasel her way onto his show. Picturing the two of them working alone together, hunched around a computer screen, didn't encourage any enthusiasm from me about her involvement in the project. Hindsight being twenty-twenty, I honestly wish the situation had just been me being a silly, jealous girlfriend. Unfortunately, at the mention of his coworker, the dismayed expression on Hudson's face revealed the reality of just how bad things at WMTG had become.

At the fundraising event where Tori first showed her interest in my boyfriend, Hudson had chalked up her flirty behavior to her being drunk. But shortly after that ominous encounter, he started coming home with stories about odd comments Tori made about his muscular arms, his kissable lips, his tight butt… Hudson would tell her to cut it out, and she'd simply laugh it off, saying she was only teasing.

As these stories became more frequent, a troubling pattern emerged. Tori Beals was sexually harassing him.

Wanting Hudson to have a safe work environment, I'd tried to point this out as delicately as possible, but my remark had put him on the immediate defensive.

"I'm probably making a big deal out of nothing." My heart ached at the sadness in his words that followed. "Besides, Tori's a big name for the station, and the network execs love her. I'm not in a position to call her out, Coco. Not when I finally have a shot at my own show."

I'd never felt so helpless, but Hudson assured me everything would be fine. Once Tori eventually got the message and tired of him, things at the station would go back to normal. *Him* reassuring *me*. God, Tori had created such a horrible situation for Hudson. He shouldn't have to wait for things to "return to normal." He shouldn't have to fear that his bosses would instinctively side with a white woman over her biracial male accuser.

With a sigh, Hudson gathered his messenger bag from the coat rack in the corner. "I guess some of the case files are so old," he continued to explain, "that they haven't been digitized yet, so Tori obtained a special pass to allow us access for the afternoon at the clerk's office in Milton. Hence, why I've been summoned."

Great, now the image of them alone at the station shifted to Tori trying to force herself onto Hudson in the dimly lit stacks of old records. Given what we'd just been discussing about Larry and Rosalynn, the irony of my worries did not escape me. Was this how Ros felt about her husband's lecherous behavior?

Hudson kissed my cheek, oblivious to my brewing angst. "I'm sorry. I know we thought we'd get a weekend to ourselves." He took my hand and threaded his fingers through mine. "And you know I hate leaving you to deal with this on your own, but the sooner I get this series greenlit from the studio, the sooner I get a new, steady schedule." He stroked my palm tenderly, although there was a haunted look in his eyes. "And then I can finally get away from Tori for good." Thankfully, Hudson's producer, Millie, still firmly believed Hudson should host his true crime show solo, but, of course, Tori hadn't stopped trying to make herself invaluable to the project.

I forced a smile. "I understand. This is a huge career opportunity for you, and I'm beyond proud. I'm sure you'll be on the air in no time." I prayed this would be the case. I hated seeing Hudson's passion for his work trampled by Tori's harassment. "I'll call Charlotte, and we'll rally behind Jasper. Besides, I'm sure everything has already been worked out down at the PD." There was an incredibly huge chance I had gotten way too far ahead of myself on this one. After all, Jasper had only been called down to give his statement and answer a few additional questions. It wasn't like they were arresting him or anything.

Hudson pressed his lips to my forehead. "That's my girl." He headed toward the door. "Be careful, babes, whatever you do," he called over his shoulder as he disappeared down the path toward the garage.

I followed him to the threshold and stood on the steps, already missing his reassuring presence. "You, too," I whispered, knowing he wouldn't hear me. Hudson didn't need reminding that he had to play it smart and safe around Tori.

It was then I spied a police cruiser parked in front of the Dunmers' condo. My insides frosted over. What were they doing back? Had Rosalynn been found?

Gavin appeared from around the back of the house, scanning the exterior of the condo from top to bottom as he circled the property.

I hastened across my front lawn to join him, stopping short of the property line Larry had continually berated me about. "Hey, Gavin. What's going on?"

Puzzled by goodness knows what, Gavin's hands went to his slanted hips. "When was the last time you saw Rosalynn?"

I shook my head, some strands of my hair coming loose from its messy bun. "At Vine with her husband." I debated a moment before asking, "Do you really think she's been killed, too?"

Taking off his uniform hat, Gavin fanned himself against the searing heat. "No, I don't. Call it a gut feeling. Larry's murder was personal. It takes a lot of anger and rage to stab someone like that. But I don't think Rosalynn killed her husband, either."

"Why not?" I couldn't contain my surprise. "Doesn't runaway bride scream guilt?"

Gavin snorted. "Sure it does, but aren't you forgetting something?" He tapped the side of his neck. "The corkscrew. If Rosalynn somehow got ahold of Jasper's corkscrew and concocted this elaborate plan to frame him for Larry's murder, why would she immediately go on the run? It's way too obvious."

My stomach flipped as I heard his logic. "So, you believe me? You know

Jasper's being framed?"

"No, I'm not saying that," Gavin corrected me. "It's just that the wife's actions don't align with the evidence we've found thus far."

I stomped my foot in frustration. "So, what? Ros's is already off the hook?"

"Stop putting words in my mouth, Coco. We've barely begun our investigation. We can't even go public with it because we haven't located Rosalynn." Gavin folded his arms. "So, I'd appreciate it if you didn't go around telling *all* your friends her husband has been killed."

I'd earned that reprimand. It really hadn't helped my relationship with the PD to run off and immediately inform a potential suspect about what we'd found down at Pelican Beach. "I'm sorry. But I only told Jasper... and Hudson."

"Hudson?" Gavin's eyes bulged. "Coco, he might be your boyfriend, but he's also a leading anchor on the most popular local news team in the state!"

"I know." I held up my hands in defense. "But he swears everything is off the record."

"Oh, super," Gavin grunted. "We'll just have to pray he keeps his word."

"Hey." I studied Gavin's drained expression. "You know Hudson can be trusted. He's a journalist with integrity. Besides, he saw some officers conducting a wellness check on Ros earlier. He would have put the pieces together even without my help." I peered at Gavin more closely. "What's really bugging you?"

He sighed. "So far, the mayor has already called my unc—Chief McInnis twice about our progress and whether we've made an arrest. Given that we haven't even located the dead guy's wife, we're not off to the most encouraging start."

I swallowed the lump of panic in my throat. I should have been relieved that the police didn't have enough to arrest Jasper, but instead, it just made me feel cold. I didn't like the idea of a killer running free any more than Mayor Sullivan.

"Well..." I trailed off, debating my words carefully. "What if someone who wasn't *really* involved with the official police investigation stepped in to help and started asking around about Larry? You know, drumming up suspects and clarifying timelines while the police track down his wife?"

I regretted my offer as soon as it was out of my mouth.

Gavin's lips pressed into a razor-thin line. "Then that person would be interfering with an active homicide investigation and could be charged with obstruction of justice or witnessing tampering or whatever other laws they'd broken in the process."

I shrank back with each offense he tossed out.

Returning his hat to his head, Gavin began to make his way toward the police cruiser. Once he arrived at the driver's side door, he glanced over his shoulder at me. "However, if this said person foolishly dismisses my advice and finds out something useful, like the whereabouts of Rosalynn Dunmer, then maybe I can overlook her meddling...again." With that, Gavin climbed into the police car and drove off.

My foundering spirits lifted at the hidden message behind Gavin's words. As long as I didn't get caught snooping and delivered some useful intel, my transgressions could be forgiven. What's more, he'd given me an official assignment: track down Rosalynn.

Chapter Ten

I retreated inside my condo to seek relief from the intense summer heat and regroup. Basking in the kitchen AC, I picked up my iPhone and checked to see if Jasper had sent me an update. Other than a few Twitter mention notifications, my cell phone was suspiciously blank except for a text from Charlotte. I frowned. As the creator of a lifestyle blog, I usually had a slew of social media notifications from followers reacting to my latest post.

Hey, gurl. Just checkin in. Maria said ur new blog isn't up...u OK?

"Omigod! My article!"

Phone in hand, I dashed into my office, heart pounding as I fired up my iMac desktop. A few clicks had the admin page of *Trending Topic* loading across the large monitor.

I shook my head as the homepage blinked into view. "No, no, no!" Last week's post featuring a variety of popular podcasts was still front and center. What happened to today's article about summer reading recommendations that was supposed to go live at six thirty this morning?

Scanning the website's navigation menu, I found my answer. "You've got to be kidding me."

I balled my left fist and pounded my desk. My keyboard, just inches away, rattled in protest. In a totally amateur move, the latest *Trending Topic* post was still marked in "Draft" status. I had forgotten to click "Schedule" when I'd written it earlier in the week.

I buried my face in my hands. "Ugh, *this* is why I don't like to rely on scheduling things ahead of time." Since launching my blog, I'd always gotten up early on Saturdays to manually upload my *Trending Topic* posts. However, in a concerted effort to not be such a control freak and give myself some time back in my weekends, Jasper and Charlotte had convinced me to begin scheduling my posts using the webpage's built-in tools. I'd been doing it successfully for about a month and a half...until now.

My eye started twitching as I glanced at the timestamp from when I'd last saved the article. Tuesday at two thirty. I mentally reviewed my work schedule to figure out how I had made such a rookie blogger error.

"Argh," I groaned as I leaned against the headrest of my snazzy ergonomic computer chair. "The Beakman call."

Beakman Emporium, a little boutique aromatherapy shop in Cherry Springs, was a new remote CoA client. I'd been working with the brother-sister duo for about two weeks. Tuesday afternoon, Astrid Beakman had called in a panic, saying she had accidentally deleted their entire website while trying to configure a newsletter. I'd been in the middle of scheduling the Saturday morning publication of my *Trending Topic* post at the time and had gotten completely sidetracked by helping her straighten everything out.

A surge of renewed pressure pounded at my temples. As much as I didn't want to admit it, my new advanced scheduling workflow wasn't to blame. This wasn't the first time I'd dropped the ball on *Trending Topic* in recent months because I was dealing with Center of Attention business. CoA clients demanded a lot of my time, which left little energy for me to interact with my social media followers. To further prove the point, I clicked away from my *Trending Topic* tab and opened the sleek application I used to manage all my socials from one spot. I had over *four* hundred unread DMs in my primary Instagram inbox alone. A quick scan told me that most were product sponsorship or collaboration requests. I just hadn't had the time to sit down and sort through them. "This is why I need an assistant." I sighed, glaring dejectedly at the screen. Monday's interviews with my promising candidates could not come soon enough.

I glanced at the little clock in the corner of my computer monitor. I *could* still post my "Booked for Summer" article, which featured my favorite beach reads across all genres. *The Cradle of Ice, Like a Sister, Husband Material,* and

The Personal Librarian were just a few of the riveting reads I'd compiled to share with my followers.

The clock blinked twelve-fifteen. I sighed, making my decision. Saturday afternoon just wasn't an ideal time to publish online content. People were out and about, living their best weekend lives. In a few clicks, I scheduled the post for tomorrow morning. My blog's followers could enjoy reading my recommendations over a cup of lazy Sunday coffee.

Once the webpage reloaded and I confirmed everything was all set for tomorrow, I picked up my phone to check if Jasper had reached out yet. My notifications center was still ominously empty. I swiped to review my iMessages. He had been down at the station for an hour. Surely, a formal statement shouldn't take that long…

The group text message I shared with Charlotte and Jasper buzzed to life.

C: Finally caught another breather. Super busy today. What's this about a drowning @ Pelican? Café is buzzing w/ theories. Cokes, u got the tea?

My fingers hovered over the keyboard. Gavin's warning echoed in my head. I knew it wouldn't bode well for the police department if word about Larry got out before Rosalynn had been found and informed. I had to play this safe, especially given the fact Gavin would likely make good on his threat to charge me with obstruction of justice if I messed up his team's reputation in the community.

I typed back. **Omw 4 quick visit. Pls have muffin w8ng.** It would be wiser to confide in Charlotte face-to-face. I couldn't risk someone spotting my response on her smartphone and spreading the news that the body on Pelican Beach belonged to Larry.

My visit to Charlotte's café would also serve another purpose. With Hudson busy at work, I needed a new partner-in-crime to tag in and help me figure out how to track down Ros.

For what felt like the hundredth time that day, I hopped into Jolly and started the engine, only this time, I navigated my itty-bitty ride toward the beach. Taking as many side roads as I could to avoid traffic along the main coastal route, it still took me seventeen minutes to reach the strip.

The residential lot was nearly full, though I suspected many tourists had snagged spots not designated for them. A ticket from the parking patrol would hopefully nip those bad habits in the bud soon. I found Jolly a spot in the back, so my walk to Brewed to Perfection took a little longer than usual.

"Hey, chica!" Maria Ortiz beamed in greeting as I entered the bustling coffee shop. "You can go right on back. Ms. Whittaker is expecting you."

I chuckled. Maria had yet to shake the habit of calling her employer "Ms." *Ah, to be young and respectful....*

"Looks like you're keeping busy, Maria," I said with a smile as I let myself behind the counter.

She nodded, her thick, dark brown hair bobbing in its ponytail. "It's been non-stop today. People are drowning their sorrows in caffeine over...." Her voice trailed off as she winced. "Sorry, bad choice of words, what with the news and all."

I patted Maria's shoulder as I scooted by, heading toward the doorway that led to the back area of the café. "I hear ya. Keep up the good work, kiddo." I grimaced at my use of the word "kiddo." I sounded like my dad. I glanced over my shoulder at the new barista. Maria was, like, six years younger than me. Yet her youthful glow and boundless energy had me feeling like a grandma around her. *Man, if this is twenty-eight....*

Maria chatted effortlessly while making an iced mocha blitz, a Brewed to Perfection summer specialty. "I love it here. Now that I've decorated my new apartment, it feels like Central Shores is my home."

I knew the feeling well. "Glad to hear it."

"Your summer trends post was such a huge inspiration, by the way." Maria winked. "Who would have thought sea glass in a bowl could look so chic?"

Maria could be quite the chatterbox, so I slowly backed into the short hallway that led to Charlotte's office, waving as I did. "You'll have to show me a pic sometime." Before she could actually pull out her phone and do so, I turned on a heel and headed for Charlotte's door. I felt bad for ditching Maria so quickly, especially since she was a massive *Trending Topic* fan, but I had a missing wife to find.

Charlotte's door was ajar, so I rapped a quick beat before I let myself inside her office, closing the door behind me.

"Hey, you." Charlotte looked up from her laptop, an effortless smile on her face. "Ready and waiting." She pointed to a cinnamon cocoa muffin perched on a bright yellow plate.

"Oh, thank God." I collapsed into the chair across her desk and broke off a chunk of the moist, homemade goodie. "I just realized I haven't eaten anything all day."

Charlotte's pert nose wrinkled. "That's not like you. I wouldn't think a drowned swimmer would keep the police that busy." She turned her laptop around so I could see the screen. She had the police department's Facebook page pulled up, my post about a drowning at Pelican Beach front and center. "Any news about who it is?"

I swallowed the delicious bite of muffin. It landed like a rock in my stomach. "You have to promise to keep this news between the two of us." I confirmed her office door was still shut tight. "Like, I-get-your-firstborn-child-if-you-break-it kinda promise." Heaven help me if she did because I did not need any kids in my life. Jasper and his childish antics were more than enough.

Charlotte rolled her eyes at my theatrics. "I promise, Cokes. Now, spill. What the heck is going on?"

I kept my voice low in case Maria walked by the office on her way to the storage room or something. "It's not exactly your run-of-the-mill drowning case."

I launched into a quick but detailed run-through of my morning. Ever the captive audience, Charlotte's grey eyes widened at every twist and turn.

At the conclusion of my harrowing tale, she glanced worriedly at the Google Home device on her desk. It displayed a picture of her and Deacon, along with the time. "And Jasper's still down at the station?"

I nodded. "I don't know why they are keeping him this long."

As if in cosmic answer, my phone rang. Jasper's contact info filled the screen. I placed my cell on Charlotte's desk and answered it on speakerphone. "Hey, I'm down at the café with Charlotte. What's the latest?"

"Sorry to keep you waiting." Jasper sounded distracted, but not in a worried way. More like an annoyed one.

My insides wriggled. "Are you done at the station? Do you need me to come pick you up?"

"Oh, sorry. I've been done for a while. Once my lawyer arrived, Detective Boss Betch only questioned me for like fifteen minutes."

My anxiety turned to irritation. "Are you kidding me? I've been waiting to hear from you! How could you leave me hanging like that?"

"Something else came up," Jasper answered vaguely.

Charlotte snorted, obviously sharing my frustration. "Something more important than being accused of murder?"

"Hello to you, too, Char," came Jasper's pointed reply.

Charlotte and I shared a knowing look. Jasper was hiding something. What was it?

"So, does this mean the police don't believe you had anything to do with Larry's death?" I asked.

Jasper's sigh carried through the other end of the phone line. "I don't know what to think about the whole sitch, honestly. I gave them a statement. They asked a few questions about my history with Larry, which Kimball answered on my behalf. She tried to wheedle from Detective Forester if a time of death had been established, but the detective wouldn't let it slip."

I assumed this Kimball person was Jasper's lawyer.

"If you were only there for a few minutes, where have you been all this time?" I drummed my fingers on Charlotte's desk. "I didn't see you come back to your condo."

"Your busybody skills need work, then. Kimball drove me home so we could go over some *Divulge* legal stuff."

I bristled at Jasper's sass, but he'd made a fair point. I hadn't been the most attentive neighbor. Once Tori's phone call to Hudson interrupted our brainstorming session, my focus had shifted to my boyfriend. Neither Jasper nor Charlotte knew how Hudson's situation at work had escalated. As much as I wanted to confide in them for advice, I would never betray Hudson's trust by sharing such a sensitive matter with my besties. It made for a heavy secret to keep.

"I would have liked to do our work at the Dover office." The worry had returned to Jasper's voice. "But Detective Forester reminded me not to leave town before we left the station."

Charlotte twisted a long lock of her amber hair. "I can't believe anyone at the police department would think you're capable of this." I noticed how her ethereal gray gaze flicked again to the picture of her and Deacon.

"Well, I plan to prove them wrong," I pledged, sounding much more confident than I felt. "Contrary to what Gavin believes, I think it's super sus that Ros is nowhere to be found. Seriously, when was the last time you saw her in public without her husband?"

Charlotte chewed on her glossy lower lip. "That's true. You'd think the police would be more focused on her as a suspect than anyone else at this point."

"As Kimball and I were leaving the station," Jasper spoke up, "I heard Gavin issue an all-points bulletin for the Dunmers' car. So that's something, I guess."

"They could be issuing an APB just to find her, right?" Charlotte looked to me for an answer.

I slid her laptop across the desk and began to click on the trackpad. "I suppose that might be their only option at this point. Gavin mentioned her cell was off, and Chief McInnis said it would take a while to obtain any prior location data."

Charlotte's brow furrowed as she watched me tap away at her keyboard. "What are you looking up?"

"There are other ways to track a person's whereabouts." I grinned.

"What's the clacking sound?" Jasper's voice whined from the speakers.

"Hang on a moment." I'm surprised the police hadn't already taken this route, but as I loaded the webpage, I understood why it wouldn't have been fruitful.

Charlotte leaned over her desk to examine the laptop screen. "What are you doing on Facebook?"

I stared at Rosalynn's Facebook profile, scanning her recent activity. "Bummer. She hasn't posted anything in the last few days." I quickly checked the "About" section on her profile to see if she had an Instagram handle but found nothing listed.

"What the heck are you doing cyberstalking on Facebook?" A burst of static distorted Jasper's voice from the phone.

"Back when Stacy was killed," I began to explain my reasoning, "my name was taken off the chief's suspect list because I posted to Facebook around the same time Stacy was murdered. The geotag and timestamp on the post proved I couldn't have been two places at once." Unless I'd scheduled the post ahead of time, but what Chief McInnis didn't know couldn't hurt him, right?

Charlotte bobbed her head in understanding. "You're looking to see if you can track down where Rosalynn is via her timeline? Clever." She studied the screen. "Maybe she has uploaded something recently, but it's not on her public profile? I'm not friends with her."

"Which is why I logged into *my* account," I countered. "I actually friended Ros a few days after she and Larry moved in. I thought I could win her over and that they'd be a little nicer since I made an effort to be welcoming. Not the case...." I trailed off, disappointed with the results of my sleuthing. "So, if Ros had posted something, I'd be able to see it as her friend unless she hid the post for some reason."

Charlotte took control of the computer mouse and scrolled down the page. "Yeesh, Rosalynn sure does share a lot of Buzzfeed quiz results."

I gave an elaborate shudder. "You know what they say, 'Buzzfeed quizzes are the eyes to the soul.'" I reached for Charlotte's wrist, silently asking her to pause on skimming the page. "Hey, look. Can you click on that picture?" I pointed to an image of a fruity-colored cocktail perched on a table overlooking the beach.

"Coming right up." Charlotte double-clicked to enlarge the photo.

"What pic?" Jasper reminded us he was still on the line. "I'm not friends with Ros, so I can't see anything on my end."

"A few weeks ago, Ros posted a photo of a drink with the caption, '*Heaven in a glass!*'" I mused over the description. "Not half bad."

"Why don't you hire her to be your new CoA assistant, then?" Jasper scoffed.

Ignoring him, I read the comments attached to the post. It didn't take long. There were only two. Someone named DeDe Marston had replied, "**Ooo, looks yummy,**" to which Ros had responded, "**Right? I'll be chugging these all summer long to survive this dreadful move.**" She also included a few crying face emojis.

"Hmmm," Jasper muttered after I read the comments out loud. "Sounds like Ms. Ros wasn't too thrilled with her husband being assigned to Central Shores."

"Maybe she's currently chugging one of these now," Charlotte suggested. "Any idea where the photo was taken?"

There wasn't a geo-tag on the post, but upon closer examination of the cocktail, I realized we didn't need one. "Look at the umbrella." I pointed to the pink accent propped on the rim of the glass.

Charlotte squinted, her nose an inch away from the computer screen. Girl needed to get herself some reading glasses. "Well, would you look at that?"

"Look at what?" Jasper wailed from the iPhone.

I grinned, recognizing the palm tree logo, as I'd featured the trendy beach club on *Trending Topic* several months back. "Looks like we're taking a field trip out to Cyprus."

Chapter Eleven

"I'll meet you guys there in twenty minutes."

I raised an eyebrow in question, only to realize Jasper couldn't see my expression. "Detective Forester told you not to leave town, remember?"

Jasper snorted. "I'd hardly label popping over to Cherry Springs as 'leaving town.'"

Charlotte chuckled. "That would *literally* be what you're doing."

"Fineeeeee." I could picture Jasper pouting on the other end of the line. "Well, then, I better get back to work. Kimball charges by the hour, so today is going to be pricy. Keep me posted, betches. My life is in your hands."

Before either of us could respond, Jasper signed off the call.

I frowned. Leave it to Jasper to throw himself into running his media empire to help him de-stress. I wondered why he needed a lawyer present for *Divulge* work, though.

A guilty look eclipsed Charlotte's face, pulling my thoughts back into focus. "What's wrong?"

She sighed. "I can't go to Cyprus today. I already promised Maria the afternoon off."

"No worries." I didn't understand why she was worked up about it. "I can go by myself."

She bit her lower lip. "Do you think that's a good idea?"

I tilted my head, wondering where this sudden concern was coming from. "It's just a little fact-finding mission. And it's even police-approved. Sorta." I shrugged as I logged out of my Facebook account and slid the laptop over to Charlotte.

She twirled a pen between her fingers. "Well, think about it. I know you said Gavin isn't totally on board with the idea, but Rosalynn could very well be the killer. If you find her and start asking questions—"

"Please, then I'll just start live-streaming the conversation. Problem solved."

Charlotte did not crack a smile. "That's not funny, Cokes. At all."

I perched on the side of her desk, meeting her disapproving gaze. "Believe me, I get how lucky I am to be alive after what happened this spring. The whole debacle taught me a valuable lesson, and I promise I won't put myself in danger, right?"

Charlotte sighed. "Just be careful. And keep us posted."

Giving her a quick air-kiss goodbye, I darted from her office and into the central area of the café. As I maneuvered through the gathered crowd, I kept an ear out for any details about the recent death at Pelican Beach. Based on chatter about strong currents and possible shark sightings, it seemed Larry's identity and murder were still under wraps.

As I walked to the car, I texted Hudson to update him. **Headin 2 Cherry Springs 4 a bit.**

His reply came quickly. **Re: Larry?**

Yup. In no jeopardy, tho.

Same. Clerk won't leave us alone, so TT has 2 be on best behavior.

A sigh of relief sputtered from my lips. Thank goodness Hudson wouldn't be plagued by "TT" or "Terrible Tori's" advances today. I hoped this meant he could enjoy a little of his research work. Despite everything going on, Hudson still really loved his job, which was probably why he was so intent on waiting out the Tori storm.

Once I was buckled into Jolly with the AC cranking, I entered the address for Cyprus into Google Maps and set off. Following the quickest route available, I pulled my car up to the valet twenty-five minutes later.

It had been several months since I'd visited Cyprus, and not much had changed about the beach club. Originally destined to become a resort, a hotel chain had pulled out of the project last minute, abandoning the new construction. The Cyprus developers swept in like vultures on a carcass. The massive compound was sleek, clean, and modern, but since the trendy spot catered mostly to singles, Hudson and I didn't really enjoy its fist-pumping vibe. We'd only been a few times and always left feeling like a shower was in order.

I handed my keys to the valet with a thank you and scanned the surrounding area. I could only see one of the club's three massive pools from out here on the portico, and it was overflowing with boardshorts and bikini-clad bodies. The place was hopping, as I would expect on a summer afternoon. I stepped into the air-conditioned lobby, where I was greeted by a tan, perky hostess wrapped in a white, impossibly tight cocktail dress.

"Hello there. Welcome to Cyprus. Do you have your member ID with you?"

I tugged at my floral-patterned sundress, feeling woefully frumpy in her presence. I had completely spaced on Cyprus's glam dress code. "Hi. I'm not a member, but I'm hoping you might be able to tell me whether a woman named Rosalynn Dunmer is here."

I might have missed the slight falter in her bright, cheery smile if I hadn't been intently watching the young woman for any telltale reaction. "I'm sorry, ma'am, but here at Cyprus, we don't share information about possible members."

Ma'am? Ugh, did I look old enough to be a ma'am? This girl couldn't have been *that* much younger than me. Still slightly irritated, I took a deep breath and pushed my wounded ego aside. "That's fine. I totally understand. Is it possible for me to purchase a day pass or something? That pool I saw outside looked super inviting."

"Of course! Let me just get your name." The hostess started clacking away on her iPad, her fake nails scraping against the screen.

"Coco Cline."

The hostess glanced up, her eyes wide. "Oh my goodness. Ms. Cline! It's so nice to meet you in person. I'm sorry I didn't recognize you. Did you cut your hair or something?" She didn't give me a chance to tell her no. "You're actually on our VIP list already. The Cyprus management team greatly admires your work. Please, go right inside." She handed me a gold-colored keycard with the Cyprus palm tree logo printed on it. "This will give you access to all member areas. Enjoy!"

I stared at the piece of plastic in my hand, giving the young woman a dazed thank you as I wandered into the center of the main lobby. Shocked by how easy gaining access to Cyprus had been, I silently thanked the universe for my good fortune. I certainly never took my local celebrity for granted, as I hadn't expected to be given the red-carpet treatment while sleuthing.

I slid the keycard into my sundress pocket and focused on the task at hand. Based on the minor crack in the hostess's otherwise cheery exterior when I mentioned her name, Rosalynn Dunmer was *definitely* a Cyprus member. Or, at least, had been at one point. "The million-dollar question is, is she here?" I murmured aloud as I took in the lively scene.

The marble lobby echoed with bubbling activity. Through the floor-to-ceiling windows on the opposite side, I spotted another inviting pool equipped with a swim-up bar. An open-air restaurant was off to my right, and a vacant dance floor was to my left. Knowing Rosalynn's propensity for Cyprus cocktails, I opted to check out the bar on the other side of the dance floor.

The bar had been modeled in the industrial style, all smooth cement, metal finishings, and glittering mirrors. A group of middle-aged women clad in flowing sarongs, oversized sunglasses, and floppy hats congregated near the buff bartender.

"Excuse me." I gave them a friendly wave as I claimed a spot next to them. "I'm looking for a friend. Any chance you've seen her?" I held up my phone, my screen filled with Ros's Facebook profile picture.

Heads shook all around. They muttered their apologies before taking their drinks and moving outside into the sun.

"May I see?"

I slid my phone over to the hulking bartender. He might have been cute if I was into moussed hair and 'roided out muscles.

With a smarmy smile, he glanced down at my iPhone. Ros's picture wiped the grin right off his face. "She's your friend?" His expression grew stormy.

I took my phone back, intent on ignoring his question. "Have you seen her?"

He grabbed a towel and began wiping down his workstation. "Not today, I haven't. But I've been stationed inside. Most club members use the outdoor bars when the sun is out."

I slapped a five-dollar bill on the counter. "Thanks for the tip." I stifled a giggle at my own silliness. It felt like I was paying off an informant.

The bartender frowned slightly before pocketing the fiver. "Word of advice. Don't let that woman's husband get anywhere near you."

Oh yes, he's totally met Ros and Larry before.

Following a boisterous crowd of bathing suits and swim trunks, I stepped out onto the back portico and surveyed the impressive spectacle. The place had a Caribbean, all-inclusive feel, which was beyond strange for a Delaware beach club. The compound boasted several facilities off the main building, including a gym, beauty salon, and shopping boutique.

With a handful of outdoor bars to choose from, I headed for the nearest one, designed to look like a rainforest temple. Careful to stay clear of the pool, where a drunken game of Marco Polo was afoot, I scanned the sea of faces in hopes of spotting Ros right off the bat. No such luck.

I waved down one of the three bartenders working the area, this one a petite Latina woman whose deep scowl had me thinking she'd rather be in the pool than serving drinks.

"Excuse me? Could I speak to you for a sec?"

Her bored look disappeared entirely. "Wow! You're Coco Cline, aren't you?"

"That's me." I grinned.

"Hi! I'm Daria. I absolutely love your Insta," she squealed. "I just started using that new face wash you recommended last week. Lovin' it, queen."

I dipped my head in sheepish thanks. It was nice to hear her appreciation for what I did on social media. Yes, I got to read positive comments from my followers—among the negative, mind you—but to have someone share their admiration in person felt special. I rarely stepped outside my little Central Shores bubble, where everyone had known me since I was a kid and treated me as such. "Thanks, Daria. I'm so glad to hear that. I love it when my followers are happy. Now, I'm hoping you *might* be able to help me out." I quickly pivoted the conversation. "Have you seen this woman at all today?" I held my phone up. "I'm trying to track her down."

Daria examined the screen. "Um, she's not a friend of yours, is she?" Her nose wrinkled.

My pulse raced. "She's my neighbor. I need to speak with her."

"Hey, Bonnie!" Daria waved to a vaguely familiar waitress carrying a tray of piña coladas. "Isn't this the old bat whose husband tried to feel you up right in front of her?"

Bonnie placed her tray down on the bar and slid it closer so she could inspect my phone. "That's her, all right."

I realized then where I knew her from. "Hey, there. You worked the Vine party in Central Shores last night."

Bonnie's cheeks darkened with embarrassment. "I didn't get a chance to properly thank you, Ms. Cline, for helping me out of that uncomfortable situation."

"Please, call me Coco." I smiled sympathetically at her. "I'm just sorry you had to go through that."

"I shouldn't have been surprised." Bonnie's slender shoulders heaved with a giant sigh. "Once I saw Mr. Dunmer roaming the party, I knew it was only a matter of time before he propositioned someone."

Daria wrestled the drinks away from Bonnie. "Why don't you two talk while I get these delivered?"

With a nod of silent thanks to the helpful bartender, I turned my attention back to Bonnie. It was clear something more had gone down between Bonnie and the Dunmers than what my friends and I witnessed at Vine. "I'm on a mission to help out a friend who's run into a bit of trouble with the Dunmers." I tried to frame my line of inquiry with a bit of truth. I didn't want to lie outright to Bonnie, but I couldn't exactly tell the young waitress Larry had turned up murdered, either. Careful to use the present tense, I asked, "Do you know Mr. Dunmer? Has he accosted you before?"

Bonnie chewed on her lower lip. "I've had a few run-ins with him here at

Cyprus. Mr. Dunmer and his wife became members only a month ago, but he's made quite a name for himself around the place already." She shuddered, a childlike innocence dancing across her face.

"Is that why he approached you last night at the party? Because he knew you from here?"

Bonnie snorted. "If he remembered me, he sure didn't show it. Mr. Dunmer doesn't spend much time looking at a woman's face. Just her—ahem, assets."

"I'm sorry you had to deal with such brutish behavior."

Bonnie's features contorted with resentment. "Leave it to a woman to apologize for the actions of a man."

"Did Mrs. Dunmer ever apologize for her husband's actions?" I motioned to the picture of Rosalynn still on my phone screen.

A harsh laugh escaped Bonnie's lips. "Yeah, right. I don't know how that woman managed to do it, but her husband could be coming onto a waitress right in front of her, and Mrs. Dunmer would just completely ignore it." She rapped her knuckles against the smooth cement countertop. "If only my boyfriend could be like that, then neither of us would be on probation."

"Probation?"

Bonnie nodded. "The last time the Dunmers were here, my boyfriend Ian got into a bit of a confrontation with Mr. Dunmer. Ian works here, too. He's on the security team." She pointed to the corner of the pool deck, hidden in the late afternoon shadows. "There are cameras all over this place, and one caught Mr. Dunmer making a pass at me. Guys make passes at us waitresses all the time, so Ian didn't think too much of it at first. But then he saw Mr. Dunmer start to get aggressive when I didn't respond, and...." Bonnie shook her head as if warding away a bad memory. "I love Ian, but he's always been a little hot-tempered. I'm just glad some of the other guys on the security team intercepted him before he could really lay into Mr. Dunmer."

I sucked in a breath. "Did Ian attack Larry?"

"No, thank goodness." Bonnie glanced across the crowded pool deck. "But Mr. Dunmer threatened the management staff with a lawsuit, regardless.

Luckily, Ian had a copy of the security footage to prove he didn't lay a hand on Mr. Dunmer *and* that Mr. Dunmer tried to touch me without my consent."

"So why are you and Ian on probation?" I didn't like where this was going.

"Mr. Dunmer made a bunch of threats about ruining Cyprus and calling the state department if 'justice' wasn't served," Bonnie replied with sarcastic air quotes. "So, to shut him up, my supervisor put Ian and me on probation for upsetting a club member."

My mouth dropped open. "Are you serious?" Any respect I'd had for the Cyprus management team evaporated on the spot.

Bonnie rolled her brown eyes. "I'd quit if I could afford to, but Ian and I need our jobs. We're applying to nursing school in the fall, and the pay here is really good." Her expression turned downcast. "And it's not as if we can easily get hired elsewhere. All the good summer positions have already been filled."

My jaw tightened as my teeth ground together. Not only had Larry violated this young woman's personal space, but he'd used his influence to mess with her future.

"Excuse me?" A woman in a barely-there bikini sauntered up to the bar and interrupted our bleak discussion. "Can we get another round of margaritas, please?"

Bonnie's lips transformed into a bright, bubbly smile with a flick of a switch. "Sure thing. Coming right up." She turned to me. "I'm sorry, Coco. I need to get back to work."

I realized I hadn't asked her the one question I'd come to Cyprus to answer. "I'm trying to track down Rosalynn Dunmer. Has she been here at all today?"

Bonnie shook her head. "No way. The Dunmers haven't been back here since Ian got into it with Mr. Dunmer, which is a good thing, too. Ian's still pretty livid about the whole fiasco." Before I could ask anything more, Bonnie dashed down to the other end of the bar, where the margarita machine chugged away.

I studied Bonnie for a moment, pity and anger on her behalf swirling in my chest. I couldn't believe Larry had the audacity to try and get her fired from Cyprus for thwarting his unwanted advances. And to top it off, he hadn't even remembered Bonnie when he'd come on to her at Vine last night. If it had been me in her shoes, I would have tossed a glass of wine in his face, maybe even a whole bottle—

A dark thought weaseled its way into my brain. What if Bonnie *had* sought out some type of revenge on Larry? I watched her carry a heavy tray of margaritas over to a boisterous group of women lounging on the sundeck. She might have been small in stature, but she was definitely strong. But was she strong enough to plunge a corkscrew into Larry's neck? I supposed anyone fueled by anger could be.

"Anything to drink, Ms. Cline?" Daria stopped in front of me. "Or did Bonnie get you what you needed?"

"I'm all set. Thanks so much for flagging her down. Enjoy the rest of your day." Figuring I'd overstayed my welcome, I left a tip for the use of the barstool and headed back inside the club. While I'd found yet another person who wouldn't mourn Larry's passing, I hadn't made any progress locating his missing wife.

"Ma'am?" A firm hand came down on my right shoulder.

Ugh, ma'am, again?

I turned to face the owner of the deep voice, surprise overtaking annoyance when I recognized the bulky figure, even without his sunglasses. It was the bouncer who'd been stationed outside Vine when we arrived.

"This fell out of your pocket by the bar." He handed me the VIP access keycard.

My fingers curled around the plastic. "Thank you." My gaze slid to his gold-embossed nametag, and my eyes widened. *Ian Miles, Security.* How many Ians could be working here? This had to be Bonnie's boyfriend. "Good catch." I wiggled the card for emphasis.

Ian glanced down at the marble flooring, his embarrassed expression reflecting on the tile. "Um, I noticed you speaking with my girlfriend on the security feed. She seemed a little upset, so I came outside to make sure everything was okay."

I couldn't decide whether his overprotectiveness was endearing or creepy.

"We were just having a friendly chat."

Ian's eyes narrowed. "I know who you are, Ms. Cline, and I know you and Bonnie aren't exactly friends."

Creepy. His overprotectiveness had just crossed into the realm of creepy. Remembering my promise to Charlotte to be careful, I glanced around the club for a way out of this increasingly tense situation.

"I overheard you asking her questions about the Dunmers." Ian loomed over me, casting a large shadow.

I gulped. "I'm just trying to find Rosalynn, that's all."

"If I were you, I'd steer clear of those two." Ian's tone held a hint of warning to it.

My curiosity got the better of my unease. "Why?"

"The Dunmers have a habit of causing trouble wherever they go." Ian folded his beefy arms across his chest.

Geez, if this guy wants to become a nurse, he should work on his bedside manner. "Bonnie told me that Larry got you both in trouble with the Cyprus management team."

Ian's scowl deepened. "I didn't even touch the man, and I have video evidence to back it up. But then he started threatening to call his friend, the commissioner of the state health department, about the cleanliness of the club if something wasn't done to punish Bonnie for *seducing* him and me for *aggressing* him." Apprehension crept into the security guard's hard features. "He even threatened to get the police involved."

"If you had video evidence, why *not* get the police involved?" I countered. "It would have at least cleared your name."

Ian's massive hands curled into fists. "Dunmer spouts off about his VIP government connections any chance he gets. Who knows what might have happened if the cops had come by? We couldn't risk Dunmer using his influence to sway them. So, Bonnie and I took our probation as the lesser of two evils."

How poetic. I noted the use of the present tense in Ian's statement about Larry. "You thought Larry might have used his clout as a state official to have you arrested?"

Ian nodded, a look of defeat masking his face. "Bonnie and I took a gap year to save our money for college, and I doubt my chances of getting accepted would increase if I had an arrest record."

And you had to take poor Bonnie down with you all because you couldn't control your temper. I frowned as I considered the situation. Ian seemed to be barely holding it together, just talking about the Dunmers. How had he managed not to pound Larry's face in when he and Rosalynn showed up at Vine's door last night? "Have you seen the Dunmers recently?"

Ian shook his head.

The knot in my stomach tightened. Was he telling the truth? How could he not have seen the Dunmers at Vine? "Weren't you the bouncer at Andre Nunez's bar in Central Shores last night?"

Ian stiffened. "Yeah. What's that got to do with anything?"

"The Dunmers attended the party." I lifted an eyebrow, giving him my most withering stare. "How could you not have seen them?"

Ian's jawbone looked like it might burst from underneath his tanned skin. "I wasn't the only person working security, Ms. Cline, and I wasn't working the line the entire time. I guess karma worked in my favor that I didn't cross paths with them."

"Did Bonnie tell you she had a run-in with Larry while catering the party?"

Ian's lips stretched into a thin line. "I need to return to the surveillance room, Ms. Cline. Enjoy the rest of your afternoon." He brushed past me, jostling me backward as he made quick, determined strides toward an Employees Only door.

"Geesh." I rubbed my shoulder where his rock-hard arm had knocked me. I glanced around the lobby to see if anyone had spotted his abrupt exit.

I noticed Bonnie leaning against one of the columns over by the pool deck entrance. Her eyes widened when I caught her staring at me, and she darted outside, disappearing into the crowd.

My nerves tingled as I headed toward the hostess to return my keycard, wondering what had spooked Bonnie.

The hostess smiled as she took the card and waved down the valet. "Did you have an enjoyable visit, Ms. Cline?"

An uneasy chuckle danced off my tongue. "It was very memorable."

While I may not have tracked down Rosalynn, my list of suspects had just grown by two.

Chapter Twelve

To my delight, Hudson had beaten me home from scouring old cold case files and greeted me with a bottle of Mike's Hard Lemonade. "I picked up some provisions on the drive back. We're dining in style tonight." He motioned to a platter of hotdogs on the kitchen counter. "The grill is ready when you are."

I kissed his cheek, glad to see him in a good mood. Not wanting to put a damper on things, I decided not to ask how his research had gone. If Hudson wished to share anything about Tori, he would. Instead, I took a savoring sip of the sweet yet tart cocktail. "Let me change, and I'll join you outside." I hadn't realized how grimy I felt from bumping into sweaty, chlorine-covered bodies until I pulled Jolly into our garage. A side effect of prying into Larry Dunmer's life.

"Why don't you text Jasper and Charlotte to join us?" Hudson called from the kitchen while I surveyed my closet. "We've got more than enough food."

A minute later, I waltzed back into the kitchen wearing cotton shorts and a Miranda Priestly T-shirt. *The Devil Wears Prada* top had been a joke souvenir Jasper had brought home for me when he'd gone to Paris. "Eh, Deacon just got back from a work trip, so I'm sure he and Charlotte will want to hang solo tonight."

Hudson picked up the plate of hotdogs and headed for the sliding door that led out to the deck. "What about Jasper? Nothing's ever stopped him from being a third wheel."

I swirled the remaining spiked lemonade around in the bottle. For the first time in my life, I was hesitant to reach out to Jasper. While I had no doubts that he had nothing to do with Larry's demise, I knew my bestie well enough to know he was keeping *something* from me. He wouldn't explain why he'd been summoned away from Vine so suddenly, who he'd met with, or why he needed a lawyer for *Divulge* business. Was something going on with the magazine? Why was Jasper being so secretive?

"Is it so bad to want you all to myself tonight?" I joined Hudson on the deck, the salty air weaving gently through my hair.

Hudson grinned, wrapping an arm around my waist and pulling me close. "I won't say no to that." He kissed me softly before turning his attention toward the smoking grill. "So, what did your trip to Cherry Springs turn up?"

"Some new suspects." Rubbing my hands with anticipation, I launched into an animated retelling of my afternoon, starting with my run-in with Gavin outside the Dunmers' condo and ending with my suspicions about Ian and Bonnie.

Hudson folded his arms at my story's conclusion. "I thought you told me you weren't putting yourself in danger."

I shrugged off his unhappy gaze, disappointed by his reaction. "I wasn't. I was just talking to people."

"Including two folks who had very real reasons for wanting Larry dead."

I rolled my eyes. "It's not like I knew that before I talked with them."

"Oh, come on, Coco." Hudson's expression grew pained. "I have cause to be concerned about you snooping on your own. You nearly got yourself killed the last time you confronted a murderer."

"I told you, I played it safe." I held up my hands in protest. "I made sure I stayed in crowded, public areas. And besides, it was the police who suggested I keep an eye out for Ros. Gavin all but outright *asked* for my help."

Tongs in hand, Hudson started yanking the charred hotdogs off the grill. "Gavin stepped out of line on this, and you know it." The grill cover clattered loudly as he replaced it. "He never should have asked a civilian to help find a suspect."

"He wasn't asking me to find a suspect. He asked me to help the police locate Larry's next of kin. Gavin doesn't think Ros is the killer," I pointed out. "The label of suspect still solely rests on my best friend, or have you forgotten Jasper's future is on the line?"

Hudson set down the platter of hotdogs on the patio table with a thud. He'd already brought out a side salad, a bag of chips, buns, and various condiments. If I hadn't been so peeved by his overprotectiveness, I would have been gushing over the lovely meal he'd thoughtfully prepared.

"No, I haven't forgotten." The fight had gone out of him. "I'm sorry, Coco. I know you're capable of handling yourself. I'm just—" Hudson choked back his words, "just still trying to let go of what happened between you and—"

I forgave him in an instant, placing a silencing finger over his lips. "No need to apologize." I studied his brown eyes, wet with emotion. I cursed myself. With everything Hudson was putting up with at work, I didn't want to be another added burden. "*I'm* the one who should be sorry. I'm just so desperate to get Jasper out of this mess that I wasn't thinking clearly."

Hudson cradled my hand, his strong fingers stroking my palm. "I don't want to be one of those control freak boyfriends, Coco. God knows I feel like the pot calling the kettle black, what with all the crap you have to hear about…you know who." His features tightened at his veiled mention of Tori. "I'm just so afraid that one day you're going to go chasing after some bad guy and never come back to me."

I shivered at his frightening confession.

"If you're not going to be concerned about your own safety, can you at least be a little concerned for my sanity?" Hudson ran a finger down my cheek, tilting my chin to meet his gaze. "Please don't go off on these little missions alone."

I nodded, unable to summon the right reassuring words. After everything that had happened this past spring, I owed it to Hudson and our partnership to be more careful.

"So," he said as he held out a patio chair for me, "are you going to let the police know that Ian and Bonnie had a bone to pick with Larry?"

Happy to switch topics and focus on the case details, I grabbed a hotdog bun and started assembling the iconic summer meal. "Gavin only asked for my help locating Rosalynn. He said if he found out I was interfering in any other way, he had a jail cell with my name on it."

Hudson managed to frown as he chewed on his ketchup-and-relish-covered hotdog.

"Besides," I continued before he queued up another lecture, "Ian and Bonnie are hardly the only people to harbor a grudge against Larry."

"Yeah, but Ian clammed up when you confronted him about seeing the Dunmers at Vine." Hudson waved a potato chip in the air. "There's no way he wouldn't have seen them there at some point."

I mulled over a budding scenario as I chewed on a mustard-laden bite of meat. "You're right. Even if Ian wasn't manning the door when Larry and Ros arrived, there's no way he missed the commotion they made before leaving."

"And if he found out that Larry came onto his girlfriend *again* after nearly getting them both fired...." Hudson looked at me pointedly. "Didn't Bonnie say the guy had a temper?"

I nodded. "If Ian was working security at the event, it wouldn't have been hard for him to swing by the table and grab a corkscrew."

Hudson skewered a hefty bite of salad with his fork. "Motive, means, and opportunity."

I deflated back into the patio chair cushion. "All of which Jasper currently has in the eyes of the police. If only I had found Ros at Cyprus, too. The police are tiptoeing around the investigation until they find her." Even though Larry's body had only turned up this morning, precious time was ticking away to track down his killer.

Hudson reached across the table and squeezed my hand. "Babes, it's not your job to find her. You followed a good lead. Now, leave it to the police, okay?"

My phone buzzed on the tabletop, saving me from having to respond. I wasn't ready to throw the towel in on finding Ros yet.

"Is it Jasper?"

Hudson's genuine concern for my best friend revealed itself in his harried question, and I gave him a sad smile. "It's Mom. She's asking me if I want to do brunch at Beaufort's tomorrow morning." I lifted my finger to the keypad to type a quick "**Can we resched?**" response. My weekend with Hudson had already taken a hit. As much as I loved my mother, spending some quality time with my boyfriend was higher on my to-do list.

I was about to hit send when a sneaky thought occurred to me. Mom had worked alongside Larry in a professional capacity. Ian Miles might have had the motive, means, and opportunity to kill Larry, but it didn't mean no one else did. The more suspects I was able to uncover, the easier it would be for the police to realize Jasper wasn't the only person with an axe—or corkscrew—to grind.

I gave Hudson a doe-eyed look. "Do you mind if I go? It's been a little while since I've seen her. She might show up on our doorstep if I prolong it anymore."

"Of course not." Hudson wiped the corner of his mouth, a sexy grin on his face. "We'll just have to make the most of what weekend we have left. In the bedroom, perhaps?" His eyebrows wiggled suggestively.

I glanced at the vacant lot next door that belonged to our beloved neighbors, the Huntingtons. The elderly couple only inhabited their Sunny Shores condo for two weeks at the beginning of August, when the Florida weather got the better of them. And with the Dunmers currently out of the picture...

A mischievous smirk formed on my lips. "It would be a shame to miss out on this fresh air, though." I tugged teasingly at the hem of my t-shirt.

Hudson's eyes widened momentarily before an ear-to-ear grin ripped across his face. "Coco Cline, you naughty little vixen." He edged out of his seat with smooth, sensual prowess and had me pinned to my chair with a breathless kiss.

Chapter Thirteen

At ten the following day, I pushed open the elegant stained-glass door of Beaufort's, reveling in the sweet smells of cinnamon and maple. I couldn't wait to sink my teeth into their Sunday brunch special: apple-cinnamon compote French toast.

Mom looked up from studying the leather-bound menu as I approached our favorite table tucked away in the corner by the window. "Oh, Cordelia!" She jumped from her seat and gave me a bone-crushing hug. "It feels like ages since I've seen you. You need to stop by the house more often."

I hugged her back before wrenching myself free from her grasp. In typical Mom-fashion, she'd waited exactly one-point-three seconds before making me feel guilty. "I hardly think two weeks would be considered 'ages.'" I kissed her cheek before settling into my seat.

Mom placed her napkin on her lap. "Thea manages to find the time to stop by and say hello every other day."

Real subtle, Mother. "Thea manages to find the time because she has to pick up her children for whom you provide free daycare," I replied sweetly with my most angelic smile, although I couldn't help but be annoyed. Not only at Mom's not-so-subtle comparison between siblings, but because Mom obeyed my sister Dorothy's request to be called Thea. Even after thirteen-plus years since I'd "rebranded myself," Mom still refused to call me Coco.

"How are the little terrors these days?" Talking about my sister's kids was always a safe subject. Thea, three years my junior and happily married, had adorable four-year-old triplets.

Mom shushed me with a stern look. "The children are absolutely lovely, Delia. Not that you would know, I gather. Thea says they haven't seen you since Memorial Day."

I sighed. At this rate, I would be filled up on guilt before we even ordered our food. "You know, Mom, some families only see each other once or twice a year."

Mom's elegant features contorted with horror. "Well, *we* are not one of those families. I don't see why it's so hard for you to visit, especially when we all live so close to each other."

I rubbed at the pressure building in my temples. There was no point in arguing with Moira Cline. Better to just embrace it. "I've been swamped juggling blog stuff, CoA clients, and my consultation gig at the PD."

This seemed to pacify my mother slightly, although she had absolutely no concept of what I really did for a living. Every time Mom heard the words "social media influencer" or "lifestyle blogger," she'd just shake her head and lament how a calculator was considered high-tech in her day. But, God love her, even though she didn't understand it, Mom tried to keep engaged with what I did for a living, so her blue gaze crinkled with obvious worry. "I thought you were hiring an assistant to help with everything."

"I am. I'm still trying to find the right person." I picked up the menu lying on my place setting to peruse Beaufort's brunch offerings even though I already knew what I wanted. "I have a few interviews tomorrow morning."

"Well, that's good." Mom took a sip of water and stared at me expectantly. "I hope you won't be too busy, though, to enjoy Salute to Summer. Council has been working hard on it this year."

"Wouldn't miss it, Mom." I'd really be in the doghouse if I skipped out on Mom's first big event as town council chair. Her predecessor, Reggie Monahan, had unexpectedly moved to Georgia two months ago to take care of his ailing father, vacating the seat. The special election that had cemented Roger Sullivan as mayor also installed my mother as chairperson.

Her veiled critique of my workaholic tendencies gave me the perfect opening to redirect the conversation. "How are things going with Council? What with the town audit and all?"

Mom rolled her eyes with exaggerated exasperation. "Ugh, that odious little man is making all our lives a living h-e-double-hockey-sticks. I can't imagine how awful he must be as a neighbor, honey."

Before I could begin dancing around the truth that my neighbor was no longer a problem, a figure appeared next to our table, startling us into silence.

"Good morning, ladies. How are the Cline women doing today?"

Both Mom and I gaped at Beaufort's newest waiter, a bit shocked.

"Melvin!" Mom recovered first. "What a surprise to see you here. How have you been?"

Melvin Beaufort smiled warmly as he refilled our water glasses. "I can't complain. Retirement suits me. If I had known just how much I would enjoy it, I wouldn't have run for that third term."

Mom and I chuckled politely, although my laughter rang a bit hollow. I wasn't sure "retirement" was the right word choice to describe our former mayor's exit from local politics. While investigating Stacy Lockner's death, I'd come across information suggesting Mayor Beaufort had had an affair with the deceased woman, and I'd shared these suspicions with Chief McInnis. Toward the end of his tenure in office, Melvin clashed with Chief McInnis on the need for a Central Shores police force and had caused quite a bit of trouble for the chief. From what I'd gathered, days after Stacy's murderer had been arrested, Chief McInnis paid Melvin a not-so-friendly visit, which ultimately resulted in Melvin announcing his resignation from public life. I couldn't help but wonder if Chief McInnis had used the salacious gossip I'd obtained to push the mayor out.

I had to admit, though, seeing the former politician beside our table did have me agreeing with Melvin that a life away from politics suited him. He'd lost a great deal of weight in the past two months, and his skin no longer had that ruddy glow of a man who enjoyed a few too many whiskeys.

Melvin set the half-empty water carafe in the middle of our table and continued, "Sometimes the endless, carefree hours do get a bit dull, which is why I'm helping Fred out with the restaurant. Gives him and Nat the chance to take a day off here and there to enjoy life."

Fred Beaufort had owned and operated the French eatery for decades, taking over the family business from Fred and Melvin's parents. Beaufort's was one of the town's oldest and most respected establishments.

"How very thoughtful of you." Mom smiled in acknowledgment.

Melvin motioned wordlessly to the pot of coffee he carried in his other hand and filled our cups after we both nodded in agreement. "And while I hate to talk shop on the weekends, Coco, after the work you did to promote Andre's new wine bar, I must say, I think Freddie should enlist in your firm's services. What a lovely party, too. My wife and I had a grand time." As one of Central Shores' more high-profile residents, Melvin had been on the guest list for Andre's event, and I was glad to know Mrs. Beaufort had enjoyed a fun night out. After learning about Melvin's ties to Stacy, I'd felt sorry for Mrs. Beaufort, who'd always been so devoted to her husband and his political career.

"How is Jeanie doing?" Mom asked, her warm personality beginning to shine. "I don't see her around as much as I used to, now that she isn't stopping by town hall to pick up her lunch date."

"She's started joining me out on the green if you can believe it. All this time, she wanted to come along, but I thought she'd hate it." Melvin shook his head. "Turns out she's already beating me by two strokes. I think WMTG asked the wrong Beaufort to participate in their little golf tournament." He tugged at his suspenders as he rocked on his heels. "Now, enough about me. You must be starving. What can I get you?"

I placed my order for the apple-cinnamon compote French toast while Mom requested eggs benedict.

"Coming right up." With a tip of an imaginary hat, Melvin disappeared through the swinging kitchen doors.

Mom let out a low whistle once the coast was clear. "He's certainly changed for the better since stepping down."

I chuckled at her obvious disbelief. "I hope being town council chair doesn't turn you into a philandering terror."

"Those were just *rumors*, Delia." Mom whacked me with her napkin. "No need to go spreading gossip. Now, what were we talking about?"

"The town audit," I prompted her, grinning with irony as I hoped she'd spill some more tea about Larry.

Mom rolled her periwinkle blue eyes. "Ugh, can we not? I'll be glad when we see the last of that man. I think the only person who can stand to be in his presence for more than five seconds is Mayor Sullivan." Her scowl deepened. "Not a day goes by that Dunmer's not threatening to cut one department's budget or another."

"Larry does like to make threats." I was careful to use the present tense. Despite being town council chair, it didn't sound like Mayor Sullivan had informed my mother about the latest murder to afflict Central Shores, and I wasn't going to be the one who let that top-secret news slip.

Mom stared at me expectantly. "I heard you, Jasper, and the Dunmers had *words* at Andre's big party."

Of course she had. A heated scene like that would have traveled through the town grapevine faster than a summer thunderstorm. I shivered to think how the story would evolve once word got out about Larry's death. It wouldn't bode well for Jasper *or* for me. "It wasn't a big deal. He was perving on a waitress, so Jasper and I stepped in."

"How his wife tolerates behavior like that is beyond me." Mom tutted softly. "I'm proud of you and Jasper for doing the right thing, honey, but you two need to be careful. Men like Larry Dunmer thrive on using their connections to punish people."

I took a sip of coffee to prevent myself from speaking. *I don't think I'm at risk from Larry's wrath anymore, Mom.*

Melvin reappeared at our table with a tray of delectable food, and we switched gears to lighter topics. While I cut into my compote-and-syrup-drenched stack of French toast, Mom filled me in on how my nieces and nephew, Blake, Parker, and Taran, were doing.

For the rest of the meal, I nodded along to give the illusion that I was paying rapt attention to every little detail about the triplets while really wondering how I was going to get our conversation back to Larry and the audit. Bonnie and Ian were certainly viable suspects, but something that Hudson had said yesterday rolled around in my mind. The two most powerful motives in the world were love and money. With Ros MIA and unavailable for questioning on the "love" front, the town audit seemed the most logical trail to follow. And from what Mom had shared already, it sounded as though Larry's short stint at town hall had been cantankerous at best. Perhaps someone had taken his threats to cut the budget seriously and, in turn, taken drastic measures to thwart it.

"Cordelia?"

The use of my given name pulled me out of my puzzling reverie. "Sorry, what?"

Mom frowned as she slipped sixty dollars into the billfold before handing it to an awaiting Melvin. "I asked if you wanted to take a walk down to Quincy's?"

My cheeks heated as I gave her a guilty look of apology. "Quincy's sounds great. I thought you were going to let me pay for brunch this time."

"Nonsense. I invited you, remember?"

I smiled at witnessing Moira Cline's Rules of Etiquette in action. "Thanks, Mom."

Bidding Melvin goodbye, we walked arm-in-arm out of the restaurant onto the busy sidewalk. As we made our way past the various shops and eateries along the strip toward the cute dress boutique, Mom cleared her throat. "I gather you lost interest in our conversation somewhere around the triplets' first gymnastics class."

She didn't sound mad, which made me feel even worse. "I'm a terrible aunt, aren't I?" I made a mental promise that I would swing by—*hehe*—the kids' gymnastics class one of these days.

"What's got you so preoccupied?" Mom's grip on my arm tightened just a bit. "Something with work?"

I sighed with a shake of my head. "I wish."

"Anything I can help with?"

I met my mom's worried gaze, touched by her concern. Thea may have been the golden child in our family, but I knew both my parents loved me deeply. The remnants of French toast did somersaults in my stomach. I hated lying to Mom, especially when I knew she'd do everything in her power to help sweep away this shadow of doubt hovering over Jasper if she knew what was really going on. "Have you heard anything around town about the drowning down at Pelican Beach?"

Her pretty features morphed into surprise. "Nothing apart from the usual. Unsuspecting tourist likely getting caught in the undertow."

My vague social media blast seemed to be doing its job.

"Why? What have you heard? Do you *know* something, Delia?"

I'd now piqued my mother's insatiable curiosity. *Like mother, like daughter.*

Instead of continuing along the sidewalk to Quincy's, I pulled my mother down the small alleyway next to Harper's Pub and toward the residential parking lot. "I need to tell you something, but before I do, you have to promise not to breathe a word of this to anyone."

Mom quickened her pace to keep in step with me, uncertainty painted across her face. "What's going on, hon?"

I unlocked Jolly and motioned for her to climb inside. Once the AC was at full blast, I turned to her. "Do I have your word? Not even Dad can know about this yet."

"Delia, you're scaring me." Mom gripped my hand. "Of course, I'll keep whatever secret you need. Just tell me what's going on."

I took a fortifying breath. "The body police found down at Pelican Beach wasn't some unsuspecting tourist. It was Larry Dunmer."

I filled my astonished mother in on everything that had transpired since the Vine party Friday night. By the end, my voice was tight with emotion. "I can't shake this worry I have for Jasper."

"Oh, honey." Mom rubbed my arms before scooping me into an awkward car hug. "The police can't seriously think Jasper had anything to do with this, can they? I mean, the fact that Rosalynn is missing seems way more incriminating than an engraved corkscrew that tons of people had access to."

"Then why did Detective Forester tell him not to leave town?" I fired back, my anxiety getting the better of me. "Jasper has no alibi after eleven thirty, he was seen having a very heated confrontation with the victim, and his name is literally on the murder weapon." I started to tremble as fear took over my senses. "I'm worried that even after the police track down Ros, they'll still pursue Jasper as a person of interest. That negative stigma could cause major trouble for him *and* for *Divulge*."

Mom cradled me against her, her maternal warmth a natural, soothing balm. "This is just awful. I wish there was something more we could do to help."

"Well, there might be." I straightened and met her bewildered gaze. "You see, I'm working on drumming up a list of folks who had it in for Larry way more than Jasper."

Mom's skin went white. "Delia!" she snapped. "I know Jasper is like family, but you nearly got yourself killed the last time you did something like this." She aged right before me, dread shining in her watery eyes.

I again reached for her hand. "You don't need to remind me, Mom. Believe me. But this is *Jasper* we're talking about. I can't sit idly by and let the police railroad my best friend."

She opened her mouth to protest, but I hammered on. "And trust me, all I'm doing is putting together a list of possible suspects I can hand over to Gavin to take the heat off Jasper. I certainly don't plan on confronting a deranged killer again."

Mom folded her arms across her chest. "I don't like it, Delia. Not one bit." Her anxious gaze traveled out across the parking lot, and for a moment, she seemed very far away. "But you're right. From what you've shared, this situation doesn't paint a good picture for Jasper. Accusations, even false ones, can linger over a person and ruin their future." She relaxed her tense posture and met my pleading stare head-on. "What have you dug up so far?"

"Very little," I admitted. "Chief McInnis is adamant Rosalynn be informed about her husband's death before releasing any details about the case to the public, and since the police haven't been able to notify next-of-kin, it's hard to ask probing questions without raising suspicion. I did take a trip out to Cyprus yesterday on a hunch that Ros might be spending time there. Instead, I ran into the server whom Larry sexually harassed at the Vine party and her bouncer boyfriend."

I then filled her in on the finer details of my visit to Cyprus.

"I see. So, you think either of these two could have murdered Larry?"

I shrugged. "I find it hard to believe that Bonnie—she's the waitress we rescued from Larry's lechery—would turn around and frame one of the people who helped ward him off." I bit my lip as I considered the theory. "But I definitely got a malicious vibe from her boyfriend, Ian. Bonnie didn't look too pleased to see me speaking with him, either."

Mom shuddered. "Well, it certainly sounds like they both have motive to want Larry dead. But did they have the opportunity to kill him? Didn't Andre's party go well into the night?"

I was absently multi-tasking, hopping from app to app on my phone, debating what to do about my suspicions about Ian and Bonnie. "That's a good point. Vine likely didn't close until at least two A.M." I frowned as I recalled the questions Detective Forester asked Jasper. She'd focused more on the fact that he had no alibi after eleven thirty rather than earlier in the evening. "I have no idea what time Larry died, though. They could have very well killed him after the party ended."

Mom pointed at my phone. "What are you looking at?"

"I'm scanning Bonnie's socials to see if she posted anything from the party." Bonnie had been relatively easy to locate on Instagram. I'd started on Cyprus's profile and began scanning their excellently curated photo collection. Proud to see that my brief CoA engagement with Cyprus had made a lasting impression, I grinned in triumph as my gaze settled on a fun snapshot capturing Cyprus waitstaff in action. Daria and Bonnie stole the show as the camera caught Daria handing Bonnie a boatload of margaritas on a shiny tray. I clicked the image for more details and saw the handle @bonniebonbon tagged. A tap of the name had me on a profile featuring a sultry picture of Bonnie.

Her Instagram, though, had no new posts in the last three days. Neither did her Facebook or Twitter accounts. I wasn't discouraged yet, though. Following a growing hunch, I clicked on the TikTok icon near the bottom of my home screen. While TikTok wasn't a part of my social media holy trinity, I occasionally swiped through the app to check out popular videos and keep tabs on pop culture references. TikTok started as a place for artists to showcase their musical abilities by posting clips of their performances. Since its introduction into the social media world, it had grown into a massive hub of viral video activity.

Mom leaned against my shoulder to get a better look at my screen. "Is that a video of a donkey?"

Indeed, someone had recorded a donkey that looked like it was lip-syncing to famous Bon Jovi songs. I shook my head at the silliness. "The wonders of the Internet."

I typed in Bonnie's Instagram handle, hoping she'd used the same name across all platforms in an effort to stay "on brand." Again, my instincts paid off. Her profile loaded and revealed thousands of videos under her account. TikTok was Gen Z playland.

Most videos featured the same apartment backdrop, with Bonnie sitting cross-legged on a simple gray couch while Ian strummed a guitar. They sang together? I would have gushed over how cute they were if I didn't consider them potential killers.

I clicked on Bonnie's most recent video. It had been posted all of five minutes ago. She was singing along to a Sara Bareilles song, leaning against a wall of wood lockers. The Cyprus breakroom, maybe?

I swiped up, going to the next video on her timeline. It was posted an hour ago. "Guess my thumb is going to get some cardio today." I gave Mom a wry glance before I started swiping with a vengeance. Keeping track of the timestamp info, it felt like I'd swiped through at least twenty clips before a video from Friday night popped up on the screen.

"Let's take a listen." I turned up the volume on my phone.

Eric Carmen's "Hungry Eyes" started blaring as Bonnie and Ian danced into the frame. Ian removed his sunglasses every time the *Dirty Dancing* crooner wailed the chorus, giving Bonnie appreciative looks while they danced around a room lined with wine bottles.

Mom chuckled at the video. "Cute stuff. Can you imagine your father twirling around like that?"

I let out a big snort. I could not. "This was uploaded around midnight," I said, examining the timestamp again. "Filmed in Vine's stockroom, I'd be willing to bet."

"And look there." Mom's manicured finger pointed at something in the video's background on the far wall.

"A clock!" I eyed her, impressed. "Good catch, Mom."

She winked. "I just got my contacts prescription updated."

Replaying the video, I snapped a screenshot when the digital wall clock appeared in the frame and zoomed in to take a closer look. While the image was blurry, I could make out the big, glowing numbers. "Well, we can confirm Bonnie and Ian were goofing off in Andre's storeroom at eleven thirty-five." I frowned, wishing I knew more about when Larry had died. "Bonnie didn't post any more videos that night...perhaps they got sidetracked with a dead body?"

Mom didn't look very convinced. "They don't look like two people preparing to commit murder, hon." She quickly continued, seeing me deflate at her comment, "But you're right. Maybe it happened later in the night." She paused. "But I wouldn't rest Jasper's freedom solely on the two of them."

She was right, of course. I needed to track down more viable suspects to share with the police, and that's what I intended to do. Hearing that Mom was on my side made everything seem a bit more hopeful. "You said Larry threatened to make budget cuts down at town hall. Would anyone have acted to prevent him from making good on those threats?"

Mom's mouth popped open in muted horror, clearly stunned by the one-eighty the conversation had taken. "I-I don't know. I can't imagine any of my colleagues doing something so awful, but..." she trailed off, her expression a dark storm, "but Larry often brought out the worst in people."

"Whose budgets was he going after? Do you know?"

Mom shook her head, the silver strands in her coifed brown hair catching the sunlight streaming through Jolly's moonroof. "Larry lorded the audit over everyone, but I'm not sure which departments he was seriously considering."

I drummed intently on Jolly's steering wheel, debating how to proceed. "Do you think he'd have notes about it in his office?"

Mom's head bobbed absently before she fully processed what I was saying.

When the realization hit her, she let out a sharp gasp. "Delia, you can't seriously be considering rifling through a dead man's belongings? You could get in trouble with the police!"

I scowled out my window. "As if the police will even bother looking." At the moment, Chief McInnis and his team were more concerned with tracking down Ros than anything. Besides, in their eyes, they already had a prime suspect with the perfect motive and evidence to convict him.

Mom's expression turned sympathetic in the driver-side window's reflection. "Honey, I know you're worried about Jasper—"

"Mom, his entire future is on the line. You said so yourself. Just being associated with this case once the news breaks could be damaging. Please, I have to do something to help him."

Mom glanced down at her lap. Her purse strap was a twisted mess. "Well, I did forget to print out a few extra vendor liability forms to have on hand at the festival. Someone always loses theirs or ruins it while setting up their booth." She finally met my gaze, a determined glint in her eyes. "Why don't you keep me company while I swing by my office at the town hall?"

I grinned at my mother's inventive excuse. Like mother, like daughter, indeed.

Chapter Fourteen

I grabbed a spot next to Mom's sedan in the otherwise empty parking lot. The town hall loomed before us, closed up tight on a Sunday morning. Its dark windows glinted ominously in the sun. The ghostly feeling permeated the rest of the town commons. Even the police station looked forlorn and vacant. The sight didn't give me much confidence that Chief McInnis and his team were hard at work trying to determine Larry's *real* killer instead of pinning his death on Jasper.

We climbed out of our cars and surveyed the scene. Mom fidgeted next to me as she hiked her purse strap onto her shoulder. "Larry's office is on the second floor," she whispered out of the side of her mouth.

I chuckled at her covert behavior. "Relax, Mom. The place is completely deserted." No doubt everyone was enjoying one last quiet Sunday before Salute to Summer shenanigans kicked off. The festival was technically hosted by the town council, but it was tradition for the entire municipal government to be involved. Especially when it came to the manual labor required to construct the grandstand for events down at the beach.

My reassurances did little to quench Mom's unease as we walked toward the building. Well, *I* walked. Mom did something more akin to a low crouch-shuffle. While my insides were practically bursting at the seams to contain my howling laughter, I needed her cooperation to get inside and couldn't risk making fun of her.

Her shrewd gaze made one final sweep of the Commons before she inserted her key into the front door.

"Thank goodness you were voted into Councilman Monahan's vacant seat, or this would be a bust." I glanced down at the key in her trembling hands. As council chair, she was one of the few government officials with a personal key for the building.

Shushing me, Mom ushered me inside and locked the door behind us. "My office is just down the hall from the lobby." She pointed to a shiny oak door with a glossy nameplate. "I should be able to hear if anyone comes into the building. You have your phone on you?"

I pulled it out of my pocket with a snort. "Of course." Before I slid my cell back into my green-and-white romper pocket, I checked the storm of notifications blowing up the lock screen. My "Booked for Summer" post had successfully uploaded to *Trending Topic* since I'd actually scheduled it to go live. I'd picked up a retweet on Twitter from Goodreads and James Rollins, the author of one of the fabulously twisty books I'd recommended. The article had also garnered quite a few reactions and comments on Facebook. Putting my phone away for now, I made a mental note to scan through them when I had the time.

This will all be so much easier to juggle once I hire someone to help me out. With another person on board, I could focus less on managing *Trending Topic* and more on expanding my efforts within the "influencer" space. There were so many great organizations and companies out there looking to collaborate and increase their brand awareness. My overflowing DMs were proof enough. With an assistant, we could properly vet requests and begin helping even more people looking to do good in the world. Just last month, I partnered with a pet company that had designed leashes with built-in water bottles to help keep dogs hydrated during long walks. To promote the startup among my followers, I'd teamed up with the county animal shelter—with Charlotte's help, as she volunteered there regularly—and featured their rescues using the H2Go Leash. Not only did the H2Go Leash sell out, but all the adorable doggies featured in the campaign were adopted. A win for everyone involved.

I did feel a little guilty, wanting to hand over the blogging reins to my new hire. In the early days of *Trending Topic*, I did my best to respond to user comments as much as possible. However, as the blog blew up and grew more popular, it became harder to give that special attention to readers. Nowadays, I found myself barely having the bandwidth to acknowledge their posts. I needed to invest more time interacting with them, or my audience would soon lose interest. Fame was a fickle friend, and there was always the very real fear that *Trending Topic* and my online platform would fade into Internet obscurity.

Would that be so bad?

The snarky thought poked at the back of my mind, resurfacing an internal debate I'd been having for a few months now. With Center of Attention busier than ever, *Trending Topic* just wasn't the passion project it had once been. I'd toyed with the idea of shutting the blog down—more than once, in fact—but I'd always shaken the rash notion out of my head. I was stressed, balancing too many projects. Once I had an assistant at my side, I was sure everything would work out.

"Delia?" Mom hissed as she scanned up and down the halls. "We don't have all day."

I pushed my entrepreneurial thoughts aside and focused on the task at hand. "Larry's office is up on the second floor. Got it." With a mock salute, I hurried toward the stairwell opposite the lobby and left Mom to her innocent printing task.

Despite the warm sunlight streaming in from the windows, the emptiness of the second floor coaxed a flurry of goosebumps across my arms. "Larry, Larry, Larry," I murmured as I scanned the army of doors lining the long, naturally lit hallway.

My searching gaze landed on a door right by the men's bathroom. A hand-written sign taped to the glass pane declared, "Larry Dunmer, State Auditor."

Prime office real estate.

I half expected the door to be locked due to Larry's overbearing personality when it came to protecting his property. However, it stood open in foreboding welcome. The sight made my heart thud against my chest. Had someone else beaten me here? Could the killer have come by Larry's office to destroy any evidence pointing toward them?

I hushed my overactive imagination. I hadn't considered the obvious. Perhaps the police had visited Larry's workspace. Hope simmered inside me. Maybe they *were* looking into other avenues rather than just focusing on Jasper and Larry's testy relationship.

I took a deep breath and stepped over the threshold. The room was oddly windowless, so I fumbled for a light switch to get a better look.

A harsh, fluorescent glow flooded the area, revealing that Larry's office was actually a repurposed maintenance closet. A collection of brooms and mops still sat propped up in the corner. I grimaced at the obvious slight, feeling a little bit sorry for my neighbor. Larry might have been sent by the state to review Central Shores' budget, but the town had quickly put him in his place by shoving him in a dingy closet. No wonder he wasn't too thrilled to be here.

At least whoever had set up the space for Larry had given him a sturdy desk, desktop computer, file cabinet, and a comfortable-looking chair. Other than those few amenities, there wasn't much to see. I did a quick sweep of his desk. No knick-knacks. No pictures. Not even a fake plant. Just a mug full of ballpoint pens, a stapler, and a stack of Post-it notes.

"What a depressing place to work." I frequently featured inviting home office décor on *Trending Topic*, but I wasn't sure even my style tips could help spruce up this cheerless room.

I debated texting Gavin to confirm whether the police had been by Larry's office, but I couldn't risk offending *or* alerting him to my snooping. Whatever the case, the police had yet to collect Larry's computer. When I wiggled the mouse, and the monitor came to life, I understood why.

"Real professional, Larry...." A comical gag burst from me as a tacky image of several women in teeny bikinis filled a security lock screen. I studied the passcode box as my plans to snoop evaporated on the spot. What had I been thinking? Larry Dunmer worked for the government. Of course, his computer would be locked when it was unattended. It also meant that the police couldn't access Larry's information without a warrant. Something like that took time to get on the weekends, if they'd be able to get a warrant to search government property at all.

Luckily, *I* didn't have to deal with conducting an investigation entirely above board.

I stared at the sleazy screensaver, willing those poor, objectified women to tell me Larry's code. How the heck was I going to get in without his password? Based on the on-screen instructions, Larry had set up a six-digit PIN. I sighed as I reached for my phone, figuring I'd start with the obvious: his birthday. I pulled up my go-to source for any and all personal data: Facebook. But while I may have been friends with Ros, I had not brought myself to send a friend request to Larry. With his privacy settings, all I could see on his profile was his grainy headshot that looked more than a decade old and the brief quote he'd selected as his intro.

"The measure of a man is what he does with power."

I frowned, knowing I'd heard the phrase before. A quick Google search revealed Plato to be the author. *Interesting.* I didn't take Larry for a deep thinker. Although, without attributing the words to the famous philosopher, the statement almost seemed braggadocious. And, considering his work as a state auditor, a little threatening.

I placed my phone on the desk, the locked monitor still mocking me. Maybe Larry had written down his passcode and hidden it in his office? It was my only option at this point. Otherwise, I'd have to toss in the towel without ever getting a chance to see whether Larry had made any decisions about the town budget.

I opened the first desk drawer. I wasn't sure what I'd been expecting, but it wasn't this. A half-empty jar of peanut butter and a sleeve of Saltines were the only contents. I didn't dare touch either. Both were covered in smudges of sticky peanut butter. Unsurprisingly, Larry wasn't the tidiest of eaters, and his workspace reflected it.

I closed the top drawer, the jar of Skippy thudding around inside. *What if…*

My gaze darted to the computer keyboard at the monitor's base. As I suspected, tiny cracker crumbs were lodged into the crevices between each key.

Gross.

Using the tip of my fingernail, I pulled the keyboard closer for inspection. It was a typical, full-size device, not like the small compact keyboards that didn't have a number pad attached.

I glanced at the lock screen on the monitor once more for confirmation. I needed a six-digit passcode. *Hmm.* I tapped my chin as I stared intently at the keys on the keyboard. Not only did I find cracker crumbs, but some letters had bits of peanut butter residue smeared on them. *Geez, Larry, ever heard of wet wipes?* I pictured the scene. Larry, stuffing his face with Skippy-smothered Saltines, plopping down at his desk and unlocking his computer. My gaze moved to the number pad and landed on the "2" key, covered partially by a thin veil of dried peanut butter. I examined the other number pad keys, enabling the flashlight on my iPhone for maximum brightness. None had any traces of peanut butter on them.

Could it be that simple? I swiped a pen from Larry's desk to avoid touching the leftover peanut butter residue and used the tip to press the "2" key down six times.

The half-naked women protecting Larry's computer dissolved to reveal a desktop featuring Kate Upton's famous 2017 *Sports Illustrated Swimsuit Edition* cover.

I didn't have time to enjoy my small victory. Mom would no doubt grow more nervous the longer I took up here. While we had little chance of being caught, I didn't want to get her into trouble, especially after she'd put so much work into coordinating the Salute to Summer festival.

Grabbing the mouse, I launched Outlook with a single click of an icon. I may have been a Mac iOS user at heart, but I was familiar with Microsoft and knew my way around. While Larry's work inbox loaded, I opened a Word document to review his recent document history. If he had typed any notes or official memos in Word, the docs would have been displayed in the history section. However, Word was woefully blank, so I closed the writing software, disappointed with Larry's lack of activity.

His inbox was another story. Larry had fifty-six unread emails. The oldest had come in around eleven thirty on Friday night. It appeared as though Larry had been opening work emails, most likely from his phone, throughout the evening. That is, until eleven thirty hit. Eleven thirty-eight, to be precise. The oldest unread email was from someone named Paul Merrill with the subject line, **RE: The Dover spot**. I clicked on the message and skimmed it, my eyes widening.

Larry had emailed this Paul Merrill guy less than a week ago about an open job posting on his team. Paul's response had been blunt: Larry wasn't a good fit. Based on Larry's flowery language in his original note, he seemed to really want this new job. If it had been me waiting for a response, I would have opened Paul's email as soon as it came in, despite the late hour. I wondered…had Larry put his phone away for the night, or was he already dead by eleven thirty-eight?

Whatever the case, this message could prove crucial to the investigation once police obtained access to Larry's government data. I couldn't risk jeopardizing evidence of his digital activity, so I backed out of the email and marked it as unread. With my tracks covered, I began scanning the other fifty-five unread messages he'd received. Most were spam or junk. Nothing about Larry's work pertaining to Central Shores. I moved to his Sent folder to see what Larry had been working on in the days leading up to his death.

An email dated Friday afternoon caught my eye, not because of the date, but due to the bold subject line: **BUDGET UNDER REVIEW**. I clicked on the message. It was addressed to margaretmorales@centralshoresgov.net. Margaret Morales? The surname sounded familiar, but a face didn't come immediately to mind.

Once the message loaded, I realized Larry's response was only part of a longer email chain. It would serve me best to start at the beginning, so I scrolled to the bottom of the message window and began reading Larry's initial outreach dated last Tuesday.

Ms. Morales,

As my review of the town's finances continues, it is becoming increasingly clear that the park's department is overspend-

ing, specifically regarding this whole Salute to Summer business. The town council is responsible for the festival. It seems unfitting that Parks and Recreation also has a budget for this event. Unless circumstances between us change, I don't see how I can allow this to continue.

Best,
   Larry Dunmer

At least now I knew why the last name Morales sounded so familiar. Peggy Morales was the director of the Central Shores Parks and Recreation department, responsible for maintaining the town's parks and beaches. The department also hosted community events throughout the year and had a large hand in the set-up and daily operations of Salute to Summer.

I scrolled to read Peggy's response.

Unless circumstances change? It's highly inappropriate to hold a personal grudge and let it affect our workplace relationship. I don't appreciate you making such crude threats. I am sorry I embarrassed you but wounded pride aside, you know very well that in order for Salute to Summer to continue being as successful as it has in the past, my team and my budget must be involved.

I reread her note. What was Peggy referring to? How had she embarrassed Larry? And was he really threatening to slash her budget because of it?

Larry's final email to her from Friday afternoon, hours before his death, sent a chill down my spine.

As per our discussion this morning, I see you've made up your mind, leaving me with no choice. Your department will not be able to operate as it stands with the budget suggestions I plan to propose to the mayor. This means layoffs and big, structural changes. Perhaps new leadership will be needed to see it done correctly? You might be out of a job before long. I'll give you until Monday to change your mind.

I sucked in a breath, floored by the invisible animosity bleeding from Larry's charged words. Change her mind? About what? I reread the exchange, making sure I hadn't missed anything. For some reason, Larry had it out for Peggy and her department, even so much as threatening to have her fired.

This didn't look good for Peggy. Had she retaliated violently to Larry's ultimatum? He'd threatened her career. I didn't know Peggy well, but I knew she'd been working her way up the ranks at town hall ever since graduating college. She'd been director of Parks longer than I'd been back in Central Shores. If she thought Larry was a threat—

My phone chirped in my hand. It was a text from Mom.

What r u doing? We need 2 go!!!!

Chapter Fifteen

Mom skillfully conveyed her unleashed panic through the number of exclamation points used.

I quickly texted back to reassure her. **Chill, Ma. We R all good. Ur just printing flyers, remember? Be down in 5.**

I closed the email exchange between Peggy and Larry. While I hadn't discovered much, I now had another lead to track down. Maybe I could convince Mom to summon Peggy for an emergency Salute to Summer pow-wow and pepper her unsuspectingly with questions.

Nothing else in the Sent folder caught my eye. With time against me, I decided to skim the trash folder and see what kind of emails Larry opted to toss.

As the subject lines loaded, it appeared the majority of them all had one thing in common. They were from Rosalynn.

Miss u, my luv

Making ur fav din din tonight, sweetums

When will u be home?

Why aren't u answering ur texts?

The list went on and on. I cringed as I read the conversational subject lines, feeling some compassion for Ros. She wasn't my favorite person in the world, but her attitude and resentment toward me made more sense the better I understood Larry. He clearly didn't pay his wife any attention, positive or negative.

I was just about to close out of Outlook completely when a message in the trash gave me pause. Sandwiched in between deleted emails from Ros was a notification from Reddit. Reddit was an anonymous, popular social media community with forums dedicated to just about every topic known to mankind. Heck, even *I* had a subreddit devoted to me and my work with *Trending Topic*.

Out of curiosity, I clicked the email. "I wonder what poor Reddit community Larry unleashed his opinions on." However, the notification wasn't signaling that Larry had unread responses on a post. It was an alert that he'd received a private chat message from another user. It was dated Thursday, the day before Larry was killed.

All the Redditor said was, "Fine."

Glancing at the desktop clock, I cursed under my breath. The five minutes I'd promised Mom were just about up. Quickly, I tapped the link to skim the full conversation on Reddit. A new browser window launched as a result, revealing Larry's Reddit inbox. Thank goodness he was still signed in. More importantly, Larry only had one ongoing chat with a user named u/merchnt_of_venyce, and the chat itself was just a few lines long.

u/MrGovtBigShot: Bring me a big ol' check tomorrow night to cover your missed payments, or I'm going to the police. I've kept silent long enough. Time's up.

u/Merchnt_of_venyce: Fine.

Ice ran through my veins. Was this some kind of joke? A prank between friends?

I read the message several more times, my stomach filling with a dark mixture of hope and dread. If this was real, I'd just uncovered Jasper's ticket to freedom. Whoever this u/merchnt_of_venyce was certainly had an axe to grind with Larry. If blackmail wasn't a motive for murder, then I didn't know what was.

"Delia!"

I jumped back from the desk, my heart feeling like it had landed somewhere outside my body. "Geez! You scared me."

Mom bounced nervously on her heels in the doorway. "Come on, honey. We've been trespassing long enough. We need to get going."

"It's not trespassing, Mom. You work here." I took a quick photo of the electronic blackmail note with my phone and scribbled the Reddit username on a Post-it. Not that it would do me much good. Reddit was well-known for guarding the identities of its users, but it couldn't hurt to check out the profile.

"Did you find anything useful?" Mom asked after we'd left Larry's makeshift office looking relatively untouched.

I nodded and was about to answer when the echoing jiggle of a lock had us both freezing mid-step.

"Someone's unlocking the front door!" Mom wheezed under her breath.

The two of us bolted with surprising speed down the staircase. By the time the town hall door swung inward, we were standing—albeit panting—right outside Mom's office.

"Hello, Moira." Roger Sullivan grinned cheerfully as he entered the lobby, looking like he'd just stepped off the Crestview Country Club golf course. "What brings you in today? I thought you'd be enjoying some peace and quiet this weekend before Salute to Summer consumes our lives."

Mom smiled easily at the town's new mayor. "I forgot to print out some liability forms to have on hand, and my daughter suggested we swing by on our way home from brunch."

Roger acknowledged me with a nod. "Your mom doesn't miss a trick, Coco. I'm sure this will be the best Salute to Summer yet."

I noted the slight twitch in Roger's left eye. He didn't seem all too confident in his own comment. Perhaps that was why he'd come into the office on a Sunday.

"I sure hope so." A crease broke out across my mother's forehead. "I know this sounds a bit crass, Roger, but I'm a little concerned the drowning down at Pelican Beach might put a damper on families looking for a safe place to swim."

I managed to keep my expression neutral. What was Mom aiming for here? Had Jasper's entanglement with Larry's death somehow unleashed her inner Nancy Drew? I continued to keep my focus on our new mayor.

Roger rocked on his heels a moment, his hands in the pockets of his crisp khakis. "I don't think there's anything to be worried about regarding the safety of the water."

Mom's nose scrunched with disappointment. She'd clearly been trying to weasel more details from him.

Roger looked like he wanted to say more, so I decided to give him a chance. "I'm going to pop into the ladies' room. It's on the second floor, right?"

Mom waved her hand. "I've got my own private bathroom, honey. Right off my office." She unlocked her door and ushered me inside the spacious room fit for a councilwoman.

I made a show of closing the door behind me before pressing myself against the wall where they couldn't see me. Since Mom and Roger were right outside the door, I could plainly hear their conversation.

"Should we add more lifeguards to the schedule rotation?" Mom skillfully wove a layer of alarm into her tone. "We want tourists to feel like our beaches are safe."

"Moira," Roger lowered his voice, "the beaches are fine. I trust you to be discreet in this, but the dead body found at Pelican Beach wasn't a drowned swimmer."

"What?" Mom gasped in elaborate shock. "But the police posted that—"

"The police are in a bit of a bind at the moment. McInnis told me that since next-of-kin hasn't been informed, the PD is trying to keep everything under wraps while they investigate discreetly."

"Investigate? Investigate what?"

Dang, I was impressed with Mom's acting skills. Maybe she should have spent her retirement doing community theater instead of local government.

"The body they found was Larry. Larry Dunmer." Roger's voice sounded heavy with emotion. Larry had made a friend in Central Shores, after all. "Someone *killed* him, Moira."

"Oh my." Mom's voice faded for a moment while she pretended to process the news. "You said next-of-kin hadn't been informed. Does that mean Rosalynn is on the run or something? Did she kill her husband?"

Roger chuckled darkly. "Please, you and I both know Ros worshiped the ground Larry walked on."

"Well, do the police think she's dead, too? Do we have a serial killer on the loose, Roger?" Mom's panic sounded genuine.

"Calm down, Moira. From what I've been told, it's not their working theory. McInnis believes this was a targeted attack toward Larry. They already have a suspect on their radar and will move forward appropriately once Ros has been found and notified. Apparently, the murder weapon was left near Larry's body, and it's pretty damning evidence."

My lungs struggled to fill with air. This couldn't be happening. Maybe Roger was exaggerating the situation to make the town seem safer. Or perhaps Chief McInnis told Roger they had a suspect on deck just so the mayor would leave the police to investigate in peace. Yeah, that had to be it. After all, the murder weapon had been found *in* Larry's body, not near it—Oh, wow, Jasper's future was now dangling in the air by semantics.

"I see. Well, that's...that's great." Mom's acting skills began to falter.

I scrambled for the doorknob, not wanting her to fall apart in front of her superior. "All set!" I popped out of her office, locking the door behind me. "We better get going, Mom. Dad will be wondering where we are." I grabbed her elbow and moved her toward the town hall entrance. "Nice to see you, Mayor Sullivan!"

If Roger thought our exit odd, we didn't stay inside long enough to find out. I hurried Mom toward our parked cars, trying to look casual but failing miserably.

"Did you hear what Roger said?" Mom's jaw hung a bit slack.

I ran a hand through my long hair, knotting it nervously in my fingers. "I don't want to believe it."

Anger blazed in Mom's eyes. "Lloyd hasn't even spoken to Rosalynn about her husband's murder, and he's ready to throw the book at Jasper? I swear, that man is sometimes too stubborn for his own good."

"Maybe Chief McInnis just told Roger he has a suspect to keep the mayor off his back. Remember, he didn't appreciate the outside pressure from town hall the last time there was a murder in Central Shores." I had to believe the chief wouldn't intentionally subvert justice before seeing an official investigation through. We may have had our differences in the past, but I knew he cared for his community, even if he sometimes came off as a bit lazy and bullheaded. "Chief McInnis knows there's a lot at stake with Salute to Summer kicking off on Friday, so I'm sure he's just easing Roger's worries."

Mom leaned against her old sedan, the fight beginning to leave her. "Did you find anything useful in Larry's office, at least?"

The Post-it note burned a hole in my pocket. "Boy, I sure did." I pulled it out and let her scope out the Reddit username referencing Shakespeare. "Do you know anyone at town hall who's a big *Merchant of Venice* buff?"

Even with her new contact prescription, Mom had to hold the note close to her nose to make out my haphazard writing. "Hmmm, no, I don't believe so. Why? What's this from?"

I kept my tone light. "Larry sent a message to this account the day before he died. I thought it was strange, that's all." If I shared the whole truth, Mom would worry about what she'd gotten me into by letting me snoop around Larry's office and, no doubt, try to convince me to go to the police.

The thing was, I wasn't sure *what* I'd stumbled into just yet, and I needed to do a little more digging on my own before I went to Gavin and Chief McInnis with my findings. I also didn't want to flaunt the fact that Mom and I had been inappropriately sleuthing around town hall without further intel to back up my suspicions.

Mom fumbled with her purse, rummaging for her keys. "Why don't you come over to the house, hon? We can chat about this more in private." Her distrustful gaze trailed over to the doors of the police station. Given what we'd learned from Roger, I could tell that Lloyd McInnis was on Mom's bad side.

"I appreciate the invite, but I should get back home. I promised Hudson I'd at least spend a few hours with him this weekend."

Mom looked somewhat crestfallen. "Well, let me know if I can be of any more help with this Jasper fiasco." Apparently, she'd enjoyed our little covert mission and was sad it had come to an end. "But for heaven's sake, Delia, be careful."

I gathered her in a tight hug. "Thank you. Jasper is going to be beyond touched that you were willing to bend the rules for him."

Mom waved the thought away. "Please, he's like the son we've never had." She stopped short once the words were out of her mouth, her face screwing into a dark glare. "If you ever tell Thea I said that about Jasper and not Lucas, I will disown you."

I chuckled, pocketing this fun nugget of information. As sibling rivalries go, I wasn't above lording over Thea that our parents treasured my fabulous best friend more than her somewhat-of-a-wet-blanket college sweetheart.

With promises to keep in touch and to come over for a backyard barbeque during the Salute to Summer celebrations, Mom and I got into our respective cars and parted ways.

I had the AC on full blast, the hot weather and adrenaline from what I'd discovered at town hall pumping through my veins. Larry's message to Redditor u/merchnt_of_venyce consumed my tumultuous thoughts. Who had he been blackmailing? Why use Reddit to communicate? And just what juicy information had Larry been keeping silent about?

An idea occurred to me as I pulled into my driveway. Larry had been in Central Shores for less than two months. Even though their Reddit chat history didn't show it, there was a very real possibility that Larry had been blackmailing u/merchnt_of_venyce for much longer. Maybe my cantankerous neighbor hadn't been killed by someone in Central Shores. Maybe he'd discovered something worthy of blackmail during one of his previous auditing jobs.

Had something from Larry's past finally come back to haunt him?

Chapter Sixteen

Hudson greeted me in the kitchen with a glass of iced tea and a kiss. "Did you have fun with your mom?"

I took a refreshing sip of the bitter, unsweetened tea and ran my fingers over Hudson's buzzed hair in appreciation. "It certainly wasn't your normal mother-daughter brunch."

My boyfriend gave me a curious stare, and I relayed a quick recap of our detour detective work.

Hudson shook his head in disbelief at my story. "I thought Moira would talk you *out* of investigating, not the other way around."

"Mom's just as concerned about Jasper as I am." My brow furrowed. "You weren't there to hear Mayor Sullivan talk about the case. It sounds like McInnis really thinks Jasper's the killer."

Hudson gave me a pointed stare. "You just said yourself the chief only shared what he did to keep the mayor off his back."

I scooted over to the refrigerator, grabbed the pitcher of iced tea, and refilled my glass. "I mean, obviously, I hope that's the case, but who am I to guess what's going on in the chief's mind? I'm really worried for Jasper."

Hudson's chiseled features softened, and he scooped me up in a protective hug. "I know. I'm worried too. So," he paused, holding me at arm's length, "did you find anything at town hall to help clear Jasper's name?"

I'd conveniently left out that part of my snooping adventure involved hacking into Larry's computer. Hudson, probably the most ethical journalist out there, would not approve of such tactics. But I couldn't lie to him. "I managed to access Larry's work email while I was in his office," I began, ignoring the reprimanding glare that morphed across Hudson's face. "Not only did he threaten people with budget cuts, but this takes the cake: Larry was *blackmailing* someone."

At that, Hudson's expression transformed into reluctant interest. "Blackmail? Are you sure?"

I pulled out my iPhone and read aloud the message I'd snapped on my phone. "If the person he was blackmailing thought Larry would really go to the police, they might have silenced him. Permanently."

Hudson stroked the stubble on his chin. "Blackmail is certainly a viable motive. Have you told the police? Gavin?"

I sighed. I should have expected this reaction. "Not yet. I just learned about it like twenty minutes ago. I thought I'd do a little digging first."

Hudson's gaze narrowed with shrewd determination. "Digging for what?"

"Whom Larry might have been blackmailing. I have a Reddit username. I can check their profile and see if anything jumps out." While Reddit prided itself as an anonymous social media platform, users could still post identifying information, either deliberately or unknowingly.

I quickly scanned our open-concept living space and found my iPad perched on the coffee table. I snatched it up and selected the Reddit app, where I typed **u/merchnt_of_venyce** into the search bar. I hoped this user's post history would paint a picture of who they were in real life.

Excitement thrummed through me when the username appeared at the top of my results page.

"Found them." I clicked triumphantly, only to have my smile wiped off my face in an instant. Nothing. No posts, no responses. Nothing to suggest u/merchnt_of_venyce had ever used Reddit for anything other than messaging the word "fine" to Larry.

"Whatcha got?" Hudson peered over my shoulder.

"Ack! It's a throwaway account." I pouted. "There's nothing here."

Hudson tapped out of the Reddit app. "Why not try searching the username elsewhere? Maybe this person uses the name on other social sites."

I doubted this. Throwaway accounts were made to be untraceable for a reason. Even on an anonymous site like Reddit, people could connect the dots by reviewing posting history, as I had planned to do. A throwaway account with no user history helped thwart such armchair detective tactics.

However, I followed Hudson's advice in the hopes our killer might be a noob when it came to online security. I plugged **merchnt_of_venyce** into Google Search. Of course, I got millions of results, all having something to do with the famous play. The first result was just a list of Shakespeare's works, including *Macbeth, Much Ado About Nothing, Measure for Measure, Hamlet, Romeo and Juliet,* and *Othello.*

I grew more discouraged as I scrolled. "I don't see profiles on other sites popping up." Whoever u/merchnt_of_venyce was, they would be too hard to trace without more time and savvy hacker skills.

I tossed the tablet back onto the coffee table and sat on the edge of the roomy sectional that wrapped around the living area. "I'm also beginning to think Larry might have been blackmailing this person *before* moving to Central Shores. His message kinda suggested that he's been keeping quiet for a while. Larry's only been in town for two months. So, instead of tracking down the owner of the Reddit account, maybe I can find out where Larry used to live before moving here. I can then cross-reference the info with Vine's guest list. If there was an attendee from a place where Larry lived previously—"

"Then perhaps they were the ones being blackmailed, snapped upon seeing Larry at the party, grabbed Jasper's corkscrew, and killed him."

I had been prepared for Hudson to debate the merits of my idea, not agree with me. "Well, yes. It makes way more sense than Jasper killing Larry, at least."

"It's not a bad theory, Coco."

I grinned at his tentative praise. I loved my mother, but it was nice to hear my "real" name again. At heart, I was Coco, not Cordelia.

Hudson headed for his laptop on the kitchen counter. "Do you still have the guest list Andre sent you?"

Excitement and relief bubbled in my chest at Hudson's offer to help. I'd much rather have him on my team than facing off about whether I should be looking into Larry's murder. "I'll email it to you." I rose from the couch and grabbed my tablet. A few taps later, I'd forwarded Hudson the Google doc Andre sent me less than two weeks ago.

I refilled our iced teas before claiming the bar stool next to my boyfriend. A quick peek at his laptop screen sent my heart fluttering. What was he doing on Zillow?

"Looking for a new place to live?" I chuckled, although my joke sounded more panicky than I intended. After all, Hudson still rented an apartment near the WMTG offices, where he'd lived before we moved into together. He'd decided to hold onto it in case he had to work late and didn't want to drive home. The place had been a sore spot for me for a long time. Milton wasn't *that* far away, and its existence made me uneasy, like Hudson wasn't ready to fully commit to our life together in Central Shores.

Hudson gave me an exasperated side-eye. "This was meant to be a surprise, but your observation skills are just too great."

I sensed I was being teased.

He pointed at his laptop screen. "I'm setting things up to sublet my apartment for the summer. Cynthia won't let me out of the lease until college kids are on the hunt this fall."

My jaw nearly hit the marble countertop. "Wait. You're giving up your apartment?"

Hudson shrugged. "Well, yeah. It's been almost two years, and I've never had to use it like I thought I would. That was the whole point of keeping the place to begin with. And since you're bringing on an assistant for CoA, I figure it might be smart to have the extra income available to help cover their salary, if needed."

Tears welled in my eyes. "Hudson…" It was one thing to hear that my boyfriend was finally letting go of the last remnant of his bachelorhood. It was quite another to learn he was doing it willingly to help my business grow.

"Oh no." His face fell at my teary reaction. "I thought you'd be happy. Please don't cry."

I burst out laughing. "These are happy tears, you goofball." I threw my arms around him, cherishing the feel of his warm, muscular body. "Thank you."

"Aw, it's no big deal."

I rolled my eyes with a snort. Even after our many disagreements about the apartment, Hudson still didn't really understand my annoyance toward the matter. For over the last year and a half, I'd viewed the Milton space as a sign that Hudson could walk away from our relationship at any time. Yet, all along, he'd reassured me that he'd only been keeping the place for practical work purposes. And now, since those reasons had never manifested, Hudson saw no sense in keeping the apartment. Whatever the case, I was happy he was finally letting it go.

Hudson minimized Zillow on his laptop and pulled up the email I'd sent him containing the Vine party guest list. His brow furrowed as he read through the file. "Larry and Ros aren't on here."

"Andre said he invited them on a whim." I collected my iced tea and headed over to sit on the couch, my preferred workspace.

Hudson released a heavy breath. "Well, if Andre did the same thing with our killer, there's a chance they aren't on this version, either."

I hadn't thought of that potential road bump. "Let's cross that bridge when we come to it. For now, I need to figure out where the Dunmers lived before moving to Central Shores."

"It could be a bunch of places." Hudson joined me on the couch with his laptop in hand. "Depending on the length of an audit, Larry could have been moving around every couple of weeks or so."

"Did Ros or Larry ever mention to you where they'd moved from?" I asked him. I honestly couldn't remember a conversation with the Dunmers that hadn't involved them dishing out some nasty rebuke or complaint.

Hudson shook his head. "The only things Larry ever mentioned to me were my 'ridiculously loud and ostentatious' car and that my girlfriend needed to be more neighborly. I rarely interacted with Ros."

My mouth dropped open. "Larry said that to you? About me? Good grief, how did you respond?"

"I told him if there's one thing I've learned in life, it's this: never purposely silence your ride or your woman."

Hudson erupted with laughter as I sputtered my distaste over his lack of defending my honor. Finally, he handed me my discarded tablet to shift my focus. "Come on, cyber sleuth. I'm sure you can dig up where Larry and Ros moved from in no time."

Sinking into the comforting cushions, I went to work. My fingers danced across the iPad screen, fueled by my simmering anxiety for Jasper.

I began on Rosalynn's Facebook page. With no new posts, I still didn't have any idea where she might be now, but I scrolled down her timeline, looking for clues as to where she and Larry had moved from. How sad was it that I knew nothing about my neighbors? Maybe if I had made more of an effort to befriend them, despite all their unpleasantness, Jasper's reputation and future wouldn't be on the line.

I scrolled passed the Cyprus photo, and for a moment, I considered whether Ian might be the one Larry was blackmailing. Maybe having Ian and Bonnie on probation wasn't enough punishment for Larry…Nah, I wasn't one to judge a movie *completely* by its trailer, but Ian didn't strike me as a Shakespeare aficionado.

I continued scanning Ros's page, browsing the numerous Buzzfeed personality quiz results she'd shared over time. Color me surprised. I would never have pegged her as Samantha from *Sex in the City* or Snow White to be her Disney Princess twin. *More like the evil Queen.*

By now, I was well into posts from last December. "What Christmas Ornament are You?" "What Christmas Cookie Represents Your Personality" and "What Your Favorite Holiday Film Says About Your Future" were just some of the quizzes she'd taken. Good grief, there was even one titled, "Which Animal in the Manger Are You?" Ros had done them all.

I was just about to give up and switch over to LinkedIn when a picture post filled the screen. Ros had shared an image of a tastefully decorated Christmas tree, lights twinkling and silver balls glistening. She'd caption it with the Facebook comment, "Forgot to share this earlier in the week!" Even though no geo-tag data was attached to the photo, my heart began to race. It was the fine print URL notated at the bottom of the post about the picture's origin that had me whooping internally in triumph: *via Instagram.com*

The image itself was a hyperlink to what had to be Rosalynn's personal Instagram. I clicked on the link, and my tablet promptly asked whether I wanted to view the website in the app.

I clicked "yes" and waited while Rosalynn's Instagram page loaded. I should have realized Ros would use more than one digital platform. When it came to all the available applications out there, age certainly did not limit one's options. Anyone could learn to use them. Charlotte's grandmother had a Bitmoji character for her Snapchat, and she was ninety-two years young.

I reminded myself that I *had* checked Ros's Facebook "About" section while in Charlotte's office to see if an Instagram page was linked to her account. There hadn't been one listed, so I foolishly assumed it didn't exist. Come to find out, Ros must have either purposely *or* unknowingly unlinked the two social media sites from one another at some point.

Once her Instagram profile loaded, it became clear that Ros was an even more avid user of the image-based platform than Facebook. Although, if I hadn't found the shared photo on her Facebook page, I never would have assumed this profile belonged to my cynical next-door neighbor. Her handle was @rosierayofsunshine, and the name listed on the account was Rosie Ray. A maiden name? A middle name? I wasn't sure.

The last photo uploaded to @rosierayofsunshine had me immediately reaching for my cell. Hudson cocked his head in question, but the other end of the line had picked up on the first ring.

"Hey, Coco, what's up?" Gavin answered through a stifled yawn. He sounded exhausted, despite it being only two on a Sunday afternoon.

I got right down to business. "Are you still trying to track down Rosalynn Dunmer?"

The shuffling noise on the other end stopped. "Do you have something?"

"I came across her Instagram account by chance. It looks like she's treating herself to a spa weekend at Reddy Wellness." I scrolled through the recent photos posted under her profile. A picture of a spacious suite. A bottle of champagne and organic chocolate. A bathrobe hanging from an ornate closet hook. Her photography skills were quite enviable, too. Either she was a master with filters, or she knew how to capture the right light. What's more, Ros had tagged @reddywellnessspa's profile in each post. The posh Crestview bathhouse had been in business for nearly a decade, a favorite haunt for those looking to pamper themselves with facials, massages, and meditation. Charlotte and I occasionally booked a girls' weekend there to unwind and recharge.

I read the caption on Ros's latest photo, which had been posted at nine twenty-eight on Friday night.

Unplugging for the weekend. In desperate need of some me time. Back to reality and my hubby on Monday! #longliveweekends #wellness #mentalhealthishealth #unplugged #blessed

Her hashtags brought a brief smile to my face. The woman was much savvier with social media than I'd ever given her credit for. And if Ros had truly 'unplugged' for the weekend, she would have turned off her cell. Now, it all made sense why the police couldn't reach her by phone.

To Gavin, I continued explaining Ros's recent Instagram activity, "She posted a bunch of photos of her suite around nine-thirty on Friday night before going dark." I frowned as I mulled over the timeline. Ros must have departed for the spa shortly after she and Larry had been asked to leave Vine.

"What's her account handle?" Gavin asked.

I read @rosierayofsunshine back to him and waited. The silence stretched on for a solid minute. Had he disconnected?

Just as I was about to pull my phone away from my ear and check the screen, Gavin released a low whistle. "Well, I'll be darned. Good work, Coco. I would never have found this with her using the name Rosie Ray for the account. It must be a nickname or something. I skimmed her Facebook page yesterday, but I assumed she didn't have Instagram since there wasn't a handle linked."

You and me, both, Gav. "Don't beat yourself up about it. That's what I initially thought, too. I only found Ros on Instagram through an old photo she'd shared on Facebook in December."

Again, there was some muffled shuffling in the background before Gavin popped back on the line. "Adrian just got off the phone with Reddy Wellness. The weekend manager said Rosalynn checked in Friday night and hasn't checked out. We're heading over there now." Gavin paused, and when he spoke again, his voice was low. "I appreciate you sharing this with us, Coco. We've got it from here."

He disconnected before I could speak further. *Geez, you're welcome.*

"Well? Don't leave me hanging." Hudson poked my arm, literally prodding me for details.

"Ros checked in at a Crestview spa on Friday night. Looks like she's been there all weekend, taking some time to unplug and recharge."

Hudson grew somber. "Yikes. She's in for an awful shock."

"No kidding." My empathy for the woman resurfaced. She had no idea her life was about to change forever. *Unless she's Larry's killer.* I wasn't about to cross her off my suspect list simply because Gavin and Mayor Sullivan seemed confident in her innocence.

"Perhaps you should give Jasper a heads up about the police knowing where Ros is." Worry stormed in Hudson's dark eyes. "Once she's been informed, there's nothing stopping them from releasing the news of Larry's murder to local media. Jasper should be prepared, especially if the police believe he's a person of interest."

"You're right." I bobbed my chin nervously up and down. Should I walk up to Jasper's house and speak with him in person? I pulled up our iMessage conversation on my phone. Last night, I'd texted him before heading to bed, asking if everything was okay at *Divulge*. The meeting he'd had yesterday with his lawyer concerned me.

Jasper hadn't responded, which unnerved me even more. It wasn't like he was one to forget to check his phone. It was practically another appendage. I knew Jasper had seen my text and purposely ignored it.

With renewed determination fueling me onward, I rose from the couch. "I'm going to stop by his condo and talk to him face-to-face. Give Jasper the reality check he so sorely needs."

Hudson reached for my hand and, with a tender squeeze, brought it to his

137

lips. "I'll see if I can do a little more digging on Larry and Ros while you're gone."

I leaned over and kissed him, my whole body warming under his touch. "I won't be long." I winked and backed away from my incredibly sexy man before desire sidetracked me from my current mission.

Chapter Seventeen

I rapped a staccato beat against Jasper's front door with my knuckles but received no response. A foreboding frown tugged at my lips. Even though Detective Forester had asked Jasper not to leave town, I should have texted to see if he was home. His driveway was empty, and with the garage door closed, I couldn't tell whether his Porsche was in residence.

I knocked again, and after standing on his stoop for a hot minute, my shoulders slumped in defeat. I turned to head down the walkway when I heard a click ring out from the door handle, and Jasper materialized.

My hand flew to my open mouth, failing to conceal a horrified gasp. "Omigod, what happened to you?"

"Hot mess" didn't even begin to describe Jasper's disheveled appearance. He had on a baggy t-shirt stained with coffee, chocolate, and who knows what else. Torn athletic shorts hung from his imposing frame. His dark hair was greasy, his cowlick out of control. His ordinarily smooth, pale skin was red and splotchy. I hadn't seen an acne outbreak this bad since high school.

"What are you doing here, Coco?"

I faltered under Jasper's annoyed glare. He had never been unhappy to see me before. "I texted you last night, but you never responded."

He rubbed his watery eyes. "I knew moving back here was a mistake."

Irritation and overwhelming concern both kicked in at once. "Listen, you can't hole yourself away like this. You have friends who are here to help you." I slipped under his arm that had been barring the entrance and stormed inside his condo. The place didn't look much better than Jasper did. What had happened here during the last twenty-four hours? An episode of *Squid*

139

Game?

"Look," I began, folding my arms across my chest as I turned to face him, "I was able to track down where Ros has been all weekend. I just got off the phone with Gavin. He and Adrian are going to break the news about Larry's death now."

Jasper stomped like a pouty child into the living room and plopped down into one of the armchairs. It groaned under the sudden pressure. Jasper's six-foot-three, body-builder-type frame shouldn't be thrown around lightly.

"Once Ros has been notified, Chief McInnis will likely release a formal statement about Larry's murder." I continued to stare him down. "You need to be prepared for word to get out about your being a person of interest if details about their investigation leak."

Jasper covered his face with his hands. "Great. Yet another piece of craptastic news to add to the list."

His reaction left me a bit confused. *Another* piece of news? I glanced around the unkempt condo. Had this mess resulted from something *other* than Jasper's unwanted involvement in Larry's case? "Okay, what the name of Gaga is going on? You've been acting totally sus since Friday night. What are you hiding from me?"

The fire in my words made Jasper stiffen, and he slowly dropped his hands away from his face. "I don't want to talk about it, Cokes. I'm too embarrassed."

Embarrassed? I snorted with offense. "Um, when have we ever been too embarrassed to share something with each other? I mean, you were there at BSU Labor Day party when I unwisely wore white and forgot about my period."

The haunting crisis was one of my most embarrassing moments to date. Jasper had come to visit me at Bayside University the first weekend of our senior year. We'd been attending a frat party when "The Red Incident" occurred. On best-friend instinct, Jasper had stepped in and strategically positioned himself as my human shield. At first, I thought he was making a drunken pass at me, but soon, I understood—well, felt—the reason for his actions. Like every challenging moment since second grade, we'd always had each other's backs. Until now, it seemed.

"Ah, The Red Incident." My trip down memory lane brought a teasing smile to Jasper's face. "That will go down in the history books of Beta Phi Omega's Labor Day parties. Thank SZA that everyone was required to check their phones at the door, or we would never have gotten you out of there unscathed."

I picked up a damp towel—*um, ew, Jasper*—and threw it at his face. "So, whatever you're hiding can't be *that* awful."

After tossing the towel aside, Jasper folded his arms across his broad chest, his chin quivering just a bit.

Wow, something was seriously bothering him.

I perched on the arm of the couch, just about the only place in the room not covered in dirty clothes, towels, napkins, empty food wrappers, or dishes. "Come on, tell me what's wrong. You know I'll still love you, even if your dirty little secret is that you really loved the *Cats* movie."

This coaxed full-on laughter from my best friend. "God, no. It's not *that* embarrassing."

"Then what's going on?"

Jasper sighed, sounding like the weight of the world was on his shoulders. "You know the super-secret meeting I scooted off to Friday night?"

The one you refused to tell us about, making me wonder for a hot nanosecond that you actually *had something to do with Larry's murder?* "Yes, I'm familiar with that mysterious little detail."

"Well, about a month ago," Jasper began, "I got wind that there would soon be an opening for a new east coast senior editor for *Variety* magazine. I impulsively sent my resume to their corporate headquarters, the whole thing entirely on a whim. I'd almost forgotten about it—okay, no, that's a lie, I've been thinking about it nonstop. But Friday night, I got an email from one of their executive editors. She was in town visiting family and wanted to connect about a position in New York. Her email said her entire team was extremely impressed by what I'd turned *Divulge* into." Jasper fiddled with his thumbs, unable to meet my gaze. "So, when she reached out and suggested we meet up—she thought I still lived in Dover—I knew this was my shot at making it big. Like, *big*, Cokes. So, I ditched you guys at the party, drove to Dover, and met her at her hotel bar. The meeting went great. She loved my ideas. She loved my portfolio. She said the team was looking to move fast and would be in touch by Saturday evening with an offer. As you can imagine, I hardly slept a wink that night."

I remembered Jasper's red eyes yesterday morning when I'd come by to fill him in on the nightmare down at Pelican Beach. Yeesh, I'd thought he'd looked disheveled then.

Jasper ran a hand through his unwashed hair. "So, obviously, I was super excited, which made it kinda hard for me to come to terms with being involved in something so ghastly as Larry's murder. The interview down at the station did nothing to burst my bubble."

I chuckled lightly. "I noticed."

"Anyway, I invited Kimball back to my place to figure out an exit plan regarding *Divulge.* I've got a stake in the company. I'm on the board…I had to figure out my options. We even talked about selling the magazine."

I raised my eyebrows. Whoa, *Divulge* was Jasper's baby. I couldn't believe he was considering selling it.

"I had everything prepared. I had my resignation letter to the board. I had a farewell email to employees." Jasper's gaze seemed far away. "Then I got an email from some rando in *Variety's* hiring department. The dude said that while I seemed very ambitious, the editorial team didn't feel like I was ready for the international arena that *Variety* spans." A pout formed on his lips. "I'm too small-town."

I moved across the room and put a comforting hand on Jasper's shoulder. "I'm sorry, betch, but you know that's not true."

He snorted at my blunt dose of hard love.

"*Variety* just wasn't ready for your brilliance. Jealous, even. You'd probably have the current editorial board all out of jobs within a month after taking over. I mean, just look at what you did with *Divulge* right out of college." I pointed to his coffee table, strewn with various issues of the culture and society magazine. "You rose through the company ranks, taking a struggling, *Delaware*-based tabloid that was ready to fold and turned it into a compelling piece of journalism. You've been invited to Fashion Week for what, two years now? How many people could honestly achieve what you have in a lifetime, let alone by twenty-nine?"

Jasper's cheeks reddened at my praise. In a rare show of humility, he thrust his head down to hide the glowing effect my words had.

"You have every right to be disappointed, but don't for a second belittle yourself. You've done amazing things, and you will continue to do amazing things. No matter what you set your sights on next."

"Thanks." Jasper's gratitude was muffled by emotion. "Although, having a murder charge hanging over my head doesn't exactly inspire great confidence about my thriving future."

I didn't dare tell Jasper what Mayor Sullivan had said to my mother about the police narrowing in on a suspect. "Honestly, it hasn't even been forty-eight hours since Larry's body was found. I'm sure once Chief McInnis and the team are finally able to go public with his death, some new development will come along and take the spotlight off you." Unable to stand the clutter surrounding us any longer, I began moving around the room, gathering food wrappers and empty bottles for the trash. "And if it doesn't, I'm pursuing a few leads I plan to pass onto the police once I have more solid intel."

Jasper hoisted himself out of his throne and came to my side, putting his hands on my shoulders. "I don't say this enough, but you're the greatest person to have ever entered my life, Cokes." He chuckled. "And I've met Oprah."

With sisterly affection, I knocked his hands away, a sheepish grin on my face. Jasper and I were not overly sappy people—we were usually quite the opposite—so it was nice to hear how much he cherished our friendship. "You'd do the same for me. Besides, I know orange isn't your preferred jumpsuit color, so…."

He laughed, picking up his dirty clothes and towels before disappearing down the hall toward the unit's built-in laundry. "So, what are these leads you're pursuing?"

While we went to work decluttering his home, I filled Jasper in on the previous day's adventures at Cyprus and the brunch I'd had with Mom this morning.

Keen to examine my evidence, Jasper watched the TikTok video Bonnie and Ian made during the Vine party. "I'm inclined to agree with Queen Moira. They don't seem to be gearing up to kill anyone. More like some weird foreplay." He handed my phone back to me once the video finished. "Besides, this whole blackmail thing seems like the real smoking gun. Do you think the police will come across Larry's Reddit message during their investigation?" he asked as he headed toward the fridge to grab us both a well-earned drink after our cleaning spree. Marie Kondo would have been proud of our quick work.

I accepted a glass of chilled rosé. Maybe after this weekend, I'd take a little break from consuming alcohol, but for now, I welcomed the relaxed vibe it elicited. "I don't know. I would hope so once they have unrestricted access to Larry's work email, but I'm not leaving it to chance. It was buried in Larry's digital trash."

"How will you bring up the whole Reddit thing without admitting you disobeyed direct orders by snooping?" Jasper asked the question that had been toiling in my mind.

I took a refreshing sip of the crisp, sweet wine and sighed. "I'll figure something out."

"Be careful, Cokes. I'd have a hard time forgiving myself if you got into trouble for helping me out." He raised his glass, and I clinked mine against his. "Although, I *would* get over it."

I giggled. Jasper seemed much more like his old loveable sassy self now. "Why didn't you tell me about the *Variety* interview before now? Why were you keeping it a secret?"

His jovial mood dimmed. "I—I didn't want to tell you about it and have it fall through. I didn't want to set myself up for embarrassment."

I squeezed his forearm in a rare show of affection. I understood his plight. But I still felt guilty that my best friend had thought he needed to keep something so monumental to himself. "Did you at least tell the police? Can the editor you met with be your alibi?"

Jasper's brow furrowed. "I told Detective Forester yesterday. But once I said what time our meeting ended, she didn't seem too focused on it."

I toyed with the stem of the wineglass. "Hmm, I guess that supports our theory that Larry was killed sometime *after* you returned to the Central Shores area." I balled my fist. I wished I could weasel more information out of Gavin or Adrian about the known details of the case but showing up at the police station and poking around would not earn me any goodwill toward my fellow officers.

My phone vibrated from the pocket of my romper. I had a text from Hudson.

Got a lead! U comin back soon?

My heart quickened with renewed hope. With Hudson's investigative journalism skills, I should have had more faith in him digging something up. I smiled as I pocketed my phone. He made for such a great partner in crime. I was glad he was on my side, helping me through this mess rather than protesting my involvement. "Hudson got a hit on the Dunmers. I gotta bounce."

"Keep me posted," Jasper called after me as I zipped toward the door. "Tell Dad I say thank you for keeping his oldest out of prison."

Chapter Eighteen

I found Hudson hunched over my tablet and his laptop, a cup of coffee in one hand and a pen scribbling away on paper in the other.

"Hey, whatcha find?" I kissed the top of his head before taking a seat next to him at the kitchen island.

"I started with Rosalynn's Instagram photos to see if she tagged any places or took any pictures that might indicate where they previously lived." Hudson slid the tablet over to me. "It took a little while because most of her pics aren't exactly of the great outdoors."

Indeed, much of Ros's Instagram profile was defined by images of food, shoes, and entertainment media. I didn't see a single picture that included her or her husband. "Her profile has been curated to showcase that she's living in style. Probably to mask her self-confidence issues that no doubt come from her husband's grotesque flirting."

A grin twitched on Hudson's yummy-looking lips. "How very perceptive of you."

I shrugged. "Social media allows us to present a carefully crafted persona of ourselves to the world. Every post has a purpose."

"You're the expert." Hudson squeezed my thigh before moving to tap one of the image thumbnails. "Out of the last six months, this was the only location shot I could find."

I examined the woodland area featured in the frame. "Oh, wow. Trees. I know for sure where they lived now."

Hudson nudged me, chuckling at my wry humor. "There's no geo-tag, but this is her caption, *'Exploring this gorgeous park in our new hometown. I love that my hubby's job allows us to live in such exotic places.'"*

I laughed at his exaggerated impersonation of our hostile neighbor. "Exotic? *Delaware?*"

Hudson grinned. "I mean, that's copium at its finest."

"Not sure if her Insta caption really counts as copium, babe. Miss Rosie Ray of Sunshine might be lying to her followers, but not necessarily to herself." I turned my attention back to the photo. Ros had certainly taken the cultivation of a sophisticated online presence seriously. In all honesty, she'd done a pretty good job of making me believe she lived an overprivileged lifestyle based on her profile aesthetic. "No wonder she doesn't geotag her photos. Ros doesn't want anyone calling her bluff."

"I agree. Besides Reddy Wellness and a few classy restaurants in Dover and Wilmington, she doesn't tag the locations where her pictures are taken. But..." Hudson held up a finger and pointed once more to the forest of trees. "Care to take a closer look?"

I studied the image. I was savvy enough with Instagram to know Ros had used the Mayfair filter to intensify the beauty of the earthy forest. The shadows made it look like the forest was denser than it probably was. It rivaled something I'd expect to grow in Maine or Vermont, not Delaware.

Nothing immediately jumped out at me, so I zoomed in on the image. An enlarged view of the photo did the trick. "There's a sign posted to one of the tree trunks!" My excitement died quickly. "But even zoomed in, it's still way too blurry. I'm not sure even my photo-enhancing hack could make it readable," I said, referencing a nifty little trick where I took a screenshot and used my Photo app to sharpen and adjust blurry images.

Hudson's grin widened. "Then it's lucky I've got access to state-of-the-art image-enhancing software. We use it all the time to make traffic camera images and photocopied mugshots suitable for broadcast." He turned his laptop screen to me. The forest image was already on display, the sign's text clear enough to read.

Welcome to Rockaway Glade, maintained by the city of Rockaway, Delaware.

"Rockaway? That's only about forty minutes south of here." My leg bounced excitedly on the rung of my barstool.

Hudson minimized the image and pulled up a spreadsheet. It was the guest list from the Vine party.

"At first pass, I crossed out folks I know conclusively do not live in Rockaway. That left me with about twenty names I didn't recognize. So, I began to Google."

I stared in amazement at my boyfriend. He'd gone above and beyond with his detective work. I couldn't be more impressed.

"None of the remaining guests lived in Rockaway."

My expression crumbled with my hopes.

Hudson raised one eyebrow with teasing precision. "...except one."

I smacked his arm playfully but was too eager for him to spill the deets to reprimand his mischievousness. "Who?"

"Have you heard of Gerald Atkins?"

"Gerald?" The name was astoundingly familiar. Gerald Atkins had been one of my first Center of Attention clients three years ago, back when I was building my business from the ground up. His gourmet cheese shop, Deco Fromage, had become somewhat of a culinary gem along the Delaware coast. I'd suggested Andre invite him to the party to establish a marketing partnership between their businesses. Wine *and* cheese? Um, yes, please.

"He was a CoA client. One of my first," I finally replied. "But Gerald lives in Long Neck, not Rockaway."

Hudson shook his head. "His business is still in Long Neck, but Gerald moved to Rockaway about a year ago."

I needed to update my client records then. "Okay, so he lives in Rockaway. But I can't imagine Gerald killing Larry. He's such a sweet, happy-go-lucky guy." I'd been hired to help Gerald rebrand his cheese shop. He wanted to evolve his store to promote a more sophisticated vibe, and, with a name like Cheese to Meet You, he wasn't exactly getting the upscale clientele he desired. Over the course of a two-month CoA engagement, I updated his website, marketing materials, and storefront to showcase the new-and-improved branding for Deco Fromage. "Did you find any connection between him and the Dunmers?" I couldn't envision a private business being affected by

148

one of Larry's municipal audits. Had Gerald sold Larry bad cheese? Had Larry threatened to give a poor review on Yelp?

Hudson clicked on another internet tab. "The plot thickens, my dear Coco. Gerald Atkins may have been on Andre's guest list, but it's his plus one I'm interested in."

I studied the webpage. The banner across the top read, "The City of Rockaway, est. 1901." It was their official government site.

Hudson scrolled down the page, adhering to the speed at which my eyes could skim the text. He paused midway, the mouse cursor hovering over a picture of a middle-aged woman, her brunette hair cut in a stylish pixie. Her wide smile beamed back at us. The name beside the photo read, "Darcy Atkins, City Manager."

"That's Gerald's wife!" I recognized her from the few times she had come by the shop.

My wide-eyed gaze met Hudson's accomplished grin. "Larry would have *definitely* faced off against the city manager during his audit."

I focused once again on Darcy's picture, scrutinizing every detail. Whether my mind was playing tricks on me or not, her expression had taken on a more sinister glare, as if she was arrogantly reveling in the power she wielded. Had Larry threatened her when he'd been working in Rockaway? Was she the one Larry was blackmailing? Had she witnessed the scene between Larry and Jasper at Vine and decided to take her revenge?

I wrapped my arms around Hudson, absolutely giddy over his brilliant detective work. If he could work this much magic in thirty minutes, his true crime show was sure to be a resounding success once it hit the airwaves. "Incredible job, babe. We have another suspect with potential means and opportunity." While I couldn't remember seeing Gerald or Darcy at Vine, it didn't mean they weren't among the crowd. "Now, to find her motive."

I brought up a new internet tab on my iPad and typed **Darcy Atkins** into my search bar. A myriad of results peppered my screen, so I narrowed my scope to **Darcy Atkins, Delaware**.

My heart thudded against my ribcage as I scanned the Google-curated description under the very first link my search returned. "Bingo!" I pumped my fist in the air and clicked.

Hudson leaned against my shoulder, eager to see the results. "What's so incriminating about her LinkedIn profile?"

I scrolled through her years of work experience, wanting to confirm what the Google search description had implied. "Check this out."

I pointed to the section of Darcy's profile that displayed her college info. She graduated from the University of Delaware. Her undergraduate degree had been in English literature, and she'd gone on to the school's master's program, focusing on literary theory.

The most thrilling entry of all was the title of her master's thesis.

"*By Abstaining from Religion, Shakespeare Confirmed Its Power*," Hudson read aloud, his eyebrows raising with slight alarm.

Shakespeare, the bard behind *The Merchant of Venice*. "She has to be who Larry was blackmailing!"

Hudson shook his head, a look of disbelief eclipsing his features. "Slow down, Cokes. We're making mountains out of molehills. We have no idea if the Reddit account belongs to Darcy. We can't go making accusations like that to Gavin and Adrian just yet."

Had I heard him right? Was Hudson suggesting that we sit on this information and investigate it *ourselves*? That wasn't like him. He'd nearly had a stroke the last time he found out I was keeping information from the PD.

"What's our next move, then?" Hey, I had no problem encouraging this kind of behavior. To get Jasper out of this mess without a cloud of suspicion hanging over him, I needed a solid suspect for the police to focus on.

Hudson tapped his fingers on the island countertop for a moment. "Let me see what else I can uncover tomorrow at work. I'm sure I can pull a few strings at Rockaway City Hall to get the inside deets on how their state audit played out. Since the news will likely break soon about Larry's death, it won't seem out of the ordinary that I'm seeking information out about him."

My lips formed a tight pout. "Um, where do I fit into this?"

Hudson opened his mouth to respond when his cell rang, the opening chords to the Goo Goo Dolls' hit "Slide" chiming loudly. He snatched it up from the counter, but not before I saw the name **Tori Beals** flash on the screen. "What the heck?" Hudson held the phone away from him like it was covered in germs.

He looked just as confused as I felt. Since when did Hudson have personalized ringtones? He always teased me about my custom selections for my favorite contacts.

He silenced the ringer by answering. "What is it, Tori?" He sounded tired at the mention of her name.

I sat there quietly, hoping to hear some of the rapid conversation reverberating from Hudson's phone, but all I could make out were the squeaky inflections in Tori's bubbly voice.

Hudson's disappointment was easy to read. "Are you sure? Why me?" His dark eyes flashed to the wall clock hanging in the kitchen.

More mumbling on the other end of the line had my shoulders tightening. *Oh no. Not* another *impromptu research session.*

"Fine. If that's what she wants." Hudson rubbed his temples. "I'm on my way." As he punched the screen to end the call, he turned to me with puppy dog eyes. "I'm sorry, babes. Looks like news about Larry's death has officially broken. Millie wants me to take the lead on tonight's evening broadcast and follow the story."

I should have been ecstatic at this development. As the investigating reporter, Hudson would have primo access to any public documents on Larry's case. It was also a great move for his career. If Hudson continued to deliver stellar content to viewers, they'd be more likely to tune into the crime show he and Millie were developing.

Instead, tendrils of unease spread throughout me. "Was that Millie on the phone?" I asked, knowing full well the answer.

"No, it was Tori." Hudson's gaze broke away from mine. "She's filling in for one of the weekend anchors and got roped into tracking me down."

I folded my arms. Roped in? I bet Tori jumped at the chance to call Hudson on Millie's behalf. "Nice ringtone."

He winced at my dry delivery. "Can you change it back for me while I get ready?" Handing me his phone, Hudson hopped down from the barstool and began gathering his things. "The song popped up on the radio while we were working yesterday. Tori made some vague innuendo about it, but I ignored her, hoping she wouldn't say anything more in front of the records clerk. I guess I should have known better." He tucked his laptop into his messenger bag. "We used my cell to take photos of those old cold case files since the clerk wouldn't let us scan them. Tori must have weaseled her way into my settings while pretending to take pictures."

There was nothing wrong with setting up personalized ringtones for family, friends, and coworkers, but if Tori had been acting professionally, would she really have chosen "Slide"?

"Hudson," I said hesitantly, "that song is literally about sliding into *bed* with someone. Shouldn't you report this? *This* is proof of her harassment."

One of the reasons Hudson refused to call out Tori's behavior was that he had no concrete evidence against her. All of Tori's pervy comments were made off-camera after she'd cornered Hudson somewhere alone, and he didn't think anyone would believe his claims over hers. He might have been a rising star at WMTG, but he feared the network would side with a prominent white woman over a young, biracial man.

Hudson waved my suggestion aside. "She'd just say *I* was the one who changed the ringtone. It's fine, Coco. Please don't worry about me. I can handle her. Everything she says goes in one ear and out the other now." He almost sounded like he believed himself.

With his back turned to me, Hudson didn't see my frown deepen. I hated that there was nothing I could do to help him. This awful woman and her inappropriate comments had him dreading the most exciting opportunity of his career.

"Babe," I tried to keep my voice level. This was a super sensitive subject for him, and I struggled with how to approach it. "You shouldn't have to work with someone who makes you uncomfortable, especially when you've made it clear to Tori that you aren't interested. She's created such a toxic environment, and it's not right. I don't care that she's a big name from Baltimore. I care about how this is affecting *you*."

Hudson paused a moment, an unreadable look flickering across his face. "It's not that toxic, Coco. It's fine. I'm fine. She's—I don't want to ruffle any feathers. So just let me deal with this my way, okay?"

My chest pinched at the genuine distress in his expression. I didn't believe for a moment this was all "fine" for him.

Hudson's lips curled into a sad smile. "I know you're only trying to help, and I appreciate it." He squeezed my hand. "But this isn't your problem. I'm sure TT's weird fascination will fizzle out soon enough. I mean, I'm not *that* amazing of a guy."

I did my best to chuckle at his attempted joke, but I didn't feel like laughing at all. Instead, my giggle became a deflated cough as I did what he asked and set Tori's ringtone back to the phone's default. What else could I do except try and support my boyfriend as best I could?

Chapter Nineteen

Not wanting to part on strained terms, I plastered on the most charming smile I could muster and grinned up at Hudson. "Well, you are amazing to me, so please drive safe." I handed his phone back to him. "Good luck with the report. Let me know if you learn anything new about Larry's death."

Hudson gave me a cheeky salute, followed by a deep kiss. "I'm sorry our weekend got cut short. I'll scoot home right after filming, though."

A few hours later, I cuddled up on the couch, watching the brief WMTG segment featuring Larry with rapt interest. I couldn't help but also admire how sexy my guy looked as he gave his remarks.

"Investigators have concluded Dunmer died late Friday, around midnight," Hudson's smooth baritone reported. "Anyone with information is encouraged to call the Central Shores Police Department."

Memories of my visit to Larry's office flashed through my head. The timestamp of the oldest unread email Larry received floated to the top. Eleven thirty-eight. My intuition had been correct. Larry must have been killed around that time, and he never got the chance to read the message.

I tapped open my Photos app to examine the screenshot I'd taken from Bonnie's TikTok video, the one capturing the wall clock in the background. Hudson's report also meant that the likelihood of Bonnie and Ian going on a killing spree minutes after dancing to "Hungry Eyes" grew more farfetched by the minute.

I texted Hudson a thumbs up once his segment concluded, and he responded shortly after.

Brainstorming coverage plans w/ M. Possibly going 2 launch show sooner than expected. And bonus, TT already left 4 the night so I don't even have 2 worry about her. Might be home a little l8r than I thought. Know u have a big day tomorrow, so don't w8 up.

My heart warmed at the obvious excitement emanating from his text. Despite all Hudson was dealing with when it came to Tori, his passion for his new project still burned brightly. I was so proud of everything he was achieving at WMTG. He had earned it tenfold.

I set my phone down and glanced around the condo. Dark shadows spread across the living room as the sun began to dip below the western horizon. A quiet evening to myself. Alone. Just me and my thoughts. Great. I stared out the windows as the inky arrival of night made its presence known across the ocean's surface. I hadn't had a whole evening to myself in a while. Since the spring, Hudson had done his best to make it home from work before I went to bed.

A sharp spasm clawed deep within me. *Oh, no. Not this again.* My eyes refocused on the window glass rather than what lay outside. I caught sight of my tense reflection. A shadow twitched behind me, and I whirled around, a shriek escaping from my lips.

"Omigod." I brought my hand to my chest, my heart thumping wildly. I could have sworn the shadow behind me had a face. The face of the person who had tried to kill me nearly three months ago.

On impulse, I reached for my cell and tapped the MindMatters icon. The app connected to my encrypted profile, and I sent a beseeching message to Dr. Ashawari. If she couldn't speak with me now, MindMatters would connect me with one of their on-call therapists.

Three weeks after my harrowing encounter with Stacy's killer, I'd still been suffering from vivid, repeated nightmares and finding it hard to focus during the daytime. Hudson, Charlotte, and even Jasper had all suggested finding someone to talk to. At their urging, I started researching therapists, a little hesitant to speak with someone in the local area. The wonders of the Internet had filtered MindMatters to the top of my search results. MindMatters was a mental health app that connected the end user to a vast team of stellar therapists from all over the country based on schedule preferences and immediate need. I could be connected with a professional at the touch of a button to talk through my mental health highs and lows. I'd been so impressed with the service that I'd featured MindMatters on *Trending Topic* and across my socials, encouraging my followers to care for their minds just as they would other areas of their bodies.

Dr. Ashawari responded to my request not five minutes later. She worked evenings, which was one of the reasons MindMatters had paired us up in the first place. **I'd be happy to speak with you. I'll send a link for a video chat.**

Dr. Ashawari's concerned expression soon filled the screen of my iPhone. "Hi, Coco."

"Hi, Dr. Ashawari." I waved at her image while propping my phone on the coffee table. "Thanks for taking my call."

"That's what I'm here for." Her smile was so incredibly comforting. "You mentioned that pinched feeling again? Another panic attack?"

I rubbed my temples, still trying to shake the memory of that haunting face encased in shadow. "I think I just psyched myself out. I'm home alone tonight, and my mind was playing tricks on me."

"Hudson's not there yet?"

I shook my head. "He has to work late tonight. He said he probably wouldn't be home before I go to bed."

"Hmm. I see. You know, he had to work late the last time you reached out for a quick chat." Dr. Ashawari paused. "It seems your anxiety is still spiking at night and when you're alone."

My cheeks warmed.

Through the video feed, Dr. Ashawari sensed my embarrassment. "There's nothing to be ashamed about, Coco. You survived a terrible trauma. It makes sense that you'd want those who make you feel safe at your side when darkness hides the unknown." She had such a poetic way of speaking.

"But I can't have Hudson feeling like he has to babysit me all the time." Tears pricked my eyes. With Dr. Ashawari, I didn't bother trying to keep my insecurities buried. "He's got enough going on. I need to deal with this myself. I need to move past what happened."

Dr. Ashawari leaned closer to her webcam. "I respect those desires, Coco. And you will get there. You're already taking the right steps by reaching out for help. You're doing the work. But you have to give yourself time to heal." She smiled. "I know you're used to moving at a hundred miles a minute, but trauma doesn't go away overnight."

"I just hate feeling like this." I ran a hand through my hair in frustration. "I used to be so fearless. Now, I literally get spooked by my own shadow."

"You're not giving yourself enough credit. You still sound pretty fearless to me." Dr. Ashawari's dark eyes crinkled behind her stylish glasses. "I can tell simply based on all we've covered during our sessions. Besides, you're going through a huge transition. On top of processing the attack, you're juggling so much with work and your personal life. You've got a lot to sift through. Last time, you mentioned your struggles with missing the spotlight. Tell me, are you still on the fence about what to do with your blog?"

"I don't know. Maybe?" I shrugged. "I love the work I'm doing with CoA. I really do. But I can't help but miss all the hype from when *Trending Topic* was at the top of its game. Now, every time we're out and Hudson gets recognized, I still long for the feelings I experienced whenever strangers recognized me. The spike in endorphins or whatever chemical reaction it caused. I'm so happy for Hudson, don't get me wrong—"

"I know." Dr. Ashawari rarely cut me off unless she needed to make a point. "Coco, this isn't about Hudson. This is about you. It's perfectly normal to miss something you once had, even if others around you don't understand. Fame is a hard thing for most people to comprehend. Remember those comments people made on your blog post?"

I cringed. Back in May, I thought a personal piece sharing my conflicting feelings about being in the spotlight might interest my *Trending Topic* followers, especially after all the media attention I received following Stacy's murder. Yeah, not my best idea. A majority of the negative comments said I was just jealous that my boyfriend was becoming a bigger deal than me. "Yeah, they said I was resentful and selfish." I still had a hard time reconciling those terms with what I was really feeling. I didn't resent *Hudson,* but I couldn't deny that *I* missed feeling special. "And aren't they right? I mean, sometimes I want what Hudson has, what I *used* to have in spades. But it's not like I *don't* want him to have it. Ugh." I buried my face in my hands. "I don't understand why I feel this way."

Dr. Ashawari steepled her fingers. "Think of it in these terms, Coco. Let's say you had the most perfect dog in the world, and people made remarks about your loving pup everywhere you went." She spoke in measured tones. "Then, your beloved dog ran away. And soon, your best friend got a dog, and everywhere you went together, everyone commented how wonderful your friend's dog was. Are you a horrible person for being sad and envious that *your* dog isn't there?"

"I don't think these are the same—"

Dr. Ashawari gave me a pointed look. "Would someone be considered horrible for being upset that their dog is no longer with them?"

"No, of course not."

"Then give yourself some slack." A soft smile curled on her lips. "Your celebrity lifestyle was—and still is, mind you—an integral part of your sense of self. But you're evolving and growing, and so is your relationship with fame. You purposely left behind life in the public eye, yes, but it's perfectly all right for you to miss it. Especially when you're reminded by it."

Her words lessened the tightness in my chest. "Thank you. It's nice to hear that from someone else."

"Now, it would be another thing if you were purposely sabotaging the people around you from achieving fame in their own right," Dr. Ashawari continued, "but from everything you've told me, it's clear you are Hudson's biggest supporter, and that you want to do right by him. The fact that these conflicting feelings are on your mind proves it."

We continued to explore my thoughts and anxieties for the remainder of the half-hour session, ending with Dr. Ashawari reiterating the breathing exercises she wanted me to use whenever that awful pinching sensation violated my chest.

"Thank you, Dr. Ashawari. Talk to you soon." We met every Thursday evening for a regularly scheduled session.

"Take care, Coco."

I ended the call, the weight on my chest much lighter than it had been. Feeling more optimistic that the work I was putting in to better my mental health would pay off, I settled into the crook of the couch and turned on Netflix.

I was four episodes into a baking show by the time my eyelids began to droop, and I realized it was getting late. My phone had no new updates from Hudson, so I sent him a final kissy-face emoji, telling him I was turning in for the night. I had to be up early to interview candidates for CoA and needed to be at my very best.

Chapter Twenty

My alarm's soft, instrumental chords pulled me out of a deep sleep. I rolled over, eager to see Hudson next to me, only to find myself alone in our California king.

I sat up, my heart in my throat. Where was Hudson? Had he not made it home? Had he gotten into an accident? Wha—

My flurry of panic subsided when I noticed the indent from his head on his pillow and the ruffled sheets. He *had* been here, at least at some point. He'd made it home.

I yanked my phone off its wireless charger to find a text waiting.

Hey, babes. Got in 18 and had 2 skip out early. Taking road trip 2 New Castle. Got a tip that Ros went there after police found her @ the spa. She's staying w/ a friend. Millie wants a clip of her 4 tonight's segment. Will catch u up when I get home. Good luck with ur interviews xoxoxo

His hugs and kisses pulled a tired smile across my face, erasing the panic and worry that had overwhelmed me just a moment ago. But, as I shifted focus to his current assignment, my smile faltered. It seemed a bit crass to ambush a woman who'd just lost her husband for a statement. Poor Ros.

I had ambled into the bathroom to get the shower going when it occurred to me that Hudson's impromptu road trip had thrown a big wrench in my own investigation. Would he have time to research Darcy Atkins and the work Larry did in Rockaway, or would he be too focused on reporting updates from the official police investigation? As Bonnie and Ian slid further down my suspect list, speaking with Darcy felt imperative to clearing Jasper's name.

I weighed my options as I washed my hair and scrubbed my face. I only had four applicants I was interviewing today, and I was scheduled to be done by noon. I *could* take a quick trip over to Deco Fromage to pop in and see Gerald. I could easily say I wanted to check in and see how his business was doing before questioning him about the Vine party. I still didn't recall seeing him there, but it had been a packed house, and I'd left the scene relatively early. Depending on the fruits of my investigative labor, I might even be able to swing by Rockaway City Hall and chat with Darcy. No need for Hudson to take time away from his work. I could easily tackle this simple fact-finding mission myself.

At eight o'clock, I waltzed through the doorway of Brewed to Perfection, inhaling the savory aroma of coffee beans.

Charlotte spotted me and waved from behind the counter as she and Maria went about serving patrons.

I grabbed a corner table by the window. Even during the coffee shop's busiest hours, most tables were vacant in the summertime. Customers tended to dart inside the café for their morning fix, only to hurry back into the sun. Knowing this pattern, I'd asked Charlotte if I could conduct my interviews at Brewed to Perfection since I didn't feel comfortable inviting strangers to my condo. The last thing I needed was for some disgruntled interviewee to harass Hudson and me at home if I didn't offer them the job.

Five minutes later, Charlotte arrived beside my makeshift office with an iced caramel macchiato in hand. "Are you nervous? Are you ready?"

"Yes, and yes." I gratefully took the iced coffee from my friend and savored a refreshing sip.

Charlotte sat in the chair across from me, taking a quick break while the café remained momentarily empty. "I'm surprised you didn't postpone these interviews."

"Why?"

Charlotte glanced around her shop. "Well, now that Larry's murder is public knowledge, I would have thought you'd be amping up your investigation."

Larry's death was figuratively old news to me. It only now just clicked that most people would be hearing about it for the first time. "Are folks talking about it?"

Charlotte's brow furrowed. "Um, are you okay? Have you forgotten where we live? Of course, everyone is talking about it!" She tilted her head with concern. "I thought you helped the police with the statement they released last night."

"Statement? What statement?" It was more rhetorical than anything because I had my answer as soon as I loaded Facebook on my phone. I'd been so focused on getting ready for these upcoming interviews that I hadn't done my social media due diligence this morning.

Sure enough, someone had posted an official statement about Larry's death on the Central Shores PD Facebook page. Short and succinct, it revealed Larry had died late Friday night around midnight and that the police were investigating his death as a homicide. Folks were encouraged to reach out to the department with any pertinent information.

"I had nothing to do with this." I glanced up from my phone screen, sharing Charlotte's worried expression. Why hadn't Chief McInnis enlisted my help? Why hadn't Gavin? He'd sounded grateful when I'd given him the tip about Ros, so why hadn't they asked for my PR services?

A chilling thought ran through me. "What if the PD is cutting me off because of my ties to Jasper?" My voice was a near whisper.

Charlotte gnawed on her lower lip. "Maybe they just didn't want to bother you on a Sunday night. You said Gavin and Adrian are star pupils. Perhaps the guys wanted to test their skills without you hovering over them?"

I appreciated Charlotte's attempts to make me feel better, but I still had a bad feeling about this whole ordeal. My CoA engagement was tailored to help the PD with situations *exactly* like this. Why hadn't they reached out for my help?

"Anyway, I overheard lots of speculation this morning, especially around opening when other business owners stopped for coffee," Charlotte continued. "Most folks think Rosalynn snapped and did her husband in, which I guess is good news for Jasper."

"Was there any mention about him or the confrontation at Vine?"

"A few mentioned the Vine party being the last time they saw Larry alive, but no one has pointed the finger at Jasper...yet. I think people are still in shock and haven't fully processed the news." Charlotte sighed. "I imagine once heads begin to clear, folks will start speculating with a vengeance, especially if Rosalynn isn't arrested soon." Her worried frown grew. "It'll indicate the police aren't sure it's her and that someone *else* might be on the hook."

I nodded in agreement. We had a brief window before Central Shores started gossiping about who else had it in for Larry Dunmer. Although, once Detective Forester began questioning people about the night of Larry's murder, it wouldn't be long before fingers were pointed at Jasper, given their public and heated scene. "Well, I picked up a lead yesterday," I lowered my voice to avoid Maria overhearing us. "Larry was *blackmailing* someone."

Charlotte's grey eyes doubled in size. "Blackmail?" she squeaked.

I filled her in on my Sunday trip to town hall with my mom. "Do any Shakespeare buffs come to mind?"

Charlotte tapped her chin thoughtfully. "Other than the AP Lit kids that come here for a study group, no."

My phone buzzed loudly against the tabletop. I snatched it up and saw an Instagram notification. "Omigosh! I forgot today's the day."

"The day for what?"

I flipped my phone around so Charlotte could see my feed. "My Crime Junkie episode just dropped!" I showed her the post I'd been tagged in on Crime Junkie Podcast's profile. The image consisted of my grinning headshot and headlines featuring Stacy Lockner's case.

A few weeks ago, Ashley Flowers had invited me to speak with her and Brit Prawat about Stacy's murder. As a massive fan of their true crime podcast, I'd jumped at the chance, although I had to be very careful about what I said. It wasn't common knowledge just how deeply I'd been involved with finding the young woman's killer. The public—outside of Central Shores, of course—believed that I had simply been at the wrong place at the right time when her murderer revealed themselves. At home, Chief McInnis and I really *had* tried to keep a lid on my exploits, but our efforts simply could not thwart the Central Shores rumor mill.

Recording the episode had been a total blast, and Ashley commented more than once about how at ease I seemed to be with the format. Brit even suggested I create a *Trending Topic* companion podcast. If I had the time and skills, I totally would, but the behind-the-scenes production work that went into publishing a high-quality podcast was beyond my current capabilities.

"Eek, this is so cool, Cokes. I'll have to listen to it in my office." Charlotte chuckled. "Although Ashley and Brit's voices are so soothing, I might fall asleep."

"I can't wait to hear how it came out." I noticed my Instagram account had already gained several hundred new followers from the Crime Junkie tag. A promising sign, as another reason I'd gone on the podcast was to name-drop Center of Attention and *Trending Topic,* hoping to expand my audience even more.

I shared the Crime Junkie post to my Instagram Stories, giving a shoutout to Ashley and Brit for having me on the show, and then navigated to my podcast app. "Why don't we listen to just a bit?" I had at least fifteen minutes before my first interviewee arrived, and the café was quiet at the moment.

"Love a good teaser." Charlotte put her elbows on the table, her expression eager. "Hit it."

Just as my finger went to touch the Play icon, the front door swung open, and Fred and Melvin Beaufort strolled in.

"Hi, ladies!" Fred beamed, looking much more refreshed than I'd seen him last. Days off from the restaurant had done wonders for restoring the fifty-year-old's boyish charm.

"Hello, Fred. Melvin." Charlotte smiled and rose from her chair, pivoting to customer service mode like a pro. "Two Americanos?"

"Yes, please!" Melvin tugged on his suspenders. "On me, this time, little brother."

Melvin followed Charlotte toward the coffee counter while Fred ambled over to my table.

With an inward sigh, I put down my phone. My Crime Junkie fix would have to wait until later. Small talk came first and foremost in Central Shores.

"How are things in your neck of the woods, Coco? It's been a while since I've seen you at the restaurant."

I managed a polite smile. One of the cons of small-town living was that everyone kept tabs on you. "Actually, Mom and I had brunch there yesterday. *You* were the one who wasn't at the restaurant."

Fred chuckled, swiping away his sandy brown hair streaked with sophisticated strands of gray. "Guilty as charged. Ever since Mel asked if he could take on some shifts and give Nat and me a break, I have been shamelessly taking advantage of him." He whipped out his phone and tapped open his picture app. "We went sailing on a catamaran yesterday. Rented one from a guy in Crestview."

I made the appropriate, appreciative murmurs he was looking for as I scanned his photos. Most were blurry and unfocused, but I could tell he and Natalia had enjoyed their ocean excursion. "That's great. I'm glad you're getting some time to relax."

Fred's jovial features darkened. "Hard to relax when there's another murderer on the loose. What's happening to this place?"

I made sure to select my words carefully. "It was rather shocking to hear."

"I hope the police can get to the bottom of things soon. I don't like this looming over our town. Of course, it's tragic what happened. Even if I wasn't a fan of Dunmer...well, I suppose I'm preaching to the choir." He gave me a knowing look.

"I certainly wasn't the president of his fan club." I couldn't help but bristle in defense. "But just because he was a rotten neighbor, it doesn't mean I'm glad he's dead."

"Oh goodness, no, I wasn't suggesting that in the least." Fred grimaced in apology. "I'm just saying the police have their work cut out on this one. I mean, it might be easier to find someone in town who actually *liked* Larry."

I had to agree with Fred on that one.

He stuck his hands in his pockets, looking a little sheepish. "Truth be told, it's not Larry I'm so much concerned about. I'd hate for Salute to Summer to have such a dark shadow hanging over it."

"I think the feeling is mutual," I admitted with a conspiratorial twitch of my lips.

"I'm surprised the police haven't asked for your help solving this one." Fred's bright, blue eyes twinkled at the suggestion.

Given my game plan for the day, my cheeks warmed with glowing embarrassment.

Fred cocked his head. "I know a guilty look when I see it. Or have you forgotten I have four teenage boys at home?" He stepped closer and lowered his voice. "*Are* you working on this with the police?"

I snorted. "Goodness, no."

"No, as in you're not working on it, or not working on it with the police?" Fred's grin widened.

Thankfully, before I could answer, Melvin returned bearing caffeinated gifts. "No sweetener, no dairy," he said as he handed Fred his drink.

Fred frowned. "Am I assuming yours *does* have sugar and cream?"

Melvin scowled at his much younger brother. "I'm allowed to have cheat days now and then, Freddie."

I glanced from one sibling to the other. Anxiety clearly radiated from Fred as he eyed Melvin's coffee cup, and then it hit me. The sudden weight loss. Fred's attention to his brother's diet. With growing concern, I wondered if Melvin Beaufort was sick.

Melvin must have seen the question in my gaze. "Type Two Diabetes. I shouldn't have been surprised. My doctor has been warning me about it for years." He took a long sip of coffee and sighed. "But dang it, I miss enjoying my food."

Fred patted him on the back, seeming eager to pull Melvin out of the melancholy funk that had settled over him at the mention of his health condition. "Coco and I were just chatting about Dunmer's murder."

Ah, yes, now there was a more lighthearted topic.

"Unfortunate, for sure." Melvin's brow furrowed. "But from what everyone is saying, I'm glad I retired before that man blew into town for an audit. Otherwise, my blood pressure might have been the death of me, not my blood sugar."

I stifled a giggle at the self-deprecating joke. "Did you know Larry at all?"

Melvin shook his head. "Never met him in person. Heard about him enough from Roger and Peggy, though."

"Peggy Morales?" The heated email exchange I'd filed way too far in the back of my mind suddenly saturated my thoughts. I had gotten so wrapped up in the blackmail note Larry had sent that I'd completely dropped the ball on pursuing Peggy as a possible suspect.

Melvin bobbed his head. "Poor gal. He was giving her a really tough time about her department's budget. She called me for advice on how to handle it, but I don't think I was much help." He rolled his eyes. "You know how those state department bigwigs can be. It's either their way or the highway."

I didn't know how state department bigwigs could be, so I prodded him for further details. "Why was Larry giving her such a hard time?"

Melvin shook his head. "I couldn't believe it when she told me. Something about him finding reckless spending in Parks and Recreation. Peggy was always so scrupulous when it came to managing her budget effectively. But Larry seemed quite intent on making some drastic cuts to her department."

"Did Peggy ever mention that Larry had threatened her?" The question was out of my mouth before I could stop it.

"Threatened her?" Both Melvin and Fred looked at me with stunned expressions.

"Yeah…" I searched for a believable scenario, trying to walk back my bold claim. "Something my mom said about Peggy and Larry had me wondering, that's all."

Fred snorted. "Well, that just about confirms it. You *are* looking into Larry's death, aren't you? Why?" He and Melvin both eyed me expectantly.

"I'm not." I didn't like lying to either of them, but I couldn't very well tell them that my best friend being a suspect was the reason for my interest. They would no doubt sound the alarm and ruin Jasper's reputation in the process. "I'm just concerned about my neighbor's death, that's all."

Melvin toyed with his well-trimmed mustache. "Peggy told me Larry was planning to make large cuts to her budget, but she never mentioned any outward threats the man-made toward her." He looked at me shrewdly. "I'd be careful what you say about this around town, Coco. Given what

167

happened to Larry, it shines an unflattering light on Peggy."

I swallowed, feeling a bit chastened. Melvin was right. Just because I was desperate to clear Jasper's name didn't mean I should be careless and throw someone else under the bus.

Fred glanced at his older brother. "I think we best keep this conversation between the three of us. Peggy has enough on her plate with Salute to Summer coming up. We'll let you get back to your day, Coco. Hope to see you and Hudson soon." He steered Melvin toward the café door. "When *I'm* working, that is."

The Beaufort brothers left Brewed to Perfection, sipping their coffees while roiling guilt festered in my stomach. I needed to revisit my investigative techniques. Melvin and Fred had seen through my questions about Peggy and all but reprimanded me for making such baseless accusations. But then again, Peggy evidently hadn't told Melvin the *full* story about her interactions with Larry. What had transpired between the two of them to make Larry so dead set on cutting Peggy's budget and trying to get her fired?

Chapter Twenty-One

A five-minute reminder alert chimed on my phone, forcing me to push my thoughts about Larry and Peggy aside to focus on the fast-approaching interviews.

I double-checked the resumes in front of me, making sure I had everyone's preferred pronouns memorized. The four candidates were the first of many applicants to make it past my vetting process and to an in-person interview. I'd posted the role online nearly two months ago and had been surprised by the flood of interest. Most likely, the media attention I received after solving Stacy's murder played a role in the applicant surge. Of course, I needed someone who lived nearby, and since I didn't want to spend all my growth budget on relocating a new employee, it was easy to pass on roughly ninety-five percent of the submitted applications.

It still left me with about sixty candidates to sift through. It had been a long time since I'd been involved with any hiring process. Back in the LiveIt days, employee relations fell to my gal pals who'd graduated with business administration degrees. Of course, I'd conducted a few interviews here and there to give my opinion about whether someone would be a good culture fit for our growing company, but Center of Attention was so much different than LiveIt. Most of LiveIt's work went on behind a computer screen, whereas my little company was hands-on and super involved with clients. I needed someone who was not only tech-savvy and detail-oriented but also an extrovert and a genuine people person.

So, with sixty remaining applicants, I had to whittle down the list to something more scalable. After conferring with Jasper and Charlotte, both successful business owners, I decided to nix anyone with no prior work experience. As much as I could have used the energy of a plucky, young high school grad, I needed someone with a definitive work ethic. Sixty applicants went to thirty-five. From there, I reviewed their skills and work experience. Those who curtailed their resume specifically to my posting made the cut. Those who sent a generic CV didn't.

With eight potential candidates, I kicked off my research. I'd requested their social media handles as part of the application process. Anyone with inappropriate tweets or posts was immediately removed from my list. In this day in age, past internet transgressions eventually came back to haunt you. Tweeting something offensive out into the world was a risk so many people took every minute of the day. I didn't have the time or tolerance for negativity, especially since it would reflect on my brand and business.

It was a long and laborious process, scouring Facebook, Twitter, Instagram, Tumblr, the works. Ultimately, I narrowed my list to four potential hires: Audrey James, Logan Jefferson, Tiffany Post, and Morgan Rose.

I kept a watchful eye on the mug-shaped clock hanging over the coffee counter as time stretched on. In between customers, Charlotte would also glance at the clock and back over at me, her forehead creased with worry.

My first interview had been set to begin at eight-thirty. Audrey James was now fifteen minutes late.

I reread her resume and cover letter, which I had printed in preparation. Audrey, who had interned at the *Washington Post* during college and worked as a marketing assistant for a Delaware-based consulting firm since graduation, lived in Cherry Springs. I found it troubling she couldn't make a meeting on time without sending any explanation. I hoped nothing serious had happened to her.

At ten of nine, a woman resembling Audrey's LinkedIn profile pic scurried into the café, frantically scanning the room. Spotting me, she hurried over, the wrinkles on her pencil skirt matching her billowy blouse. "Ms. Cline! Audrey James. So nice to finally meet you. I couldn't believe my luck when I heard back from you." She approached the table with a hand outstretched for a shake.

I smiled at her, noting she made no apologies for being twenty minutes late. Strike one.

"This shop is so cute. I forget how cute Central Shores is." She tucked a strand of sleek, black hair behind her ear. "So cute."

My smile already felt like it was beginning to tire. Describing Charlotte's shop as cute was fair enough, but to use the word repeatedly? Couldn't she come up with a better descriptor for her assessment of Central Shores? Where was the woman who had such creative captions on her Insta posts? Strike two.

"So, why are you looking to change roles?" I asked once we'd exchanged a few more pleasantries. Since she'd arrived late, I had to ensure I wrapped this up by nine-thirty or risk running into my next appointment.

Audrey gave an elaborate sigh. "I need a new challenge."

Not a bad start to an answer.

"I've been in marketing for, like, six years now. All day long, I work with clients who complain their business just isn't attracting the attention they want, and it's starting to get old."

I stopped scribbling on my notepad. Did Audrey not understand that Center of Attention essentially boiled down to being a social media *marketing* firm?

"What kind of challenge are you looking for?" I struggled to keep a barb of sarcasm out of my tone.

"Well, exactly what CoA does."

Which is helping our clients' businesses attract more attention. Strike three.

After thirty minutes of listening to her excruciating answers to the questions I'd prepared, I thanked Audrey for her time and told her I'd be in touch. As she skipped out of the café, I stared dejectedly at her resume, praying my vetting process hadn't been a total bust.

Logan Jefferson's arrival lifted my spirits. He was a tall, gangly Penn State graduate who had worked for two years in Apple customer service. When I asked him why he was looking to change jobs, he gave me a solid answer.

"I enjoy helping people, but not necessarily troubleshooting their tech problems." He gave me a sheepish grin as if embarrassed to admit that being a Genius Bar rep wasn't all it was cracked up to be. "I'd like a more creative space to thrive in."

While I enjoyed our conversation, his lack of *being* creative concerned me. No doubt, Logan could grow into a fine member of the CoA team, but I didn't have the bandwidth to allow him time to find his footing. *Maybe I'm being too tough on the guy, but I don't think I can take the risk right now.*

Tiffany Post ended up being a colossal disappointment. I'd been excited to meet her and was willing to overlook my concern that she lived nearly two hours away in Wilmington. Tiffany already operated a blog of her own, *Another Woman's Treasure*, which featured unique finds she'd uncovered at thrift stores all along the East Coast. The site had about ten thousand subscribers, so she knew a thing or two about building a brand.

What she did not know anything about were humility and self-awareness.

The first thing Tiffany said to me after breezing into Brewed to Perfection was that I should feel *lucky* she had availability to see me today. She began our interview by commenting how she couldn't believe she was entertaining working for someone other than herself. I'm all about being a lady boss, but her condescending attitude started things off on a sour note. It only continued to go downhill from there.

"Of course, I need major flexibility with my schedule." Tiffany rolled her eyes like this was a given. "I was thinking like ten hours a week would probs be all I could spare at the moment." She snapped her bubblegum with a loud *crack.*

"How generous of you."

Tiffany then studied her glossy nails. "And I would, of course, need to be reimbursed for any commuting expenses. You know, gas to get to Central Shores and such."

Yeah, no. This wasn't going to work. I might be a diva, but I prayed to Saweetie I wasn't this cringeworthy.

"Why don't I get back to you? I wouldn't want to take up any more of your time." I mustered a sickeningly sugary smile to end this painful interaction. At this rate, I'd have to put all my hopes into Morgan Rose.

Morgan texted ten minutes before the start of their interview that they'd accepted a P.R. position out in L.A. and would not be making our meeting.

"Good for you, Morgan." I sighed and tossed my phone onto the table. What a total disaster of a morning. How could I have been so wrong about the candidates I'd chosen? They'd all seemed so perfect on paper. I guess I had to chalk it up to the fact that they were *really* good at cultivating a presence online. Maybe I could take a chance on Logan and teach him the creative branding ropes. He was the only person who showed any promise out of my applicants.

"Ah, there you are, Cokes! I feel like I haven't seen you in forever."

I recognized the singsong voice at once and glanced up from my stack of resumes, bracing myself for the encounter to come.

Chapter Twenty-Two

Amanda Highgrove glided across Brewed to Perfection, slipping her chic sunglasses into her buttery blond hair. A beaming smile stretched across her beautiful, perfectly made-up face. "How have you been? Arthur was just saying the other day that we need to have the gang over soon."

Amanda's comment was so friendly and endearing that it was hard for me to resist her charms. "I can't complain too much. Life is good."

Without waiting for an invitation, Amanda plopped down in the chair that had served as my interviewing hot seat. "I'm relieved to hear that. When I heard about Larry Dunmer's death, I immediately thought of you."

I stiffened. Why had *I* popped into Amanda's mind?

"I remember you telling us how awful Larry was to everyone in Sunny Shores and how he seemed especially fixated on you." She lowered her voice dramatically. "And obviously, I heard about the scene at Vine. I'm so sorry neither Arthur nor I were there to step in and assist. What a horrid man! To say something so savage to poor, sweet Andre."

I nodded, keeping a tight lid on my surprise. Amanda and her tech-guru husband, Arthur Bushman, had invited Hudson and me out to dinner only a few days after Larry and Ros moved in. Leave it to the new-and-improved Amanda Highgrove to remember such a trivial conversation.

Settling into her seat, Amanda gave a cutesy wave over to Charlotte behind the counter. Charlotte, busy with a customer, returned the greeting with a bright smile.

"Gosh, I wish I could look like her without wasting two hours of my life in front of the mirror every morning." Admiration for Charlotte's natural beauty emanated from Amanda's every pore.

I choked back a scoff of disbelief. Although Amanda was prone to covering herself in makeup and expensive designer clothes, she didn't need them to look beautiful. Her perfectly tanned skin, sparkling blue eyes, and self-confident grace only enhanced her pretty features.

"Soooo…." Amanda stretched out the word as she surveyed the clutter around me. "What's with the makeshift office? Are you questioning suspects or…." She raised a salon-threaded eyebrow in my direction.

My jaw dropped. "What are you talking about?"

"Oh, please." She batted away my protests. "There's another murder in our hometown, and you're *not* involved? I know you a little better than that by now."

If someone had told me my senior year of high school that one day, Amanda Highgrove would be doing everything in her power to become my close friend and confidante, I would have advised them to seek professional help for delusional thinking. Yet, here we were, conspiring like old pals. At least, Amanda was. I was still working on forgiving all the terrible things she'd said and done to me growing up, but she was wearing me down little by little.

"Besides," Amanda giggled, "Hudson texted us."

Us? Who was this "us?"

"About what?" Since when did my supposedly loving boyfriend have a text chain going with my former high school nemesis?

"He messaged Jasper, Char, and me that he's been helping you dig into Larry's case but got called into work. Hudson's worried you might try to fly solo and asked one of us to check in on you." Amanda reached across and gave my forearm a reassuring pat. "So, I volunteered!"

I shot a quick look at Charlotte behind the café counter, throwing daggers at her with my eyes. She responded by doubling over in silent laughter. Clearly, she was enjoying my discomfort. *The traitor.* I knew Charlotte had to work, but why hadn't Jasper offered to step in?

Returning my gaze to Amanda's animated expression, I struggled to push aside the less-than-fond memories of torture I had endured at the hands of this woman's teenage self. Yet, I couldn't deny Amanda had been a good friend in recent months. People *could* change. While she'd never said *outright* she was sorry for how she treated me in high school, Amanda's kind and thoughtful actions spoke louder than words these days.

"Did Hudson explain *why* I'm looking into Larry's death?" I asked, extending a tentative olive branch.

"No." Amanda's lips twitched. "But Jasper sure did. I had to read his texts like three times to make sure I hadn't misinterpreted any of it." She shook her head in disbelief, her blond hair cascading around her shoulders. "I get their confrontation at Vine isn't a good look, but how anyone at the police department can remotely entertain the idea that Jasper would be involved is beyond me."

If Jasper, the king of grudges, could succumb to Amanda's charms and forgive her for tormenting him in high school, then maybe it was time for me to finally bury my reservations toward her once and for all. Besides, if Amanda knew that Jasper was a person of interest in Larry's murder and the whole town didn't...well, maybe she could be trusted.

She slid a piece of paper out from my pile and skimmed it, her pert nose wrinkling. "Is this Audrey James person a suspect?"

I chuckled. "No. I'm actually taking a break from detective work and trying to find an assistant to help me. I'm up to my eyeballs in client engagements and blog admin." I sighed as the daunting to-do list floated through my mind. "I have three webinars tomorrow about online newsletter management that I haven't brushed up on, and I have yet to even draft my new twenty-first-century dating feature."

Amanda's brow furrowed. "I did notice your *Trending Topic* post went out a day late. I usually look forward to reading your stuff on Saturdays. Not that I didn't race to download your recommendations on my Kindle yesterday morning."

I gave her a sheepish smile while swallowing my shame. Amanda had been a loyal follower of *Trending Topic* since its launch. If she had noticed the delay, other long-time readers would have, too. "Yeah, a CoA engagement threw me off my blogging game."

"So, did you find anyone who meets your standards?" Amanda pushed the resume back toward me.

Charlotte appeared at our table with three iced teas. "It sure didn't look like it from where I stood." She giggled as she pulled up another chair to join us.

I stuck my tongue out at her. "Don't bask in my misery. It was a disaster. The only one who shows potential has a solid tech background, but I'm worried he doesn't have the strongest creative skillset. I need an assistant who can hit the ground running."

Amanda took a thoughtful sip of the cherry lime green tea Charlotte was featuring this month. "An assistant, huh? What tasks are you looking for help with?"

"Well..." I took a moment to tally everything I did with my clients and where having an extra set of hands would be most helpful. "For starters, I'd like someone who can schedule *and* conduct webinars about online branding, advertising, profile management, etc. I'm not too worried about that one. They just need to be able to read my PowerPoint decks. I'm also looking for a person who can develop creative marketing campaigns *and* help me manage some of my *Trending Topic* activities. Not to mention, I'd love it if they could handle smaller CoA engagements all on their own."

Amanda tapped her chin. "So, it sounds like you're searching for a client engagement manager, not an assistant."

I opened my mouth the protest, but the words sputtered in my throat. I guess I *was* looking for someone to take the reins on client projects. Had I been hunting for the wrong person this entire time? No wonder all my applicants had come across as juvenile and inexperienced for what I needed. "I guess I thought an assistant could do all of that for me."

Amanda shook her head. "Not in today's job landscape. People see the word 'assistant' and assume it's scheduling meetings, booking travel, going on coffee runs, the works. An assistant isn't in charge of solving client problems. You need someone to manage clients for you."

Charlotte bobbed her head in agreement. "I didn't realize you wanted someone to help *manage* your client load. Otherwise, I would have suggested the same thing sooner."

I dropped my elbows onto the table, my head collapsing into my hands. "I'm a horrible business owner. I can't even hire my first employee properly." I sighed, a wave of anxiety washing over me. "I have to go back to the drawing board. Not only that, but I'll have to cancel a few upcoming contracts to manage my workload."

"Nonsense." Amanda waved my worries aside. "Why don't you hire me in the interim while we work to find you someone who fits the bill? I'm more than happy to step in and help."

Both Charlotte and I stared at Amanda as if she'd sprouted another head.

"What?" She gave us an innocent shrug. "I serve on the boards of five non-profit organizations. I've organized and promoted numerous fundraisers. Successful ones, I might add. I know how to manage projects *and* people." Amanda counted out her surprisingly relevant qualifications on her manicured fingers. "I'm well-versed in all things social media. And I know how to work a room." She folded her arms with confidence. "I'll have your clients drinking the CoA Kool-Aid in no time."

My brain struggled to compute what she was saying. Amanda Highgrove wanted to work for *me*?

"W-why?" I finally sputtered. "Why would you want to do this?" Didn't she realize my little company might get in the way of her high society galas, afternoon tea at the country club, tennis lessons, sunbathing...

Amanda's graceful posture deflated a tick. "Because I want to help you. If you're struggling to manage your workload, I'd like to lend a hand."

Her selfless offer touched my heart. Lord knows Amanda wasn't in it for the money. The Highgroves were one of the wealthiest families in Central Shores, if not the state. They had been one of the first affluent dynasties to settle in Millionaire's Row over two decades ago, launching the trend for wealthy city folk to relocate to our town's beachside shores. And even if Amanda didn't have her own money, her husband, a cybersecurity genius, had a *billion*-dollar empire to his name.

"Well..." Was I really considering hiring Amanda to work at Center of

Attention? Could I put aside everything in our past and work alongside her?

Absently, I unlocked my phone and tapped the screen. I glanced at the events on my calendar app, knowing there was no way I could handle the next few weeks by myself without giving up a few client engagements. I couldn't afford to disappoint prospective clients, not if I wanted my business to grow.

"If you're serious, Amanda, I'd love the help."

She clapped with unrestrained glee. "Yes! Oh, Coco, thank you. This is going to be so much fun!" she gushed, shaking Charlotte's shoulder as if to reiterate her point.

My lips instinctively curved into a smile, sharing Amanda's enthusiasm. "Can you come by the house tomorrow around noon? I'm giving a few back-to-back webinars about newsletters that I'd love for you to listen in on." The truth was I hated online newsletters, but they were such a useful marketing tool that my clients couldn't afford for me to skip out on them. I hoped that my new *engagement manager* could take the lead on this particular presentation in the future.

"Of course!" Amanda had her phone out and tapped away at her screen. "What else do you need help with? I'm free to start shadowing you now if need be."

"Actually," I said, chewing on my lower lip, "I don't have anything else scheduled for today. I cleared my calendar after these interviews wrapped up. I thought I'd need some time to process my thoughts on each applicant."

Charlotte studied me with interest. "Why do I get the feeling you have something else in mind for your afternoon's activities?"

I rolled my eyes. *Busted.* She was way too perceptive. "All right, you got me. I'm planning to take a little field trip over toward Rockaway."

Amanda's doe eyes widened. "Does this have something to do with Larry?"

I nodded and was just about to share my latest theory in the case when the café door clanged open, and Charlotte swore under her breath. A stream of beachgoers overwhelmed the coffee counter. The lunch rush was upon her.

"Don't suppose you can wait a few hours to fill us both in?" Charlotte gave a wry grin as she rose from her chair. "No? Okay, well, give me the rundown later." She dashed off to help Maria process the slew of orders.

Amanda gave an encouraging wave as Charlotte retreated. "What's Rockaway got to do with Larry?"

Unsure how much Jasper had shared with Amanda in this secret Who-Can-Babysit-Coco text chain, I kept the details light for now. "Larry was assigned to audit Rockaway's finances. I want to poke around and see if anyone there had reason to kill him."

Amanda bobbed her head along with my words, gathering my papers strewn across the table. "All right. Let's get going."

When I didn't immediately respond, Amanda released a heavy sigh. "Come on, Coco. It will put Hudson at ease if you have company. And besides, you can use the time to fill me in on your current clients and your business goals for the quarter and such."

Do I have goals for the quarter? When does a quarter even end? Or start?

Amanda made some valid points. If hiring her for Center of Attention was going to work out, even temporarily, she had a lot to learn. However, it was her point about Hudson that won me over. He knew me well enough to know I'd continue my investigation without him. Having a buddy tag along would at least reassure him that I was perfectly capable of handling this safely and responsibly.

"Okay, sounds like a plan. I have a CoA new hire packet already prepped at home. Why don't we swing by, you can leave your car in my driveway, and then we can head down the coast?"

Amanda rubbed her hands together. "Investigating a murder feels like a great way to initiate someone into your life, Cokes."

I whacked her arm as we cleared the table, hiding a smile that threatened to give away the secret giddiness bubbling inside me.

"So, Gerald Atkins is a former client?" Amanda asked as Jolly crossed into the city limits of Rockaway. I'd spent the drive filling her in on my findings.

I pushed my worn Tom Ford shades—a treasured T.J. Maxx find—up the bridge of my nose. "One of the first. We rebranded his cheese shop into a gourmet connoisseur's dream."

"Daddy and I use Deco Fromage all the time. The cheddar sculptures make for beautiful and purposeful party centerpieces."

I winced at the not-so-subtle privilege seeping from Amanda. Her "Daddy" was Thurston Highgrove, a retired businessman, philanthropist, and President of the Central Shores Chamber of Commerce. He was a nice enough old man, but I still held a grudge that he'd raised such an obnoxiously mean teenage drama queen.

From the corner of my eye, I noticed a frown on Amanda's glossy lips as she read through the binder I had prepared in anticipation of a new employee. It held all my presentations, walkthroughs, one-pagers, and processes used for executing a successful client engagement, as well as current trends in social media and valuable features on various networking platforms. Now that Amanda had seen what she'd signed up for, was she getting cold feet?

"I can't help but wonder," she finally said, suspicion lacing her words, "are *all* your clients bloodthirsty killers?"

This time, I didn't hide the snarky grin that crossed my lips when I swatted her arm. "I don't think *Gerald* killed Larry."

"You're right. I'm sorry. You think your client's *wife* did in your odious neighbor."

"Darcy Atkins is, or at least used to be, a big fan of Shakespeare," I explained. "You don't write a two-hundred-page thesis on something you're not interested in."

"And since the Reddit user Larry was blackmailing references *The Merchant of Venice*, you think she's the one he was threatening to report to the police?"

Hearing Amanda say it out loud made me realize just how big of a mental leap I'd taken. "It's possible," I said, giving myself some wiggle room to be wrong. "I'm interested in learning how Larry's time in Rockaway went. Was he as unpleasant there as he had been in Central Shores? If so, he might have made more than a few enemies."

"Indeed." Amanda closed the binder, hugging it to her chest as she gazed out the window.

Rockaway was much larger than Central Shores and was one of many municipalities overlooking Rehoboth Bay. Yet, despite its size, it exuded an old-timey charm, which made it a well-known tourist destination in its own right.

It was nearly one by the time we turned into the parking lot of Deco Fromage in neighboring Long Neck. I wanted to start by questioning Gerald about the party and whether he knew anything about his wife's working relationship with Larry.

"How are we going to play this?" Amanda asked out of the corner of her mouth as we approached the purple-framed glass door.

I had our cover story ready. "I like to stay connected with my clients even after an engagement is complete, hoping they'll refer CoA to their friends or need help with a future rebrand or marketing campaign. Since I'm bringing a new client engagement manager on board," I paused, welcoming the excitement in Amanda's gaze, "I want to introduce her to some of CoA's most important and appreciated clients, so they can get to know her."

"It amazes me you can just come up with these things on the fly."

I laughed. I didn't bother mentioning that I'd already established a cover story for my impromptu check-in with Gerald before I left the house this morning. I just had to tweak it to fit Amanda's presence by my side.

Chapter Twenty-Three

Heavenly scents of savory cheeses wafted through my nose as we entered the bustling shop. Seeing how busy Deco Fromage was for a Monday afternoon pleased me. Based on the various red, white, and blue getups, many folks were already on vacation and anticipating the long weekend celebrating Independence Day.

Amanda and I wandered around the tantalizing cheese displays, taking hearty offerings of the free samples scattered around the store.

"I'm going to need a salad after all this dairy," Amanda murmured before picking up a slice of camembert and popping it into her mouth with a blissful sigh.

I swallowed a cube of smokey gruyere. "Lunch is on me. Can someone say tax write-off?" I winked.

We had moved onto the asiago samplings when Gerald emerged from one of the storerooms off the main showroom. He carried a large basket filled with an assortment of wrapped cheeses and handed it to an awaiting customer.

He must have spied me in the crowd as a broad, welcoming smile stretched across his face, and he waved in my direction. I returned the greeting and pulled Amanda toward him while Gerald muttered something to one of his nearby employees before meeting us halfway.

"Coco, darling! It's been too long." He kissed both my cheeks in wannabe French fashion. With his eclectic European style and a light (not to mention fake) accent, Gerald seemed to forget that he'd grown up in a small farm town in Minnesota, not Lyon. "What brings you to my humble market?"

I eyed a nearby wheel of Pule cheese sitting on prominent display. At six hundred dollars a pound, it appeared Deco Fromage had grown into anything but humble. "I wanted to check in and see how you were doing. We haven't touched base since the CoA Facebook trends webinar." The presentation had been my very first remote webinar with multiple clients, and Gerald was a vocal participant. I motioned around the shop. "Looks like business is good?"

Gerald swelled with pride. "Business is grand! Your idea to feature a cheese of the week has really got folks returning. I'm even putting out notecards with recipes using the cheese as an ingredient to entice customers to buy the other supplies I'm now selling in the store." He pointed to the back wall. Rows of newly constructed shelving displayed everything from seasonings and gourmet olive oils to pasta makers.

"I'm glad to hear CoA can still be of use." I turned to Amanda. "And speaking of CoA, I'd like you to meet my new client engagement manager, Amanda Highgrove."

Amanda beamed brightly as she and Gerald shook hands. "I'm delighted to meet you in person, Mr. Atkins. I'm a devoted Deco Fromage patron."

I fought against rolling my eyes at Amanda's use of the word "patron," but Gerald ate it right up.

"Oh, Ms. Highgrove, what an absolute treat!" He pulled her in to exchange an air kiss on each cheek. "My staff and I are extremely grateful for all the business you and your father have referred our way."

I sighed with relief. Amanda's initiation was complete. "Amanda will be managing mostly new clients going forward, but both of us are at your disposal if you ever need any assistance."

A gust of wind vaulted into the room as the front door opened, and a slew of new shoppers breezed into the store. With a distracted glance, Gerald patted down his silver-streaked auburn hair. "How thoughtful. I'm so glad you stopped by, Coco."

Sensing his desire to greet the new arrivals, I knew our time was limited. "Of course. I would have introduced you to Amanda at Vine on Friday, but I'm sorry to say we didn't cross paths at the party." To say nothing of the fact that Amanda hadn't been there *or* even hired yet.

Gerald's brow furrowed. "Oh, I'm sorry, dear, but I didn't make Andre's little soiree. I had a prior engagement with a potential seller I'm wooing." His attention again drifted to the cluster of patrons, now gathered around a display of gorgonzola, so he missed the disappointed looks Amanda and I exchanged. "I know Vine is interested in collaborating with Deco Fromage, though, so Andre and I set up a meeting next week to talk shop."

I bobbed my head repeatedly, trying to pick up the pieces of my suddenly shattered theory. If Darcy hadn't attended the Vine event with her husband, she wouldn't have been able to swipe the corkscrew used to kill Larry. *So much for means and opportunity.*

Amanda recovered before I did. "Well, Mr. Atkins, if anything comes of those discussions that requires assistance from Center of Attention, please let us know."

Gerald waved formalities away. "Please, call me Gerald. And I certainly look forward to our future collaborations. Now, if you'll excuse me, I see some uncultured palates that think bleu cheese and bubblegum pair well together." Then, after another round of goodbye cheek kisses, Gerald fluttered over to educate the latest arrivals.

My demure smile spiraled into a frown as my former client dashed across the room and out of earshot. "Well, that was a bust."

Amanda threaded her arm through mine and guided me toward the front door. "Maybe not. Could Darcy have gone to the party without Gerald?"

I glanced over my shoulder to examine Gerald one final time before we stepped over the threshold and into the balmy summer breeze. "He didn't give that impression, but maybe she went without him knowing?" I whipped out my phone and shot a quick text to Andre.

Hi, Andre! When you get a chance, can you confirm whether Darcy Atkins attended your event on Friday? I stared at the little message on my screen, hoping Andre wouldn't find the request too odd or ask any follow-up questions.

I showed Amanda my text, and she nodded. "While we wait for his response, why don't we head to Rockaway for some lunch? I wasn't lying when I said I needed a salad."

I chuckled. The last sample I'd noshed on had been a spicy Bleu d'Auvergne, so I didn't mind grabbing something to wash down the saltiness it left behind. "Sounds like a plan."

Fifteen minutes later, we were seated on the deck of a small Greek restaurant overlooking Rehoboth Bay. Over salads and grilled veggies, we chatted about CoA and my upcoming projects. Amanda continued to surprise me with her willingness to take on whatever work I felt comfortable delegating to her.

"Arthur has been teaching me a thing or two about Squarespace." She polished off her iced tea. "A few non-profits I help out with had sites in desperate need of a makeover, so I took it upon myself to step in."

Wow. The Amanda Highgrove I knew in high school would never have taken the time to learn such a "nerdy" skill, let alone help anyone. "Most of my remote engagements focus on overhauling existing webpages and redesigning them to entice more traffic. Two new clients with Squarespace sites are scheduled to kick off next week. Why don't I let you take the lead on their redesign and have you run your client deliverables by me for sign-off?"

Amanda gave me a mock salute. "You got it, boss lady."

As we waited for our server to swipe my business credit card, our conversation returned to my fledgling investigation.

"Any word from Andre?" Amanda asked.

I glanced at my phone for what felt like the hundredth time during our meal. "Nothing yet."

"Well, since we're here, why don't we just head over to city hall and ask Darcy ourselves?"

I mulled over Amanda's suggestion for all of a second. "I'm sure we can come up with some reason for checking in. What have we got to lose?"

With our bill paid, we decided to enjoy the midafternoon sun and walked three blocks from the restaurant to Rockaway City Hall. The building, while styled to look like the Parthenon or Lincoln Memorial, was relatively new construction and much livelier than the Central Shores town hall had been during my last—albeit unsanctioned—visit.

We found the city manager's office on the first floor, although drawn curtains blocked our view inside. With a hopefully believable cover story in place, I knocked on the polished wood door barring our entry.

"Come in," a muffled voice replied on the other side.

Amanda gave me an encouraging nod as I pushed the door inward.

Darcy Atkins glanced up from her imposing desk, a government-regulated smile pinned to her face. "Hello, there. How can I help you?"

I gave her a shy wave. "Hi, Mrs. Atkins. So sorry to bother you. I'm not sure if you remember me. My name is Coco Cline, and this is my assistant, Amanda. I did some work for your husband a few years back."

"Of course. How could I forget?" Darcy gave us each a firm handshake before returning to her seat. "To what do I owe the pleasure? It's not every day I get a visit from a local celebrity." She raised an eyebrow, clearly curious about why a lifestyle blogger had stopped by her office.

I gulped down the tsunami of nerves that welled in my throat. "I'm afraid I'm here to deliver some sad news as the spokesperson for the Central Shores Police Department." I muttered a silent prayer, hoping word about this visit wouldn't get back to Chief McInnis. "I'm not sure you've heard, but Larry Dunmer, a former Rockaway resident, passed away this weekend."

Darcy visibly stiffened in her chair. "Larry? Gosh. No, I hadn't."

Amanda shifted on her feet out of the corner of my eye. I didn't dare risk a glance at her to see if she was thinking the same thing I was. How could an upper-level government official not be aware that a murder had occurred only a few towns over? Central Shores may have been small-time compared to Rockaway, but murder certainly wasn't an everyday occurrence in this region of Delaware.

"On behalf of the Central Shores community, I'm very sorry for your loss." I quickly added, "Since Mr. Dunmer worked here at city hall, I thought the unfortunate news should be shared in person."

Darcy nodded, her gaze trailing out a large window overlooking the bay.

"My department also has a few questions." I edged closer to her desk, hoping she'd invite us to sit down. "About Larry's time here in Rockaway."

"You said you're a spokesperson for the police?" Darcy's brow pinched with growing horror. "They're investigating? Are you saying he was murdered?"

"I'm afraid I cannot go into details, but the police are treating this as an active homicide investigation." I continued to pull references from every crime show I'd ever watched, trying to sound as official as possible. I was in incredibly dangerous territory, skirting along the lines of impersonating a police officer. But, in my defense, I was only reiterating what the local news had reported, and I had clearly introduced myself as the PD's spokesperson, which I was…for now. "Did you know Larry personally?"

Darcy shuffled a few papers, straightening them on her desk. "I did. He wasn't a city official, mind you. He was appointed by the state treasurer's office to conduct an audit." She sighed as she deflated into her chair. "I just can't believe he's dead. Larry was such a great guy."

This time, I couldn't resist sharing a dubious glance with Amanda. Larry Dunmer? A great guy?

"I mean, as far as state auditors go, he was a big ol' teddy bear," Darcy continued, seemingly unaware of the silent disbelief Amanda and I expressed. "Why someone would have reason to kill him, I don't know."

Darcy had to be mixing Larry up with someone else, another state auditor, or something. Maybe a picture would set things right in her mind. I dug out my phone and opened my mouth to clarify we were talking about the same Larry Dunmer when Darcy's soft features twisted into an ugly scowl.

"Actually, I take that back. His wife was certainly a nasty piece of work."

Chapter Twenty-Four

My heart quickened, hammering against my chest. "You know Rosalynn?"

"Unfortunately, Ros and Larry were a packaged deal." Darcy winced at some phantom memory and finally invited Amanda and me to take a seat. "That poor man couldn't go two hours without his wife barging into his office to check up on him. He certainly regretted renting an apartment so close to City Hall."

"Why did Ros drop in so much?" I asked.

Darcy rolled her eyes. "Oh, she always had some inventive excuse, but I think she was keeping tabs on her man. Larry was just so naturally charming, and he was quite popular here. I think it made her jealous."

My jaw dropped reflexively on its own. Larry, *charming*? It was then I noticed the hint of blush blossoming on Darcy's cheeks as she continued to sing Larry's praises. Had Gerald's wife developed a crush on the state auditor during his time in Rockaway?

"Larry was more than annoyed by her obsessive attention when his assignment here wound down." Darcy lowered her voice and leaned forward in her wing-backed desk chair. "I even overheard him tell her that he'd consider filing for *divorce* if her overbearing behavior continued."

I gave Darcy a simple nod of understanding when on the inside, I was reeling. Larry had threatened to *leave* Ros if she didn't give him his space. Was that why she let her husband get away with such lecherous acts in Central Shores? Was she afraid he'd divorce her if she spoke out against him?

I toyed with this new information. Had the scene at Vine pushed Ros over the edge? Had she confronted her husband about his treatment of Bonnie? If Larry justified his actions by threatening her with a divorce, maybe Ros had snapped and killed him in a fit of humiliated rage. Whatever the case, I bet once Gavin and the others learned there was trouble in paradise, the police wouldn't be so dismissive of Ros as a suspect.

"What can you tell us about the audit Mr. Dunmer completed for the city of Rockaway?" Amanda spoke up, abruptly changing the topic of conversation. "Did he make any major budget cuts? Was anyone unsatisfied with the results of the audit?"

Darcy chuckled. "Larry located about ten thousand extra dollars for Public Works, which they were elated over. He found ways to save the Parks and Recreation folks nearly five percent each year. He even got us three more school buses. We were all very pleased with the thoroughness of his work."

I shook my head in muted astonishment. How was this the same man who had been my horrific neighbor? "No one was let go?" I asked, hoping Darcy had misinterpreted Amanda's question.

"Nope. Not a one. And our budget has never been healthier." Darcy glowed with a satisfied smile.

"When was the last time you saw Mr. Dunmer?" Amanda continued with her astute questions.

Darcy's brow creased in recollection. "Well, we had a going-away party for him back in April, but I ran into him again at the Crestview Country Club a few weeks ago. Gerald and I were golfing and came across Larry out on the links."

"By himself?" I gave Darcy a furtive look. "Or was Ros trailing after him?"

Darcy smirked. "She must have allowed him out of her sight for once. But, no, he was with a few gentlemen. I didn't catch any names, but I believe one of them was the Central Shores mayor."

While I wondered who the others in the group were, her words further confirmed Roger Sullivan had indeed been one of the only people Larry had befriended during his time in Central Shores. It also suggested that Darcy had not seen Larry at the Vine event on Friday night.

"Mr. Dunmer was last seen in public attending a private event at Central Shores' new wine bar, Vine. We've obtained the guest list," I delivered the misleading context with gritted teeth, "and saw you and your husband were on it. Did you happen to see anything at the party that might be helpful to us—I mean, the investigation?"

Darcy sighed. "I'm afraid not. I wasn't able to attend the function. My husband and I were at a business dinner."

The last glimmer of hope I'd been holding onto blinked out of existence. After listening to Darcy praise Larry's virtues so profusely, I couldn't help but wonder if she'd been trying too hard to give the impression that she had no problems with Larry to cast off any suspicion in his death. But if Darcy hadn't attended Vine, then she wouldn't have had access to the murder weapon. However, her virtuous descriptions of Larry still seemed disingenuous compared to the man I knew. Larry Dunmer hadn't become a total sleazebag overnight, and I found it hard to believe he'd been a complete angel during his time in Rockaway. The more likely scenario was that Larry knew how to behave around people in power, which was why Darcy, as city manager, remembered him so fondly. He'd certainly suckered his way into Mayor Sullivan's good graces somehow.

But the chances of Darcy Atkins brutally murdering Larry over blackmail threats grew nonexistent after speaking with her. The shelf behind her was filled with books and pictures, not a single Shakespeare work among them. After handing in her master's thesis, it was quite possible that she never wanted to touch Shakespeare again. I'd taken one line from her extensive resume and blown it way out of proportion to suit my own ends. I'd wasted valuable time tracking down a false lead while Larry's killer was still out there. Well, maybe not "wasted." Darcy's insight into Larry and Rosalynn's blissfully wedded union had shone a new light on things.

"I see." I rose from my seat, signaling to Amanda our impending exit. "Well, thank you for taking the time to speak with us, Mrs. Atkins. And again, on behalf of Central Shores, we are sorry for your loss."

We left Darcy with a vaguely confused expression, like she'd just realized she wasn't quite sure what we'd been doing in her office all this time.

"I didn't get the feeling she was our killer," Amanda whispered once we were safely out in the bustling hallway.

"I don't think she's our *Merchant of Venice*, either." I sighed. "I still believe whoever Larry was blackmailing is our guy. Or gal. I just wasn't right in thinking it was Darcy Atkins."

"What about the claims she made against Ros?" Amanda lowered her voice as we passed by a group of six or seven young women, all gathered around a vending machine.

I opened my mouth to respond when I caught a snippet of their conversation.

"—Dunmer, dead. Can you believe it?" a tall, pretty brunette burst out.

A petite blond scoffed. "That's karma for ya."

"Crystal, you're awful!" came a chorus of nervous giggles.

I halted in my tracks and whirled around. "Excuse me, did you say Dunmer? As in Larry Dunmer?"

The women all nodded simultaneously.

"Omigosh! You're Coco Cline, aren't you?" an auburn-haired beauty squealed. "I'm a huge fan! I just love your blog."

I managed to rework my cringe into a cheery grin. In Central Shores, nobody batted an eye at me when I talked to them, as most folks had known me since I was in diapers. They didn't get the whole "fame" thing, which was one of the reasons I had moved back to my hometown in the first place. Besides, being well-known online didn't necessarily transpose to being popular in the real world. Yet, this group's age demographic described a majority of *Trending Topic*'s audience to a T. I hadn't been prepared for that when I stopped to butt into their conversation. The last thing I needed was for word to spread online amongst my followers that I was asking about dead bodies. Again. *That* would definitely make its way back into Chief McInnis's ear.

"Aw, thank you so much. You've made my day." I smiled warmly in return. It *was* very nice to hear, and I wished I had more time to chat about why she enjoyed *Trending Topic*. Unfortunately, I had bigger fish to fry. "I'm sorry, but I couldn't help but overhear you mention my neighbor, Larry Dunmer."

"Dunmer was your *neighbor?*" Gianna, the only one among her friends to have a nametag on, glanced skeptically at me.

I decided to play dumb. I didn't advertise to my followers that I worked for the Central Shores PD, and I doubted these girls would go digging too much into what I did outside of *Trending Topic*. "What do you mean 'was'?"

The long-haired brunette who'd caught my attention gasped. "You mean you haven't heard? He's dead! Someone *killed* him. Can you believe it?"

"What?" I stifled my own gasp of shock. These young women didn't need to know *I* was the one to I.D. Larry's body.

Beside me, Amanda struggled to morph her smirk into a frown. Evidently, my acting skills were a little over the top.

Gianna bobbed her head furiously. "It was all over the news this morning."

"How have you *not* heard? Isn't your boyfriend a TV reporter?" The auburn-haired *Trending Topic* fan tilted her head to the side, a confused expression spreading across her features.

Oops. I pretended not to hear her. "Yeesh, that's…terrible," I said in answer to Gianna's remark. In my quest for more information, I did not bother to sound sincere.

Crystal, the petite blond admonished for mentioning karma, snorted. "You sound real broken up."

I shrugged sheepishly, this time not having to act at all. "Larry wasn't exactly the world's best neighbor." I quickly amended my statement. "Not that he deserved to die or anything."

"You sure about that?" Crystal cocked an eyebrow. "I bet he was all over you with your looks."

I suppressed a triumphant grin. My brewing suspicions had been on the mark. Darcy may not have experienced Larry's unwanted advances, but this group certainly had. "Well, I didn't consider myself to be *that* special. The guy made a pass at anything with boobs."

Gianna hugged herself, shivering. "He was a total skeeze. We were so glad when he left town." She glanced at her friends, who all nodded their agreement.

Again, Darcy's claims about a fond farewell didn't hold up. "You said someone killed him, didn't you?" I feigned cluelessness, hoping to get them to spill more deets without me looking like I was poking my nose into things. "Like, in an accident?"

"Nope. My newsfeed said police are treating it as a murder." The brunette reached into the vending machine slot and pulled out a bag of trail mix. "Another murder in a town as small as Central Shores, can you believe it?"

This young woman seemed to have difficulty believing anything, considering this was the third time she'd used the phrase.

I gave each girl a skeptical look. "He may have been a sleazebag, but I can't think of anyone who'd want to *kill* Larry."

Gianna took the bait first. "I bet his wife finally snapped."

"Please, Ros worshiped him." Crystal rolled her eyes. "She let him walk all over her. It was so sad."

"But remember how mad Ros got at Zoe when Larry touched her knee out in the courtyard?" The brunette pointed to her raven-haired friend.

The girl I assumed was Zoe scowled. "As if it was *my* fault that her husband found every 'innocent' excuse possible to brush up against me."

The brunette nodded. "I wouldn't be surprised if it finally dawned on Ros that her husband was the problem."

I had to agree with her. Rosalynn Dunmer had clearly been territorial of her husband for a long time. Add Larry's threats of divorce into the mix, and maybe the mortifying incident with Bonnie had taken Ros one step over the edge.

An uneasy silence settled over the group. I watched confusion and calculation dance across their expressions, and I knew my time here was up. I didn't need these young ladies asking questions about what I was doing in Rockaway.

"Well, thanks for filling me in," I said with a wave. "Enjoy the rest of your day." Then, grabbing Amanda's hand, I dragged her outside into the hot sun.

"Wow, smooth exit." She chuckled as we resumed normal walking speeds back to my car. "I'm sure those girls won't think twice about running into you at all now."

Embarrassment heated my cheeks. Or maybe it was just the three P.M.

sun. "I never said I was *good* at this whole undercover thing."

"I'd hardly call this 'undercover.'" Amanda used air quotes to emphasize her point. "Let's hope our little excursion doesn't make it back to Chief McInnis, or CoA's engagement with the PD may cease to exist."

It pleased me to hear the note of concern in her voice. Amanda may have been a CoA employee for all of three hours, but it was nice to have someone else vested in my business's future. "Maybe he won't be mad once we tell him what we've learned. A handful of people who have no interest in proving Jasper's innocence whatsoever have all said Ros was capable of killing her husband. That has to count for something, right? They can't just write her off?"

Amanda squeezed my shoulder as we arrived at Jolly. "I know you're anxious about Jasper, but I'm not so sure it's a good idea to tell Chief McInnis about all this. You blurred the lines a bit back there, Cokes. Telling the chief could cause more trouble for Jasper *and* you."

Before I could reply, my phone chirped from my pocket. I pulled it out, and my heart skipped a beat. Andre had finally responded.

Darcy? Doesn't ring a bell. Sorry. And I already trashed the attendee roster the bouncers used, so can't check to see if she's on it.

A frustrated sigh growled across my lips. Andre had thrown away a valuable networking tool by deleting the names of the party's confirmed attendees. His vague message didn't exactly absolve Darcy of suspicion, either. If she had snuck away from her husband's business dinner early, she *could* have attended the party and flown under the radar of its host.

I showed Amanda the text once we were both buckled in the car. "Any suggestions as to what I should do next?"

"You mean, what should *we* do next?"

I smiled at her before pulling out onto the street. In high school, I could never have imagined Amanda wanting to be my crime-fighting partner. She hadn't even wanted to be my lab partner for fear of catching "fat." But it seemed the days of her calling me "Gourdy Cordy," a nickname I'd earned for buying non-zero-sized jeans, were thankfully over.

Neither of us had an immediate answer and lapsed into companionable silence during the drive home. While Amanda studied her new hire binder, I mulled over what I had learned about Larry, which amounted to very little the more I thought about it. He liked to harass young women he found attractive. His wife didn't appreciate it, but she tolerated his behavior for the sake of their marriage. The person I'd hoped would be the owner of the u/merchnt_of_venyce Reddit account turned out to be one of the few people to ever praise Larry.

I still had no clue who Larry was blackmailing, and despite everything we'd learned about Ros, I couldn't shake the nagging suspicion that Larry's extortion scheme was central to this crime.

A little before four, I pulled Jolly into my driveway, next to Amanda's sleek Mercedes.

"Looks like Ros isn't home," Amanda commented as we got out of the car.

I stared at the dark, lifeless windows of the Dunmers' rental home. "She must still be visiting her friend."

Amanda headed over to her car. "Once we're done with the webinars tomorrow, maybe we should track her down and check in on her?"

I easily read between the lines. Ros wasn't our blackmail recipient, but we couldn't ignore that more than five people had suggested she'd killed her husband in a jealous rage. A conciliatory chat might help determine whether those suggestions had any merit. "Of course. A neighborly visit is expected in situations like this, after all."

Amanda laughed, and after we exchanged goodbyes, she drove off.

Before I had time to figure out a game plan for the rest of my afternoon, Hudson texted right as I set my bag down on the kitchen counter.

Miss ur face. Working 18 but need a break 4 dinner. Want 2 come by & grab a bite 2 eat?

His thoughtful invitation warmed my heart. After all our weekend disruptions, it was nice to know Hudson felt as disappointed as I did about our lack of quality time together.

I checked the time and sent a reply. **Just got back from an outing with my new CoA hire. Will tell more soon**

Need to prep some work real quick. Be @ studio by 5 – Chinese or Indian? U choose!

With my reply on its way to Hudson, I headed to my office to ensure everything was ready for tomorrow's presentations. Not only did I have remote clients attending, but I'd also opened my sessions to anyone willing to pay an attendance fee. For eighty dollars, an interested individual could register for a training webinar without needing a CoA engagement. I found that for every forty or so people who signed up, I got at least a handful of future contracts out of the process, as well as an easy chunk of change.

I'd hosted this newsletter presentation several times, so there wasn't much to update. However, I did need to address some new features MailChimp had recently released. With technology constantly changing and evolving, I strove to give my clients the most accurate information about how my preferred marketing platforms worked.

After refreshing the PowerPoint deck, I noticed the time. Yikes, I needed to get moving, or I would be late. Drafting my online dating feature would have to wait until after I returned home from dinner. It sounded like Hudson was in for another late night at the studio, so I could write my new *Trending Topic* piece while I waited up for him. Mapping out the article would be a great way to keep myself focused on the here and now and *not* the fears that crept into my mind when I was alone at night.

Shaking off the uneasiness unfurling in my mind, I put away my work. As I shut down my computer, I did my best to ignore the growing guilt over not giving my blog more attention. I needed to up my game, and not just for *Trending Topic's* continued success. Center of Attention relied on me maintaining my online popularity just as much as *Trending Topic* did. No one wanted brand management advice from a has-been blogger.

Chapter Twenty-Five

At five on the dot, I entered the spacious, sleek lobby of WMTG. The horde of receptionists had already gone home for the day, leaving only the evening security guard, Wally, to greet me.

"Ms. Coco, it's been a while since we've seen you around here." Wally flashed me a toothy grin and tipped the brim of his cap in a chivalrous greeting. "How you been, sweetie?"

Usually, terms like "sweetie" and "honey" made me cringe, but Wally's grandfatherly delivery of the endearment tugged a smile across my lips. "Life is good, Wally. How about you? How's Eunice?" I asked after his wife of forty-five years.

"Can't complain." Wally winked. "Although Eunice does."

I joined in his jovial chuckle. I'd met Eunice a few times at WMTG functions and was well aware of her fiery spirit.

"We're looking forward to taking a drive and checking out Salute to Summer. Eunice is thinking about submitting her lemon meringue for the pie bake," Wally continued, the soft glow of the lobby lights shimmering on his dark brown skin. "I've heard great things about this year's festival."

"My mom will be delighted when I tell her. She's been working hard to make it the best Salute to Summer Central Shores has ever had."

Hudson materialized beside me, a teasing grin on his face. "With Moira Cline at the helm, I'm sure it will be." He draped an arm around my shoulder.

Having not seen him in over twenty-four hours, it took my breath away at how much I had missed him, even though it had only relatively been a short amount of time. I leaned into his secure warmth, appreciating the feel of him. "Hey, you," I murmured, hoping Wally wouldn't catch the intimacy that laced my greeting.

Hudson squeezed my shoulder in return. "I went with Indian for dinner. The Grubhub guy should be here soon. We can chill in my office while I wrap up some work. I hope you don't mind?"

A little disappointed I wouldn't have Hudson's full attention, I reminded myself that just being near him was enough. "It's a date."

Hudson had coordinated our food delivery perfectly with my arrival, for a young man hustled into the lobby carrying a large paper bag.

"You kids enjoy," Wally said as Hudson thanked the Grubhub driver. "I'm off to do rounds." He waved before disappearing into the security suite.

Hand-in-hand, Hudson led me toward his new office space. He'd gotten the upgrade a few weeks ago when he and Millie went full throttle on developing their true crime pilot. The last time I visited, the place was spotless and virtually untouched. Tonight, the couch, worktable, and computer desk were covered by folders, newspaper clippings, maps, and printouts.

"Busy day?" I leafed through a stack of papers lying on the arm of the couch.

Hudson scooped up a bunch of documents, making room for me to sit. "Trying to make some headway on a cold case from five years ago." He cleared off the coffee table for our food. "It's back on as our pilot episode since we're having a tricky time getting enough details on Larry to create a full show."

I frowned. He sounded a bit defeated on that front. "Were you able to speak with Ros?"

"Nope." Hudson sighed. "She barricaded herself inside her friend's house all day. Millie and I waited five hours to speak with her, but no luck." He reached into the bag and produced a large vat that smelled tantalizingly like lamb biryani. "Millie is not happy."

I pulled him away from the food and started to massage his tense shoulders. Hudson clearly needed a moment to unwind.

After a few minutes of relaxing silence, my boyfriend turned to face me.

"Tell me about your day." Hudson wrapped his arms around my waist. His eyes brightened with interest. "You hired someone for CoA?"

"I did. And you won't guess in a million years who it is."

I gave Hudson five attempts before revealing Amanda was CoA's new client engagement manager. He was understandably floored, as he knew our turbulent history, but proud I'd decided to put the past aside and give her a chance.

"I feel like I should be awarded a headhunter's fee or something," Hudson joked once I had explained my decision.

I raised an eyebrow in question.

"Well, if I hadn't asked her to track you down, this fortuitous turn of events may not have happened."

His teasing remark was the perfect segue into the rest of the day's adventures. "Speaking of your keeping tabs on me—"

But before we could settle into our food and I could tell him about my visit to Rockaway, an errant wail came from outside Hudson's office door.

"Could this day get any more discouraging?" Millie Stabler barged into the room, tossing her arms in dramatic frustration. With three-inch stiletto heels adding height to her already six-one frame, she nearly punched the overhead light fixture. "First, that odious woman denies us an interview after stringing us along for hours, then our servers go haywire, and we lose valuable data, and now—Oh, hi, Coco!" Millie flipped her personality switch, going from raging boss to delighted friend. "How lovely to see you." She planted a rather forceful kiss on my cheek.

"Everything okay?" I eyed her warily, trying to spare Hudson her wrath.

Millie released a hurricane of a sigh. Hot, minty air blew straight into my face. "Everything will be once we get all our ducks in a row."

"What's happened now?" Hudson perched on the side of his desk, his arms folded.

"Jessica Barnes's agent just called." Millie slumped against the wall. "Due to *personal reasons*, she won't be able to fly out to host Wednesday's golf tournament."

My heart plummeted at the news. The young Hollywood starlet's name was all over the Salute to Summer marketing materials and had drummed up a great deal of public interest in the tournament. I hoped this change in plans wouldn't affect the fundraiser's success too greatly. Many local charities counted on the donations it was meant to generate.

"What?" Hudson hopped off the desk, concern written across his face. "She's bailing? What about the contract she signed?"

"She's paying the fine our lawyers negotiated." Millie rubbed her temples, her reply coming out as a moan. "Like money makes up for it. We have no one to replace her!"

"What about someone on the anchor team?" Hudson suggested. "I'm sure one of us would be willing to take her spot. I don't mind dropping from the tournament to host."

Millie scoffed. "No offense, but we need someone our viewers don't get a chance to see every night. Someone fun and fresh to make watching four hours of golf somewhat less mind-numbing. Someone who—" Her sharp gaze halted on me. "Coco? Would *you* consider stepping in?"

"Me?" My response sounded as dumbfounded as I probably looked.

Millie's sleek black bob swung furiously across her cheekbones as she nodded. "Yes, you! You're a well-known figure, you have experience in front of the camera, and I know you can think on your feet to keep the crowd entertained." Excitement twinkled in her eyes at this surprising solution. "What do you say?"

"Well...I...uh." I sure wasn't displaying my usual eloquence now. So much for being able to think on my feet.

"You'd be amazing, babes," Hudson offered his encouragement. "It'd be great press for CoA. I'm sure we can throw a line or two about Center of Attention being a contributor to the event." This statement he directed toward Millie.

"Yes, of course!" Millie clapped her hands eagerly. "Think of the boost in business, Coco. Free promotion!"

I'd been ready to say yes as soon as Hudson had voiced his support, but free airtime for CoA sealed the deal, especially since I now had the bandwidth to take on more clients with Amanda's help. "All right, all right. I'll do it. But I know absolutely nothing about golf."

Millie laughed, clutching the air in front of her in triumph. "And you think Jessica Barnes does? We have golf pros commentating on the game itself. We just need you to mingle with the crowd, chat with golfers about the charities they're supporting, and talk up the various Salute to Summer events before sending us to commercial break. I'll have all the participants' info sent to you tomorrow morning, along with filming logistics."

She made it sound so simple, but my stomach coiled into knots. There had been a time when I sought the spotlight, but ever since returning home to Central Shores, I had retreated from it. Online fame was easy enough to step away from by silencing notifications or turning off my cell phone, but I still remembered the days when LiveIt saturated the mainstream media, and reporters followed me around everywhere I went. Fame hadn't been as glamorous as I'd imagined when I was younger, even though a small part of me still did miss it sometimes. Not that I expected anything as extreme as paparazzi groupies to stem from hosting a local charity golf tournament. It had just been a long time since I had done anything to knowingly enhance my celebrity status.

Hudson placed a hand on my shoulder, giving me an encouraging squeeze. "You're going to knock this out of the park."

His warm brown eyes instantly quelled the anxiety bubbling within me.

"Well, now that one crisis is resolved," Millie said, giving Hudson a knowing glare, "you can work on solidifying the pitch. We present to the network board on Thursday."

Hudson chuckled and gave Millie a mock salute. "I'm on it, boss."

"Good. Now, I'm scooting out for some fresh air before the six P.M. taping." She bid us goodbye, promising an assistant would email me the deets for the golf tournament.

"Still hungry?" Hudson asked after she'd gone.

"Still have time?" If Hudson had to pitch his new show later this week, I didn't want to get in the way of his prep, and we only had about forty minutes until he was due on set for the evening news.

Hudson circled his arms around me and pulled me close. "For you, always."

We settled into our now-lukewarm food. Hudson had ordered tandoori chicken and lamb biryani to share. While we ate, I launched into bringing him up to speed on my trip to Deco Fromage and Rockaway and where things currently stood with Larry's case.

Hudson chewed thoughtfully on a bite of lamb. "The theory that Larry pissed someone off during his previous auditing assignment seems to be losing steam."

I swallowed a bite of tangy chicken. "But it doesn't mean he didn't discover something during his time in Rockaway that he used as blackmail. Maybe he found all that extra money in the budget because someone was hiding it."

Hudson's brow wrinkled. "I'm not sure government budgets work like that, babes."

"Well, I'm not even sure anymore that blackmail was the reason Larry was killed," I admitted. "The women I spoke with today all pointed the finger at Ros."

"I wish I could have gotten a read on her." Hudson sighed, scooping the last bits of chicken out of the tandoori to-go container. "Millie wants to try speaking with Ros again tomorrow."

It was then I noticed the dark circles under his eyes. Between his pilot project and covering Larry's death, Hudson was being run ragged.

"You heard anything from Jasper?" he asked.

A small smile twitched on my lips at his concern for my friend, despite everything Hudson had on his plate. "Not today. I'll check in tonight and see if he's heard anything new."

Hudson glanced at the clock above his door. "Shoot. I need to get to makeup."

"I'll clean things up here." I motioned to the used napkins, dishes, and silverware on the coffee table where we'd had our makeshift picnic. "Do you want me to grab anything to have at home on my way back?"

"No, I'm good." He pushed himself off the floor and dusted the wrinkles from his suit pants. "Thanks for coming down. I needed to see you to make it through the rest of the day." He planted a soft kiss on the top of my head. "Lock the door behind you, please!" His voice echoed as he disappeared down the hall.

Three minutes later, I closed his office door, fumbling for my phone and car keys in my bag. It didn't help that this wing of the building was rather dark this time of the evening. Only a few dim lights peppered the corridor. All broadcast activity occurred at the soundstage on the opposite side of the compound.

"Well, look who it is," a cheerily insincere voice sneered behind me.

I stiffened and reluctantly turned to greet the unwanted visitor. *Play nice, Coco. For Hudson's sake.*

Chapter Twenty-Six

"Hi, Tori." I waved unenthusiastically, my keys and phone clanking together in my hand.

Tori Beals sashayed toward me, her high heels clacking on the tile. "Hudson's friend, right? Cece?"

Her spiteful attitude never failed to irk me. "Coco," I seethed through gritted teeth, knowing full well she knew my name and that I was more than Hudson's friend.

Tori didn't bat an eye, not bothering to apologize. "Well, I hate to burst your bubble, but Hudson's not available to deal with distractions right now. We have a broadcast to prepare for." She twirled a buttery brown ringlet with a finger. "Sorry."

"Thanks, but I've already been a *distraction*." I kept my tone level. "Hudson and I had dinner together. He just left for the soundstage."

Tori moved closer. The height of her heels gave her at least two inches on me, forcing me to look up to meet her irritated gaze.

"Well," she began with a little *humph*, "I suppose he told you about our new show, then. It's being pitched soon."

I replied with a raised eyebrow. "Don't you mean Hudson's show?"

Tori smirked. "Oops, the cat's out of the bag. I have it on good authority that Millie will soon add me to the roster. The higher-ups think the chemistry Hudson and I have is too magnetic to pass up." Her eyes narrowed. "I can't wait to tell him. Hudson will be *so* excited. Late nights, just the two of us, working to create a juicy story. I'm looking forward to it."

I pressed my lips together, trying to keep my flaring temper at bay.

"Aw, don't pout." Tori wagged a finger at me. "It's just business. With Hudson and me lighting up the screen, viewers will be captivated. Who cares what the show is about? They'll be tuning in to see *us*." Then, with an innocent laugh, she added, "Besides, as hot as he is, the guy can't carry a show by himself, whereas *I* already have a built-in fanbase from my Baltimore days."

My fists balled at my side before I knew what I was doing. The edges of my keys and phone dug into my skin. *Easy, Cokes, violence is never the answer.* Instead of smacking her perky little nose, I took a deep breath to calm the fiercely protective fires burning inside me. Hudson could carry eight hundred shows by himself, but since he had asked me not to do anything about Tori's ongoing harassment, I opted for a Michelle-Obama-*when-they-go-low-we-go-high* response, as much as it pained me. "What good news for you, Tori. Bye now." With a tight smile, I turned away from her and headed toward the lobby.

My lack of a comeback must have left Tori momentarily speechless, as she didn't reply until I was nearly out of earshot.

"I get what I want, Coco," Tori called after me. "It would be best for Hudson *and* his career if he realized that sooner rather than later."

Her unabashed threat toward my boyfriend stopped me in my tracks. Then, without thinking things through, I whirled around and marched toward her.

Tori took a startled step back as I approached. Good, let her fear me. Sorry, Mrs. Obama. The high road wasn't going to work for me this time. Not when I could help Hudson take down such an abusive snake.

"What did you just say to me, Tori?" I snapped.

She quickly regained her superior attitude. "I said it would be best if Hudson realized that I get what I want."

I folded my arms across my chest, hoping she wouldn't notice how awkwardly I clutched my phone. "I don't get it. What do you want?" I couldn't shy away now. I couldn't continue to let Hudson carry this burden alone.

"Gosh, you are dumb." Tori's lip curled in a snarl. "Don't be a sore loser,

206

Coco. Why would Hudson want a washed-up blogger when he could have someone as successful as me? It's only a matter of time before I convince him to take our on-air relationship off-screen." She glanced at her perfect French manicure. "*If* Hudson wants to continue working here, that is. I have friends in much higher places than he does."

It took all my strength to simply tap a button on my phone and not chuck the device at Tori's head. "We'll see about that." I swallowed all the nasty insults I wanted to hurl her way. I had to get out of there before she realized what I'd done. "Good luck with your life, Tori." I summoned my most withering glare before turning on a heel and stomping away, for real this time.

I didn't dare look over my shoulder or check my phone until I was safely alone in the lobby. I opened my photo app with quivering fingers and pressed the video thumbnail. There she was, in all her harassment glory. I finally had the proof Hudson needed to blow the whistle on Terrible Tori.

Once I made it outside to the studio parking lot, the adrenaline from my intense encounter with Tori began to fade. My knees began to shake. I was rapidly losing steam. I needed to sit down and collect my thoughts.

As I hurried toward my car, I replayed the wild scene. I couldn't believe I'd caught Tori Beals on camera saying those arrogant, awful things about Hudson. Did she really think I wouldn't fight back? Was she *that* used to getting her own way?

I considered my options. My petty side wanted to blast the video all over social media to unmask Tori as the gross bully that she truly was. If anyone deserved to be canceled, it was her. But that was just vengeful me thinking. I wouldn't share Tori's callous words with anyone other than Hudson. He could decide what to do with the evidence I'd obtained. While I wanted to text him and let him know what had transpired, this warranted an in-person conversation. I'd have to wait until he came home.

With a long-winded sigh, I checked my notifications and messages, eager to decompress and forget about Tori's antics in the meantime.

I had several texts from Jasper and Charlotte, each wondering what I had been up to all afternoon. Charlotte had clearly filled Jasper in on my hiring of Amanda. His latest message asked if I had sacked her yet. Maybe he still held a *bit* of a grudge toward Amanda 2.0.

Amanda had also texted a family recipe for homemade aloe vera lotion, saying she thought it might be useful for a *Trending Topic* feature. Reading through the recipe, I replied with a hearty thank you. Homemade skincare remedies would be a great concept for a summer beauty blog post. I copied and pasted her text into my Notes app, where I kept ideas for future *Trending Topic* content. I winced as I scanned the list. It had grown dangerously long.

By the time I found my car and sank into Jolly's comforting embrace, I was checking my Instagram and Twitter accounts for recent activity. Day-old posts about my summer reading recommendations were still getting traction, and I'd been tagged by a few followers in a Twitter thread about one woman's disastrous Tinder date.

@CocoCline uve got to feature this poor gurl

@CocoCline this sums up dating in the 21st century like no other

I saved the original tweet for reference. I already had enough material to draft a trial post. If my readers enjoyed the new relationship column, I would need all the real-life dating drama I could get for future installments.

I did a quick sweep of my direct messages, noting that I'd also received several dating horror stories through this channel. My Twitter followers were definitely taking the assignment to heart. I couldn't afford to disappoint them. I needed to focus and deliver the new content I'd promised. Maybe with Amanda's help, I could find the time to get it off the ground.

Just as I was about to close my Twitter app, a username in the DMs section caught my eye: @meazur4meaz. Why, I wasn't quite sure. Something about the name tickled the back of my brain.

I clicked on the message to see what dating disaster this person had submitted.

Stop pokin into Larry's life or ull end up like him.

My hands shook so badly that my phone clattered to the car floor with a *thud*. Frantically, my searching fingertips brushed against the glossy screen wedged under my seat. I tugged the device free and wiped away bits of sand stuck to the case. With a deep breath, I reread the message, convinced I was having a nightmare. I'd just been speaking with Terrible Tori only a few moments prior, so I couldn't dismiss the notion entirely.

Stop pokin into Larry's life or ull end up like him.

Even though my car had been baking in the evening sun, I sat shivering against the warm leather. This was real. Someone was *threatening* me.

I clicked on the @meazur4meaz username to investigate the profile. Unsurprisingly, the account had no real name tied to it, nor did it have any personal information in the "About" section. What's more, Twitter displayed the date a user joined the community. It appeared that @meazur4meaz joined in June of this year and had no tweets or geographic information listed on their account.

"What do you bet this was created today?" I asked Jolly's steering wheel. He offered no reply.

I clicked back to my direct messages. The note had been sent earlier in the afternoon, around when Amanda and I departed Rockaway City Hall. Had one of the girls we'd run into sent it? They certainly would know how to create a basic Twitter bot account on the fly...

Who was I kidding? Anyone who could Google would be able to do it, meaning Darcy was also very capable of creating the shell account. Had I been wrong about her? Could she have been the one Larry was blackmailing after all?

My head spun with wild theories, each more unnerving than the last. I had to get somewhere safe. I had to get home. Locking my fears away into a tiny mental box, I tossed my phone aside and made the thirty-minute drive back to Central Shores.

Once I was huddled in the arms of my sectional couch, clutching a glass of red wine, I allowed myself to fully process everything. My life had been threatened. Someone wanted to harm me. What in the name of Olivia Rodrigo had I gotten myself into?

Clearly, I was making someone nervous, but who? How did they even know what I was up to?

I fired off rapid texts to Jasper, Charlotte, and Amanda. **U haven't told** anyone about my investigation, right?

While Jasper didn't respond, Charlotte and Amanda each replied quickly.

No way! Why?

Of course not. Where's this coming from?

My fingers hovered over the keyboard. I didn't want to worry my friends. What's more, they'd try to convince me to stop digging into Larry's death. And if I was being threatened, didn't that mean I was close to uncovering the truth?

Hope rekindled within me. Receiving a threat *had* to mean I was on the right path to tracking down Larry's killer, right? The trouble was, I wasn't even sure which path I was on at this point.

I considered the people I had interviewed since kicking off my little investigation. I'd spoken to Bonnie and Ian before an official statement about Larry had been released. If they had seen his death on the news, maybe they'd figured out the real purpose of my visit and freaked out.

I shook my head, nixing the idea before it fully formed. Bonnie's TikTok proved she and her boyfriend had still been busy working the Vine party when Larry was murdered.

Then there was Darcy Atkins. It wasn't exactly a secret that I'd been tangled up with bringing a killer to justice before. It had made national news, after all. Maybe she'd seen right through my visit as the PD's spokesperson and decided to warn me away…

A flash of light coming from the kitchen window caught my attention. Car lights? Was Hudson already home?

I dashed off the couch and pressed my face against the glass. A nondescript sedan pulled into the Dunmers' driveway next door. The headlights blinked off, and Rosalynn Dunmer stepped out into the fading sunlight.

With sunglasses hiding her eyes and a scarf covering much of her head and hair, I couldn't make out her expression from this distance. But as I watched Ros hurry toward her dark and empty house, I couldn't help but wonder if we now had a killer living next door.

Chapter Twenty-Seven

Beep. Beep. Beep.

The sound of Hudson's alarm jarred me awake the following morning. I was surprised to find myself tucked under the bed covers. When had I fallen asleep? Last I remembered, I was waiting for Hudson to get home, so we could talk about Tori and the unsettling Twitter threat.

"Sorry, babes. Go back to bed." Hudson kissed my forehead after he'd silenced the alarm.

"What time is it?" I wiped the sleep from my eyes.

Hudson was already making for the bathroom. "Six. I've got to record a few new scenes for our pilot, and it needs to be in the editing room by noon."

I winced. Hudson was up against a time crunch. Not the best time to dump a bunch of drama on his lap, but the sooner, the better. "Do you have a moment to talk?"

"Sure, be out in a few."

The sound of the shower drowned out anything further.

I remained snuggled among my pillows, my brain slowly preparing for the delicate conversation ahead of me. There would be no way I could go back to sleep once I came clean about everything. And besides, getting up a six probably wasn't such a bad idea. It gave me plenty of time to polish my dating post for *Trending Topic*.

"Millie wants to know if you got her PA's email?" Hudson's head appeared in the doorway, his wet hair dangerously close to dripping on our bedroom carpet.

I scrambled for my phone. An email notification from one of Millie's many production assistants greeted me. "What time did you get in last night?" I asked as I scanned the lengthy PDF attachment outlining the tournament logistics.

"Twelve thirty," he replied, his voice muffled by the bathroom wall. "Found you passed out in here with your laptop."

I glanced at my silver laptop perched on my vanity. Hudson must have moved it before tucking me into bed. "I tried so hard to stay awake until you got home."

"You had a big day at work. I'm sure you were drained."

I *had* been exhausted by the time I curled into bed to draft my blog post in comfort. But not from my "big day" at work. "Listen, Hudson. I have something to show you."

He appeared in the doorway, his face a mask of concern. "What's up? Is something wrong? Are you okay?"

I swallowed. "I'm fine. It has to do with Tori. She kinda cornered me on my way out of the studio last night."

"What?" Hudson's bronze skin lost its luster. "Cornered you? She didn't hurt you, did she?"

I tapped my phone screen and held it out for Hudson. "Just watch this, please."

He took my device and pushed play. Tori's snide voice rang out from the speakers, and he physically recoiled.

Tori's upsetting words became background noise as I carefully monitored my boyfriend's reaction. Fear, anger, and hatred radiated from every inch of him until Tori spoke her final, condemning lines. Only then did Hudson's eyes well with tears of unfettered relief.

"Coco." His voice broke.

I jumped out of bed to wrap my arms around him, searching for the right words. "The file is yours to use. However you see fit." I squeezed him hard.

His arms tightened around me, and even though I couldn't see his face, I felt his tears soaking through my nightshirt. "Thank you."

"I know you told me you could handle this by yourself, but we're a team, Hudson." I stepped back and held him at arm's length. "As long as I'm around, you'll never have to go through anything alone."

He nodded, wiping his wet cheeks. "I know that, babes." He cleared his throat, regaining his stoic composure. "Thank you for not posting this on your socials. I bet you wanted to."

I laughed at how well he knew me. "You have no idea."

Hudson sent himself the video and handed my cell back to me. "I'll pull Millie aside today and show her this." He snorted. "She'll probably be angrier that Tori lashed out at her favorite influencer than her employee."

While I was pleased to see his sense of humor return, I knew lingering fears about his future at the station fueled his wry comment. "Millie will have your back," I reassured him. *She better, or she'll have to answer to me.*

"Anything else life-changing happen last night?" Hudson cracked a smile. He was ready to put the weighty topic behind us for now.

With a sinking heart, I went to open my Twitter app to show him the threat from @meazur4meaz, but my fingertip paused over the icon. Hudson had been a good sport about my latest foray into crime-solving. I didn't want to mess that up. I didn't need him worrying about me when he already had so much going on.

I could just picture Hudson's stern expression once he learned about the threat. *You have to reach out to the police, Coco.*

With what information? I imagined myself saying. If I involved the police, I'd have to come clean about breaking into Larry's office and snooping through his government-issued computer. That could lead to major trouble for me, not only professionally, but personally.

"Any new developments in Larry's case?" Hudson had clearly noticed my extended silence.

"Nothing too earth-shattering." I tossed my phone onto the bed. There was no sense in worrying Hudson about the threat. After all, I planned to listen to @meazur4meaz. Not because I'd been scared off by the menacing message but because I had no clue what to do or whom to speak with next. Problem solved.

Hudson studied me a moment before adjusting the buttons on his shirt cuffs. "I sense there's more to this story, but I really need to get to the station. Talk later? I'll be home right after tonight's taping. Gotta get my rest for the tournament tomorrow." He kissed me, his lips lingering. "I'm glad you'll be there."

"I was planning to go anyway." I whacked him with a pillow. "I wouldn't miss cheering you on."

He chuckled. "You better brush up on your golf game etiquette, Miss Celebrity Guest Host. You don't really cheer during them."

He backed away from the bed before I could knock him with another pillow. I raced after him, catching up to him at the front door. "Coco Cline will redefine the game of golf," I boasted in pompous assertation.

"I have no doubt you will." Laughing, he scooped me into a big hug. "See you tonight. And thanks, babes. I'm glad to know you'll always be in my corner."

From the front steps, I watched Hudson disappear into the garage, his car emerging onto the road a few moments later. I stood outside and waved, enjoying the dewy morning breeze as he drove off, my mind savoring the peace he filled me with. Despite our neighbor being murdered and the hardship Hudson was dealing with at the station, we were good. Beyond good. Better than ever. Last night during our studio dinner, he'd even told me he already had someone lined up to sublet his apartment and that perhaps we could celebrate with a weekend getaway soon.

As I surveyed our seaside home's exterior, I chided myself over all the time I'd wasted being angsty about the whole apartment situation. Hudson was clearly dedicated to me. Never, in our four-plus years of dating, had he ever given me a reason to distrust him. Hudson had only kept the space in case he needed a spot to crash after work, and since that had yet to happen, he was giving up the apartment. Simple as that. My boyfriend didn't play stupid mind games.

I was lucky. After reading the dating stories my followers had sent me, it had become quite clear that mind games were the norm in today's dating culture and that no one believed another person's motivations could be trusted. Young couples emulated what they saw on reality TV, creating drama for the sake of drama. Maybe that had been why I'd been so insecure. I hadn't trusted that Hudson was above playing games with me. But he'd proved, time and time again, that he was as levelheaded and straightforward as they come. Something I didn't truly appreciate until this very moment. He was my person, and together, we could get through anything.

Filled with relief that Hudson's saga with Tori would also soon come to a close, I turned to head back inside the house. But my happiness was fleeting. Could I be a bigger hypocrite? Here I was, appreciating Hudson's trustworthiness when *I* was the one being deceitful. Why hadn't I told my boyfriend about the Twitter threat? Why had I skirted around the truth?

I could tell myself it was because I didn't wish to worry him, but there was a more selfish motive behind my actions. I didn't want Hudson talking me out of solving this mystery.

My investigation into Larry's death may have been on life support, but I had a solid lead only twenty yards away. Amanda had mentioned tracking down Rosalynn after we were done with our webinars, but why wait? Yes, I had promised not to snoop alone, but Ros didn't know Amanda and would probably clam up around someone so glamorous and beautiful. If I showed up solo on Ros's doorstep, I had no doubt she would give me the tongue-lashing she always did and, in the process, potentially let something about Larry slip. Plus, I'd have my phone with me, so I could always call for backup.

Putting my work on the back burner (again), I jumped into the shower and got ready for the day. It took a few moments to decide what to wear for this mission, as I didn't want to encourage any of Ros's insecurities to come out to play. Finally, I settled on a violet, tastefully cut sundress, no makeup, and my hair gathered into a twisted bun.

I also couldn't just show up at a grieving widow's home empty-handed or at seven A.M., either. Murderer or not, I had to follow proper houseguest etiquette. Although did I *really* think Ros had killed her husband? The women in Rockaway certainly thought her capable, but I couldn't get passed the blackmail note. The timing of Larry's random Reddit message and his death couldn't be a coincidence. I wondered if he'd told Ros about the scheme.

After checking my kitchen cabinets to ensure I had the necessary ingredients, I whipped up a batch of my mom's delicious espresso chocolate chip cookies. It was one of the few things I could bake without setting off the fire alarm. There was a reason why I steered clear of posting recipes on *Trending Topic*. No one in their right mind needed cooking advice from me.

By eight-thirty, the cookies were cool enough to be boxed in a Tupperware. I prayed Ros wouldn't notice the enduring red and orange residue glued to the container's interior. The Tomato Alfredo Mom had sent home with me a couple weeks ago had sure left its mark.

Cookies in hand, I knocked lightly on the Dumners' front door at eight fifty-five. The time might have been a bit uncouth for a social call, but Ros struck me as an early bird.

A few moments passed before I knocked again.

No answer.

I pulled my phone out of my dress pocket. Eight fifty-seven. Maybe I had come by too early. She was grieving, after all. I wouldn't be able to get out of bed for months if something ever happened to Hudson.

Peeved that my eagerness to question her had outweighed reason, I began to retreat when the click of a lock caught my attention.

The Dunmers' front door swung inward. Ros stood there, wearing a loud, pink-and-teal plaid robe.

"Coco?" Her nose crinkled.

"I'm so sorry. I didn't mean to wake you." My guilt doubled as I studied her. She looked exhausted. What had I been thinking, coming over here to pump her for information?

"You didn't wake me. I was sitting on the deck and didn't hear the door." Her watery, red eyes narrowed, sizing me up. "Are those...?" She nodded with interest at the cookies tucked under my arm.

"For you? Yes!" Regaining my footing, I handed the Tupperware to her. "I thought you might need...Ros, I'm so sorry about Larry."

She accepted the cookies with a half-hearted smile. "Thank you. I appreciate that. I know you and my husband had grown close since we moved in."

My jaw dropped despite my best efforts. What kind of reality did this woman live in?

She opened the door a little wider and invited me inside. "Care to join me? I don't like sitting in all this oppressive silence. I'll put on a pot of coffee."

"Oh, please, that's not necessary," I said as I stepped inside. "I don't want to impos—"

"*I* need coffee, so if you want some, you're not imposing in the least." Ros steered me with surprising force into her kitchen. The condo's layout was similar to mine, albeit smaller.

Ros busied herself at the coffee maker while I sat on an uncomfortable metal barstool. I squirmed in the awkward silence as I tried to figure out how to tactfully ask whether she killed her husband or, at least, knew who might have wanted to.

"Larry insisted we buy those." Ros pointed to the stools with her free hand while setting a hot cup of coffee in front of me. "He saw them at some state senator's home and said we *must* have them."

I nodded, my gaze surveying the living area, filled with gaudy statues and modern artwork.

"Practically everything in this place Larry saw in someone else's home." She sighed. "He sure did like to look the part of a bigshot."

A traitorous snort shot out of me before I could stop it. I recovered by pretending to choke on my coffee. "Sorry, didn't realize it would be so hot," I lied.

Ros studied me carefully. "We were married for twenty-two years." Her eyes misted over. "But these last few had been a bit tough for us."

Goosebumps perked up across my skin. Oh, God. Was this a confession? What had I been thinking, coming to speak with her alone?

Ros didn't appear to detect my sudden wariness. "I'm just glad I get to move out of this sleepy little town and back to Dover. Larry's work offered to cover the remainder of the lease on this condo. I'm leaving as soon as I can. I can't wait to be done with this wretched place." She paused, giving me a sheepish shrug. "No offense."

"None taken. You never seemed very happy to be living here."

Ros glanced down at her own coffee mug, her cheeks coloring. "I'm not the best at making new friends."

Gee, I wonder why?

"Larry's job was hard on me with all the moving around we did. I kept begging him to put in for permanent reassignment, but he just wasn't having it."

I frowned, remembering the email Larry had sent someone in the state department asking about the open position on their team. For a moment, I considered sharing that Larry *had* been trying to get a more permanent job but that it just wasn't working out. Yet, it probably wouldn't make his wife feel any better, and I certainly couldn't risk her blabbing to the police that I had been snooping around Larry's personal communications.

"Larry liked the change of scene," Ros continued. "He liked to 'conquer' places." She scoffed. "Conquering. That's what he called it. What person enjoys coming in and looking for people to fire?"

I nodded sympathetically. "I can see how that would have made it hard for him to stick around once the damage was done." I thought back to Darcy's claims that no one in Rockaway had lost their job. Had it been a fluke in Larry's tenure? Or had she lied to me?

"Oh, yes. He racked up quite the body count throughout his career." Ros massaged her left temple. "Although, the last place we lived in, he simply couldn't justify firing anyone, and boy, did it irk him. Just be glad he didn't get the chance to bring down the axe on Central Shores."

Her candor intrigued me. "Was Larry planning to make a lot of cuts?"

Ros bobbed her head. "He was preparing to present his findings to Mayor Sullivan this week. But of course, he—he didn't get to." The emotion I'd been expecting from the grieving widow suddenly overwhelmed Ros. She reached for a paper towel and furiously dabbed her eyes. "I'm sorry. I'm a roller coaster of emotions. Gosh, I miss him so much."

"You don't need to apologize." I gave her a light pat on the forearm, still uneasy with her odd attitude. Why was she treating me like we'd been cordial neighbors these last two months? Had shock dulled her hatred for me?

Ros stifled another sob. "You should have seen me at the PD's office yesterday. I was a blubbering mess. I thought I had finally cried everything out."

Now we were getting somewhere. I was eager to learn about her interactions with the police thus far, and this gave me the perfect opening. "I hope they didn't pummel you with questions. I can't imagine how distressing it must have been."

"To be asked whether you killed your husband? Yes, it was quite surreal." Ros whimpered. "I thought I was just going in for some follow-up questions, but no."

I pretended to be aggrieved on her behalf. "Why would the police even *think* you could do such a thing?"

"Well, after that embarrassing scene at Vine, I was a little miffed with Larry." Ros huffed. "I know that young waitress was flaunting herself, but it would have been nice if he'd shown *some* resistance toward her charms."

I glanced down to examine my Picasso-inspired coffee mug. I couldn't risk Ros seeing my incredulous expression. Had she really deluded herself into believing *Bonnie* was at fault for the incident at Vine?

"We'd planned to go on a weekend getaway after the party, but I was so mad that I told Larry he could find his own way home. I was taking a vacation by myself." Ros's knuckles grew white as she clenched her coffee. "We already had our bags in the car, so I drove to Reddy Wellness on a whim and booked a room. Of course, Larry kept calling to apologize, so I eventually turned off my phone." She swallowed, her eyes once again tearing up. "I just keep going over the last thing I said to him before driving off."

I waited for her to tell me.

"*I don't care if I ever see you again!*" She collapsed against the counter in soul-wracking sobs. "But I do care, I do! And now I'll never see him."

I rushed to find Ros a box of tissues and patted her gently on the back as she wept.

"Of course," she continued as she wiped a nasty river of snot from her nose, "the police latched onto our argument and asked if anyone could verify where I was the rest of the night."

"Could they?" I prodded.

"Not really. All I did was check into the spa and go to bed." Ros shrugged. "I told them to check the security footage at Reddy Wellness."

"I'm sure that will clear your name." I gave Ros what I hoped looked like a convincing smile. Inwardly, I crossed her off my mental suspect list. Even without photographic proof, I was confident that Ros hadn't killed her husband.

She blew her nose, tossing the used tissue onto the growing pile beside her. "I think it must have. The detective left the room for a while, and when she returned, she switched topics, asking whether Larry had any enemies." Ros rolled her bloodshot eyes. "As if Larry was important enough to have *real* enemies."

"Didn't you just say that he's fired a lot of people over the course of his career?"

She suddenly chortled. "No one *kills* someone over losing their job, Coco."

Um, had Ros never heard the phrase "going postal" before? Had she never watched cable news? People killed each other over chicken sandwiches these days. "Well, what did you tell the detective?" My seemingly innocent question would hopefully convince Ros to tell me who she believed killed her husband.

Her chin quivered. "I told the police to look into the horrid woman harassing Larry at work."

I straightened in my seat. "What?"

"Larry kept telling me he was handling it internally, but that tart was messaging him at all hours of the day." Ros folded her arms with a *humph*. "She tried to pass it off as being concerned about the future of her department, but Larry told me that the woman threw herself at him the first week he arrived. He, of course, turned her down, but she kept bothering him."

"What woman? Do you remember her name?"

Ros's forehead furrowed. "I think her last name was Parks. That's what he called her, anyway, and that's what she was listed as on his phone."

Parks? I didn't know anyone who worked at the town hall with the last name Parks— "Oh, do you mean Peggy Morales, the director of the park's department?"

Ros shrugged. "Maybe?"

The heated email exchange between Peggy and Larry filed in the too-far-back recesses of my mind sprung forward. Larry had painted a very different picture for his wife than what the email suggested. While I'd forgotten much of its exact wording, I remembered one line with resounding clarity: *I am sorry I embarrassed you but wounded pride aside...* Given the context Ros had just provided, I was willing to bet that *Larry* came onto *Peggy*, and she refused his advances. Then, to cover his bases, Larry told his wife that Peggy was harassing him at work should it ever become a battle of he-said, she-said.

As for Peggy's frequent messages to Larry, I suspected she was afraid he would take his injured ego out on her beloved department. But would she kill for it?

Whatever the answer, I'd put off speaking with Peggy Morales long enough.

Chapter Twenty-Eight

I successfully extricated myself from Ros's house five minutes later. A friend called to check in on her, allowing me to make a graceful exit. I waved a wordless goodbye to my grief-stricken neighbor and headed home.

It was time to track down Peggy.

Sunlight bathed the deck, enticing me to set up my command center outside. I grabbed my laptop and settled into my favorite patio chair. Moments later, I found myself on the Central Shores government website. Clicking past all the promotions for Salute to Summer, including the patriotic countdown clock I'd helped Mom embed into the announcement bar, I made my way to the staff directory. Peggy Morales's photo was not your standard LinkedIn profile headshot. It featured her outdoors, in hiking gear, giving a friendly wave to the camera. I clicked on her name, and a short biography loaded. Peggy graduated from the University of Virginia with an environmental science degree before moving back to Central Shores to begin her public service career. She'd joined the parks department as an office admin, working her way up the ranks to Director. I stared once more at her smiling picture. Could Peggy have killed Larry if he threatened to ruin her reputation and storied career?

The Twitter threat floated through my mind. Was @meazur4meaz some hiking motto? How had Peggy even figured out I was looking into Larry's murder? Did Mom accidentally let something slip? It was possible.... They *had* been working closely together on Salute to Summer prep.

I dropped my head into my hands as the questions continued to swirl.

Maybe I'd made a colossal mistake dismissing Peggy's testy email, instead choosing to pursue the blackmail trail. Part of me knew why I had zeroed in so intently on the vague Reddit chat. I didn't want to believe another member of our community was capable of killing a person, especially over something as remediable as losing one's job.

If Peggy reached out to Larry as often as Ros made it seem, the parks director sounded pretty desperate. But then again, Ros was known to embellish the truth if the truth painted an unflattering picture of her husband.

The only way to figure out what was going on between Peggy and Larry was to ask Peggy myself.

I glanced at the clock in the corner of my laptop screen, wondering if I had time to track down Peggy before Amanda arrived to prep for our afternoon webinars. The perks of waking up early. It was only nine forty. Amanda wouldn't be here for at least another two hours.

I closed my laptop with a snap and gathered my things to bring inside. While I could leave my electronics on the deck without fear of them being stolen, I didn't want to chance an impromptu summer shower and have them ruined by rain.

Finding Peggy was my next task, and luckily, I had an insider source. I tapped her contact info on my cell and waited while the phone rang.

"Delia? What a pleasant surprise!" Mom gushed on the other end of the line.

Her obvious pleasure at receiving a call from her eldest daughter caused a twinge of remorse to reverberate through me. As a millennial, I wasn't conditioned to enjoy talking on the phone, always preferring to text rather than chat. But, clearly, my mother favored hearing my voice as opposed to reading my words.

"Hey, Mom. How's the week going so far?"

"Oh, just peachy."

I didn't miss the sting of sarcasm. "Are you down at town hall?"

"Oh, yes. Been here since seven thirty for two days in a row. We're being inundated with questions about Larry's death. Hardly anyone cares that the festival is kicking off on Friday."

I sympathized with her frustration. I knew from previous experience how it felt to have your hard work overshadowed by a murder. "Well, I'll promote the heck out of it while I'm hosting the golf tournament tomorrow."

"What?"

I chuckled at her strangled shock before bringing her up to speed on my latest gig.

"Well, that's wonderful news, hon. I can't wait to see you in action. The town council will be there since Salute to Summer is a sponsor." She lowered her voice, so perhaps she wasn't in the safety of her private office. "How are things with Jasper?"

I glanced out my kitchen window, spying on Jasper's condo up the road. "I haven't heard anything from him today, so I'm hoping no news is good news." I made a mental note to check in on him later. "Anywho," I continued, wanting to wrap this conversation quickly, "I'm on my way to a meeting,"—not entirely a lie—"and I have a few questions about Salute to Summer that I need clarification on before my hosting gig tomorrow. Any chance Peggy Morales is in her office so I can swing by and speak with her?" I grabbed my bag and headed for the door.

"The parks department is down at the beach, overseeing the setup of the grandstand. Not sure how long they'll be there, but you might have a better chance of catching Peggy near the Boardwalk than in the office." Mom used the rebranded term for the strip that the town council continually fought to implement. In a polarizing effort to make the strip sound more sophisticated, the council and wealthier residents of Central Shores referred to the town hub as the Boardwalk while the rest of us peasants still called it the strip.

"Perfect. Thanks, Mom. I'll try to find you and Dad at the tournament tomorrow."

We said our goodbyes just as I hopped into Jolly. I fired up the engine and set off for the strip, strategizing my next move. The beach was sure to be crowded, so I felt no fear about questioning Peggy in public. Besides, if she was Larry's killer, she already knew I was looking into his death because she'd have to be behind the threatening Twitter DM.

I pushed an image of Hudson from my mind. He would not be happy that I was throwing caution to the wind, but my insatiable desire to uncover the truth won out. Peggy's name had popped up one too many times throughout this investigation, and I needed answers.

I parked in the residential area and strolled toward the beach. As predicted, it was already crawling with tourists and beachgoers, towels and umbrellas covering nearly every inch of sand for the entire stretch. It made it easy to spot the dark contrast of the stage equipment at the southern edge of the main beach, where the grandstand was being erected.

I arrived near the construction site, shading my eyes with a hand as I scanned the crowd. A bright ginger ponytail caught my eye, and I spotted Peggy hunched over a clipboard with another colleague. Both sported the same forest green polo and tan shorts, looking more like park rangers than government bureaucrats.

"Excuse me, Peggy?" I called out, waving in her direction.

Peggy glanced up, sliding her polarized sunglasses down the bridge of her nose to get a better look at me. "Oh, hi, Coco. Haven't seen you around in a while. What may I help you with?" She paused to instruct her coworker with the clipboard before taking a few steps to close the gap between us.

Hmm, her neutral reaction didn't give me much to go on. If she'd sent me an online threat, wouldn't she be a little warier of my presence? "Hi, there." I smiled brightly. "I was wondering if I could ask you a few questions about Salute to Summer. I'm filling in for Jessica Barnes at tomorrow's golf tournament and wanted to make sure I did my best to promote the festival events."

"You mean the Hollywood princess bailed?" Peggy brushed the sand off her hands, her snark evident. She then chuckled. "Sure thing. Why don't we head over there where it's less chaotic?" She pointed a thumb toward a large tent next to the grandstand site.

"Lead the way." I didn't hesitate to accept her offer. The tent was still surrounded by buzzing activity, so I was hardly putting myself in harm's way by speaking to her. *Geez.* I shook my head as I walked behind her. I couldn't believe I was thinking these things about sweet Peggy Morales. Amateur sleuthing was a weird, twisty business.

Once under the relieving shade of the tent, Peggy put her hands on her hips. "Fire away."

I began the carefully crafted line of questioning I'd come up with during my drive. "Central Shores relies on the profits from Salute to Summer to fund the town budget, right?"

I detected a brief wrinkle in Peggy's nose. She obviously hadn't been expecting a question like this, and who could blame her? "That's correct."

"Town Council has gone all out promoting Salute to Summer this year. Ads, online features, radio spots, the works." I counted the marketing tactics off on my fingers. "Is that because the budget isn't where it needs to be? Is Central Shores in some kind of financial trouble?"

Peggy reached for the tip of her ponytail and gave it a nervous tug. "Coco, I'm not sure these questions are necessary for you to host a charity golf tournament."

"Did Larry Dunmer find something wrong with the budget? Was he planning to make a bunch of department cuts to resolve the town's financial issues?"

Peggy froze at the mention of Larry's name before narrowing a frosty glare in my direction. "You're not here about promoting the festival, are you?"

"I have it on good authority," I continued, ignoring her question, "that Larry planned to make serious changes to the parks department's budget."

"He did." Peggy folded her arms. "Although not because the town's in any financial crisis."

"Then why?"

Peggy's gaze turned haunted. "Because he wanted to punish me."

The vulnerability in her words made me stop short. "Punish you? Peggy, what happened?"

She sighed. "The first week Larry set up shop here, he summoned me to his office to 'chat' about my department goals." She shivered. "I'd barely sat down before he was perched on the desk in front of me, stroking my thigh.

I pushed his hand away, but when he reached for a second time, I stood up and headed for the door. I told him if he ever touched or even looked at me again, I would report him to Roger." Her chin quivered as her words petered out.

Larry's behavior was worse than I'd imagined. Based on what Ros told me, I'd thought Larry had likely made harassing comments toward Peggy. I hadn't even considered he'd been physical with her. "Oh, God. I'm so sorry."

She shook her head. "I should have told Roger right away, but not long after our encounter, I heard Larry talking to someone in the break room that *I* had been the one to come onto *him*. I-I-I was mortified. So, I decided to keep my head down. But then Larry started threatening me with budget cuts and overhauling the department." Peggy's fists balled at her sides. "He said he'd found a surplus of funding in my budget and that I was being irresponsible, hoarding it all. As if. I told Larry to show me the numbers, but he kept claiming state privilege or something ridiculous."

"When did you last speak with him about this?"

"Friday morning." Peggy sighed. "Larry cornered me in a conference room. He told me he'd consider revisiting my budget if I joined him for dinner one night." Her face contorted in disgust. "That was the final straw. I just couldn't work in those types of conditions, Coco. I couldn't let him bully me any longer."

My throat tightened. *Oh no.* Was this heading where I thought it was? Was Peggy about to confess to Larry's murder?

"I made an appointment with our HR rep, Linda Wright." Peggy's words cascaded out like a waterfall. "I spoke to her Friday afternoon, just before I left for the day. I showed her the emails Larry and I had exchanged and told her about our in-person interactions. Linda was going to launch a formal investigation on Monday. She said it could get messy but that I was doing the right thing by speaking up about his aggressive behavior." Peggy wiped a stray tear from her eye. "I know this is a terrible thing to say, but when I heard he was dead, I couldn't help but feel relieved. The investigation, the budget, my job...All my problems disappeared when he died."

I raised an eyebrow.

She saw the suspicion in my expression and scoffed. "Which is undoubtedly why the police asked me to come into the station earlier this morning."

"You've spoken with the police?" I was stunned. Here I was, giving Gavin and his team no credit at all when they'd already beaten me to the investigative punch.

Peggy bobbed her head. "Yes. I was grilled by both a county detective *and* Gavin. Gavin said they'd been granted access to Larry's emails the night before and had some questions about our terse exchange."

My heart skipped a beat. It sounded as though the warrant to search Larry's work computer had come through. I wondered if Gavin had found the Reddit notification buried in Larry's trash folder.

Peggy's scowl deepened. "It also came to their attention that I'd been 'harassing' Larry in the days leading up to his death." She crossed her arms, anxiety brewing in her gaze. "Someone believed the horrible rumors he was spreading about me."

Ros, no doubt. "So, the police think you killed Larry?" My heart raced. Yes, I'd believed the same when I'd arrived at the beach, but after speaking with Peggy...

"Sounds ridiculous, right? As if I'd throw away my life over that horrible man." Peggy's athletic frame trembled with indignation. "What's even more strange is that Detective Forester's entire line of questioning all rested on me attending the Vine party on Friday. Since I was on the guest list, it somehow made me guilty."

I nodded as if agreeing with the absurdity, but I knew full well why Detective Forester was focused on Vine. If Peggy had killed Larry, she would've had to pick up the murder weapon at the wine bar. I didn't recall seeing Peggy there, but with the considerable crowd, that didn't mean much.

"Did you attend the party?" I asked.

Peggy shook her head. "I went on a camping trip to unwind. With all the stress from Larry and Salute to Summer, I needed a break, or I was going to explode." She grimaced. "Of course, neither Gavin nor the detective seemed too convinced when I told them. I mean, a solo camping trip is hardly alibi material."

CHAPTER TWENTY-EIGHT

"They didn't believe you?"

Peggy's chin quivered again. "Detective Forester told me not to leave town." Her fear suddenly morphed into fiery anger. "As if I would drop everything and bail on a festival I've spent months working on."

Hope and anxiety simultaneously warred within me. If Detective Forester had told Peggy to remain in Central Shores, the police considered her a valid suspect. Maybe Jasper was totally in the clear. But chatting with Peggy had proved to me one thing: she wasn't Larry's killer. And there was no way I'd let an innocent woman take the fall for a crime she didn't commit. Not when I'd come this far in my own investigation.

"You don't have any proof you went camping other than your word? What about someone tending to the campsite?" I asked.

For the first time, Peggy smirked. "I didn't go to a designated campsite. I'm a bit of a camping snob. I just parked on the side of a road, took a hike, and found a spot up by Eldrich Pond."

My brow furrowed. "And you didn't see any other hikers?"

Peggy shook her head. "Nope. Just me and a beautiful summer sunset over the water. Man, I got some great pictures of the pond at night."

"Pictures?" My ears perked up. "May I see them?"

"Sure." She pulled her smartphone out of her pocket, unlocked it, and handed it to me.

My whole body hummed with anticipation. Peggy had the latest Google Pixel, which utilized GPS tracking to label the location of photos taken and stored in the Google Photos app. "Did you share these photos with Gavin or Detective Forester?"

She tilted her head. "No. I didn't see the point. They would have just accused me of adding old pictures to my camera roll to cover my tracks."

"Sure, you very well could have. But if you took these with your phone, it's a whole different story." I excitedly tapped on an image of a breathtaking golden moon, its reflection sparkling across the glassy waters of Eldrich Pond. "Google Photos records all kinds of data when you take a picture with your phone, including the location, time, and source." I pointed to the timestamp and geographic location embedded into the details of each photo.

"This info proves you took these photos the night Larry was murdered. These pics are your alibi."

Chapter Twenty-Nine

Peggy's mouth dropped open. "I had no idea that much detail was being tracked. I thought it only recorded when the photo was added to my library." She grabbed the phone, holding it an inch from her face. "Coco, I think you just saved my life. I've got to show this to Gavin. Thank you. Thank you!" She lunged forward and squeezed me in a fierce hug. "Omigod, I have to go." In a hassled frenzy, she gathered her belongings from a nearby chair and called out to the nearest worker. "Hey, Carlos, gotta take care of something. Be back before lunch, I hope."

She gave me a distracted wave as she dialed a number on her phone and took off across the beach toward the residential parking area.

I smiled at the bounce in her step. A weight had been lifted from her, but not from me. Once the police realized Peggy was miles away from town the night Larry had been killed and not attending the Vine party, would they be forced to shift their focus back to Jasper? Had I inadvertently set my friend up to take the fall for Larry's death by simply finding out the truth about Peggy?

As I walked back to the parking lot, my intestines felt like spinning knives. I'd come down here to confront Peggy as a suspect in Larry's murder, only to unequivocally clear her name. My list of potential suspects was, once again, unsatisfying blank.

I dialed Jasper's number as I approached Jolly, the call switching to Bluetooth once I was inside the car.

"Are you all right?"

Jasper's suspicious greeting had me chuckling. Apparently, I was surprising everyone by making phone calls instead of sending text messages. "I'm fine. I'm just checking in to see how you're doing."

"I've been waiting around for you to be at home. Where have you been all morning? I thought you had some webinar today?"

"I had an errand to run. I'm heading home from the strip now." I didn't feel like going into the details of my morning when Jasper obviously had something he wanted to share. "What's going on? Any updates about Larry?"

"Yes. You're speaking with a free, no-cloud-of-suspicion-hanging-over-me betch."

"What?" I squeaked, nearly veering off the road as I drove back toward Sunny Shores. "Tell me everything!"

"If you're on your way home, I'll just meet you in front of your house. This needs to be discussed over a spiked seltzer or something."

I glanced at the clock. "It's not even eleven."

"All right. Mimosas, then." With that, he hung up.

Instead of calling back and demanding answers, I drove a little more above the speed limit than usual, and five minutes later, I pulled into my driveway.

Jasper waited with an impatient glare on my front porch, tapping his foot.

"Start talking, and I'll start pouring," I ordered as I waltzed passed him to unlock the front door.

"Kimball called me this morning to let me know I'm officially off the hook." Jasper beamed with profound relief as he sank into a barstool.

My hand hesitated before grabbing two champagne flutes. "This morning? Like, what time?"

"Eight-thirty." Jasper shuddered at the early hour.

I swallowed. *Oh no.* What if the police had cleared Jasper only after speaking with Peggy and finding out about her flimsy alibi…that wasn't so flimsy anymore?

"Did Kimball tell you what made the police clear your name?" My words were a bit stilted.

Jasper's grin had a dastardly gleam to it. "Security footage."

I grabbed orange juice and a bottle of cheap, opened champagne from the fridge. "Security footage? From where?"

His devilish smile widened. "This is the juicy part I wanted to talk with you about. Did you know the Dunmers have been *spying* on us all summer?"

"What?" Orange juice splashed over the rim of Jasper's glass and onto the marble countertop.

He bobbed his head furiously as I wiped up the mess. "Turns out, Larry had cameras installed all over his property, all angled—not at his home—but at our condos! He's been keeping tabs on us for weeks."

I poured a liberal amount of champagne into Jasper's flute, opting to skip out on adding it to my glass. I still had three webinars to get through this afternoon. "How..." I had trouble forming the proper response to this weird and violating development.

Jasper quickly continued, "He wasn't using it for pervy reasons or anything like peeping in windows. He just wanted to make sure we were adhering to all the asinine rules he'd laid down for us."

I prayed Larry's cameras hadn't been recording my deck two nights ago when Hudson and I had spent an intimate evening in our hammock. Otherwise, whoever had the footage would be in for an R-rated shock. "How did the police find out about this?"

Jasper grabbed his drink and took a refreshing sip. "According to Kimball, it came out during Ros's interview. She told the police Larry had installed cameras around their home. They could review the recordings to confirm whether Larry ever made it back to Sunny Shores after the Vine party." He paused for another drink. "Come to find out, none of the cameras were set up to capture the Dunmer's property, so it was a bust on that front. All the police found was footage of *our* homes. But, lucky for me, the police have video of me arriving home at eleven thirty-one, going inside, and never leaving until you stopped by the next day."

I almost collapsed with relief. "That's incredible, Jasper. You have no idea how happy this makes me." I raised my glass of OJ, clinking the rim of Jasper's flute.

"Indeed. Not that it changes the whole *Variety* fiasco. I didn't make it out of this debacle completely unscathed." Jasper's features darkened. "Turns out, Detective Forester did reach out to check whether I had met their editor in Dover. Not a great look to have your interview followed up by a police inquiry. I asked Kimball if the police could call and retract their questions, but *that* request was denied."

I studied my best friend. Word about his possible involvement in Larry's murder had thankfully never spread too viciously around town, but his future had still been soured by the experience. "Their loss. Just think about what an outrageous chapter this will be in your memoir."

Jasper chuckled. "I'm already picturing Beyoncé's narration of it on Audible."

We continued sipping our drinks in companionable silence.

"Sooooo," Jasper finally ventured, "I feel like it is my duty as your best friend to officially relieve you from investigating this case going forward. My name has been cleared, which is what you set out to do."

A gloomy cloud of doubt hovered over me. "But *I* didn't clear your name. The police did."

"By conducting a *proper* investigation," Jasper pointed out. "They aren't as inept at their jobs as you think, Coco. You had me seriously believing they were going to railroad me for a crime I didn't commit." He gave me a sage, if searching, look. "I'm beginning to think you just convinced yourself of that so you could investigate on your own. Maybe it's time to get a vaccine or something for this mystery-solving bug you have."

A bubble of defiance swelled within me. I didn't like hearing that I'd purposely convinced my friend he was in danger of going to jail, simply so I had a reason to stick my nose into police business. But...was he right?

"I'm sorry, Jasper. After what happened with Stacy—I guess I thought I knew better than the police." I prickled in sudden defense. "And I *was* worried they'd come after you. They had evidence pointing to you, a solid motive, and opportunity. What friend wouldn't be concerned?"

Jasper waved his hand. "I know, Cokes. I know you went into this with the best of intentions. And I will forever appreciate it. But I need you to promise me you'll let the police take it from here. They are more than capable of tracking down a killer without your interference—*help*." He coughed as he corrected himself.

I sighed, staring at my nearly empty glass of orange juice. I regretted not adding champagne. "I have no problem promising you that because I'm at a complete dead-end myself. Everyone I've suspected either has an alibi or just doesn't feel like a killer."

Jasper snickered. "*Feel* like a killer? So what, have you got some connoisseur's eye when it comes to murderers now?"

I took the balled-up paper towel I'd used to wipe away the spilled orange juice and tossed it at his forehead. But before Jasper could retaliate, a knock sounded on my front door.

I glanced at the clock. "That's probably Amanda."

"Then that's my cue to let you get back to your regularly scheduled programming." Jasper slid off the barstool and followed me to the entryway. "I appreciate you going out on a limb for me, Cokes. I really do."

"I know." I rolled my eyes, not wanting to get all sentimental before a CoA webinar.

Amanda and Jasper exchanged quick, friendly greetings before I ushered her inside and waved goodbye to Jasper as he sauntered toward home.

"He seemed to be in good spirits," Amanda commented as she placed a Tumi messenger bag on the kitchen counter. Wowsa. Someone was ready to work in style. "Any news about the whole Larry thing?"

I filled her in on my visit to the Dunmers' house, my talk with Peggy, and Jasper's name being cleared as we began setting up for the webinar in my office.

Amanda released a low whistle at the conclusion of my recap. "You've covered a lot of ground today." She straightened the white photo screen, checking the iMac monitor to ensure it completely blocked the bookshelves and decorations I had hanging in my office. I used the photo screen to keep my clients focused on me speaking during a webinar and not zoning out, studying my office décor.

"I had an early start to the day." I studied her pensive expression. She seemed a little put out all of a sudden. It took me a few seconds to realize why. "I'm sorry I didn't wait for you before chatting to Ros."

Amanda dipped her chin in acknowledgment of my apology. "It's fine. I just feel like I let Hudson down by not keeping an eye on you." She chewed on her lower lip, her flawless red lipstick not even smudging. "And I also had fun yesterday. I get why you like doing this sort of thing."

I laughed. "I had fun, too. But since Jasper's been cleared, I have no reason to keep poking into Larry's death."

Amanda raised a coy eyebrow. "Are you sure? Jasper might be off the hook, but there's still a killer skulking around our hometown."

I shook my head and turned away from her, hiding the slight grin on my lips that she and I had been thinking *exactly* the same thing. Not only was Larry's killer still out there, but they had made a serious mistake by threatening to take me away from the people I loved. I could not let something like that go unchecked. Their Twitter warning also meant I was close enough to the truth to make someone nervous. I couldn't just give up. That wasn't my style. But I had no idea what else I could do to expose Larry's attacker...except tell Gavin about the unresolved blackmail note.

Did I *really* need to get myself in trouble by telling him about the Reddit chat, though? Jasper had made it very clear the police were taking this investigation seriously. They weren't rushing to judgment. Peggy had mentioned that Detective Forester and Gavin had gotten approval to access Larry's work emails. They'd probably found the Reddit notification in the trash already...right?

"Let's put a pin in this for now and talk CoA," I said, intent on changing the subject. "I'd like to introduce you at the beginning of each webinar, so clients can become familiar with you and put a face to the name once I start transitioning engagements and projects to you."

Amanda happily switched focus. "I was reviewing the PowerPoint you sent me last night, and I feel like I *might* be able to help run the third session once I see you in action a few times. You know, tag-team the two-thirty presentation? It would help me get my footing."

Surprised she was willing to take the initiative and jump in, I nodded with enthusiasm. It wasn't like I was giving a presentation on rocket science or anything. "How about I let you take the lead on the last session once I do introductions, and if you need help, just shoot the topic over to me?"

CHAPTER TWENTY-NINE

Amanda beamed. "Let's do this!"

It was four o'clock by the time Amanda departed. After our last presentation, we'd shared a pitcher of iced tea, taking some time to debrief. I couldn't have been more pleased by her performance during the webinars. Amanda exuded confidence and expertise on the subject and engaged the attendees with such ease. I was a little bit envious. I would never have believed she hadn't been doing this her whole life.

With plans to get together tomorrow after my hostessing duties at the golf tournament concluded, I bid Amanda goodbye and retreated into my office once she was gone. I wanted to review the post-session survey results before sending Amanda any additional feedback. After each online presentation, Zoom sent clients a survey about the speaker's performance, knowledge, and engagement on the subject matter, as well as recommendations for future areas of focus. I might have enjoyed Amanda's performance, but I wanted to see if clients caught anything I missed.

My phone chimed before the results loaded.

H: OMW w/ good news!

I glanced at the clock. Hudson was on his way home this early? Something big had to be up.

Seeing as I'd spoken with my mom and best friend on the phone and managed to survive their calls, I dialed Hudson's number. "Hey, there. Can you tell me this good news now?"

Hudson's velvety chuckle warmed me all the way down to my toes. "I suppose. I talked with Millie and showed her the video. She immediately took it to HR and demanded they suspend Tori and launch a full investigation. You were right, Cokes. Millie's got my back." His relief was evident.

Honestly, so was mine. While I wanted to believe Millie would do right by her employees, it felt good to hear confirmation of her ethics.

"Millie's giving me time off from the anchor desk to 'refocus and begin healing.' Her words, not mine." Hudson explained, as if I'd ever think he'd come up with such emotionally charged terms on his own. "She stressed it was in no way punitive. She wants me at my best for pitching our show later this week."

"That's wonderful, Hudson." I sagged against my desk chair, a torrent of emotions washing over me.

I could hear Hudson smiling through the wireless connection. "Be home soon, babes. I hope you're ready to celebrate. I love you."

"Love you, too. Drive carefully."

As I ended our call, I happily savored the big wins of the day. Not only had Jasper's name been cleared, but Hudson had finally been able to take action to protect himself against Tori's behavior.

Now, all I needed to do was figure out how to nab Larry's killer without them knowing I was still on the case. I massaged my temples in thought. I'd talk to Ros and Larry's former colleagues. Who did that leave?

A Gmail notification popped up on my desktop screen. I minimized the Zoom survey results and clicked the alert. It was a message blast about Salute to Summer. Mom's latest email campaign was making the rounds. I smiled as I read through the activities list, my attention caught by an image near the bottom of the email. It was a photo of Mayor Sullivan waving an American flag. The caption beneath him read, "Come see your favorite local figures in action at tomorrow's Swing Well, Save Lives tournament. Use #SalutetoSummer to show your Central Shores pride online."

A metaphorical lightbulb dinged above my head. I'd interviewed Larry's wife and colleagues, but I never tried speaking with his friends. Mostly because I didn't think he had any. But Larry *had* somehow managed to ingratiate himself with our new mayor, and he'd wiggled his way into Roger's inner circle with surprising ease. Was their friendship genuine, or was there something more unscrupulous at play?

"Don't worry, Mr. Mayor. I'll be there, ready to hashtag my heart out."

238

Chapter Thirty

The morning of the tournament, Hudson had a bagel toasted and smeared with cream cheese waiting for me by the time I finally emerged from the bathroom, dressed for my TV hosting debut. I'd opted for a pale pink blouse, linen slacks, and Chanel flats I'd scored from T.J. Maxx. The last thing I wanted was for a dress or skirt to blow up over my head on live television, so pants seemed like the safer choice.

"You look lovely." Hudson admired me as I gave him a runway turn. He'd joined me briefly in the shower and was already dressed in his usual golfing attire. Khakis and a striped blue-and-white polo. However, there was a noticeable difference in my man: his buoyant attitude. I hadn't seen Hudson this happy or carefree in a long time. It almost brought tears to my eyes, thinking about everything he'd gone through to get to this point. I was beyond thrilled that, together, we had vanquished Terrible Tori.

I tore my gaze away from his handsome smile and tugged self-consciously at my top. "You don't think this will wash me out on camera?"

Hudson chuckled, kissing my neck before replying, "No, this will contrast nicely with the green. That's why so many golfers wear light hues." He returned to his coffee mug.

I bobbed my head with a nervous glance at the clock. "I don't think I can eat anything, or I might be sick."

Hudson reached for my hand. "Take a deep breath. You're going to knock this out of the park. Just be yourself." He grinned. "The camera loves you."

I rolled my eyes but secretly basked in his praise. "It's been a long time since I've done anything like this in public." That was the beauty of being a social media influencer. All my work was done behind closed doors and with the right camera filter.

"I know. I remember how nervous you were before your big *Today* interview with Savannah Guthrie and Hoda Kotb." Hudson dumped the rest of his coffee down the drain and placed the mug in the dishwasher. "But I also remember how much fun you said you had after it was done."

"Okay, okay, you've convinced me." I laughed. "I'm awesome."

It was a twenty-five-minute drive to the Crestview Country Club, where the charity tournament was being held. Millie had asked me to arrive an hour and a half before the live broadcast kicked off, and since Hudson was participating in the tournament, we drove together.

Once we arrived at the picturesque green, I was whisked away to a trailer where three women hovered over me, touching up my makeup and hair. Well, not so much touching up, but completely starting over from scratch. I may blog about everyday makeup tips, but I had nowhere near the incredible skillset of these professionals when it came to styling a person for the silver screen. I watched in muted fascination as they transformed my face, contouring and highlighting my features with their superior abilities. No wonder celebrities on the red carpet always looked superhuman.

A production assistant stationed in the corner of the small trailer pressed her earpiece to her head before nodding. "Ms. Stabler is on her way to speak with you, Ms. Cline."

I couldn't nod in acknowledgment because one of the makeup artists was painting liquid mocha eyeliner on my lids in an understated cat's eye. "Black eyeliners often come off as too severe and aging on video, so we're going with more natural tones," she explained as she worked within an inch of my face.

Unable to move, I winced internally at my rookie error. I had come to set wearing midnight luxe eyeliner, as black always made my eyes pop in photos. Obviously, TV styling was a completely different ball game that I knew very little about.

My lips were being painted a rosy nude color when Millie arrived with her usual fanfare.

"Coco, darling," she drawled as she came up behind me so I could see her reflection in the mirror. "You look wonderful. The camera will not be able to get enough of you."

"Thanks, Millie," I mumbled incoherently, unable to move my lips as lipstick was applied.

"Everything okay?" She lowered her voice, although the makeup artists could obviously still hear her. "You, good? Hudson, good?" Millie was clearly speaking in code about the Tori situation.

"We're good. You?" I raised an eyebrow, the only expression I could muster without disrupting my makeup team.

"Trust me, Coco. I'm going to rain fire on that repugnant woman," Millie seethed through gritted teeth, her expression deadly convincing.

Even though Hudson had told me Millie had taken his side, it was good to hear confirmation for myself. "Good."

"Good." She gave a curt bob of her head. "Okay, so, once you're done here," she continued, giving me whiplash with her topic change, "head over to the sound tent. Gary will get you mic'd up, and then we'll kick off the pre-show."

"Pre-show?" I squeaked.

"Yes, I thought it might be nice for you to do in-depth sit-downs with some of the golfers. You know, *why* they've chosen their particular charity and such." She animatedly waved her hands like she was conducting the Royal Philharmonic Orchestra, not a local TV program. "We can then use those clips and replay them throughout the event when it gets undoubtedly boring."

Her "and such" didn't give me much clarity as to what else I was supposed to interview these golfers about, but I grunted my agreement. I knew from Hudson's personal experiences that there was no use arguing with Millie once she'd set her mind to something.

Fifteen minutes later, I thanked the makeup artists for their excellent work. With contour and highlighting, they'd somehow shaved at least five pounds off my face and enlarged the size of my sea-green eyes into a doe-eyed, innocent manner that male viewers found appealing—according to their own network research. The hairstylist had given me a beautiful French twist, a much more polished and sophisticated updo than the ponytail I'd arrived with. A final glance in the mirror made me feel like I could actually pull this off. I looked like a real TV host.

At the sound tent, Gary bashfully hooked up my mic, mumbling his apologies every two seconds as he snaked the wire up my back, under my shirt. I felt sorry for the poor guy. In the age of #MeToo and with people like Larry and Tori roaming the streets, Gary's actions could be construed as inappropriate *if* taken out of context. However, I assured him I knew this came with the territory and to not worry.

"Okay, Ms. Cline, I want to check your levels before we start the pre-show." Gary returned to his impressive soundboard. "Can you stand over there and just talk like you normally would?"

I followed the direction of his finger to the shade of a large tree looming at the side of the golf course. "Sure thing." I hurried over to the spot he indicated.

"Right there is fine," came Gary's voice in my ear.

"What do you want me to talk about?" I looked over to the sound tent.

"Anything is fine. Feel free to use the time to brainstorm ideas. And remember, you don't have to whisper or shout. Just talk like you normally would."

My mouth dried. I hated the open-endedness of his request because it made my mind go completely blank. "Okay..." *Hmm*, I could figure out how I was going to approach Mayor Sullivan, but I doubted that's what Gary meant by brainstorming. So, instead, I searched around the golf course, hoping to catch a glimpse of something I could talk about or read. *Read! Duh, Coco.* I could just read stuff on my phone.

I pulled my cell from the pocket of my slacks and checked my notifications for something to recite. Maybe a CNN news alert or something.

However, an email from Andre Nunez caught my eye.

"*Coco*," I spoke out loud, adhering to Gary's request that I could talk about anything. "*Please see the attached images. I'm posting a slew of pictures from*

Friday's party soon, and I'd love it if you could check them out beforehand. To see how I did with captions and hashtags, you know? I need to make sure the student really has become the master before I upload them on Vine's socials."

Gary's voice chimed in my ear. "Sounds great, Ms. Cline. You can head to set."

I gave him a thumbs-up before shooting a quick response to Andre.

I'd be more than happy to take a look. I'll try to get back to you within the hour.

With my sound check completed, I strolled over to the designated "set" for today's event. Production had roped off a roomy area of the green and situated a few director-style folding chairs in the center.

Millie stood in front of them, surveying the scene with a practiced eye. "Let's move some of the onlookers over here for the pre-show. Tell them it's an exclusive VIP area or something. Anything to make it look like people are actually happy to be here."

I chuckled as I arrived next to her. "You're not really a fan of golf, are you, Millie?"

She stuck her tongue out. "Whatever gave me away? Here, Coco, this will be your seat." She pointed to the chair on the far right. "Smith, take these other chairs away," she barked at a nearby gangly, pale PA. "I just want Coco to do a few one-on-ones for now."

While the chairs were removed, another PA held a piece of paper in front of my face.

"Ah, yes." Millie scanned the document before thrusting it back at me. "This is the updated roster of golfers. You're familiar with the names?"

"Updated?" My nose wrinkled.

Millie sensed the hesitance in my voice. "Did you not receive a list in the packet we sent you yesterday?"

I shook my head, already feeling bad for whoever dropped the ball.

Millie's cheeks ballooned with irritation. "Who failed to send Coco the list?" Her gaze snapped around to examine her scrambling assistants.

I grabbed her forearm to refocus her energy on me. "No need to worry, Mil. I recognize everyone here, so I won't be stumbling over unfamiliar names." I lowered my voice once she had calmed down. "But you mentioned this was updated. Did someone drop from the competition?"

Millie waved a hand. "You could say that. The dead guy, Larry Dunmer, was on our original lineup and didn't get taken off until last night." She grumbled under her breath, but loud enough for me to hear, "If you want something done right, you have to do it yourself."

"Really?" I stared down at the updated list. "Since when does being a state auditor make you a local celebrity?"

Millie snorted. "It doesn't. Someone, I can't remember who, pulled some strings higher than my paycheck to get him on the list. The guy had friends in high places. I'll give him that."

It was hard to believe that Larry had friends willing to call in such a strange favor. But then again, Darcy Atkins had mentioned seeing Larry out on the green with Roger Sullivan. Had Roger used his political influence to secure Larry a spot in the tournament? Why? My list of questions for the mayor continued to grow.

Millie's irritated voice yanked me from my thoughts. "But we don't have to worry about him anymore, now, do we?" With guiding hands on my shoulders, she plopped me down in my assigned chair for the foreseeable future. "For the pre-show, I figured we'll start you off easy." She smiled and waved to someone nearby.

Hudson materialized and took the seat next to me, giving my forearm a quick squeeze. "You ready?"

I chuckled. If I could make effortless chatter with anyone, it would be Hudson. "Ready."

With cameras rolling and production lights stationed around us to combat the natural shadows on the golf course, I summoned my inner talk show host and kicked off the pre-show by reading the teleprompter in front of me. "Welcome to the tenth annual Swing Well, Save Lives tournament, benefiting charitable organizations around the globe and here at home. I'm your host, Coco Cline. Today's broadcast is sponsored by Salute to Summer. Join us in Central Shores for an Independence Day tribute, the likes of which you've never seen." I flashed a bubbly grin at the camera, hoping my cheeks wouldn't split from the strain. "Before the first swing takes place, we're catching up with some familiar faces taking part in today's competition. I'm joined by Hudson Caruthers, WMTG's very own star news anchor."

The interviews that followed passed in the blink of an eye. Besides Hudson, I interviewed the resident golf pro at the Crestview Country Club, Delaware state senator Mark Tybert, and Jerry McClain, a bestselling fantasy author who lived in Cherry Springs. By the time I concluded the segment, my whole body thrummed with excitement.

"Flawless!" Millie squealed as she approached after we'd gone to commercial. "Jerry, thanks so much. Best of luck on the links. Coco," she said, turning her sharp gaze on me. "You were born for this." She didn't give me a chance to bask in her hyperbolic praise or to thank Jerry for his time off-camera. "Now, we must get you to your post by the first hole. The game tees off in ten minutes." She flagged down a golf cart driven by yet another PA. "Get Ms. Cline to the start, stat." She even pounded on the hardtop of the little vehicle for emphasis.

With an apologetic grimace at the skittish driver, I climbed into the cart. As we drove the length of the back nine, I busied myself with my phone, as I hadn't had time yet to attend to Andre's request. I downloaded the attachment he sent along with his email, having embedded the photos and their captions together in one document for easy access. I tapped on the first image to get a closer look. A glamorous, well-lit picture of Vine filled my screen.

Andre had selected a few pictures of the decorated wine bar before guests arrived, giving people an idea of the space his bar offered. With the caption, "**The perfect setting for any engagement**," he'd followed it with various wedding hashtags targeted at catching the eye of couples looking for reception venues.

"Not bad," I muttered to myself.

The next series of pictures were of Vine in full party mode. I blushed at the first photo. It featured me, Charlotte, and Jasper, laughing with our wine glasses raised in the air, a blurry crowd out of focus in the background. *Wow.* It was an effortlessly chic photo, capturing Vine's classy, fun essence. I made a note to ask Andre for a copy. This pic of my fabulous besties deserved to be framed on my desk.

I started swiping through the other photos, all of them equally high caliber. Andre had done an amazing job at curating the images to showcase the ambiance of his bar.

Yet, even all the filtering and contrast in the world couldn't hide the hideous Hawaiian shirt floating in the background in a shot featuring four glamorous Mill Row residents sharing a laugh over a plate of hors d'oeuvres.

Larry. I grimaced at the sight of his fuming jowls in the background. I studied his blurry expression a little longer. Man, if looks could kill. I wondered who had been on the receiving end of his glowering anger. *Probably me or Jasper,* I thought with a snort.

I was just about to examine the final image Andre had sent when my golf cart driver deposited me at the first hole, and I was forced to put my phone away.

A wall of very familiar golfers greeted me with warm smiles and mild-mannered clapping.

"So, you're the one who stepped in to save the day!" Arthur Bushman helped me out of the golf cart. "Amanda refused to tell me who the studio got to replace Jessica Barnes. Now I know how she found out before me."

"I hope you're not too disappointed," I teased, giving Arthur a warm hug in greeting.

Amanda's tech genius husband beamed. "When you're involved? Impossible to be disappointed."

"I'm just glad we have someone hosting a *local* celebrity golf tournament who's actually a local." Mayor Sullivan broke away from the crowd and shook my hand.

I didn't get a chance to respond to Roger's comment before another recognizable face stepped in.

"Imagine the flack a Hollywood star would give us for thinking we were anything to write home about." Fred Beaufort winked at me.

I laughed, knowing the restaurant owner had hit the all-too-humbling nail on the head. If Jessica Barnes had turned up here and seen whom the surrounding communities considered to be "celebrities," she probably would have turned around and headed back to the airport faster than you could say SAG Award winner.

"I would have enjoyed putting the young upstart in her place." Former mayor Melvin Beaufort joined his brother, puffing his chest out.

The other golfers nodded their agreement, all save Lloyd McInnis. The police chief looked particularly put out by my arrival and barely acknowledged me before stomping away to do some practice swings. Since his hopes of meeting Jessica Barnes had been dashed, I decided not to take his rudeness too personally.

Hudson arrived by my side, draping an arm around me as he whispered in my ear. "I watched the footage you got during the pre-show. It's great, Coco. Millie is over the moon and ready to offer you a full-time correspondent gig."

I grinned with anticipation, my adrenaline from the pre-show fueling my positive energy and keeping my nerves at bay. Today had the potential to be a lot of fun. But I needed to find time to chat with Mayor Sullivan about his friendship with Larry. If anything, maybe he had some idea about who had it out for his new golfing bestie.

Ethan, the PA who'd driven me over in the golf cart, cleared his throat behind me. "Excuse me, everyone, we're about to get started. Golfers, please remain in this area until you are called forward. Ms. Cline? If you'll come with me."

"Good luck!" Hudson and I both mouthed to each other.

"We have a prompter set up with your introduction," Ethan continued to explain. "At the end, you'll send the viewers to our panel of golf pros, and then you'll have some downtime until our first commercial break. Just listen for us in your earpiece, and we'll let you know when it's time. You'll return to this same spot."

I nodded understanding as we arrived at another roped-off area, a growing crowd of onlookers gathered around.

Two figures in the back waved wildly at me from the sea of faces. I had to squint to make them out clearly.

From what I could see, Jasper and Charlotte were decked out in their country club finest. Jasper in a polo and sports coat and Charlotte in a form-fitting aquamarine sundress. Next to Charlotte, I spied Deacon, looking equally dapper in a polo and golf cap.

I waved, letting them know they had been spotted, but I had to turn to face the teleprompter to kick this whole shebang off.

"Hello, WMTG viewers, and welcome to the tenth annual Swing Well, Save Lives tournament…."

Chapter Thirty-One

I made it to the end of my spiel without stumbling too badly over the words the prompter threw at me. After sending viewers to the panel of golf experts and their commentary on the first hole, a WTMG producer gave me a thumbs-up from behind the camera. "We're clear."

My shoulders slumped in relief as I reached for a water bottle Ethan had set aside for me. Taking an eager gulp, I savored the cold liquid. The marathon of speaking had my mouth feeling like the Sahara Desert. It had been much harder to stand here and talk by myself than to chat conversationally with the golfers during the pre-show.

"Ms. Cline, return to this spot in thirty minutes, please," an unfamiliar voice instructed through my earpiece. "It's been decided that you'll welcome us all back from our first commercial break."

Nodding to no one in particular, I lifted the rope barricading me from the sea of spectators. Folks were now moving closer to the first hole to watch the start of the game, so it was easy to navigate the thinning crowds toward the spot my friends had claimed.

"We have no idea what you were saying to the camera, but you looked good doing it." Charlotte hopped up from the ground and gave me a one-armed hug as I arrived at their little picnic area.

"Yes, a Maria Menounos in the making." Jasper lounged in a collapsible chair, a hat covering his pale face. "Your mom and dad were also here for a bit, but then Moira had a Salute to Summer emergency pop up, and Simon went with her."

I winced at this development. I hoped everything was all right and that

Mom was just being extra sensitive about the festival. My mother had a tendency to blow things out of proportion—I know, Pot meet Kettle.

Deacon remained seated atop the blanket he and Charlotte had been cuddling on moments ago. "Hey, Coco." He smiled at me as Charlotte returned to his side. "I thought I'd see you around the station a bit more these past few days than I have."

Jasper handed me a chilled bottle of Perrier that I accepted gratefully. "Why?" I asked Deacon.

Deacon pointed to Jasper. "Well, since he's been persona non grata in the Dunmer case, I'd have thought you'd be all over Gavin and the chief about it. In fact, both have mentioned more than once how odd it is that you haven't decided to butt in to clear a friend's name. Especially after you did it for a client."

My cheeks burned under the layers of foundation expertly applied by the makeup team. "I didn't think it was appropriate to bother them," I replied as demurely as possible.

Deacon continued to stare at me expectantly. Why did I feel like I had walked right into a trap?

"Before you say anything further, Cokes—" Charlotte's crimson cheeks mirrored the color mine felt like they were. "I *may* have filled Deacon in on some of your recent exploits."

I shot an accusatory glare at her. "You sold me out?"

"Don't get too mad at her, Coco." Deacon chortled. "She didn't cave until I grilled her yesterday afternoon to see what you knew."

My hands went to my hips. "How did you know I was looking into things?"

"Things clicked into place for Gavin and me around the time Peggy Morales came rushing into the station, shoving her phone in our faces. She showed us the GPS details embedded into all her recent Google Photo files." A smile curved on Deacon's full lips. "When she mentioned *you* were the one to point all this out to her, we figured you had to be up to something. Otherwise, why would you be talking to a person of interest in a murder investigation about the night Larry Dunmer was murdered?"

I couldn't meet Deacon's twinkling gaze.

Jasper slid down his sunglasses and eyed me knowingly. "See? I told you that at least some of the Central Shores PD have a clue."

"So..." I folded my arms across my chest, feeling incredibly foolish and self-conscious. "How much did you tell him?" I glanced at Charlotte.

"I only told him you *thought* Larry was blackmailing someone and that you were trying to figure out who." Charlotte's pleading expression had me forgiving her in an instant. I couldn't be mad at her for being honest with her boyfriend.

"Yes, although Char has failed to mention *why* you think your neighbor was part of an extortion scheme." Deacon's narrowed gaze bounced from his blushing girlfriend to my stoic mask. "*But* after digging into Larry's recent communications, we did find something on Reddit, of all places, to corroborate your theory."

"Really?" My voice squeaked in a traitorous fashion. "Guess my hunch was right then."

The corners of Deacon's lips twitched. "Chill, Coco. I'm not here to berate you. I'll leave that to Gavin. But next time you're sitting on some helpful intel, clue us in a little sooner, will you?"

Stunned that he wasn't reaming me out for breaking probably fifty laws, I relaxed. "I wish I had more to share, but I didn't get very far investigating Larry's blackmail scheme."

Charlotte shuddered. "Blackmail, murder...this is Central Shores, not an episode of *The Wire*. It's scary to know Larry's killer is still out there, walking free around our hometown."

"Not for long, I hope." Deacon pulled her close to him. "This stays between the four of us, but Gavin submitted an emergency disclosure request to the Reddit legal team. We should have some data retention info on the user Larry was blackmailing in a day or two."

A day or two. I stared out across the golf course. A day or two seemed like a long time to wait around for Larry's killer to be apprehended. What if the killer decided to strike again? What if other people were unknowingly involved in Larry's blackmail scheme? Were they also in danger?

"So, you're just in limbo?" Jasper asked the question I'd been thinking.

Deacon shrugged. "You'd be amazed by how much police work is spent waiting around for information to come through. I mean, look how long we had to hold off on going public with the details of this case. We were practically sitting ducks until next-of-kin was notified. To say nothing of the special warrant Gavin had to obtain to access Larry's government emails."

I bobbed my head in acknowledgment. My way of sleuthing certainly had been more expeditious. "But there must be something more you could do in the meantime? Interview everyone who attended the Vine party, see if they saw anything suspicious?"

"We've already spoken to most of the people Mr. Nunez invited—"

"Ms. Cline?" a voice buzzed in my earpiece. "This is just a time check. We need you back at your post in twenty minutes."

"—with all the wine that was consumed, it was hard to get a clear picture of the evening, to begin with."

I caught the end of Deacon's reply, having missed most of what he said due to the PA in my ear.

Charlotte tilted her head in concern. "What's wrong, Coco?"

"Nothing. I just have to report back to my spot in twenty minutes." I tapped my earpiece. "Sorry, Deacon, I missed what you said about interviewing people from the party."

Deacon pointed to Jasper. "Other than the altercation Larry had with you guys, no one had much to say about the Dunmers." He shifted on the ground and pulled out his cell, which buzzed in his palm. "Lait, here. Really? Okay. Give me a sec." With a hand covering the mic of his smartphone, Deacon rose from the picnic blanket. "Gavin's checking in. I'm gonna head somewhere a little more private."

Jasper and I shared disappointed looks with one another as Charlotte gave her boyfriend an encouraging wave.

"Seems pointless to slink off like that." Jasper snorted. "He knows we're going to bug him senselessly over whatever Gavin's calling about, right?"

Charlotte threw him a reprimanding look. "You will do no such thing. You're a free man now, Jasper. There's no need for us to concern ourselves with this case anymore."

252

I raised my eyebrows in question. "But *you* just said that Larry's killer is still out there. Roaming the streets of Central Shores, plotting who knows what." All right, Charlotte hadn't said *that* much, but still. "Aren't you the least bit curious as to who did in our ornery neighbor?"

Before she could respond, Jasper scoffed. "I'm curious who tried to *frame* me for it."

"I'm sure the police will get the job done."

Charlotte sounded a lot more confident than I felt.

"But what if they're too late?" I countered. "What if his killer decided to skip town? By the time the police track down the Reddit user Larry was blackmailing, they could be halfway to the Caribbean. *My* investigation could have scared them off." I prayed that wasn't the case, or I'd feel horrible for the rest of my life.

"The Caribbean?" Jasper chuckled darkly. "You make it sound like a James Bond villain did in Larry."

I shrugged. "It would have to be someone with money if Larry was blackmailing them."

My phone hummed in the pocket of my slacks while Jasper and Charlotte debated prodding Deacon for more information about the case. I had a text from Andre.

Hey, gurl. Checkin 2 see if u can sign off on those pics? I want 2 upload & tag peeps b4 S2S kicks off. U know, drum up buzzzz.

I smiled at his informal message. **Hey, Andre. Yes, I reviewed ur email. Pics look great! Upload & tag away!**

A thumbs-up emoji popped up on my screen.

"Ms. Cline?" the deep voice rang through my ears once more. "We need you back in fifteen."

I nodded as if the voice in my head was somehow looking down upon me.

"You agree with him, Cokes?" Charlotte's expression looked like a mix between mortification and disappointment.

"What?" I glanced between my two friends. Jasper stood with his arms folded across his chest. Charlotte had risen from her picnic blanket and stood with her hands on her hips. Neither looked happy with the other.

"I'm sorry, I have no idea what's going on here." I tapped on my earpiece again in apology.

Charlotte huffed. "Jasper was just complaining that my boyfriend is too—" she cut short and pulled out her phone. "Oh, it's just an Instagram notification."

Jasper and I checked our buzzing phones as well.

Instagram tag notifications cluttered my screen. "Andre must have been chomping at the bit. I bet these are the Vine pics from the party going live." I swiped open the app. "You guys have to see a total glam shot of us. It's legendary."

Their own vanity won out as Charlotte and Jasper scanned their phones for the photo instead of pursuing whatever topic they'd been fighting about.

"Wow!" Charlotte's jaw dropped.

"Wow, indeed." Jasper's grin widened. "We look like we could be on a vodka billboard."

I admired the photo of the three of us on my feed. "This is definitely the best of the bunch. I'm glad Andre led with it." I noted that our handles had been tagged, meaning anyone connected with Charlotte, Jasper, or myself could be drawn to Vine's Instagram profile and, thus, Andre's business.

"You taught Andre well." High praise from Jasper. "All these shots look gorg."

Charlotte bobbed her head. "Yeah, Andre clearly captured the festive vibe of the evening."

Her statement subconsciously resurfaced something Deacon had mentioned earlier in our conversation before departing to take his call.

"—with all the wine that was consumed, it was hard to get a clear picture...."

Clear picture, clear picture...

"Wait a sec," I yelped aloud. We had a ton of clear pictures right here in our hands. "Maybe there's something in these photos that could help us figure out who might have had it in for Larry."

Both Jasper and Charlotte gave me funny looks.

"Hear me out. Take a look at this pic." I showed them the photo of the Mill Row darlings having a laugh, with a brooding Larry hovering in the background. "See his face?"

Jasper examined the image. "Larry always looked like that when he wasn't ogling a woman's assets. I doubt he's staring down his worst enemy."

"See if he's in the back of any of the other shots." I ignored Jasper's ribbing.

"Um, Coco?" Charlotte's voice trembled. "Take a look at *this*."

She flipped her phone screen toward me. She'd already swiped through the carousel of images, displaying the last photo Andre had uploaded.

It was one I hadn't seen. I'd either overlooked it in the email Andre sent, or he'd added it later. Either way, it was a snazzy, black-and-white number of Mayor Roger Sullivan and our former mayor, Melvin Beaufort. A changing of the guard shot. Each man was laughing, hands clapping each other on the back. Andre had shadowed the background so that it made for a nice portrait. Nothing, though, to tell me what had been happening in the restaurant at the time it was taken. It certainly hadn't captured Larry anywhere in the shot.

"What am I looking for?" I raised a finger to zoom in on the image when my heart shuddered to a brief stop. Instead of zooming, I'd tapped the photo by accident. The tagged accounts in the picture popped up. Andre had tagged each man using their personal Instagram handles. Roger Sullivan was marked by @golfgreenwithenvy, likely an ode to his love of the sport. Melvin Beaufort was tagged as—

"@merchofvenice!" A strangled gasp escaped my lips as I met Charlotte's wary expression. "That's practically the same Reddit account Larry was blackmailing!" Still using Charlotte's phone, I clicked on Melvin's handle and pulled up his profile. Under his name and preferred pronouns, his short bio read, *Retired politico. Philanthropist. Lover of golf, whiskey, and Shakespeare.* "Omigod, guys. We might be onto something."

Handing Charlotte back her device, I used my own phone to pull up the image of the two mayors. With quivering fingers, I zoomed in closer, noticing Melvin was clutching something in his left fist. Since I didn't have Hudson's high-tech photo-enhancing software at my immediate disposal, I used my nifty trick from the days before Instagram allowed users to zoom in on images. I took a screenshot of my iPhone, capturing the picture of the two men, and then opened the saved screenshot in my Photos application. It took mere seconds of image sharpening to see what Melvin clutched in his hand: A braided corkscrew bearing the name *Jasper Hastings*.

Chapter Thirty-Two

"Holy Harry Styles." I released a low whistle as I shared my findings with my friends.

Jasper stiffened at my side. "That slimy piece of—"

"You guys, we have a *clear picture* of what happened right in my hand." I stared at the enhanced image as a stunned silence settled over us. The evidence beaming up from our phones suggested Melvin Beaufort, Central Shores' former mayor, had taken my friend's party favor and stabbed Larry Dunmer in the neck.

Shuffling back to Vine's Instagram post, I added, "This is too big of a coincidence. Melvin had to be the one Larry was extorting. The Reddit account Larry sent his threat to is almost the same as Melvin's Insta username." Yet, it was different enough that Melvin's profile hadn't come up in my Google search for u/merchnt_of_venyce.

"What did our old mayor do to warrant blackmail?" Jasper asked.

Charlotte and I shrugged.

"Do you think it's something related to Stacy Lockner?" Charlotte suggested, twirling a strand of her amber hair in thought.

I recalled how Beaufort had handed in his resignation shortly after I told Chief McInnis about the mayor's possible affair. "Maybe. Or perhaps it has something to do with the town budget. Larry could have stumbled across something shady while doing his audit."

"What do we do?" Jasper waved his phone in our faces. "Do we call the police?"

"Why don't I go find Deacon and show him what we've found," Charlotte countered. "That way, neither of you gets on the chief's bad side for poking your nose where it doesn't belong." She stared at Jasper and me pointedly.

"Fine. But hurry up. I need to get back to my hosting spot soon." I glanced at the time in the corner of my iPhone.

Charlotte nodded and took off toward the clubhouse, where Deacon had gone.

"I can't wrap my brain around this." Jasper's head hung from his shoulders. "Why would Melvin want to frame *me* for murder? What have I ever done to him?"

I patted him on the shoulder. "I know this probably sounds silly, but try not to take it too personally. No doubt, he witnessed the argument between you and Larry. Between your harsh words and Larry's threats, you literally *teed* up the perfect motive."

Jasper gave me a critical glare, not at all impressed with my pun.

With a light smirk still on my lips, I turned my attention toward the cluster of people gathered along the first hole. Were they nearing completion? Scanning the crowd, I found Hudson standing among a group of tournament participants, chatting away. Arthur was there, and so were Roger and Fred. Where had Melvin gone?

I spotted the former mayor making his way through the onlookers, barely bothering to acknowledge the claps on the back he received, I supposed, for his performance. In fact, he barely noticed anything. His heated gaze appeared to be glued to his phone.

I gripped Jasper's arm before glancing down at my cell. Vine's post of Roger and Melvin still occupied the screen. Yet, when I again tapped the picture for more details, only Roger Sullivan's @golfgreenwithenvy handle showed. My gaze darted back to Melvin's somber features as he pushed through the crowd. He'd already untagged himself as @merchofvenice.

My breathing quickened as I typed in the username in the Instagram "Discover" feature. "No! He's even deleted the account."

Jasper followed my wide-eyed gaze as the former mayor worked his way toward the edge of the crowd. "Coco, I think he's making a break for it."

Melvin Beaufort definitely wasn't heading in the same direction as the other golfers. He appeared to be snaking his way toward the parking lot, not the second tee.

"Ms. Cline? We need you back in five." The deep voice in my earpiece nearly gave me a heart attack.

Ignoring the command, I grabbed Jasper's hand and pulled him away from the shade of the tree. "Come on. I have an idea."

With Jasper in tow, I hurried along the golf course, parallel to Melvin's path, but being careful to keep the horde of onlookers between us.

Jasper, a good seven inches taller than me, kept me apprised of Melvin's location among the crowd. "I think we can intercept him near your little hostess area."

Choosing to ignore the slight drip of snark lacing his "little hostess area" comment, I moved faster, glad I had worn flats to traverse the golf course terrain.

We arrived at the small, roped-off production set, where I was required to report in less than three minutes. How fortuitous. I did like to be early, after all.

Beaufort pushed through the last of the stragglers beginning to make their way to the second tee and stepped onto the soft turf only a few feet ahead of us.

"Hi, Melvin!" I waved cheerily, giving him my most charming smile. I searched wildly around for a way to prevent the older man from leaving. Jasper and I only had to detain him long enough for Charlotte to fill Deacon in on what we'd discovered. "Can I get a quick interview about how the first hole went for you?" I pointed at the lone blinking camera to which I'd delivered my welcome message, relieved it was powered on to sell my lie. Hudson had explained that all cameras were to be left on during the tournament, their footage being monitored and selected for broadcast from the production booth.

Melvin released a flustered sigh. "Sorry. I need to use the restroom before the next hole."

Jasper pointed in the opposite direction Melvin had come from. "Bath-rooms are over there, Beaufort. Looks to me like you're heading toward the parking lot."

Melvin puffed up at Jasper's clipped reply. "I need to swing by my car to get a granola bar." He looked at me, seeking sympathy. "You know, low blood sugar and all."

I nodded with sage understanding. "Craft services is over there." I pointed to a table overflowing with delicious goodies not far away from where we stood now.

"I really just want my granola bar." Melvin made to bypass Jasper and me.

"I have a granola bar." Jasper reached for his back pocket. "Since I know you enjoy taking my things and using them to meet your own needs."

Melvin's brow furrowed with annoyance. "What in the world are you talking about?"

Instead of pulling a granola bar from his pocket, Jasper held his phone in front of Melvin's flushed face. "Looks like you made off with something of mine from the Vine party."

I didn't need to see the screen to know Jasper was showing the former mayor the incriminating Instagram pic.

Melvin's jowls slackened, and his ruddy skin drained to pale white. "W-whatever do you mean? This is just a photo of me holding my party favor from Andre."

Based on his stunned tone, I suspected that Melvin hadn't even seen the traitorous details etched into the corkscrew when he'd untagged himself from the photo. He'd been spooked by the mere use of his telltale Insta handle. "Actually, it's not *your* party favor, Mr. Mayor." I showed him the enhanced image on my phone, the name *Jasper Hastings* staring back at us.

"So, I took the wrong party favor by accident." Melvin shrugged, but his forehead brimmed with rivulets of glistening sweat. "There's no crime in that."

"Oh, the crime isn't that you *took* the corkscrew," Jasper seethed between his teeth. "The crime is that it ended up in Larry Dunmer's neck a few hours later."

Melvin's gaze narrowed sharply as he straightened.

"You witnessed the heated confrontation between Larry and Jasper," I continued where Jasper had left off. "You heard Larry threaten to upend Jasper's career at the party. So, when Jasper failed to take his engraved party favor, you scooped it up, figuring you could kill Larry, and Jasper would be blamed."

Melvin just stood there, his entire body shaking. Either with anger or fear, I couldn't yet guess.

"You killed Larry because he was blackmailing you," Jasper growled. "He had something on you that you couldn't risk getting out."

A piece suddenly clicked into place as Larry's message to u/merchnt_of_venyce danced through my thoughts. *Bring me a big ol' check tomorrow night to cover your missed payments, or I'm going to the police. I've kept silent long enough. Time's up.*

"No..." I trailed off a moment while my thoughts arranged themselves into a coherent fashion. "You killed Larry because you couldn't afford to continue paying him for his silence." Larry must have sent the threatening message because he was getting antsy over not receiving payment. The memory of Sunday brunch with my mother filled my mind. Melvin hadn't been working at his little brother's restaurant because he wanted to help the family business and give Fred a break. He needed the extra cash to pay Larry.

Melvin stood his ground. "This is the most ridiculous thing I've ever heard."

"Then it's just a huge coincidence that your—since *deleted*, mind you—Instagram account is @merchofvenice, and Larry was sending blackmail letters to practically the same Reddit user?" I countered.

Melvin visibly swallowed but did not break. "Yes, of course. I barely even know what Reddit is."

"Then why did you send me a message warning me to stop looking into Larry's death?" I snapped back.

"Wait, what?" Jasper whipped his head in my direction.

Oops. I'd yet to tell my bestie—or anyone—about receiving the nasty Twitter DM.

Eh, I'd fill him in later. For now, I kept my focus on Melvin. "You knew

I was looking into the matter after you and Fred dropped by my table at Brewed to Perfection on Monday." That was why the Twitter account @meazur4meaz sounded familiar. I finally remembered where I'd seen the unabridged phrase before. *Measure for Measure* was a lesser-known Shakespeare play, but one an aficionado would most certainly appreciate. The title had been wedged among the results when I'd Googled the Reddit username to no avail.

Melvin suddenly chuckled. "Goodness, the police must be more desperate than I thought if they're hiring social media consultants instead of real detectives." He sighed. "But no one listened to me when I said we should relocate everything to the county level."

"The police know Larry was blackmailing someone, and they'll soon have definitive proof the Reddit account was accessed from your home IP address," I lied with unabashed confidence. I had no idea what Reddit information the police could trace, but my theory sounded believable enough.

Melvin's left eye twitched involuntarily. He must have believed in my bravado, too.

"Coco," a warm, familiar voice whispered in my ear. But it wasn't the PA who had been reminding me to report back to my designated spot. It was Hudson. "Deacon is en route, and so are the chief and Gavin. Keep Melvin talking. Ask him why Larry was blackmailing him. Make Larry out to be in the wrong."

I stared at the camera for a moment, the continuous beam of red light no longer blinking. "Um, are we on the air?" I whispered into my mic.

My body relaxed under the magic of Hudson's chuckle. "Leave it to you to confront a killer on live TV."

I didn't miss the fear and anxiety simmering underneath his teasing comment. Jasper and I had to be careful how we proceeded.

I shot a warning look at my bestie, willing him to let me take the lead. "I just can't believe Larry resorted to blackmailing such an esteemed member of our community. How could he stoop so low?"

Jasper's eyebrows rose. "Have you met the man?"

I resisted a slight grin. I could always count on my BFF to know when he needed to play along in a charade. "Being a horrible neighbor was one thing. But blackmailing one of Central Shores' most respected residents?" I stretched out an arm toward Melvin.

Melvin lifted his chin as if trying to prove he still had some dignity left. "Dunmer was about as egotistical and self-serving as they come. He thought he was such a big shot, rifling through the town's finances and telling us all how to use our money."

Our money? I frowned at Melvin's off-the-cuff remark. Melvin hadn't been in office when Larry began his audit. What money did Melvin have from his time as mayor that Larry would be interested in?

I frantically searched the inventory of information I'd collected while looking into Larry's death. I needed to keep Melvin talking to find out what he'd done to warrant extortion. I found myself comparing Larry's time in Rockaway, where he'd found extra money in the budget and left with the higher-ups being happy, to his berating of Peggy for her department's surplus, an accusation she vehemently denied.

The solution suddenly seemed clear as day. "Larry found financial discrepancies tied specifically to *your* office. But instead of doing his job and reporting the missing money to the authorities, he began extorting you."

Melvin scowled. "That's enough, Ms. Cline. We're done here."

I'd clearly hit a sore spot to make Melvin so uncomfortable. "Not only was Larry blackmailing you, but he was also trying to cut the parks department budget to cover the hole you left, committing fraud himself in the process. Was that your idea or his?"

"His, of course!" The words were out of Melvin's mouth before he realized what he'd said. "I-I..." He trailed off and slumped in knowing defeat. "I didn't want anything more to do with that man, but I couldn't very well turn him into the state department for embezzlement...."

Jasper and I exchanged satisfied looks. "Without implicating your own crimes," I finished off.

Before Melvin could say anything further, a shadow loomed from behind us. "Melvin Beaufort," thundered Chief McInnis, still clad in his golfing attire as he appeared beside me. "You're under arrest for the murder of Larry Dunmer."

The chief rattled off Beaufort's Miranda rights while Gavin swooped in behind the former mayor and cuffed him. As Jasper and I watched with elated relief, I noticed a crowd beginning to swell around us. Whatever was happening on the second tee was clearly not as entertaining as what was going on here.

"I don't remember this being anywhere in your CoA consulting contract," Chief McInnis muttered under his breath so that only I could hear him.

I glanced sheepishly up at him, only to find that his stormy gaze had a playful twinkle to it. "How did you all get here so fast?"

Deacon came up on the chief's right as Gavin escorted Melvin off the green. "Gavin called me from the squad car. He was already on his way here since he knew Melvin was playing in the tournament. Because we submitted an emergency request last night, Reddit came through with the account data pretty darn quick. From there, the county tech guys were easily able to trace Melvin through his internet service provider and IP address."

I shook my head in wonder. I actually hadn't been that far off in my guess.

"We planned to question Melvin *quietly*," Deacon said with a smirk, "but then Charlotte found me and showed me the pictures from Vine's Instagram page."

Charlotte popped out from behind her boyfriend's tall, muscular frame and gave a tinkering wave. "Deacon and I tracked down the chief on his way to the second hole and were bringing him up to speed when Hudson called me."

"That sounds like my cue." Hudson gave me a sexy grin as he snuck under the rope barrier, keeping the crowd at bay on the other side. "After finishing the first hole, I went to the broadcast tent to chat with Millie. I spotted you and Jasper on Camera 2 talking to Beaufort. Millie and I listened to your mic, and when we realized what was going on—"

"Hudson called me as to your whereabouts," Charlotte finished with a triumphant smile.

I raised one eyebrow Hudson's way, knowing he was omitting another

264

important detail. "And?"

"And?" Deacon, McInnis, and Charlotte all parroted.

Hudson avoided eye contact with the police chief. "And…started broadcasting the takedown for our viewers. Millie wants to use it as a teaser for our new crime show."

Chief McInnis's jaw dropped dangerously close to the grass.

Jasper held his phone up to me. "#CocoClineStrikesAgain is already trending on Twitter."

Hudson chuckled. "I left the broadcast tent just as Millie was fielding calls from MSNBC and CNN."

I slowly turned to face Chief McInnis, steeling myself for an eruption of anger, only to find the disgruntled man shaking his head in disbelief.

"You know, it would be really nice if Central Shores could solve a murder without having it end up on national news."

Epilogue

"And without further ado, enjoy Salute to Summer, folks!"

Brilliant canopies of fireworks burst high overhead, drowning out the cheers from Mom's speech at the beachside grandstand. The opening Friday night celebration was officially in full swing.

I leaned into Hudson's comforting embrace and admired the kaleidoscope of color against the inky sky.

"Wow." Jasper whistled on my other side. "Did the town council use Beaufort's stash of embezzled dough to pay for all this?"

Deacon's chuckles got lost in Charlotte's hair. "No. That money is long gone, I'm afraid."

"I can't believe Melvin used town finances to pay for his reelection campaign," Charlotte murmured, pulling Deacon's arms tighter around her. "I mean, I know we suspected him of having an affair with Stacy Lockner a while back, but stealing from his own community? That's *real* low."

"He did more than steal from his hometown." Hudson's hand clutched my forearm as if he were holding onto me for dear life. "He killed a man and threatened to do the same to Coco once he realized she was poking around into Larry's death."

I shivered. "Gavin said Melvin was onto me even before the news about Larry's death broke."

I'd spent most of Wednesday afternoon down at the police station, helping the chief and his team manage the media blitz that had arisen from the WMTG broadcast. In between interviewing Melvin and processing the evidence, Gavin had filled me in on what transpired during Melvin's confession. "It turns out my brunch with Mom raised the first red flag. Melvin overheard me peppering her with questions about Larry which immediately put him on edge. Then, when I saw him and Fred at Brewed to Perfection, my comments all but confirmed for him that I was investigating Larry's death. Heck, Melvin even tried to throw me off the blackmail trail by alluding to Peggy having a good reason to want Larry dead. His ruse worked for a time."

"You're lucky all he did was threaten you, Cokes." Jasper stared me down.

I gave a nervous chuckle. "The perks of being born and raised in Central Shores. Melvin might have been capable of killing a stranger, but he's known me since I was a baby. He told Gavin he never intended to harm me. He thought a threat would be enough."

Jasper didn't let me off the hook that easily. "I'm still mad you didn't tell us about the DM."

"I know. And I'm sorry. I won't keep something like that from you guys ever again." It was a promise I intended to keep.

Hudson pulled me closer to him. "Only you would take a threat on your life as a personal challenge."

I squeezed his thigh under the table. His teasing was a good sign. He, too, had been hurt that I'd kept such a big secret, but the journalist in Hudson had ultimately understood my drive to find the truth.

"So, what happens now?" Charlotte glanced from me to Deacon, her worried gaze searching for answers.

Deacon cleared his throat. "Well, we let the justice system take it from here. The state prosecutor is going for first-degree murder."

"Won't his lawyers argue that it *wasn't* premeditated?" I asked. "That Melvin killed Larry in a fit of anger when he couldn't deliver the payment Larry wanted?"

Deacon grinned. "Glad to see at least some things are still a secret from you down at the station," he teased. "Detective Forester searched the Beauforts' home and found *both* Melvin and Jeanie's personalized corkscrews in their kitchen."

My hand flew to my mouth. "Omigod. That basically proves Melvin purposely took Jasper's corkscrew to frame him."

Deacon nodded. "Once Harriet revealed all the evidence building up against him, Melvin cracked and told us how it went down. After witnessing Larry and Jasper getting into it at Vine, Melvin scooped up Jasper's corkscrew, a plan already hatching." Deacon swirled around the contents of his drink. "He mingled around Vine until eleven, hoping to establish an alibi, before driving his wife home. After she went to bed, Melvin used *67 to block his number and called Larry to tell him he finally had the money. Since Ros had taken the Dunmers' car to the spa, they arranged to meet near the bluffs south of town. Larry could easily walk there from his Sunny Shores rental. Upon Larry's arrival, Melvin plunged Jasper's corkscrew into Larry's neck and pushed him over the bluff into the ocean."

We all shivered at the gruesome mental image.

Jasper grunted beside me, taking a sip from his twelve-dollar plastic cup of beer. "My lawyers are gearing up for an *epic* civil lawsuit against ol' Mel for trying to frame me. I should be sitting quite pretty in the near future. Maybe I'll even move to Mill Row."

"You're already sitting pretty," Charlotte tutted, and I glowered at him in disappointment.

"I'm obviously kidding." Jasper rolled his eyes. "I'm donating whatever I get to the charity Melvin screwed over with his abysmal Swing Well, Save Lives performance."

Hudson patted him on the shoulder. "Heart of gold, this one."

"If Melvin was working extra shifts at his brother's restaurant to pay back Larry," Charlotte clarified with a raised eyebrow, "how is there any money left for you?"

"Oh, there's money," I chimed in. "Did you know most of the Beauforts' fortune comes from Jeanie's family?"

Charlotte shook her head in surprise.

"Melvin's wife asked about the large withdrawal he made from their joint account pretty soon after Larry began blackmailing him," I explained, having picked up the answer to this bothersome question down at the police station. In the aftermath of Melvin's arrest, Gavin had been more than generous with the information he let slip about the case. He'd also apologized for the cold shoulder I'd been given regarding my role as department spokesperson. Chief McInnis had been concerned whether I could be objective about a case involving Jasper—I couldn't deny it; the man had good instincts. But now that my best friend was no longer a suspect in a murder investigation, I was once again back in good standing with the Central Shores police.

"When Melvin couldn't come up with a good excuse to explain away his first payment to Larry, Jeanie immediately froze his access." I sliced the air for emphasis. "Come to find out, Melvin had a history of mismanaging their money, so she thought cutting him off would put a stop to whatever he was up to."

"No wonder Melvin siphoned money from the town to fund his last reelection campaign," Hudson murmured, his breath warm against my ear. "He didn't want to dip into personal funds and tip off his wife."

"I still can't believe Melvin thought he could get away with paying off a blackmailer on a waiter's salary." Jasper chuckled. "It's a miracle Central Shores survived under his leadership for as long as it did."

Hudson nudged Jasper in the arm. "Speaking of miracles…."

Amanda and Arthur glided across the sand toward our little group, bearing two heaping trays. Amanda carried an assortment of staple festival foods from vendors peppered along the beach: fried dough, deep-fried Oreos, curly fries, fried Twinkies…basically anything bad for you and fried. Arthur skillfully balanced our drink refills.

Tossing our empties into a nearby recycling bin, everyone eagerly rubbed their hands in anticipation of the feast. The guys all snagged beers from Arthur while Charlotte and I took our requested frozen margaritas. Amanda set down the cholesterol-inducing food on the picnic table we had claimed for the evening's inaugural Salute to Summer ceremony.

"This is a business dinner, right?" She giggled as she motioned for us to help ourselves to the smorgasbord.

"I wish." We'd all insisted on going Dutch for tonight's meal, even though the Highgrove-Bushmans offered to pay for the exorbitantly-priced festival cuisine. It was clear Amanda and Arthur still felt like outsiders amongst our tight-knit gang, and I didn't want them to feel like they had to buy their way into our good graces.

I promised myself I would do better at making them feel part of the team because, truthfully, they were. Arthur had become one of Hudson's closest friends in the years since he'd moved here, and Amanda's help had been invaluable, both in my investigation and when it came to running Center of Attention. Together, we'd finally polished my *Trending Topic* dating feature, and Amanda had really stepped up when it came to dealing with the media scrutiny that followed the on-air takedown of Melvin Beaufort. Not only had the clip trended on YouTube and TikTok, but I'd received an influx of requests for new client engagements. Of course, I'd had to reject quite a few of them because they'd been soliciting my services as a private eye, not a social media consultant. I guess two nationally televised murder cases *did* make me somewhat of a crime-solving influencer.

"Attention, everyone." Hudson cleared his throat and raised his frothy beer. "I just want to say thank you for getting Coco across the finish line unscathed. From going undercover with her," he paused, smiling at Amanda, "to helping her corner a murderer," he glared a little bit at Jasper, obviously still somewhat displeased we'd gone after Melvin in the first place, "you all went above and beyond to keep her safe." He finally turned his gaze to me. "I shouldn't be surprised that you're willing to put everything on the line to help a friend, Cokes. Even your own safety. It drives me completely nuts with worry, but it's who you are, and I would never want to change that. Cheers, babes, to a job well done." He tipped his glass against mine.

In typical Jasper fashion, my best friend scoffed. "Oh boo, I thought he was finally going to propose."

Amanda and Arthur, still learning our group's little quirks, let out tiny gasps of horrified shock. Deacon, Charlotte, and Hudson simply chuckled at Jasper's joking, if a bit brazen remark.

"Well, then, at least *I* have an announcement to make." Jasper cleared his throat to claim the spotlight. "After the world saw how I commanded the silver screen, overshadowing Coco at every twist and turn during Melvin's confessional…." He gave me a sidelong glance, a playful smirk stretched across his lips. "*Variety* magazine called me again and offered—no, begged—for me to take an editorial position with them."

"Woohoo!" Charlotte punched the air.

Hudson whistled his approval.

"You're leaving us already?" My deflated reaction surprised even me. I wanted to feel happy for my friend, but the thought of him moving away to New York just about broke my heart.

Jasper waved a hand, brushing my comment aside. "Of course, I told them to shove it. It's their loss for not realizing I was a star sooner."

"No, you didn't!" Charlotte rounded on Jasper, knocking his arm. "Working for *Variety* is an incredible opportunity. Think about how many more doors that could open."

"Oh, I thought about it. And I'm already opening doors all on my own." Jasper's calculated grin widened. "You're looking at the new face of *Divulge Direct*."

Arthur chuckled nervously. "Is that supposed to mean something to us?"

"Maybe not now, but soon, *Divulge Direct* will be all anyone can talk about." Jasper clapped his hands in glee. "I'm partnering with some fiery executive producer at WMTG to bring the words of *Divulge* to life with my own talk show. Talk show! I'm going to be the next Oprah!"

I shot a suspicious glance at Hudson. "Millie?"

He shrugged with a smile. "Jasper made me promise that I wouldn't tell you before he had a chance to."

"Just like he made me promise not to tell you that the network finally set a date for the premiere of his crime show—" Jasper held a hand over his mouth. "Oops."

"WMTG set a date?" My head whipped toward Hudson. Some detective I was, what with all these secrets my companions were keeping.

Hudson's brow furrowed, but he took Jasper's feigned slip of the tongue in stride. "Three weeks from today. We're going with *Crime Sweet Home: A Look at Local Mysteries*."

"Brought to you by your host, Hudson Caruthers," Jasper said, mimicking Hudson's studious on-air voice. "I heard him record the intro like a thousand times when I was at WMTG yesterday."

"The one and *only* host." Hudson eyed me knowingly, the relief and elation in his expression apparent.

I couldn't contain the enormous grin that spread across my face. This day just kept getting better. Millie called earlier to tell us that Tori Beals had officially resigned, hoping that WMTG would drop their investigation into the allegations against her. Not a chance. Already, other staff members were coming forward with accusations of their own, so armed with their testimonies and my video evidence, WMTG was prepared to take Tori to court for all the pain she'd caused.

"Of course, Millie wants me to scrap all the work I've done on the pilot and lead with a segment about Larry's murder." My boyfriend wrapped an arm around me and pulled me so close I could see a dusting of confectionary sugar on his kissable lips. "I hope you're not planning on saying goodbye to the spotlight too soon. You know she'll drag you into the studio for an interview, if not try to wrangle you into being a correspondent for the show."

I gave him a dramatic sigh. "I guess I can tolerate fame and notoriety for a little while longer."

Jasper snorted. "What a saint."

Ready to move on from the tumultuous past week and enjoy the present, we all settled into animated conversation about the Salute to Summer events everyone planned to attend over the next several days. Mom and Dad came by our table to say hello. A heartbeat later, Thea and the kids appeared alongside them. My nieces and nephew peppered me with sticky kisses, likely leftover from the cotton candy covering their faces. Their attention spans being what they were, it wasn't long before the kiddos were begging Thea to let them try fried Twinkies.

Charlotte happily offered hers to share. "I got a cavity just looking at it." She reassured my sister that she had no need for the yummy treat.

Deacon frowned as he looked at his plate. "No wonder. You already ate mine."

"This group lives by the motto, *your plate is my plate*." For emphasis, Jasper swiped a funnel fry from Hudson. "But *my* plate is *my* plate." He swatted

Charlotte's stealthy hand away from his fried pickles.

I leaned into Hudson, enjoying the sight of everyone I loved gathered around me. Safe and happy, once more. Whatever obstacles the future held for us here in Central Shores, I knew everything would eventually turn out just fine. With my family and friends beside me, life always trended in the best direction.

Acknowledgements

As my writing journey continues, my list of people to thank grows and grows. Many thanks to my editor, Shawn Reilly Simmons, for being an invaluable partner in this process. I'm so happy to have Shawn and the team at Level Best Books in my corner. Thank you to my agent, Dawn Dowdle, for nurturing my career and my creativity. I also want to give a special shout out to Laura Darrell for her portrayal of Coco and her friends in the *#FollowMe for Murder* audiobook.

I must express my gratitude to *The Bookish Hour* community, and all the support our viewers have given us as our little podcast empire has grown. And of course, many thanks to my Sisters in Crime siblings, my BRLA family, and the *Writers Who Kill* blogging team.

Thank you to J.C. Kenney, Lori Robbins, Sarah Wu, Melissa Green, and Marilyn Levinson for your support, encouragement, and knowledge.

Just as Coco has her followers to thank for her success, I am beyond grateful to the wonderful readers who enjoyed their time in Central Shores in *#FollowMe for Murder* and came back for more fun in *#TagMe for Murder*. You're the reason why I write these stories; thank you for sharing your time with me.

About the Author

Sarah E. Burr lives near New York City. Hailing from the small town of Appleton, Maine, she has been dreaming of being Nancy Drew since she was a little girl. After not finding any mysteries in corporate America, Sarah began writing some of her own. She is the author of the Trending Topic Mysteries and the Court of Mystery series. Sarah is also the author of the award-winning Glenmyre Whim Mysteries. *You Can't Candle the Truth* was a 2022 NGIBA Best Mystery Finalist and a 2022 Silver Falchion Best Supernatural Mystery Finalist.

Sarah is a member of Sisters in Crime, currently serving as the social media manager for the NY-TriState Chapter. She is also the creative mind behind BookstaBundles, a content creation service for authors. Sarah is the co-host of *The Bookish Hour*, a live-streamed YouTube series featuring author interviews and book discussions. She writes as a member of the *Writers Who Kill* blogging team. When she's not spinning up stories, Sarah is singing Broadway show tunes, video gaming, and enjoying walks with her dog, Eevee.

SOCIAL MEDIA HANDLES:
  Instagram: https://www.instagram.com/authorsaraheburr
  Facebook: https://www.facebook.com/authorsaraheburr

AUTHOR WEBSITE:
https://www.saraheburr.com

Also by Sarah E. Burr

Trending Topic Mysteries: *#FollowMe for Murder*

Glenmyre Whim Mysteries: *You Can't Candle the Truth, Too Much to Candle*

Court of Mystery: *The Ducal Detective Mysteries, Paradise Plagued, Burdened Bloodline, Sovereign Sieged, Crown of Chaos, Harrowed Heir, Ravaged Reign, Innocence Imprisoned, Ardent Ascension*

www.ingramcontent.com/pod-product-compliance
Lightning Source LLC
Chambersburg PA
CBHW050148120726
47903CB00002B/533